Bloodline:

Forged Spears

Book One

Kellan Duell

ISBN:979-8-9949498-0-1

DEDICATION

To those who have left their stories with me, I thank you. Good, bad, or ugly, it has brought us here, and I hope you find yourselves in these books as I've tried to stay as true to your character as possible. The sweat, the experiences, and the blood we've spilled together have left an indelible mark on mine, and hopefully I can start a ripple to reach many more who have enriched my life from working the sweltering, closed-custody Texas prison runs to welding on the frozen prairies of North Dakota pipelines. When you spoke, I was listening.

ACKNOWLEDGMENTS

To my bride of all these years, an uncommon woman who usually raised children alone while I was off working, I can never say enough about what you have done. Any mistakes I've made here are my own and do not reflect anyone else who helped me with this book. The places mentioned are real, but I have altered the landscape slightly to suit my literary needs.

1 Gideon

Death was here, and I felt its presence, whether for me or my prey, I wasn't sure, but in this new world, it had become a constant companion like hunger. Silence settled over me as the birds stopped, and I sensed a change. Sitting against a beech tree, with an oak to my right, I waited for prey and watched for whatever disturbed the forest. These woods differed from home, but both revealed when you're no longer alone.

My sister and I were running low on food, and I wanted to add some fresh meat to stretch out our meager food supply, so I came to hunt along a small game trail armed with my friend's plundered recurve bow and pistol. The pistol was for emergencies only, as the sound would give me away, and that could be more dangerous than starving now. I had practiced with the bow for only a few days and had yet to kill anything with it, and with the pistol, only a few more times, so my best option was to remain hidden from potential danger.

I was here early enough to see the first glow of light across predawn, and the forest had come alive. Once the bare branches and trunks were discernible, something had disturbed the creatures here, forcing them into silence. Minutes dragged by, but the silence remained, warning me that something was amiss and still present. The cool, damp Wisconsin morning and dew from the leaves I sat on seeped into my pants, further eroding my patience, which I never had in abundance, and I had to force myself to remain still. I strained to see any predators or prey in the eerie silence, sitting still and relying on my ears and peripheral vision to detect movement, just as my father had taught me.

A squirrel started jumping overhead, a return to normalcy,

and I assumed I was being overly cautious. Then again, I've killed many an impatient squirrel, so I couldn't put too much trust in them. I sat still and watched others skitter in the branches to my right, and a flash of fur ran along the tree limbs, needing one to come to ground so I could risk an arrow. I know that if I missed it when it was off the ground, the arrow would be gone, and a miss was likely. A deer would be best, but even a squirrel or two would help.

Moments later, I saw movement to my right, not in a tree but on the ground. Good, I thought, and slowly turned for a better angle. A flash of black and brush-moving revealed a dog stepping from behind two small oaks on the other side of the creekbank. I wasn't to that point yet, and I imagined my sister, Maryn, would scratch my eyes out for bringing in fresh dog meat, so instead I watched it walk closer to where I'm sitting, I'm covered in all camo, taken from the same house I got the bow and pistol and like the bow, a little too large for me, and it got within twenty yards without seeing me.

That's when I got a good look and saw it was blue, not black. The heeler turned its head and looked back to its right, and I followed its gaze. Not seeing anything and knowing the hunt was over for the day, I stood up, wood chips and debris exploded from the oak I had been half hidden behind and stung my face. The loud sound reverberated through the woods, sending a wave of panic through me. A gunshot. *MOVE,* my brain screamed. I circled the tree and sprinted the way I had come. I heard shouting behind me and barking, and another shot went wide as I scrambled through the brush that led back to our home, just over four hundred yards away.

I realized, after clearing the trees, that I couldn't go directly to my house; whoever was shooting could likely see me if I crossed the street, so I cut to my left and skirted along the forest edge. I remembered there was a huge culvert for the creek I was hunting by, one that cut under a bike path leading to my street, just a block away, so I sprinted to it. Arrows jangling across my back, the pistol belt and holster seemed to drag me down, but I pumped my arms and ran as hard as I could. I left the neighborhood behind and to my right while I rushed for the bridge. Near the edge, the bow slipped out of my hand and got tangled in my feet. I went crashing into the water face-first, hitting rocks and piled debris.

The spring rains had been light this year, so the water was low, but it was enough to get me soaked. I scrambled back up, dazed, and looked around for the bow. Finding it in the overgrown grass at the edge, I pulled it close and lay still, scanning the wood line. Ten seconds later, a young boy ran from the cover and stopped at the edge, looking both ways. He turned and shouted something in the woods and pointed off to his right, away from where I'm hiding. Soon after, a man emerged and looked at the way the younger man was pointing. They both took off in a jog in that direction, leaving me in the ditch for the moment, safe from their discovery.

I crawled slowly back to the culvert and took in my situation. My head was bleeding from a gash, but I can't tell how bad it was. It runs from my hairline back, and my hair was sticky from blood. With no first aid kit, the only thing I can do is put mud on it. It's black here, not red like the clay back home in East Texas, but it's the best I've got for it until I can get back and let Maryn take a look. For the time being, I washed the blood out of my face the best I could and hid further into the culvert, waiting for dark. I pulled out the pistol, kept it ready in case they came back this way, and checked my hiding spot.

2 Maryn

I quietly walked from room to room in the familiar house directly behind ours that I shared with Gid. He was out hunting this morning, so I am finishing up by going through the house to look for anything useful: ammo, medicines, food. He's already taken some hunting clothing, and the rest we left until later. I was looking for something that was missing from my mother's supply. Not really expecting to find the thing I needed, but I knew Mr. Davenport, who lived here, wouldn't mind if I took anything we could use. He was the only person in the neighborhood who had been friends with my father and was always glad to see us. In fact, Gid had Mr. Davenport's bow and hunting knife with him right now. I think he secretly had a crush on my mother, but it's odd to think that a 66-year-old would have feelings like that. Jess Spears was a rare beauty, and many men, as well as some women, were often struck by her looks, so it wasn't too far-fetched, I supposed. Her auburn hair and soft brown eyes hadn't been passed on to her children, though; we both got black hair and blue eyes from our father, Charles.

Fortunately for him, Mr. Davenport didn't have to watch Jess die as he went just before her. He even had the decency to drag himself with a cast on, outside, and onto a chair before doing so. Trying to save us the trouble of carrying him out, I supposed. He left a note telling us to put everyone we intended to bury into one of the farther houses, so no fresh graves in a yard would attract scavengers, the four- or two-legged kind.

We found him while going to let him know about our mama, and we placed both in a home at the end of a cul-de-sac, isolated from the others. It was far enough away from other homes that it wouldn't alert anyone to where we lived, but we had to wait until full dark to make sure we weren't seen. We gently loaded them onto an old garden wagon from Mr. Davenport's garage and took turns pulling it to the house.

Mr. Davenport's hand-scrawled note included the address and instructed us to put him there and to lock the basement door behind us. The home was north of us by Camelot Park, and I remembered seeing it on the way to have picnics. He knew the owners, and they lived in Arizona during the winter and wouldn't return (if ever) until the full summer. He kept an eye on the place for them during the winter months and wrote that the front door key was on his key ring. He wrote us a goodbye at the bottom, saying he enjoyed hearing me laugh and that he was sorry about the turkey hunt with Gid, since he knew Gid had been looking forward to it. He also took a moment to thank my mom for always being kind to him. He was adamant about leaving him in the basement, not digging a hole someone would see, or an animal could dig up, so we couldn't refuse to honor his final wish, and it seemed a solid idea to us.

The sight of my beautiful mother, lying wrapped in a sheet atop Mr. Davenport, almost broke my sanity. Gid wouldn't look me in the eyes, and I suspected he would have burst into tears if he had. For the first time in my life, I felt like a balloon being blown away after the string was cut. I couldn't focus, and it's a lucky thing no one saw us, because we weren't going to put up much of a fight in our state.

Gid insisted on getting a mattress from a bedroom, and we placed both of them on it. Seeing them both rolled in sheets, I could almost pretend they weren't two of the most important people in my life. I wondered what my father would think about this, knowing they were so close together in death, and that caused even more pain, as he was still missing.

I don't see my brother cry, but I did unashamedly. Gid read a Psalm of David, and we said our goodbyes and locked and bolted the door. I turned to look back, but Gid gripped the wagon and trundled off back toward Mr. Davenport's. I wanted to yell at him that he didn't have to return the wagon immediately and that he could take a minute to grieve. He always put things back, and it was ingrained. Maybe it was something comforting for him to cling to while everything was in a tempest, so I kept my outburst to myself. My mind was numb on the walk home, and I kept remembering how she laughed and the sound of her voice. Always kind, caring, and full of mischief, teasing us gently. Her wit was as sharp as her sewing needles, and my father and brother bore the brunt of it. I only heard her raise her voice once, and that was when Gid was playing near a hot stove. Of course, that was before we left Texas and moved here. She doted on us, and I knew no one would ever love me that unconditionally again. Mr. Davenport had grown close to us over the last year, and we had spent a lot of time together with that kind soul as well. If only I could call my grandparents, it would help some, but phone service and internet were both down, and I suspected they would be for good.

The next few days were a blur as both of us tried to deal with our loss and figure out what to do next. We took everything we thought we needed from a quick sweep of Mr. Davenport's, but it was done quickly and without too much enthusiasm. Gid wanted to check the gun safe, which he didn't remember to unlock when he got sick, so we were without the weapons he had inside. We were trying to avoid encountering anyone else in their homes, dead or worse, alive and looking to take what little we had. Our father had gone to Green Bay for work, and we waited to see if he would return. I figured it would take seven days to get back, even if he had to walk, so after eight days, I started to worry that he had gotten sick, too. My last text had been read, but no reply came before things went dark. I called my grandparents, and no answer there either.

3 Llewelyn

When I got out of the shower, I turned on the TV in my motel room. The news on a local station showed a hospital with patients waiting in beds along the hallways and a packed waiting room. Was COVID back, I wondered?

When I pulled into the parking lot, it was lightly populated, but that was nothing new. I got to work early and liked having time to drink a coffee and focus my mind on the day before the rest of the crew came in. Pipefitters, welders, and apprentices weren't the quietest of folks, and once they drifted into the turnout room, the silence was over, and the day really got underway.

I drank my coffee, was still alone in the shack, and didn't see a soul until the union steward walked by. I called to him when he was past the door.

"Cadillac, where is everyone?" I asked, and he walked back over to me, shaking his head.

"You are going to be loaned out today. I think most of the hands are out with the flu; it's so scarce out here that they may have to shut the job down. Sit tight here, and I'll have someone come and get you if they can fill a crew." I nodded and walked around outside now that the sun was coming up. No noise, no ironworkers on the steel, no hungover boilermakers hammering on flange bolts. Strange.

When I got to the other side of the unit, I knew something worse than the flu had happened. Four trucks are in the parking lot, including mine, out of two hundred craftsmen on this shutdown. I'm eight stories up, so I have an overall view of the world bathed in the early morning sunlight. Nothing on the roads, no people walking around. I went to the north side and looked at the administrative buildings. One car. Oh shit, something has come off the rails.

Opening my lunch box, I called my mama back in Texas and got no answer. I called back immediately, and she answered.

"Mama?" I asked unnecessarily.

"Llewelyn, is that you? Go to the children, something is wrong. Don't bring them here; everyone is sick and dying. Do you hear me? Llewlyn? DON'T COME HERE!" I'm talking, but she can't hear me. The line went dead. I tried to call right back, but my call wouldn't go through. What the fuck, I thought, starting to get worried. I tried to call my brother Charles and his wife, but still nothing. A text from Charles appeared on my screen: "Come a-runnin," a phrase we joked about as kids that our old man said our family used for years to let others know to drop what they were doing and come help. No joke now, though. Frustrated with the cell service, I grabbed my lunchbox and headed back down to the parking lot. Firing up my truck, I sped out of the parking lot. They will have to finish this outage without me, as I gunned it north on OH 45.

4 Maryn

The news said thousands of people were sick across the nation on Monday. On Tuesday, the military was being called out for looters and protesters. On Wednesday, the news stopped airing altogether. By Thursday night, Mama and Mr. Davenport were laid to rest in the abandoned house. Something swept across the country, and it seemed nothing could stop it. Onset of symptoms, hours later, death. With no known cure, the sickness had upended the country, probably the world. We didn't get sick and weren't sure why, but if you did, there seemed to be no hope of recovery. Of course, we hadn't seen anyone but each other so far and were trying to hide from people who had panicked, jamming the highways with wreckage, fighting and looting, so surely some of the ones that didn't die of the sickness did then.

The small town of Oak Creek, where we had lived for the past year, had been spared from violence for the most part. Gunshots and fires were common enough that we avoided going out in the daylight as much as possible. Packs of stray dogs were also starting to form. So far, they weren't desperate enough to try to get into our house, but who knew what would happen if they caught you unarmed? Of course, the power went out after three days, and I suspected the water would be next. We decided to stay as long as possible before leaving and try to make our way back to our grandparents' place on the Neches River in Texas. We decided to give our father more time to reach us before we gave up and abandoned the house. Before we left, I wanted to check one more time at Mr. Davenport's house, and that's how I came to be here now.

The quiet house, coupled with being alone, made it even

more eerie. I heard a faint shot in the distance while climbing the stairs, hoping that it was Gid with some fresh meat. Our neighbor had been an avid hunter, and he had all types of camo gear, so I thought I'd inspect that room first. I opened the door, and the closed-in air in the stale room had a moldy smell.

Racks of waders, coveralls, and boots lined the walls. I overheard the outdoorsman talking with my dad about making his camo to suit his needs, which would require sewing, and hopefully what I needed. A new sewing machine sat on a small desk pushed into a corner. As soon as I reached for the drawer, I heard a dog barking close by. Too close. I hadn't thought to lock the back door when I came in, and the barking grew louder, meaning either the dog had moved closer or someone had opened the door and made it seem so. I turned and headed back through the bedroom door, and I heard a male voice telling the dog to hush. I closed the door quietly and spun back into the room. Near panic, I looked around for anything I could use for defense and saw nothing, but the gear strewn around. Reaching back to the desk, I quietly opened the top drawer and found only a pair of pinking shears. Unfortunately, it was the only item that could be used as a weapon. As I snatched them up, I heard someone walking around on the bottom floor. I left the drawer open and looked around for somewhere to hide. The hanging clothing on racks against the wall wouldn't cover me, so I quietly opened the closet. Nothing in here but more boots and waders. The dog has stopped barking, but I heard the stairs creak as the man started up. I quickly stepped into the closet and closed the door gently.

I could hear a door open, and a few seconds later, it closed. There are only two other rooms up here, and one is a bathroom with the door already open, so that he would come here next. I tried to slow my breathing and focused on being quiet as the door opened to the room I'm in. My knuckles turned white around the 'weapon' I'm holding as I heard him walking around in front of the wooden door I'm behind. He rummaged through the hunting gear, possibly taking some with him. Hoping he would find what he needed and leave, I stayed crouched down. The closet was dark and musty, and I felt panic crawling up my back like an insect. The floor creaked, and footsteps shuffled around. The door whipped open, and I sprang toward him.

After the impact, we both fell to the floor, and I heard the air slam from his lungs. Clothes covered both of us as I knocked them off the hanging rack, and I scrambled not to lose my advantage of surprise, so I grasped a handful of his medium-length dark hair and twisted it up into my left hand. The other, I put the shears to his throat and pressed them against his skin. His eyes were wild, and he was gasping for breath. In his desperation, he managed to roll over to his knees and flipped me off to my right side. I never let go of his hair, and I'm right back on him before he can recover any further.

"Don't move again," I said as I wrench his head backward and place my blade against his throat again.

He slowly put his hands up and managed through tortured breathing, "I'm sorry, I don't want any trouble. I didn't know anyone was here. I'm just hungry."

"Do you have any weapons on you?" I asked through gasping breath, myself.

"Uh, n-n-no," he stammered, slowly putting his hands up.

"Who are you?"

He gasped out, "Jimmy, Jimmy Weaver."

"Is there anyone else with you?"

"Yeah, old man Burns." He replied

"Crazy old man Burns? Is he armed?" I asked, alarmed.

"Yes. I went to his camper this morning outside of town, thinking he would be the most likely to have food put away. My dad said he is a survivalist. He caught me about to open his front door, and he pointed his rifle at me. He thinks I'm someone named "Tex," and I was too terrified to answer his questions." I shifted to my feet and nodded for him to continue, "He drew a map in the dirt of our next 'op, which was to scrounge food from town. The old man showed me where he wanted me to set up an ambush. He asked me about my missing rifle, but before I could answer, he nodded his head and said he left his plastic piece of crap behind for the VC, too. He terrified me, so I had no choice but to come along. We got separated when he sent me down a bike road looking for a man he shot this morning. I panicked and ran into the first unlocked home to get away, but there were dead people in there, and I came here next."

Panic flared in my mind. "You shot someone this morning?"

"I didn't shoot at anything, told you I wasn't armed, but he did, I think he missed. We were about to cross the creek when Burns shot at some guy who took off and disappeared before we saw which way he went. He didn't chase him at first, afraid of an ambush, saying it was a trick they often used. I'm not sure what he means, because you know he's crazy. Anyway, this dog was there too, so maybe it belongs to the man who got shot at? I couldn't tell who he was because he was camouflaged.

“You didn’t see the man who got shot at?”

“No, I only got a glance before he ran off. The shot surprised me, and I was looking in the wrong direction to see him when Burns fired.” he shook his head.

“Oh, I think he was carrying a bow, but I can’t be sure, like I said, it happened so fast- “

“Get up slowly and let's head downstairs. If you move too fast, I’ll slide this knife into your throat, do you understand?” I bluffed.

“Now slowly,” I prodded the scissors more firmly into the right side of his neck, and as he stood up, I found he was no taller than me, so no trouble holding his hair while walking him from the room. I remembered Mr. Davenport had a lock on the outside of his upstairs bathroom door because he left his duck dogs in there during the day instead of putting them in a kennel when he was training pups.

“This way, I have a better idea,” I turned the boy, and I say boy because he couldn’t be older than fourteen, and a couple of inches shorter than me, and skinny as a rail. We got to the bathroom door, and I explained what I needed him to do.

“I’m going to leave you in this bathroom so you can have access to water and the toilet. Don’t make any noise. There’s light from the window, but it's too small for you to crawl out of. I’ll bring you some food in an hour or so.”

“Please don’t leave me here locked up,” he pleaded.

“I don’t have much choice, either leave you in here locked up for a few hours or dead on the floor because I can't have you bringing Burns here or attacking me." He nodded and walked into the room.

"Go sit on the tub with your feet in it so I have time to shut the door."

He walked over and complied. "Please don't leave me here too long, I'm scared," he sobbed.

I can see him starting to tear up, but I must make sure I'm out of danger before worrying about his fears. I closed the door quietly and rammed home the bolt.

"There are towels in the pantry you can use to sit on, and I'll be back as soon as I can. Remember, no noise."

5 Gideon

Around noon, the damp clothes began to bother me, and it was growing harder to wait for dark before getting out of the culvert. I kept reminding myself of the dangers of moving around during the day and focused on that. A few minutes later, I heard something clicking on the pavement. After the hours of quiet, the sound seemed to echo through my dank hiding place, and I gripped the pistol more tightly. A man was talking, but I can't quite make out the words, just the deepness of the voice. It comes closer, muttering.

"Stay alert, Tex-..." The voice became quieter, and I could hear the footfalls going over me and away from the neighborhood, in the opposite direction of the place where I came out of the woods.

Once I couldn't hear the man any longer, I crawled from the pipe and checked the way he walked, making sure he was still heading away from me. I peeked from the tall grass and didn't see anyone at first. An old man with wild, white hair sprang from the opposite side of the road about forty yards away and started sprinting further down the road. What the hell? I can't see him well for the grass, but that must be old man Burns.

He wasn't wearing his trademark yellow slicker, but I felt confident it was him. My father told me he was a veteran who had severe mental issues and that he had never really left "the delta," whatever that meant. The locals shortened his name from Burnette to Burns after he accidentally blew up the old camper he was living in last fall by leaving the propane on and trying to light a cigarette. He had to spend several weeks in a burn unit over in Milwaukee, but he survived. The left side of his mouth was pulled and shrunken, so it always made him look like he was leering, and spittle would often run from his mouth without him knowing or caring, I supposed. Burns never did any harm that I knew of, just rode around on his old beach cruiser bike with sheepskin mud flaps and picked up beer cans to subsidize his VA pension. One of the local churches had raised enough money to purchase the old RV he now lived in, which was all-electric and had no gas appliances, of course, and I never heard of him harming anyone, but he had shot at me today, so something had changed. Hell, I saved our Dr Pepper cans to give to him when I had enough, I'd get my dad to run me over, and I'd leave them on his porch, bagged up with some food my mom fixed. The church had moved him, though and I don't know where he lived now.

I supposed the new reality had affected everyone, and he had lost whatever hold of sanity he had before, so I made sure I didn't move until he was out of sight, around the curve on the bike path. I knew I shouldn't, but I started back home even though it was early afternoon. I needed Maryn to check out my head and sew it up if needed. She's good with a needle and maybe a little too eager to try it out, but I'd have to wait and see. Also, my clothes were wet, and a cold right now could turn nasty or worse with no help around.

I gave old man Burns another few minutes, then, checking around, I ran to the house. After entering the door, I laid down the bow, arrows, and camo by the back door. I checked throughout the house, but I couldn't find Maryn. I looked for Mr. Davenport's old Remington 12-gauge that we had taken a couple of days ago, and it, too, was gone. Alarmed, I headed out the back door to the house directly behind us. It's the only place my sister had been since the sickness, so I went there first. I went through the gate between our yards into his backyard and saw the same blue dog lying on the back porch.

Easing my pistol out just in case he gets grumpy, I walked to the back door. He got up, stretched, and walked off without giving me a backward glance. He's not starving, so he's been eating well the last week. I didn't want to think about WHAT kept him so well fed. I opened the door and stepped in.

6 Llewelyn

I went back to my room and brought out the only thing I really needed from there. I slid the stiff plastic case from under the bed, grabbed the smaller one from the bottom drawer of the cheap particleboard chest of drawers, and left everything else behind. My mama wasn't a fool or an alarmist, so taken with what I was seeing myself, I needed to make a move west.

I got on I-80 without any problems and reached a cruising speed of 85. Four miles of that, and I hit an exit and pulled into the nearest fuel station, but the pump wouldn't accept my debit card. I opened the smaller case and put my pistol in the small of my back and walked into the store.

A teenager was behind the register and didn't even look up when I walked in. His dark hair hung limply around his face, and he was wearing an Iron Maiden shirt. Must be from his dad's closet, I assumed as I walked to the counter.

"Good morning," I said, and he looked up in surprise. His eyes were bloodshot, and one nostril had a sheep's leg of snot hanging out of it.

"Hey," he responded and slid his dad's shirt sleeve across his nose.

"I need some diesel," I explained.

"The machine is done," he croaked out.

"Will the machine still pump fuel, or is it just the payment wrecked?"

"I dunno," he said, uninterested.

"Turn the pump on for me, will you?" I said and waited for him to unlimber from his seat.

"Why don't you go home? You look sick." I asked as he worked the buttons.

"My mom is coming to get me," he sniffed, withdrawing the new leg that was forming back into his nostril.

I opened my fuel tank and the reserve in the bed and topped both off with diesel. I looked at the pump and saw the $370 price tag. Well, I hoped the sick kid valued his life more than that. The door alarm clanged again when I walked in, and he had his forehead on the counter this time.

"Hey, kid, I got some bad news, I don't have any cash," I admitted with my hand under my jacket on the pistol in my belt.

He raised his head slowly and blinked, not understanding, so I repeated it.

"Mister, I don't give a shit if you took the cash register, none of this is mine," fair point, I thought as I went back out and gunned it back to the interstate. Luckily, the toll road was mostly empty, with a car or truck on the shoulder every few miles, and the electric cameras would have a heavy toll to mail me.

7 Gideon

The air inside was warmer but stale and closed off. The creaking floors of this old house couldn't be avoided, and so I started searching in as much silence as I could muster. Nothing was downstairs, and as I headed up the stairs, Maryn was standing at the top with her finger to her mouth, silencing any talk. She headed down toward me, and I moved out of the way to let her pass. She tugged my arm with her left hand, her right hand holding the missing shotgun, and walked to the back door to check that it was locked. It was because I locked it in, and she beckoned me to follow her to the kitchen, where Mr. Davenport had a small table along one wall where he prepared his meals. He only ate with us or in front of his TV, which my mother good-naturedly scolded him about. As a widower, he protested he didn't need a table.

She sat at the table, and I sat across from her. She looked at me and asked, "Did you get shot?"

Surprised, I asked, "How did you know about that? No, I hit it on a rock falling into the dry creek bed."

"Let me look at it first," she said, and went to the sink to grab a cloth. After motioning me over, she lowered my head and began rinsing it. Fresh blood dripped as she washed away the mud. She stopped, brought a chair over, and told me to sit so she could get a better look. I do, and she started scrubbing harder as I gritted my teeth.

"Stay here, I'll be right back." Maryn took off quickly, and I heard the back door open.

When she returned with a bag, she took out a medical kit. "Are you going to cry when I start putting these stitches in?" she teased.

"Strange that every time it ends up hurting me, you think it's funny."

She giggled and rolled her eyes, bringing the kit over. "Be still and lean over the sink."

It was the first time she had done stitches on a wound, and I can't lie and say it didn't hurt like hell, but no worse than the alcohol rub she poured on first. That made my eyes water, but I had to bite down and not let that out. I'd never hear the end of it from her, and that wouldn't do.

She packed everything back up and told me she thought it would hold, and I'm surprised she didn't want to shave my head first.

She giggled again and said, "I didn't think of it, but I will next time. Now tell me what happened this morning."

I went through everything, and she's surprised Burns would shoot at me, but I can't explain why. I told her about the boy who was with him and that I'd never seen him around before. After teasing me about wearing a football helmet the next time I need to run, she looked at me seriously and said.

"About that boy you saw this morning..."

8 Maryn

We stood in front of the door, and I turned to Gideon. “Are you ready?”

“Ready to pistol whip him for trying to kill me this morning,” he growled.

“Hush that kind of talk, you’ll understand when you meet him.”

“Hmph,” he grunted.

“Jimmy, my brother Gid is here, and I’m going to open the door. Stay in the tub for your safety, okay? We’ll figure out what's going on. Did you hear me, Jimmy?’

“Y-y-yes, I hear you.” He said barely above a whisper. “Okay, I’m in the tub.”

I handed the shotgun to Gideon and opened the door slowly. Jimmy was indeed inside it and had his hands up to make sure we didn’t see him as a threat.

“C’mon out and let’s go downstairs.” Jimmy almost fell out of the old claw-foot tub.

“Put your hands down before you break your neck,” I told him, exasperated.

“You care about that?” he asked.

“Not if you can do it quietly,” Gideon warned.

“Of course, I don’t want you hurt. We need to make sure you aren’t a danger to us,” I said softly to encourage him.

He clambered out awkwardly, and I moved aside and waved him forward.

“Down the stairs and to the right,” Gid said, and we headed down, handing the shotgun back to me.

“Have a seat in the chair and let's find out what’s going on around here.” Gid pointed out Mr. Davenport's old La-Z-Boy covered with a blanket depicting flying ducks.

Gid picked up one end of the sofa and quietly swung it around so that it was mostly facing the nervous Jimmy. We both sat with me at the far end, away from Jimmy, and he folded his hands into his lap and looked nervous and jumpy. Understandably, since I had technically kidnapped and held him hostage, I supposed. The rules were gone, and we would all have to change the way we lived, but protecting my brother and me was paramount. Even though I felt bad about the situation Jimmy found himself in, it was necessary for now.

“Where did you come from and why were you with old man Burns?” Gid was straight to the point.

“My dad lives here, and I moved here last weekend. I've been living with my grandmother in Reedsburg, and this was the first time I’ve been with my dad since he was released from prison. She only sent me because the doctors put her on hospice. I don’t have any other family, but him, and it was either try with my dad or go to foster care. The kids at school told me horrible stories about what happens in foster care, so I chose him. I was checked out of school on a Friday, and we came here. He got so sick on Saturday night that he went to bed early without really saying much to me, and Sunday morning, he wouldn’t get up. I called 9-1-1, and they said they would send someone as soon as they could. Sunday night, looters broke into the house and set the place on fire when they took what they wanted. I think he had drugs or money they knew about. I hid in the basement until the smoke got too bad, and luckily, I could fit out the small window, or I would have died in there. I've been looking for people ever since, and the old man was the first person I met who didn't chase me off or point a gun at me. He called me Ace and Tex, talked like we were war buddies. Of course, that isn't my name, but he didn't try to kill me either. It was weird, but he did feed me this morning, and I didn't know what else to do. I saw him shoot at a man in the woods, and that decided it for me that I needed to get away. I don't want to be mixed up in a killing."

"Stop right there for a sec and let's back up. I'm not clear about what's been going on with you for the last week or so. Why didn't you go back home after your dad died? Aren't you worried about your grandmother? Have you been with Burns for a week? It took you that long to figure out he was crazy?" Gideon questioned.

"I'm not sure I can find my way back to Reedsburg, but if I did, my granny is dead by now. If the sickness didn't kill her, the lack of electricity for her oxygen machine would have. The batteries only last a day without recharging, and it's been days since the power was out. I've never been away from my hometown, and I'd wonder until I starved or worse till someone caught me...." he trailed off. "I just met Mr. Burns this morning, and I ran off when he shot at someone."

"Jimmy, how old are you?" I asked the skinny boy. "August, I'll be thirteen," he said.

"Gid, it's time to go eat, so let's head home and fix something," I said, standing up.

“Hold on a sec, I’m not so sure I want to bring someone to our house who tried to kill me earlier today. What is your last name, kid?” he stared directly into Jimmy, making him squirm.

“Weaver is my name, Jimmy Weaver. I-I-I didn’t try to, that was you this morning?” His face paled.

“Yeah, jackass, that was me, and it was a damn close thing too.” Gid also stood up.

“Well, you know I didn’t shoot at you, I don’t even carry a gun.” Jimmy managed.

“Yeah, it’s the only thing that’s saving your life right now,” Gid said with his hand on the holstered pistol.

“Gid, let's talk out here for a second, please. Jimmy, stay here and don’t move. We’ll still be close enough to see you and remember to stay quiet.” That last part was probably unnecessary. He looked too scared to do anything and seemed completely at our mercy. We walked into the hallway, and I asked Gideon what he wanted to do with him.

“Well, we only have two choices. Either let him go or kill him.” His answer didn’t surprise me, as I knew it really would have come down to this.

“You want to kill him?” I asked him, shocked.

“Of course not. He knows where we are now, and if we bring him home, he’ll know where we live. I don’t want to release him and risk him bringing that crazy old man crashing down on us, either, or a group of other people he may get caught up in. Hell, for all we know, he murdered his dad and his old granny.” He exclaimed.

“That boy couldn’t murder anything except maybe a Pop-Tart, and that’s only if someone unwrapped it for him. I don’t think he’s any real danger. I certainly don’t want to murder him in cold blood.”

Gid rubbed his face with both hands. “Okay, let's take him back to the house, but we must keep it secret, and we have to always have one of us with him to make sure he isn’t giving us away to any outsiders.”

“Agree, and that’s the best we can do.” I turned to the living room and started back in with Gideon on my heels.

“Before we go back in there, stop twisting your hair; it makes you look nervous,” he teased.

“I am nervous. Why aren’t you?” I asked.

“He can’t be too much to handle if my sister was able to kung fu him into submission.” He grinned and glided past me into the living room, irritating me even in the most serious of circumstances.

9 Llewelyn

That good run of highway ran out three miles from the gas station, and I had to slow to a crawl, sometimes even leaving the road for the shoulder, and it took me till dark to get west of Cleveland. I saw a pile of cars stacked up on an overpass in a town called Berlin Heights, and I had to come to a complete stop for the first time. Someone ahead was waving their hands in the air behind a crashed Lincoln Town car, but I couldn't make them out in the twilight. I stepped out, opened the larger case, and pulled out my POF-USA Rogue .308. Whoever that was ahead must have gotten spooked by that and opened fire on me, hitting my GMC and sending me to cover behind a parked ice cream truck on the shoulder. Another shooter joined in what sounded like a .22, and I heard the rounds hitting my truck. Goddamn them for that. I eased off into the bushes beside the highway and headed north through the dense trees along the shoulder.

They couldn't hear me because they were firing their rifles at my truck foolishly, and I supposed they didn't see me slip into the woods. I got to a hog wire fence along the road that ran under the overpass, then headed back to where the firing was coming from. When I reached the concrete barrier, I saw two men looking downrange, one of whom was reloading his rifle. I eased the barrel up, switched off the safety, and shot the one firing first. The surprised man dropped his unloaded rifle and shot his hands into the air.

I stepped over the barrier with my rifle pointed at him and told him to kick his rifle away, and he did so.

"Why are you shooting at me?" I asked, but seeing the other shot-up vehicles here, I could guess.

"We' re trying to keep people out of our town; the disease is spreading."

"Did you drive up here?" I asked.

"Yes, that's my Jeep," he pointed back with his thumb to a mid-80's Wrangler piece of shit.

"The keys?" I asked.

I walked over and picked up his rifle, a Marlin, as I had as a boy, one that I'm sure my old daddy still had hanging in the hallway gun rack, collecting dust. I dropped my rifle onto its sling and crashed this one against his skull, sending him to the pavement. I left him there bleeding and looked back at my truck in the distance. From here, I could see steam rising from the grill, and with the pile they have here blocking the road, I'm forced to get in his scuffed-up Jeep.

I drove the stolen Jeep until an overpass in Perrysburg, where some idiots were taking potshots at me from up high. They shot it all to pieces, and I was fortunate to get out alive. Once again, I used the darkness and trees to sneak up on these highwaymen. The rustler's or fingernail, my mama would call it, moon didn't cast much light on the bridge, but I could see moving silhouettes. I hefted my rifle and sent one to the concrete, and the other two remembered somewhere else they needed to be. Lesson learned, no more noisy vehicles on this stretch for sure.

10 Gideon

“Jimmy, here’s the situation. My name is Gideon, and my sister Maryn. Our house is nearby, and we're going to take you there too, so we can figure out what to do. Maybe get you some gear so you can make out on your own. We’ll address all that later; in the meantime, I’m going to put this blindfold on you, and we’re leaving. Just stay quiet while we’re walking, and we’ll have a nice supper. Do anything to attract attention to us, and none of us may ever eat another meal? Do you understand?” I asked.

Jimmy went white at the mention of that, and I felt a twinge of guilt for scaring the boy so much, but hell, we were scared too, and it was serious. I didn’t want to kill him, but I wouldn’t trade his safety for Maryn’s. Keeping her out of danger was top priority. We hadn’t turned eighteen ourselves, and I’m not sure we could survive long as things were right now. Indeed, it may make things more difficult with Jimmy around, but the alternative was bleak.

I went back upstairs and got the old squirrel vest that was collecting dust in Mr. Davenport’s hunting room, as he called it, and headed back downstairs to the living room. I fashioned it to cover Jimmy’s eyes and most of his head.

“Ready?” I asked Jimmy.

He nodded but didn’t speak.

“Not a sound on the way. I don’t care what happens, not a peep from you, okay?”

He nodded again, and I slid the vest over his head. I know the old vest was stained with old squirrel and duck blood, and no telling what else, but it would have to do.

“Stand up.”

He did, and I grabbed the duck blanket from the chair he had been sitting in. “Hold onto this blanket so you don’t wander into anything.” I placed a corner of it into his outstretched hand and led off to the door.

“Maryn walk behind in case he gets any weird ideas and shoot him if he makes a sound,” I said loud enough for him to hear clearly through the vest. It would be easier if he genuinely believed the danger was real and kept him quiet. At least I hoped.

“Stay right here,” I said, dropping the blanket and walking to the door, leaving them in the hallway. Slowly opening the door, it's almost sundown. I look around for a few seconds and don't see anything suspicious, so I head back to gather them up, and I take up the blanket.

“Looks clear, so let's be quick but quiet. Jimmy, slow and smooth, you with me?”

He nodded, and we went through the door. Just outside, I stopped so Maryn could close the door behind us. Jimmy kept walking, and I put my hand out to prevent him from running into me. When she turned back to me, I saw a flash from my right and swiftly reached for the pistol at my side. That blue heeler was still here waiting.

“Is that your dog?” I asked Jimmy.

“Dog? What dog? I’ve seen lots,” he said.

“The blue one,” I said, observing the stray warily.

"No, the first time I saw it was this morning near the old man's place."

"Maryn, keep your eyes on that dog; it may be like you and your Uruk-hai," I said with a smile.

"What?" Jimmy asked, muffled under the vest.

"Hungry for man flesh," I grinned even wider, and she rolled her eyes at the reference I always used on her friends, who had heard the joke before.

I walked them next door, then back to our yard to disorient Jimmy in case things went sour, so that he couldn't go directly to our home from Mr. Davenport's. I told Jimmy to stop so I could drop my end of the blanket, reached into my left pocket, and fished out the house key. We didn't want to come home with someone in our house.

I opened it quietly and swung the door inside. I picked up the end of the blanket with a slight tug. We were through the door, and Maryn asked," Can we let the dog in?"

"Hell no," I replied, "it may start barking in here, and we don't need the noise. Close it quick." I heard her turn the locks into place. I took him to the basement door and opened it.

"Jimmy, take one step down, and you can remove the vest."

He tentatively put his foot out and down until he touched the step, then the other. Maryn stepped in and closed the door, and I reached for the flashlight we keep on the ledge. Switching it on, I had him take it off. He does, and I gave him a few seconds to adjust to the light, then beckoned him down with me. I reached the bottom, and he's right behind, looking around terrified. I pointed over to two empty beds and told him to have a seat. He sat nervously, with disheveled, unwashed hair.

“He doesn’t have any gear or supplies that were left behind at the other house?” I asked Maryn.

She shook her head. “Jimmy, we’re going to feed you, but first you need to bathe, and we’ll find you some clothes until the ones you have on can be washed and dry out. Washed by you, understand we aren’t the Red Cross here. We aren’t going to be babying you, so get ready to pull your weight for a couple of days until we figure out what’s your best move.”

“The best move for you or me?” he asked quietly.

“The best for US,” Maryn interjected, boring her eyes into me. She hustled over and gently touched his arm.

“C’mon, let's get you a bath. Luckily, our water heater is gas and still works.” She stared at me like I tracked dog shit into the house. I'm not sure why she’s upset with me, so I shrugged my shoulders and grabbed three cans of beef stew. We only have thirty or so left, and they wouldn’t last us much longer, especially with Jimmy to feed as well. We were going to have to start looting other homes in the neighborhood. I'm not sure how much longer the gas will last on our stove, but for now, we can at least heat canned meals. I took the three cans upstairs after them, struck a match, and got the stew going.

Ten minutes later, they came back to the dining room with Maryn holding a candle (we had already put extra blankets over the curtains to block out any light, but didn’t need to risk anything too bright inside), while Jimmy wore a towel draped over his shoulders, revealing his bony ribs fighting to break free of his skin across his narrow chest. A pair of Maryn’s light pink satin shorts completed his outfit. No wonder she overpowered him so easily, and it made me ashamed of being so gruff to him. Maryn brought out a pair of her old overalls and a light-brown shirt that should have been donated when it became too small two years ago. He turned his back on us, and we did the same as he got dressed.

"Go ahead and eat. I'm going upstairs to wash some of this mud off, don't wait for me." I pointed to the steaming bowls of stew on the table and half a loaf of stale bread. I cleaned the rest on my head besides the cut, and got out of these damp clothes. Coming down the stairs in nothing but a pair of shorts, Jimmy stared up from his food. I know what he sees, or what I saw several days back, before this catastrophe occurred. At seventeen, I am already 6'2" and well-muscled for a boy who didn't spend any time in the gym except what the coach required for football. Short black hair, the cut of which I'm unsure, as Maryn was my latest barber, and I am half scared of studying it too closely in the mirror. Blue eyes that match Maryn's. Our hair and eyes match, but not our skin; she was more like our mom with pale skin that would burn but didn't seem to tan. On the other hand, my skin would darken, and I could spend hours in the Texas sun without burning. Of course, that had been over a year ago, when we were home, and if you know Wisconsin, it's not the same sun. Going shirtless outside for most of the year here was impossible for me. My teammates from school easily accomplished this, but I haven't yet mastered it.

Working, fishing, and swimming took up most of my time back then, but last year I put on some weight from limited activity, which I've since addressed through football and basketball. Anyway, that was starting to melt away, too, from the one-meal-a-day diet I had been on since we found ourselves in this emergency, so I was probably under my toned weight of one eighty-five. I noticed Maryn had begun to slim down as well, and she wasn't much to begin with, so we would have to establish a regular meal routine. I learned in my health class that poor nutrition was linked to illness and physical decline.

Now, here it was just like back home, you couldn't eat at my mama's table with your shirt off or even wear a hat in her house, so by habit I fished a shirt out and put it on before sitting down with them.

"Maryn, can you look at this again? It's opened back up." I pointed to my head. She motioned for me to lean down, and she peered at it using the candle that I had walked to the bathroom and back with.

"Tilt your head over, I can't see anything like that." She gently pulled my head forward.

"It's too wide to stop bleeding on its own. Want me to glue it?" she asked. "No stitch it for me so I don't have to keep fooling with it."

"We'll do it after supper, so you two finish up, and I'll fix you up. I need more light, and my kit is downstairs."

We stacked the bowls and spoons in the sink; she ran water into them and hustled us off down the stairs. Jimmy was the first one down, so he went straight to his bed and wrapped his sleeping bag around his shoulders.

"Come over here where I can see better." She pointed to my bed, and I sat on it.

She gathered up the medical kit and laid everything out on the bed. “This is going to hurt some, and I need to shave some hair back.” What did it matter? I wasn’t impressing girls now.

She got our dad’s straight razor and scraped away from the cut until she was satisfied.

She poured a liquid into my scalp, and it felt like a bucket of hot coals dumped on my head. I gritted my teeth and tried not to make a sound. My eyes involuntarily watered, and she moved to grab the needle and thread. “I’ve never done this; it may not be pretty.”

I gave myself a few seconds to regain my voice before answering. “Just make sure it holds, that’s what’s important. Oh, and clean.”

Yeah, I’ll pour some more alcohol rub on it to make sure.” She smiled sweetly.

“No, it doesn’t have to be that clean.”

She giggled and scrunched my cut together with latex fingers, and the needle going into my skin made me grit my teeth again.

An eternity later, she snipped the thread and proclaimed it a masterpiece in sewing. My mind was made up that from now on, it’s going to be glue and only stitching if there’s no other option. I had to know if I could take the pain, though. I felt everyone must see how much they can take to test themselves, even in silly ways. Not just with pain but with everything from physical activity to stress. I wanted to be tough, but I thought I was going to swoon and embarrass myself in front of Jimmy. The worst would have been never living it down with my sister, but fortunately for me, when I was on the cusp of breaking, she declared the job done. From now on, glue for the win.

I didn't need to worry about Jimmy seeing me in dire straits because when I looked over at him, he was passed out on the bed with food on his face.

11 Gideon

Maryn used a washcloth to wipe away the blood that had leaked out after my shower, then went to the plastic sink beside the water heater and ran another washcloth under cool water. She returned to Jimmy and gently washed his face off while I put up the leftover supplies from the emergency kit. I put it back up with our dwindling supply of food and caught a glimpse of her gently washing Jimmy's face.

It dawned on me that when I came down the stairs, Jimmy had been the only one eating, and in my worry about the freshly opened cut, it didn't register with me until now.

"You let him have your supper, didn't you?" I asked sternly.

"He hasn't eaten well in days, and I wasn't hungry." She headed back to the sink to rinse the cloth out.

"I don't give a damn how long it's been for him, but I DO care if you skip meals. We haven't eaten since yesterday and can't give away our food. No, sit down, and I'll get another ready for you." She started to protest, but I shook my head. "I can make it without Jimmy, but not without you, so let's get you fed and tomorrow I think we can start to find some better sustenance for the immediate future."

After handing her a bowl, I went out to make sure the dog had a couple of strips of beef jerky before heading down to the bed. He sniffed the first piece before eating the second one, which didn't even hit the ground before he devoured it. I relocked the door and headed downstairs, leaving Maryn sitting at the table eating while I got into my bed and fell asleep almost immediately.

Hours or minutes later, I couldn't tell, bolted upright, sending my sleeping bag sliding to the floor, reaching for my pistol that was at the head of my bunk. Something in the dark woke me, and I slowly swung my feet to the cold concrete floor. My head felt like it was on fire, and I thought for a second I would throw up. Taking a second to fight down that sensation, I listened for... what? Something was off. A noise? I heard Maryn's gentle breathing in the bunk next to mine, while I tried to concentrate on what had awakened me.

Carefully, I reached over to grab a flashlight and switched it on with a click, shining it immediately to the bunk where Jimmy was sleeping. He's sitting upright with feet dangling over the edge, staring at me. Is he still asleep? I got out of bed and walked over to him. I put my hand on his bony shoulder, and he sat there shivering in Maryn's shorts. His sleeping bag pooled at his feet, and I shook him more firmly to get his attention. He turned to stare at me, but he probably can't make out my face behind the flashlight. "Jimmy, are you okay?" I asked quietly, not wanting to startle Maryn.

"I-I-m hungry and cold." He stared in my direction.

"Pick up your blanket for a start, and I'll get you something to eat. After that, we'll get you some better clothes, okay?"

He stared ahead, not moving.

"Jimmy, did you hear me?" I asked.

I put the light on his bunk and grabbed him with both hands. "Hey, get the blanket and warm up; if you get sick, you very well may die from it." The pain in my head started to crescendo, and my patience unraveled as he sat there. I reached down, grabbed the blanket, and tossed it to him. It wrapped around his face and head, and one corner hit the flashlight, causing it to spin off the bed and crash onto the floor. The spinning light and bending down for the blanket made me feel queasy again. The noise woke Maryn, and she muttered to me from her bunk.

“Gid? Are you okay?” she asked sleepily.

“Fine. When you’re ready, Jimmy is hungry again.” I groaned as I reached down to get the light from the floor. Well, at least it has finally stopped spinning.

“I’m going to start looking into the neighborhood for more supplies and maybe propane canisters for the camp stove,” I told her as she crawled from her covers. She nodded as I laced up my sneakers. May have to run today, so no boots. I slung the gun belt with my revolver around my hips.

“If I can find something we can use, I’ll come back, and we’ll get started on it together,” I told Maryn.

“You don’t think it’s any danger leaving you here alone with Jimmy?” I asked only half seriously.

“Go do what you need to do, we’ll be fine here. We can sort through what we have and make a list of what we need the most. I’ll keep him occupied so he won't be any trouble. Probably not a good idea to cook anywhere else, though. I don’t want to be walking back from somewhere after dark, do you?” She turned, grabbed Jimmy by the hand, and said, “Let's go upstairs and try to find you clothes that aren’t pink.” She giggled and winked at him.

My mama used to say she got half the height but double the kindness when we were in the womb together. She was right about that, just as she was about everything else she told us, I decided. I asked one day, when we were doing homework at the kitchen table, what I was better at as she extolled how well Maryn could color, how neat her handwriting was, etc., etc., and she told me how fast I was and how strong, but my father yelled from the living room.

"You'll always have a bigger dingus than your sister," which shocked all of us because he wasn't known for making jokes.

My mom's face flushed red as we all burst out laughing, and she scolded him for being crude. She was usually the jokester in the family, and he was often quiet, never cruel, but standoffish to us for the most part. We didn't think much about it; lots of kids didn't even have a father living with them, so we never thought it was odd. We didn't have a TV family, but hell, who does? My father worked most of the time, and days would pass without him being at the dinner table or us speaking.

He took us to the UP with Mr. Davenport last summer for a couple of weeks. Of course, he left after the third day for work, but we stayed behind at his cabin, and it was one of my best memories. The Upper Peninsula was a wild place and exciting for a young man to explore. I had my first sip of beer with my dad and Mr. Davenport that night after unpacking. They both guffawed when I screwed up my face at the bitter taste, and I suppose it's a rite of passage for men to expose kids to things they will find hilarious in the trying of. Mr. Davenport insisted we call him by his first name, Cliff, but my folks would never put up with that. That fell into the "no hats inside, shirts at the table" rules. Adults not in your immediate family were always Mr., Mrs., or Miss, with very few exceptions. The old man who ran the country store near our old homestead in Texas was Mr. Bill, and my grandparents had known him for a hundred years or so.

My father, Mr. Davenport, Maryn, and I shot about two thousand rounds of various ammunition over the two weeks we stayed at the cabin. My father, though he went to law school and became an attorney, was raised on guns, and of course, Mr. Davenport was an enthusiast. We went through the variety of pistols he brought, along with several rifles and, of course, my current pistol. The .357 Ruger Vaquero Mr. Davenport had was my favorite to shoot, and he explained that it was the most versatile for using .38 ammo that wasn't too expensive and didn't kick as much.

We practiced shooting and learned recurve bow skills and animal tracking from Mr. Davenport. The forest around the cabin was vast with no neighbors for miles—he joked that the distant store owner probably mistook our noise for thunder.

As I mentioned, my father was called back to work due to an emergency. He had to drive nearly ten miles just to get phone service and check in, and, as expected, he needed to go. Mr. Davenport and Maryn went with him so they could use their phones, while Mama stayed behind. I asked Maryn to take screenshots of any social media photos of her friends in bikinis, but she just stuck her tongue out at me. Meanwhile, I decided to put my new tracking skills to the test. It proved more challenging than I thought. Locating and identifying tracks was straightforward, but determining their age was much more difficult.

When they returned, my dad said goodbye and headed off to his job. He promised to return when he could, then left down the gravel road in a cloud of dust. Mr. Davenport was also returning to Oak Creek. He would be back in a few days, but an essential package was being delivered to him and had to be signed for, so we loaded most of his weapons, except the 12-gauge Remington, which we still have.

We cooked outdoors, my mom told us jokes and funny stories, we went on walks, and even to the shore of Lake Superior. We camped at Salmon Trout Point, and that night I saw true magic for the first time. The pink, purple, and green lights danced in the sky, and we sat dumbfounded by the sight. None of us had ever seen anything like this display before, and at the time, I didn't know I'd see it only one other time in my life.

When we returned to the cabin, Mr. Davenport had been there the day before and had seen the note my mother had left on the table. He was happy to find us alive and admitted to being somewhat worried that we had been out overnight. His eyes bugged out when my mother told him we had been out four nights, and he looked like a fish out of water for a second. My mom laughed at this, and we sat down to lunch and caught him up on our travels. He was genuinely amazed that she could navigate her way there and back, and she explained that, as a girl, she had been wild and lived outdoors for most of her life.

We played dominoes and cards until late at night. I walked outside before bed and tried to get a look at the aurora borealis again. No shimmering lights, but the night sky looked like spilled sugar on black paper, and the stars seemed close enough to reach out and touch.

"Quite a sight, isn't it?" Mr. Davenport asked right behind me, startling me out of my daze.

"Yes, sir, I haven't ever seen a clear sky like this."

He slapped my shoulder, "Won't either unless you get away from other people."

“What do people have to do with it?” I asked, confused.

“People are mostly afraid of the dark, and light pollution is why you can’t see a sky like this unless there’s a major power outage.”

I felt foolish for not thinking of that before asking. “C’mon, let's get some sleep, tomorrow I want to show you how to catch fish, and I don’t mean the little kind you grow in Texas.” He snorted with laughter as we walked back to the cabin. He teased us about our home state, but never cruelly. He showed kindness and respect to everyone I ever saw him interact with, and he was funny, too.

A couple of days later, my father returned, and we stayed four more days running through most of his ammunition. We fished, ate, played games, and were all teased by my mother to varying degrees. While playing Scrabble one night, my mom spelled out the word ‘cervix’. I wasn’t entirely sure what it was, and my sister blushed bright red. My dad looked upset for some reason. Maryn, seeing my confusion, asked through her blush, “Gid do you know what that is?”

Mr. Davenport, sensing my confusion, cut in, “Yeah, my mother had two of these when I was a boy.”

“WHAT!” my mama exclaimed, fighting back her laughter.

“Yeah, she put them on the wall in the main room of our house.” He shifted in his chair.

“Two CERVIXES?” my mother asked incredulously.

Mr. Davenport looked at me with his weathered face and warm eyes and gave me a quick wink. “That’s the thing they nailed Jesus to, right?”

The color drained from my father's face. Maryn just gaped at him, but I had never seen my mama laugh so hard. Amid all the teasing, jokes, and pranks, this was the first time I had seen her laugh uncontrollably. One thing I was sure of when we loaded up to return to Oak Creek was that these were the best two weeks of my life.

12 Maryn

Mr. Davenport showed us a lot during the camping trip up to the UP. My mama also showed me something important as well. She wasn't just a pretty face, full of wit and sarcasm, but a competent woodsman and tracker. I was nervous about her taking us out into the wilderness, but she just laughed off my reservations and told me that if you knew the stars, you knew where you were.

"The stars aren't the only way to travel, though. Any time the sun doesn't rise in the east and sink in the west, you have worse problems than being lost," she chuckled around her canteen.

"Your father is good at this stuff, too," she said as she sat on a fallen log and patted a spot beside her.

"I couldn't imagine him out here hiking," I admitted to her. She smiled and took another drink.

"He's a woodsman, too, though he was never comfortable with it like your uncle and me. He's the real deal, and I'm only passable. Good enough to get you two to the show tonight and back home again.

"The show?" I asked, confused, as we were surrounded by trees and streams. She laughed at that and got back to her feet.

"We have to go, or we will miss the opening act and remember it's not over until the curtain call." She smiled at me slyly, and we continued.

The ride home from the trip was a high point for me. I had spent some quality time with most of my family, and the show she had told me about was indeed worth it. Now, though we were heading back to civilization and I could check in on my friends that I haven't seen from back home, and the new ones I made here in our neighborhood. My Texas friends, of course, would all be online, but I wanted to know how they were getting on and what the latest gossip was about the boys.

Gid was lost in his own thoughts as we turned onto the first pavement we'd been on in days, and I ignored him and immediately tried to get on social media. The familiar app opened, and I checked everyone's stories, then uploaded the photos I had taken. The girls begged for more pics of Gid, shirtless, and even teased me about being lost in the woods with the ruggedly handsome Mr. Davenport. The post and the comments under the pics were not for the faint of heart, and luckily, my mother didn't follow me on here, or she would have been furious with me for some of these hashtags.

I spun through my phone's camera roll and landed on one of Mr. Davenport, where he was handing over a walking stick he'd cut for me. His smile was captured on the screen, and he was the sweetest man I had ever been around. Patient, warm, and with a great sense of humor, I wondered whether he had a family or was considering remarriage. Surely, he was lonely over there by himself.

The ding of my phone brought my thoughts to what my friends were saying, and the sweet ones about Mr. Davenport and the envy of my mama's photos were replaced by the vulgarity of the shameless harlots over Gid.

13 Llewelyn

I've had two vehicles crippled by gunfire before I could even get out of Ohio, I thought bitterly. You know how it feels when you are in a hurry, and everything seems to get in the way? Now my patience had run out, and I silently vowed that the next person who hindered me on my way to Wisconsin, I would hunt down. I'd had enough pot shots and hiding in the woods; from here on out, I would be the aggressor.

I walked sixty miles until I caught a break. I had to constantly hide off the interstate as armed people rode by in pickups, sometimes weapons bristling out of the bed like Afghanistan. Sometimes only a couple, but all armed, driving up and down the highway like they were patrolling. I haven't seen any active law enforcement, and since the National Guard wasn't out, the brakes had truly come off.

I came to an overpass that was thankfully empty of people and saw a farmstead off to the side of the road. I cut through the thin trees here and had a look around. The farmer who had lived here had a mess to clean up, if he was still alive, because his fence had been kicked down and all his livestock were gone. Too bad, I thought, I could have ridden a horse with no problems. I went through the barns and found nothing I could use, just old tack and hay. I started for the shop next to the house, but figured I may as well check the house first, because if he was here, I didn't want to be in the shop and catch an ass full of birdshot.

The front door was unlocked as farm folks do, and I walked into the gloom and instantly smelled that I needn't have worried about him. The old couple was dead in their bed, and I left without disturbing them and headed for the kitchen. I used their gas stove and pot to heat a can of chili. I went outside and sat down away from the smell to enjoy the first food I'd eaten since yesterday morning. Mixing in crushed saltines, I ate every bite.

I set the pot down on the back steps, walked to the metal building, and looked inside. I tried the switch on the wall, and of course, it didn't work, and I flicked on my penlight. Between that and the door I left open, I could make out a couple of chairs and an old fridge that men trundled from their homes into the workshop to operate for twenty more years, keeping the coldest beer around. Opening it, I found cool beer, and that would have to do as I cracked the top and swilled it down. I looked around and found a pair of mountain bikes stowed overhead in a custom rack the old man probably built himself. I pulled the larger one down and checked the tires. Good to go, so I had some transportation at least.

I dusted off the old cot he had stowed against his work bench and rolled my jacket up for a pillow. I looked at the ceiling, wondering what had happened to Charles and Jess. If their twins were even still alive, I may be walking through this madness and find an empty home or worse, their bodies inside. My old mama back home, worried sick, didn't sit too well with me either. She told me not to come home for a reason, but I don't know if she was already sick or just concerned that I would get infected if I traveled there. She had made her wishes clear about the children first, I was duty-bound to our bloodline to find out for sure if they lived and to help any way I could; them's the rules and always has been, my old man would say.

14 Gideon

Mr. Davenport became a staple in my life the year we lived here. He expressed his opinion on several subjects, and I absorbed it like a sponge. Explaining to me that a man's physical fitness was his responsibility to maintain, and nothing should stop you from doing anything you can to stay healthy. He fought in Panama and had been wounded by a grenade that a fellow soldier had thrown too close to him. He couldn't walk without a limp, but it didn't slow him down too much. Enough to get him discharged from the Army, but he came home and worked at the post office for the next thirty-two years, retiring last year. He exercised regularly and still hunted and fished, so he was in great shape for an old man about to turn 67.

We spent a lot of time together, and I probably asked him a million questions. He wasn't resentful that he was crippled from battle, but he was upset with the US selling or using weapons that ended up turning brown kids into skeletons. Not sure exactly where that was happening, but he didn't believe America had any business in the Middle East, or militarily in any other country. He explained that one of America's greatest assets was soft power, wielded through aid and infrastructure rather than rockets and guns.

He didn't give a damn about Americans feeding children with food stamps, but was furious over our government getting federally funded healthcare and insider trading. Most of what he talked about went over my head, but I did understand that he showed respect to everyone he met. Young as I was, he valued my point of view even if it wasn't completely developed. Mr. Davenport told me the most dangerous thing you can do is judge someone without getting to know them. I know for sure he gave old man Burns food on the regular, and he volunteered at a homeless shelter in Milwaukee every week. He never spoke of his family, at least not with me – and I didn't think to ask, though I never met any of them, whether he had one. The old pictures on his walls and fireplace mantle showed a younger version of himself with a wife who died some years back in a car accident. He never spoke of her, and I didn't mention her again after learning of her tragic death.

We spent a lot of time together that first summer in Oak Creek, and he never ran out of patience with my company. He ate at our home often, claiming that my mama brought the only thing worth a damn from the south with her cooking. They constantly teased each other, and even my father was somewhat at ease in his company. Mr. Davenport grew a garden in his yard, and we had a steady supply of fresh vegetables. He gave us advice on how to deal with the winters here, and my mama introduced him to spices beyond salt and pepper. He took us to his cabin in late summer, and I hunted with him that fall after football season. Maryn and I both cleaned fish we'd never seen before, like Walleye and Brook trout. We had Thanksgiving at his cabin and hunted in the surrounding woods. We already knew how to dress game animals from hunting in our childhood, and Mr. Davenport was impressed by how quickly and efficiently we both cleaned deer. He promised a turkey hunt the following spring, and I looked forward to it, having never even seen a wild turkey before we moved here.

Spring came, and instead of preparing for the turkey season, he promised me this year, Mr. Davenport got a hospital stay due to slipping and breaking his leg, and then three weeks later, the world almost died. Well, I don't know about the world, but most of mine did.

I stepped out of the back door slowly, looking around for any danger. Hand on my pistol, ears straining for any sound of danger. I checked the thermostat nailed to a post on the back steps, and it read a balmy 48 degrees. Girding myself against the cold, I quietly shut the door and stepped off.

A whirl of movement to my left, and I spun that way, expecting danger. A blue blur in the early morning light, that dog was still here. It walked to within six feet and sat down, staring at me. I cautiously looked around for anyone with it. No one seemed to be around, so I squatted down and extended my hand. The dog was wary but seemed unafraid. It sat up, stepped toward me, stopped, and sat again. I reached into my jacket pocket and took out the pack of beef jerky. Hearing the package crinkle, the dog stepped closer, nose twitching. Pulling out a piece, I coaxed it to come closer. I could see a frayed rope loop around its neck, and I'll slip it off if he just comes close enough. One more step, and it stretched out to reach the morsel. Not even bothering to chew the jerky, it's gone in an instant.

"If you're going to eat my lunch, I'm at least going to pet you," I said quietly. The second piece went without hesitation, and the third I hold closer. Not waiting anymore, I placed my hand on its neck and rubbed gently. It reached for my hand with the food, ignoring the petting and me pulling the rope off. The last piece was gone just as fast as the others, and the dog turned and trotted away a few steps, no longer seeing any more food. That's when I noticed he was male. I stood up, tried to step toward him, and he shied away.

"You're welcome, ingrate," I mumbled as I started through my back yard. I walked slowly from house to house until I reached the end of Madison Drive and then turned east into the neighborhood. In the opposite direction from where old man Burns had walked yesterday, hoping to avoid him, I turned left onto Crane and walked to the dead end at the park. I tried the front door of the last house on the street, a two-story house with a brick base and a tan top. A younger couple lived here, but I had never spoken to them, just waved to them in passing.

I opened the door as slowly and quietly as possible, listening for any signs of life. One hand on the pistol, I quickly enter and close the door behind me, more worried about someone outside seeing me than in here.

It's a strange feeling being in someone else's home. Even the house we live in now doesn't quite feel like home, but a stranger's home was unsettling. A stranger's house with a high chance of them being dead inside really ratcheted the eeriness.

Luckily, the home was abandoned, and I found plenty of clothes that I could wear and maybe some for Maryn, too. I'm not a good judge of clothes, so I would bring her later to look for herself. I emptied their canned goods from the pantry into my backpack, though it wasn't much. They probably ate out a lot, I thought, as I checked for batteries and flashlights. Finding none of that, I saw a small bag of unopened dog food by the back door, so I made a mental note to grab it for the new acquaintance. One place left to check, and I put it off till last: the refrigerator. Although it was still cool here, the power had been off for several days, and the food inside was turning. Bracing myself for the stench, I opened the door and quickly glanced inside. I pocketed the pack of D and AA batteries I found on the shelf and closed the door. The stench was too fast, though, and dressing animals hadn't made me immune to the smell of long rotten and decaying food in such a small space. I nearly gagged and took a few moments to compose myself. Once the dry heaves passed, and I could breathe deeply again, I exited through the back door, the pack full, a small bag of dog food in hand.

Before I made it to my back door, the dog came running up, looking at me expectantly. I tried to pet him again, but he wasn't having it. I shrugged my shoulders and headed inside to make sure everything was in hand.

15 Maryn

I heard Gid knock quietly on the basement door before opening and descending. He dropped the backpack onto his made-up bunk and sat beside it.

"Everything good here?" He looked over at Jimmy, still lying under his blankets.

"Yeah, did you see anyone?" I asked while he unzipped his bag and dumped the contents onto the bed.

"Just that blue dog." He set the cans on our plastic 6-foot table.

"He didn't try to bite you?" I asked as he stood up and slung his pack over his shoulder.

"No, he just ate my lunch and wouldn't even let me pet him." He shook his head slightly. "I'm going back out; I'd like to find some more weapons if I can. Not sure how many of the city folks here were hunters like Mr. Davenport, but I want to find at least another pistol for you."

"I don't know that I need anything except the shotgun for protection," I said to him as he headed back up. "You going to carry a shotgun all day?" he threw back at me and went up the basement door before I could say anything.

Carry all day? What is he talking about, I wondered. I shook my head and refocused on the task that needs doing most today: getting Jimmy up and properly dressed in something that will fit better.

"Jimmy?" I shook him gently, and he sprang up, eyes wild and hair a mess. "Let's get ready for the day. It's going to take half the morning to tame your hair, so let's get started." I smiled at him to let him know I'm only teasing. He didn't seem to notice, and he stood up and stretched with a yawn. The pink shorts are almost falling off his skinny hips as he reached above his head. "Throw these old overalls on for right now, and I've got you a pair of socks and one of my shirts here." I handed him these and turned my back while he got dressed.

I sort out the cans Gid has brought back and try to think where we could start the search for him for some suitable clothes. The Bakers lived on the corner of E Michigan Avenue and had younger kids who often played in the street. Not sure how many, but that's where the street hockey net was always pulled in, so it's probably worth checking there first.

"Maryn?" I turned, and Jimmy's ready to go. We always left our shoes by the door, so I went up the stairs and motioned for him to follow. I turned and put my finger on my lips to remind him to be quiet before opening the door. He nodded, and we stepped into the living room. I looked around, holding the shotgun, making sure we were alone.

"Close the door," I whispered over my shoulder to Jimmy. The sun was full, and with reflective tint on the windows, you can see out, but not in, so there's enough light to see by. We closed the heavy curtains when we cook up here and add the blankets just as an added precaution.

Jimmy grabbed the door and pushed it closed. Well, truth be told, he tried to close it, but it sticks sometimes, so I helped a bit.

"Sorry," he said sheepishly.

"No worries," I told him with a smile.

He's holding one hand onto his stomach, and it dawned on me that we probably needed to eat again. Not sure what has happened to him since this started, but regular feedings weren't it.

"I'm hungry, let's warm something up while we wait on Gid." He smiled weakly while I walked over to the kitchen's one window and drew it shut.

"Raviolis?" I asked him, and he nodded.

"You know how to cook?" I asked.

"N-no." he stammered.

"Well, you won't learn over there; come over here."

He shuffled over, and I went through the simple task of heating the food. "Watch the sauce, when it bubbles for a bit, I know it's ready," I said to him as he watched me bring the pot over.

We shared the can of ravioli, and I brought him over to the sink. "Got to learn this part too," I said as I walked him through washing the pot, plates, and silverware. I washed them and handed him the clean dishes to put in the drying rack.

The front door opened, and I grabbed the shotgun. I peeked around the hallway corner and saw Gid facing the door, shutting it back. When he turned back, he saw me and smiled.

"Ready?" he asked.

"What's the plan?" I asked.

"We need to start going through these houses that we suspect are empty and look for more supplies. Clothes, weapons, batteries, food, etc. After that, a decision has to be made on how long we are going to wait for him before we take off."

"Let's check the Baker home for sure and search for Jimmy some clothes," I said, and he looked at Jimmy.

Nodding his head, he says, "Okay, we can go there first, and that will be the furthest we search today. We can work our way back here from there. I don't like moving during the day, but I sure as hell don't want to be walking into these houses in the night."

"Are there going to be dead people in there?" Jimmy asked.

"Yeah, I suspect so, Jimmy. It isn't dead people I'm worried about, though. Dead people can't hurt you, but the living sure can." Gid said.

"W-w-what if they're zombies?" Jimmy wrapped his skinny arms around himself and shook slightly.

"Jimmy, there aren't any zombies, but if you see one, yell out, and I'll handle it. The important thing to focus on is staying quiet and looking for dangerous, live people. Think you can do that, or do I need to leave you here?" Gid growled at him.

"Maryn, are you going too?" he looked at me.

"Yes, I'm going."

"Oh, I can't stay here alone." He was on the verge of tears at the thought of being left.

I looked at Gid, and he scowled. He shrugged and walked over to Jimmy, putting both of his hands on his shoulders.

"We aren't going to leave you alone if you don't want to stay, but you will have to be quiet and not put us in any more danger than we are in already. Understand that we ARE in danger, and the more desperate people are, the more dangerous they become. You saw that old man shoot at me yesterday, so you know anything can happen. When a dead person takes a shot at me, I'll start to concern myself with them."

"I'm scared, Gideon, I'm not brave like you," he said, and I saw him for what he was for the first time—a terrified little boy. Softening my tone, I kneeled in front of him.

"I know you're scared, and being scared is the only time you can be brave. I'm afraid, too, so let's pay attention and be brave together, okay?"

Seeing him be kind to Jimmy made me proud of Gid, but it saddened me to think about what this little boy had been through for a week on his own, afraid of everything. I'm not sure what he saw when he looked at him, but all I see is a boy who is on the edge of a mental breakdown. It's not his fault the world was in an uproar no more than it was mine, but he would have to adapt to it. I'm determined to do what I can to help him while also learning, myself, the new reality we live in, and I can already see a harder skin starting to form on Gid, and I'm honestly not sure how far the change in him will go or if I can do anything to help. I know he is grieving still for our mama and even for Mr. Davenport; it didn't seem to trouble him that our dad was missing, but surely that was on his mind as well.

We found the Baker house empty, and it had precisely what we needed for Jimmy. There are some clothes and boots he can wear, and we fold as much as we can into a bag we found in one of the bedrooms. No guns and not much in the way of food, but Gid did find a nice knife and sheath that he liked, so he tucked that into his belt.

“Let's leave the doors to the houses we already checked unlocked, so if anyone comes looting, they will not skip these, and maybe they will waste time searching these and may buy us time to stay hidden,” I said as we leave the Bakers.

“Good idea, we aren’t coming back here for anything else, so why not?”

The home next door was even less productive, and the one after that had its back door locked. “I’ll go check the front, so stay here and listen for anything,” Gid said and took off around the corner.

16 Llewelyn

I woke in the cot and wondered where in the hell I was for a second. It's completely dark, the way I kept my motel room, and I wondered for a few seconds if it was time for me to go to work. I sat up and remembered that work was canceled, probably forever, in the current situation we found ourselves in. I stepped into my boots and heard the rustling again. DANGER, my mind screamed, and I picked up my rifle and searched for my light. I flicked it on, shone it around the immediate area, and saw two raccoons taking off back toward the house.

"Little fuckers scared me," I mumbled, looking at my watch. Five minutes after four. Well, may as well get this day started, I told myself, standing up and feeling the weight of the years. People talk about how they could withstand this or that when they were younger, and I suppose that's true, but the one thing I remember, and miss is how quickly I recovered. I still felt the heat and pain, thirst and hunger as I do now, but I could rebound from them so much easier then. I was closing in on forty since my birthday a few days ago, and it was bringing a change in me. Standing up and raising my arms above my head with a yawn, I felt the slick scar on my back and side tighten and stretch. Those Afghans had some hard boys over there, and they left their marks on me, but fair is fair, I supposed.

I rolled up the main door to the shop, pushed the bike out to the road in front of the house, then sat on it and tried to pedal. I wobbled at first, it had been twenty years since I had been on one, and I smiled at the memory of that ride. Flying down the hill by Mr. Bill's country store, not using the handlebars, and hitting a wet spot on the pavement that sent me crashing into the pines. I was trying to impress Jess and her friend Rachel, but I made a fool of myself instead. It was worth the scratches, though, to see her look down at me with so much concern, I remembered.

The wind rushing past me and the hum of the tires on the pavement may have blocked out noises from far off, but when I pulled off to let people drive past, the quiet afterward felt the same as when I was kicking doors in Iraq. You know people were watching, you just didn't see them, and it's a strange sensation. I gave trucks plenty of time to get down the road before I resumed my trip and only stopped afterward to scout overpasses and piles of wreckage.

A pair of men ran off into the woods when I came upon them looting a Lincoln. Seeing me, they rushed off, but not before I caught a glimpse of a wad of money in the younger one's hand. Not sure what he was going to do with that, but the unlucky, the infirm, and the foolish would soon die off. It wouldn't be long, and those boys would learn you can't eat money.

17 Gideon

I walked stealthily around the front of the house and noticed the garage doors were open. Two Mercedes were parked inside, and my hopes sank. I didn't expect folks who drove this type of car to have any firearms, but my dad drove one; and he had the pistol. Besides, we were here, and you could never tell. The front door and the garage were both locked, so I headed around to the back to Maryn and Jimmy.

Jimmy, now dressed in better-fitting clothing but still wearing the oversized overalls so he could stuff several shirts under them for warmth, didn't look as pathetic, and it seemed to cheer him, so if nothing else, that was worth the trip.

"All locked up," I told them as I looked up at the split-level home. "Jimmy, you think if I boost you up that you can crawl into one of those windows and unlock the back door for us? I really don't want to break out the glass if we can avoid it." Jimmy looked up at the window and nodded nervously to me.

I clasped my hands into a stirrup and lifted him, surprised by how light he is, until he was shoulder-high against the window above the back door. He fiddled with the screen for a sec, then it's free, dropped it beside Maryn and me. He tried to slide the window open, but it won't budge.

"I'm going to let you down, and we'll try another."

All the windows on the back are locked, but we are in luck on the side opposite the garage. He easily slid this one up, and I boosted him higher, and he folded over into the room.

Looking down at us, he said, "It's scary, Gid."

"I know, but in twenty seconds we'll be together again. We aren't going anywhere, okay?"

He nodded and reached into his back pocket for his flashlight. I thought he was gone when he popped his head out the window again, and Maryn smiled at him, and I gave him the thumbs up. He disappeared into the house, and we waited. Seconds ticked by and nothing: twenty, thirty, forty seconds, and nothing. There's a loud crash and screaming from inside. In a near panic, I pulled the new knife I had acquired from the Bakers and hit the back door glass with the handle, shattering it inward. I snaked my hand through the broken glass and felt for the bolt. The screaming intensified, and I fumbled with the lock. It seemed to take me a couple of moments to open, but when I did, the screaming was still going on, and I pulled my arm out, and blood was running down to my fingers. Ignoring that, I opened the door, and I told Maryn to stay here till I see what's going on.

I rushed to the screaming, pulled my pistol out, and bounded up the stairs. The smell of decay was awful, but it didn't fully register with me. At the top, I turned and looked up the next set. Jimmy was lying at the top and screaming like hell, but I couldn't see what had terrified him so. Taking the next set of stairs, I saw in the gloomy hallway someone lying across his feet. A flipped-over wheelchair and a corpse have pinned him to the floor, and he was still screaming and trying to scramble out from under them.

He saw me and yelled, "ZOMBIE, ZOMBIE!!" I hooked him under his arms and pulled him, and the corpse rolled to its back, and the chair came with him. He shrieked again, and I looked and saw his bibs caught the wheelchair handle and were tangled. I sliced it with my knife and dragged him down the stairs away from the "zombie". Maryn rushed to him and wrapped her arms around him. He's sobbing, and I growled at him to be quiet, and Maryn gave me a withering look and took him to the back door that I had broken into.

I slowly headed up the stairs this time with my flashlight out and gun in hand. Rounding the top, I shone the light on the carnage on the floor. An old man who was wheelchair bound from the looks of it had died here, and somehow Jimmy had bumped the chair going around it, and the chair handle had snagged on his overalls strap. The man and chair had been dragged forward and pulled over on top of him, and his feet had tangled in the oxygen line, and in the struggle, the chair was flipped on its back with the small wheels in the air. The body was sprawled on its back with arms pointing back at the stairs. The oxygen bottle was overturned, and a tube ran to the mask still on the man's face with his wispy white hair splayed across Jimmy's stomach as his legs churned trying to escape, but only managing to drag the entire contraption with him toward the stairs until I cut him loose. What looked like a hospital gown was splotchy with stains and was almost hiked up to his crotch. The smell was eye-watering, and the sight was nightmarish. No wonder Jimmy lost his shit; I was about to do the same.

I turned to head back down the stairs when I saw the body move. Surely the play of light in the dark hallway and shadows has tricked me. It twitched again. Even then, I told myself it's not real. It's almost imperceptible, a slight shudder rippled through the body, and I felt a scream building in my brain. A violent twitch at the man's crotch, and I knew I should run, but I'm frozen in place, terror gripping me as I've never felt before. Until then, I had forgotten the pistol in my fist, and I extended my arm to the corpse to pull the trigger. Recalling all the movies, I knew a shot in the head would be the only thing that would stop it, and I prepared for the noise. The bottom of the gown wiggled, and in my terror, I had to force down the hysterical thought that even a zombie still got erections, and I almost laughed out loud like a madman. I thumbed back the pistol hammer as a large rat poked its head from the hem of the gown and skittered off down the hallway. I sank to my knees in relief. Sweat had broken out on my face, and my muscles seemed to give up.

A couple of breaths of the fetid air, and I regained my composure. Shakily walking down the stairs, unwilling to turn my back entirely on the carnage up here, I made my way to the front doorway. Maryn and Jimmy stand just outside, and she still holds him and speaks to him quietly. At least he had stopped screaming.

“We have to go, quickly now,” I said as I joined them outside.

“Close the door,” Maryn said to me, and I shot back over my shoulder, “To Hell with that door, let's get home, everyone in a mile heard that screaming.”

18 Gideon

We came through our backyard gate, and that blue dog was sitting at the door. He got up and moved away when we got close, then watched us walk past him. He ran up to Jimmy and put his head into his hand. Jimmy didn't really seem to notice at first, and I'm afraid the incident with the corpse had broken his mind. The dog nuzzled him, and he looked down at him, smiling a little. Though still in a daze, he seemed to understand the comfort the dog was giving him, and he dropped down on one knee and wrapped his skinny arms fully around him. The dog patiently stood still and looked at me like he was daring me to try to break up this intimate moment.

I shook my head, walked to the door, and unlocked it with the key. I opened the door and waved Maryn inside.

"Bring me a towel out here, will you? I don't want to bleed all over the floor." I looked back at Jimmy, still holding the dog, kneeling in the grass. I turned to Maryn and shrugged my shoulders. She handed me a white towel, and I wrapped my hand in it so we could get inside.

"Bring the dog in," she whispered. Not wanting to argue in the doorway, I told Jimmy to come inside and bring his friend. He got up and walked to the door, looked back, and motioned to the dog. He followed and walked right in, as if it were his home. I shook my head, stepped inside, closed the door, and locked it. Boots off, and we headed into the dining room.

I ran my hand under the bathroom sink to assess the damage from the glass and saw it wasn't so bad, some scarring, but I had full use of my hand, at least. I poured some peroxide over it, letting the excess fall to the tub, and Maryn handed me some antibacterial ointment. I lathered it on, and she examined it. The index finger, the back of my hand, and the wrist got the worst of it. We went back to the dining room, and Jimmy was standing by the door, not wanting to let us out of his sight. Maryn put her arm around him and guided him to a chair, where he sat, blue dog under the table between his knees.

"I'm sorry for sending you into that house alone, Jimmy, but that wasn't a zombie, so that we can clear that up. Now tell me exactly what happened." I sat on my chair, giving him my full attention. Maryn wrapped bandages over my hand and wrists, while Jimmy looked shell-shocked.

"I saw him sitting there and knew he was dead. I tried to walk around him and reach the stairs, but the chair caught on my shirt. That's why it's ripped." He turned to Maryn and said, "Sorry about that. I know you put yourself in danger to get me some clothes, and I already tore my shirt." His shirt was indeed torn, and he looked horrified at ruining the new clothes. It wasn't just his shirt; those bibs weren't letting go of the handle either, but I didn't mention that.

"Hush about that shirt, silly. We are worried about your well-being. We can always get you more clothes." She said to him with a smile.

"I tried to pull away, and the chair fell over on top of me, and I couldn't get up. I didn't mean to scream, but I was stuck, and I DID see the man move, so he's a zombie for sure. I was afraid he would bite me and turn me into a zombie, too. Oh my God, did he bite me?" he started to shake with panic.

"No, he didn't bite you, and he wasn't a zombie," I told him with my arm out to stop him from undressing.

“I saw him moving even though he was rotted. I cross my heart, Gid,” he pleaded.

“I know, but it wasn’t him moving it was rats inside eating him,” I said.

Maryn and Jimmy both looked sick to their stomachs with this news. “Y-y-you’re sure?” he stammered.

“Yes, I saw a rat come from his body,” I said to assuage his fear. “You kicked his chair over, and the oxygen tube was caught on his body and made him jerk. Rats were eating him on the inside, and they came out when I checked up there again.”

“It was eating him?” he asked. I nodded, and he ran to the sink and vomited. The dog followed him and rested against the back of his legs as Jimmy let breakfast raviolis go.

Maryn ran over, put her arm around him, and turned on the water. She grabbed a washcloth, dampened it under the running water, and washed his face with it.

“You need to take those clothes off because you may have gotten corpse juice on you while you were wrestling with that dead guy,” I said with a grin.

He turned back to the sink and chums some more. Maryn shot daggers at me with her eyes and mouthed the word “Asshole”. That made me grin wider, relieved that we had made it through the altercation relatively unharmed. Of course, Jimmy was on his tiptoes, emptying himself of everything he had eaten from first grade till this morning, but he was alive and intact.

I realized I had made serious mistakes today, though I learned a valuable lesson. If cars were at a home, they most likely would contain people alive or dead. I should also have checked the open garage for a ladder instead of sending Jimmy into danger like that, and I would apologize to him for it when he was done retching. Maryn was right about my teasing, but I was relieved that we were safe, even after the mistakes I made.

19 Maryn

Bathed and dressed, Jimmy was starting to get his color back. I felt so bad for him this morning, and unlike Gid, I knew the trauma from this morning would probably stay with him for a while, if not forever. We were lucky it wasn't more serious, and I could tell Gid felt the same way by the brooding he did. I made sure Jimmy and his clothes were cleaned. The dog had followed us through the house to the bathroom and back, and we were back down in the basement again when Gid asked, "What are we going to do about this dog?"

"What do you mean, do about him?" I asked.

"We can't have him barking and giving away our position here. I don't think we should keep him around, and if we put him outside, someone may see him and know that we are in here feeding him."

"The dog stays, but we can compromise." I see that he thought we were going to put him outside, but I followed up with, "He stays, but you can name him."

He furrowed his brows and started to say something. Changing his mind, he nodded and started unpacking his cleaning kit.

"I can see he helps Jimmy so that we can give it a try, but if he barks, then he must go. Maybe I can train him to help me hunt rabbits." He announced as he began cleaning his gun. Jimmy and I looked at each other and smiled. He reached down and gently petted him.

We spent that day at home. I cooked for us, and Gid washed the dishes. That evening, we took the dog out, and he seemed content to be around us and seemed housebroken. Gid told us later, over a game of Monopoly, that he would resume the search for more food and gear the next day.

“I can’t hunt where I was yesterday again with that crazy old man wandering around armed, so I’ll try some more houses. Soon, we are going to have to make a big move from here before it gets too late in the year,” he pondered.

“How long do you think it will take to get to Texas, Gid?” I asked.

“Riding bikes, maybe six weeks or so. Hard to say how bad the roads are going to be, weather, bridge conditions, things like that. We need to be there by early summer to plant, but we really need to start getting ready for the trip. I don’t think it will be practical to use a tent, so we will have to use the sleeping bags we have. Food and medicine will be most of the weight we have to carry —oh, and water. Also need to find suitable weapons and ammo. Speaking of that, Jimmy, come over here and let’s go over the guns we have so you will be familiar with them.”

They huddled together with the dog and went over the shotgun and pistol while I read a book, but Jane Austen couldn’t take my mind off today. The screams from Jimmy were still ringing in my ears, and soon I just closed the book, turned over, and stared at the wall. What felt like hours later, I must have drifted off because I was dreaming about those screams when I realized someone was shaking me awake. I turned over and could make out Jimmy’s slight silhouette in the nightlight. “What’s wrong?” I asked sleepily.

“I had an accident,” Jimmy said softly, clearly embarrassed.

“It's okay, let's get you cleaned up,” I said as I swung my sock feet to the cold floor. We headed upstairs and back to the bath.

“I'm sorry,” he said as I waited outside the door for him to get cleaned up.

“It's okay, Jimmy, you had a terrible day, and we're all scared,” I told him.

“Gideon isn't afraid; he came in there and got me,” Jimmy said muffled through the door.

“He's afraid in a different way, but he is afraid too. He will always come for you, he's mental that way for family, we all are. It's okay to be scared, and you shouldn't be ashamed of it.” I told him, realizing how afraid I am.

“But I'm not family,” he said, sadly.

“No? You think Gid would cut his hand up and run into a zombie house to save just some random stranger?”

“Yes, that's what heroes do, silly.” He walked off back to the basement door, and I followed him.

After we got downstairs, he asked if he could sleep in the bunk with me. I moved over, and he crawled beside me, dragging his blanket with him. Soon, I can hear his even breathing, and I hope he sleeps nightmare-free through the night.

Gid was up and already cooked breakfast before we got to the kitchen. He left a note on the table, letting me know he would be on Chapel Drive, searching for houses today. We ate the breakfast he had made and fed the scraps to our new dog, and I cleaned up the dishes. Afterward, we made our beds and went through the leftover food so I could figure out what to cook for supper tonight. We had eaten twice a day since Jimmy joined us, and I knew Gid was worried about how scrawny and underfed he was. We washed all the clothes and hung them outside on a makeshift clothesline Gid had built in the backyard. We have a high fence, so unless someone opened the gate or stood on something, they wouldn't be able to see into our yard.

"High fences make good neighbors," Mr. Davenport said to my dad when he brought up the idea of putting up a fence not long after we moved in. My father looked uncomfortable, and my mother laughed brightly.

"What kind of fence could keep you away?" she teased.

"The wall that a million Chinese worked on wouldn't keep me away from your porkchops," he shot back. They laughed together while my father just stood there looking awkward. Daddy and Gid put up the fence, causing a minor scandal, according to my mom and Mr. Davenport. After finishing up, we were having supper when my mom said she was happy they were done with the fence so that things could get back to normal.

Gid and my dad both looked confused. Mr. Davenport put in, "Yeah, I hear the neighborhood has been in an uproar, and the HOA was bringing down charges. Things have gone to Hell since I've been gone all weekend."

"HOA charges?" my dad asked, confused.

"Yeah, apparently two men have been seen making unregistered milkshakes in our backyard." My mom smiled mischievously.

"Milkshakes?" Dad wondered, not seeing the joke coming.

"Yes, you've brought all the girls to the yard with your milkshakes," I said, and my mom was about to burst.

Gid laughed, and the realization hit my dad, finally, he's being had. He shook his head, and we all fell into fits of laughter except him.

Gid said, "Where did you go this weekend, Mr. Davenport?"

"To a gun show over in Door County. Got an old army buddy that lives over that way, and he puts me up when I get over." He took a sip of sweet tea, but didn't let us off the hook, yet.

"I heard the neighborhood ladies were all a flutter over you two working shirtless in the back yard. The divorce rate is going to skyrocket in this neighborhood because you two are out here making the women pant and the men envious." He guffawed at the look on my dad's face.

"I heard even Mr. Connors turned out to watch the show." He said with a wink at Gid. Mr. Connors lived two houses over with his partner and proudly displayed a rainbow flag on his front porch year-round. I don't know about Mr. Connors, but I did see several women and girls, ranging from middle schoolers to grandmas, suddenly take an interest in the bike path that ran in front of our house. My best friend, Stephanie, texted and begged me to take some pics and post them on Instagram for her to devour. She was away in Wisconsin Dells, or she would have been here, lusting over Gid like usual. She and her mother lived two streets over, on the street Gid is searching according to his note, and I suppose she had let Steph know what she was missing while she was with her father at the water park.

"You wasted your trip up there, Cliff, because the real gun

show was right here in our backyard. I'm sure Mr. Connors would agree." Mom giggled, and Gid grinned like an idiot, flexing his muscles for everyone.

Jimmy took me off memory lane by shaking my arm. I looked down at him, and he was pointing at the sky. The black and dark blue hues signaled rain, but I had already hung my clothes out, and it didn't make sense to take them all down now.

I shrugged my shoulders and said," Oh well, we already got them up, and they won't dry in the house, so let's head inside." Drops started hitting the ground before we were inside, and by the time we made it to the basement door, we could hear the pounding on the roof.

20 Llewelyn

I rode the bike with a few stops for a little over a hundred miles before I just had to stop and rest one full night. I stashed it behind a kicked-down fence in Dolton, IL, and broke into the home through the back door. It was empty, and I slept on the couch, barely able to get my boots off before drifting off. I woke before dawn the next morning and looked through the house for something to eat, my crotch hurting from the seat and my back aching. A sleeve of Ritz and a box of Oatmeal Cream Pies would have to do, I supposed, as everything else had gone bad or been gnawed on by rats.

I was chewing on one of the oatmeal cookies when I stepped out of the house and came face-to-face with a man and his teenage-looking son standing in the middle of the road. They were both armed but not as fast as me to get their rifles up.

“I'm not looking to hurt anyone,” I told the older man as he stood there, undecided about what to do. “I'm just passing through.”

“Where are you going? The whole world is fucked,” he said in frustration.

“I got some kin up north I'm going to check on. Why don't you two just head south a bit and give me a chance to get on my way, and then you can carry on with your business?”

“I don't know if you realized it, but everyone is dead, mister. Why would you go looking for someone if they're most likely dead?” The older man was bewildered.

“I got to see for myself, they're my people. Now I'm going to point my rifle down, and we aren't going to have a problem, are we?" I asked, and the older man shook his head.

"We've got enough problems as it is. Be on your way, we're trying to find food." He said, and the younger version nodded.

"I hate to tell a man his business, but you won't find much food that will last long in cities. From now on, it will have to be grown."

"Man, I ain't no farmer, we won't survive without food." Well, he wasn't wrong, just nothing I could do for him, and I suppose he was just expressing his frustration with our new situation.

"What do you have in that bag?" he asked of my backpack.

"Nothing worth dying over, I assure you. Just a knife and a map. Your best bet in the short term is to break into the Guard Armory and get some MREs. I'm not from around here, so I can't point you in the right direction, but it's time for me to go. If you would, go that way," I jerked my head south, "so there's no misunderstandings." He nodded, and I could tell by the way they carried their rifles that they were inexperienced. Well, they would get hard or die out here now, not much of a learning curve anymore.

When they got out of sight, I grabbed up the bike and pedaled my way to the freeway, anxious to get away from them because desperate people do desperate things, and I didn't want to be shot in the back by novices or pros, so I made haste. The highway sang beneath the tires, and the cool breeze blasted past my face as I raced north.

I rode through greater Chicago without too much trouble. I heard gunfire, but it wasn't directed at me, and I pedaled on. I saw a woman pushing a shopping cart across an overpass, but she just watched me pedal beneath her without saying a word.

I dodged car wrecks, bodies in the freeway, some killed from the sickness, others from accidents, and gunshot wounds. I didn't stop to search for them or try to find anything to eat that night until I was standing in a cul-de-sac on Lancaster Lane in Libertyville, IL.

The third house I tried was vacant and unlocked, and I helped myself to their store of canned goods. That night I dreamed of that hill again on my bike, and instead of running into a wet spot, the two men I had found earlier were lying in the road with blood pooled beneath their black skin, bullet holes riddled their bodies. I felt like it was slow motion as I rode past on the way to my accident in the trees, eyes glued to their bloody torsos, flies lifting off from the pools of blood. I forced my eyes away from the imminent crash that was happening and braced myself for the impact. I woke before the collision and panted in the dark, breathing in the musty, closed-in air of the house, though I had left the door open to vent some of it.

Had I left them to die? Probably, but it was possible I wouldn't be alone soon, and I was focused on Jess and her kids. Even if Charles were still alive, even though we didn't care for each other, he was still my brother. One more grueling day, and I should be there according to the map. Satisfied with that info, I got myself ready to go.

21 Gideon

I was leaving the home next to the "zombie" house, finding little, when I smelled the rain. Looking up, I saw the same sky that had sent Jimmy and Maryn inside and knew if I didn't get somewhere fast, I would be drenched. I dashed to the next house on the corner of Chapel and Montana Ave.

Climbing up the back step, I grabbed the door handle at the same time the rain started. The handle didn't turn, and I gritted my teeth in frustration. Walking in the rain around the front, I don't notice any vehicles in the drive, and I try the front door. Same, locked up. Again, at the back, I stood by a window, and when thunder rumbled, I hit the glass with my knife handle. This time, I made sure all the glass was knocked away before reaching in with my sore hand to feel for the latch. Switching it to unlock, I clambered into a laundry room. The washer and dryer were against the wall with the window, making it awkward to navigate around the broken glass. My pistol holster caught on the window seal, and I almost fell face-first onto the tile floor before catching myself on the dryer. The jarring opened the deepest cut on the back of my thumb, and I looked at it in frustration.

Getting free of the window and curtain, I pulled my pistol and switched it to my left hand while wrapping my right thumb into the hem of my shirt to stop the bleeding. I don't smell anything dead here, but that doesn't mean there isn't any danger. I immediately started looking for a bathroom and band aids. I left my light off and used the dim lighting in the house to make my way down a hallway. I couldn't hear anything except the storm outside, but I could barely see an open door at the end of the hall and two closed doors before reaching it.

Bedrooms? Closet? I would check them on the way back, but first, I needed to stop this bleeding. The bathroom has an outside window, so there's a little light here because of the clouds, but not enough to see clearly.

I opened the cabinet door under the sink, and there was a box of mixed-size Johnson and Johnson band aids. I grabbed it up, set the seat down on the toilet, then sat. I bandaged myself as well as I could and put the remaining box into my kit. I checked the bedrooms, and it seemed a single man lived here alone, for there wasn't anything in one room at all, just a bed with no sheets and the other room had only a single bed, a dresser, and a closet with a few pairs of pants and what looks like western shirts from the 1980s and cowboy boots in the bottom—no pictures of family, art, or anything distinguishable at all. The kitchen was a motherlode, though. Canned goods, ready-to-heat meals, and packaged soups filled the pantry. I stuffed my bags as full as possible and set everything else I couldn't carry by the back door. On my last trip back to the pantry, I saw a small shadow dart across the kitchen floor and ran behind the fridge. A mouse? I grabbed the rest of the food to stash and turned out of the pantry, and it isn't a mouse but a rat scurrying across the floor. I set the food down on the pile I've already started, unlocked the back door, and stepped out onto the small back step.

Seeing that rat triggered something in my brain that I had never considered before. I knew what I had to do to fix a mistake I had made, and I felt ashamed that I didn't do it the other day. I headed back to Mr. Davenport's house, peeled off my pack, and went to the garage. I dumped the food and supplies out and went back twice more to the old man's house until I had everything piled up by the door. After slogging through the storm, drenched, I had one more task to do before heading back home. Leaning against the closed garage door, I sat down and let my grief rage over the loss of my mom and Mr. Davenport. The image I have of them is two white-faced corpses, being trucked along like firewood, a sad end for two people who were so important to me. Still important to me, I thought, as I recalled the laughs and love I received from them. I grabbed road flares from Mr. Davenport's old Bronco, and a five-gallon gasoline can he kept for his generator. I read the instructions on the flares, picked up the gas can, and headed back out.

22 Maryn

Gid came home and told us about the supplies he stashed at Mr. Davenport's, so I started putting on my boots to help him bring them home.

"No," he shook his head. "I'm already soaking, and it's starting to pick up again, so I'll just run back there and get them, no big deal."

"You smell like gas. How did that happen?" I asked.

"I moved the tank at Mr. Davenport's and some sloshed on me," he added quickly, but it didn't sound truthful, and I looked at him sharply. Hmm.

"Leave your pants outside then, and let the rain wash some of it out," I told him, and he agreed, then ducked out to bring in the supplies.

He came back after two trips, went straight to the bathroom, and showered without saying a word to either of us. I cooked up some Ramen, and Jimmy was on his second bowl when Gid came back down dressed in shorts and a T-shirt.

"Did you see anyone today?" I asked as he sat down at the table, and I handed him a bowl. He shook his head and started to eat. Jimmy was tucking away his second bowl, so we ate in silence. The three of us are in our own thoughts, the blue dog gnawing on a piece of jerky between Jimmy's legs.

"Tomorrow we'll all go out again with you," I said.

"Jimmy, you feeling better?" Gid asked as he stood up to put his bowl in the sink. Jimmy nodded and continued eating. We all finished, and the dishes were sitting in the sink when Gid looked at us.

"The world is different now and will never go back to the way it was. I know what we see and do now is a shock, but if we are to survive, we must change. We are going to have to get used to seeing the dead, scrounging for food, and soon we will have to live in the wild. The longer we stay here, the more likely we are to be discovered by someone."

"Isn't that a good thing? Maybe they will help us." Jimmy said, looking at me.

"We can't trust anyone to help us, and we should assume anyone we meet only wants to take what we have. Everyone is struggling right now, and I'm sure many are worse off than we are. Assume that when we meet people, they don't want to help us, and we should avoid them whenever possible. I think by the end of next week we should head out." He looked at me.

"What about Dad? That may not be enough time for him to get here?" I asked, feeling the dread of leaving without him. On Tuesday, he was finishing a deposition and heading home. It was the last time any of us heard from him.

"That will give him time to get here. I've calculated it, and even if he's walking, it's 150 miles from here, and it shouldn't take more than four days to get here. We'll give him two extra days in case something happened, but we must leave soon," he said.

"He told me he had a cold when he called; he could be at his hotel needing our help. We can't just leave him. What if he shows up here the next day after we leave?" I asked. I dreaded leaving here without him because something told me that if we did, we would never see him again.

“He probably had the penny virus,” Jimmy put in without any explanation.

“The what?” I asked him.

“The penny virus is what they called it on the news. Some people bombed a town called Penny in Russia or somewhere, and they had a secret lab there. It got loose and killed most folks,” he said, looking at us like we had heard this already.

“Some people bombed some Russians, and they released this disease, is that what they said on the news?” Gid asked.

“No, we hadn’t heard that. Did they say anything else about it?” I followed up.

“Not that I heard.” He went back to petting the dog, leaving us looking at each other in puzzlement.

“Okay, then. We’ll leave him a note with the date we leave, so IF he does come here, he’ll know we are alive and heading for home. Our real home. If he were sick, he’s probably gone. The news says no one recovers from the illness. We can’t survive the winter here and remain hidden. Not if, but when the gas goes out —we’re in real trouble. We must go back home; our people have lived there for hundreds of years, and most of them without electricity, so we will, too. We know how to farm that land at least, and we can grow our food. The winters are too harsh here, and even if we did stay in Wisconsin, we couldn’t live in this house. We need room to hunt and farm, and that needs to be away from other people. Can’t risk every hunting trip with someone taking a shot at us or catching us in a field plowing. Hopefully, Papa and Granny are still alive at home and can show us how to live like that now, because I didn't pay attention when they had us working the garden, did you? You know how to lay out a field, plow, sow, and harvest? When to plant, what to plant beside which crop? Outside of the three sisters, I don't remember any of that shit because I never thought I would have to grow my food."

"Outside of picking the vegetables, I don't remember much about farming," I admitted.

"That won't help us survive, and if we get there and they're both gone, we can dig through Papa's old farming books. Worst case, we take a few seasons to figure it out, but we can still hunt and fish there, and, just as important, we won't freeze. If what we saw on the news is accurate, then the grid won't be back online anytime soon, if ever. Since we survived and old man Burns, we know it misses some folks, but not how many. It could be millions of people still out there or none, we don't know. My point is, no more electricity, water, processed foods, or garbage removal. We saw the riots on TV before they went off the air, so we know that any survivors are desperate, so we need to be careful."

Gid made sense with his points, I just felt terrible leaving without knowing what happened to our father. He wasn't an outdoorsman like Mr. Davenport and might struggle to survive in this new world. He wasn't rough like his father, my papa, even Gid was starting to show signs of hardness I'd never seen in my father. He could shoot, hunt, and fish like most folks where we're from, even kids did all those things and were often alone, but he liked poetry and plays. He was educated and gentle. "He's thoughtful and tough like you, just not like your brother." My mom once told me, and I didn't understand exactly what she meant at the time, but I'm starting to see it now.

In bed that night, silently crying, thinking about him out there, hurt, and us not helping him, but I know deep down we couldn't save him if he needed it; we probably wouldn't even be able to find him. We never thought of asking where he was going while working in Green Bay, and we would probably end up lost or run into other dangers. Anyway, Gid's idea of going back to Texas did seem the most logical, but it was disheartening to leave without him. I would always miss my mama, but I KNEW what happened to her. I saw it with my own eyes, but with him, I was afraid I would never know.

23 Gideon

The next day dawned clear and still. The air was still too cold for short sleeves, but it warmed up close to noon and became comfortable. I asked Maryn to take Jimmy to Oak Creek to catch some fresh fish. Mr. Davenport had provided us with plenty of fishing gear from his stash, and it would give them something to do outside the house for a few hours. Maryn carried the shotgun and book, and Jimmy brought the fishing poles and tackle box. She took a small can of whole-kernel corn and a can opener in her pack as bait. They didn't believe me about using corn for fish, but I insisted that Papa told me he used it years ago in Virginia to catch rainbow trout. I figured there may be rainbows here, too, so I convinced them to give it a try. The three of them took off across the street to the bike patch just after daylight, and I went on my way to keep the search going.

When I came to a house that had the stench of death in it, I didn't go inside; I skipped it and looked for one that was unoccupied, either living or dead. I slowly found things we could use —peanut butter, packaged foods, and, of course, canned goods. Our medical supplies also increased steadily, and I started to worry about how we would pack them all. It didn't stop me from collecting it, though; transporting it would be a problem I would have to solve later. Right now, I just got what I could.

Not much luck with firearms yet, though. That surprised me because growing up where we did, everyone had guns, and I mean everyone. I'm sure parents with young children were somewhat worried about guns in the home, but they could be disabled until you needed them. To me, a gun was a tool, no different than an axe or shovel. It had a specific use and, when you needed one, it was hard to find a substitute. Maybe city people didn't think they had a use for guns, I'm not sure. Having been raised around them, it seems silly to me and downright dangerous, really, but different strokes, I suppose. The ones I did find were hidden in safes I couldn't open, and another thing I didn't think to learn when I had access to the internet was how to safe crack.

I trudged back to the house with pack after pack of food and medical supplies, and on my third trip back, I saw Maryn and Jimmy emerging from the woods. It's midafternoon, so I figured Jimmy had gotten hungry and they had given up on the fishing, but as they cross the street, I see Maryn carrying the shotgun and fishing poles, and Jimmy with the tackle box and a half dozen fish on a stringer. When he saw me, his face split into a grin, and I could see him almost jumping with excitement. They walked to the back door, and I noticed they were indeed rainbows.

"That's a great catch, Jimmy," I said, admiring them. He beamed with pride and started yammering like a monkey about how he fought them onto the bank. I put my finger to my mouth to silence him, and he clamped his mouth closed so hard I could hear it. I smiled behind my finger to let him know I'm not upset, then motioned for them to go inside. After getting inside, I bragged about his catch over the kitchen sink.

"Fine job, Jimmy, I've never seen rainbows this big before," I told him as he glowed. Maryn was all smiles, and they both deflated when I said. "We field dress any game before we bring it home, though," I said and shook my head.

"Let's get these cleaned up and on the stove," I said as the thought of fresh fish made my stomach growl. Jimmy grinned again, and his good mood returned when he saw I'm not upset about their oversight. He was so excited that neither of them even thought of cleaning them before coming home. Understanding, I reached into the drawer, withdrew the filet knife, and showed him how to filet the brown trout he'd caught.

Jimmy looked a little green during the cleaning process, but after seeing the first two, he did a decent job on the last four. I searched our pantry and found some cornmeal my mom had in a plastic airtight container. We skinned some potatoes, and Maryn taught him how to cut them into fries. I put a small pinch of the cornmeal in and showed Jimmy what it looked like when the grease was ready—I dropped them in and fried them up. We dumped Cajun seasoning on the fries, and into the cornmeal we'd coated the fish in, and it was the best meal I'd had in several days. Mr. Davenport had taken it personally the first time he saw my mama frying them this way instead of baking, claiming she had ruined them. Once he took a bite, though, he conceded it was a great way to prepare them.

"If I needed to know how to live like a bachelor and wear the same underwear three days in a row, I want you to know I would come to you for advice, but when it comes to cooking, I would appreciate the same courtesy," my mama had teased him, his face reddening with embarrassment.

Our blue dog seemed to like French fries, and I had yet to find anything he wouldn't eat. I hand-fed him under the table as Jimmy regaled me with a play-by-play of how he reeled the fish in, making it sound like he had battled Moby Dick. Maryn seemed happy for the first time since this all started, and I saw a glimpse of how it could be: even a simple life like this could be enjoyable. I felt relaxed, and that meal lifted my mood.

"Can we play Monopoly?" Jimmy asked.

"Sure, let me get rid of these fish bones, and I'll put you into bankruptcy again." I smiled at him. The scrawny kid sitting there, swinging his legs and starting to feel more at home around us.

"I'm going to do it this time, but remember to clean any game in the field from now on." He nodded at me. I grabbed the plastic bag with the fish guts and bones and headed to the back door.

"Can I be the battleship this time?" Jimmy asked as I put on my boots.

"Sure, whatever piece you want. Get a hold of the dog, I don't want him following me and eating fish bones," I told him.

He patted his legs, and the dog lumbered over to him. "Let's get our showers done while he's gone," Maryn said to him. "The dog needs one too." She wrinkled her nose at his smell. Showers and young boys are enemies, and Jimmy's no exception.

Grinning at his complaints, I slipped out the door quietly and closed it behind me. The sun had set, and the sky was losing its pink and orange hues, deepening into purple. I could still make out shapes, but I knew the return trip would be almost entirely in the dark. Silently, I chastised myself for being idle so long with work still left. Now I would have to bumble around in the night. Consequences and repercussions, I supposed, and I turned to the corner of the house. The small shed where my father kept our lawnmower and rake was to my right, and I stopped by it to open the gate to the front yard when I heard or felt something moving to my left. I turned my head, and an arm snaked around my face from the right. Panic flared in me, and I dropped the bag to reach for my pistol, and I felt a knife blade touch my neck.

"Let go of that pistol. You understand?" I nodded, and the rough hand slid from my mouth. He reached up and grabbed my hair with one hand and guided me to the back door.

"Open it, I wanna take a look at you." I heard the gruff voice command.

"No," I said, and the grip got tighter on my hair.

"What do you mean, no?"

"Kill me if you must, but you aren't getting in there," I said. I feel the blade again, and I hear him say. "What's your name, boy?"

"Gideon," I said through clenched teeth.

Here it is, I think, a quick slice, and I'm gone. I needed to yell out to warn Maryn, though, and I took a deep breath to do just that when he moved the knife away.

"I'm your uncle Lew. You remember me?" he asked, spinning me around to see his grin.

The tempest of my situation, going from certain death to having a relative show up here, has taken control of my speech. I nodded, recognizing him.

"Well, let's go inside and say hi to my niece." I could see his teeth flash in the dim light.

24 Maryn

When I stepped out of the bathroom, Gid was standing in the doorway with a man. This man had his face painted in dark hues and held a knife in one hand. Seeing someone other than Gid or Jimmy shocked me so much that for a second, I couldn't move. As soon as I got my wits, I sprinted to the kitchen table and reached for the shotgun.

"Maryn, it's okay, it's Lew." I barely heard him with blood rushing in my ears, and it doesn't register what he's saying until I have the gun halfway up to my shoulder. I slowly lowered it, and the man sheathed his knife and raised both hands. He smiled brightly.

"Uncle Llewellyn?" I asked in disbelief.

"That's right, honey. Now, be a good girl and point that shotgun somewhere else," he grinned.

"Where did you come from?" I asked, in a shocked state; this was the most important thing I could think of saying.

"Let's gather around that table and have a sit. We can go over everything."

Gid walked over to him, unbuckled his gun belt, and slung it over the back of the chair before sitting.

Lew notices and says slyly, "You went outside armed? Hmmm."

I leaned the shotgun back against the island where it was and sat down myself. Remembering Jimmy, I jumped back up, and a streak ran out of the half-opened basement door. It's him, with a wild look on his face, wielding the knife Gid had given him earlier to fillet the fish. He charged at the stranger in our house and tried to bring the knife down overhand. Llewellyn easily deflected it and pushed the small boy against the wall. He slammed into it with a crash and crumpled to the floor. Jimmy's feet were kicking to get back up, and he had a scowl on his face. The dog ran out right behind Jimmy and stood over him, growling and showing his teeth to Lew. Gid rushed over and told the dog to hush up and wrapped up Jimmy's flailing arms. I got to him a second later and called his name, but he couldn't seem to hear me for a second. When he could focus on me, I told him the man was part of our family and didn't want to harm us. Gid pulled him up by the arms, and he stood there, chest heaving like a bellows, face flushed red.

"Seems I walked into a snake den here. Got one willing to die to protect his family and two others coming at me with weapons, all in forty-five seconds, not to mention a dog that wants to murder me now. This is probably the most dangerous home in all of Wisconsin." He grinned at his joke.

After calming down, Jimmy sat at the table meekly, and the unhinged person who came rushing from the basement was nowhere to be found. He petted his dog and sat quietly, eyeing Llewelyn warily. I made us some hot chocolate, and Lew asked about coffee.

"We have some, but I don't know how to make it without electricity," I told him. He moved to the pantry and dug out my mom's old percolator, which belonged to her grandma. I've never seen her use it, but Lew went right to work on it. While it brewed, he went to the bathroom and washed the paint and dirt from his face.

Lew poured himself a cup while we all declined, sat back

down, and took a sip. His hat was on the chair beside him, and I could see the tan line just before it met his jet-black hairline, where the sun never reached. Besides the small scars on his face, neck, and knuckles, he looked like an older version of Gid. Just taller and more muscular. I could see he was having trouble with something, and I figured he was worried about his brother, tired from wherever he came from, and when he picked the cup up and brought it to his lips, I noticed an enormous, fresh scrape on his left forearm.

He took a deep breath and asked, "Where's your mama?"

Seeing my look, he nodded solemnly. "Tell me everything that's happened since this started." So, we took turns pouring out our story. He didn't interrupt or ask any questions until we'd finished recalling the last few days. I also told him we planned to head home, but we were waiting for our dad. He nodded at this.

"Where did you lay her to rest?" he asked me.

"Over by the park," Gid says quickly.

Strange, him being so anxious. Lew prodded him for more details.

"North of here, a few blocks." He told him curtly, still evasive.

"Well, keep an eye on that direction for the next couple of days because there is a home still smoking up that way when I come in."

I looked at Gid, and he's staring at the floor, not saying a word. Why is he acting so weird, I wondered?

Lew broke into my thoughts by speaking, "I talked to your

granny, and she told me to come here and not return to Texas. She said to protect our family, and that's here. Your father texted me a code phrase from our boyhood, and it means to drop what you are doing and come to the family; do you two know what it is?" We both shook our heads. "We'll get to that later. Our main concern now is getting you back home; that's the move. It's dangerous, and you have a lot to learn along the way. Tomorrow we'll start on that education. I could use a day of rest to catch up on my sleep, so if I don't wake up early, leave me alone until I get up on my own. I've been doing some hard traveling, and honestly, I'm worn out."

"Well, I can make you something to eat, and we have hot water still for showering," I told him.

"Sounds great, but first let's go handle the business you were about when we met outside earlier, Gid." He jerked his head toward the back door.

"Just taking out the trash, I can handle it." He said morosely. I wonder about that, but I think I'll talk about it later.

"I left my gear outside, so I'm heading out anyway. C'mon, let's get it done." He stood and headed for the door. Before opening it, he turned back to Jimmy and me at the table.

"I'll be back in a few minutes, so no more knife or gun play tonight." He flashed his white smile again and stepped out the door, with Gid following.

25 Gideon

"You seem upset. What exactly is the problem?" Lew asked me as I grabbed up the sack again.

"You mean besides you holding me at knife point?" I asked, letting the sarcasm really seep in.

"I didn't know who you were at first, and I wanted to make sure no one had you held hostage or worse. You didn't piss yourself, and I didn't cut you, so no harm, no foul, right?" Though I couldn't see it, I could hear the smile in his voice, and it irritated me even more.

"So, let's start over. Tell me what is making you so surly?"

"It's embarrassing that you were able to sneak up on me so easily," I admitted.

"Don't take it personally, I've been doing that since I was your age. I got started on animals back home, and I honed it on men in Iraq and Afghanistan."

"Can you teach me?" I asked

"Sure, there's a lot that you and your sister are going to have to learn. It's going to be hard, but one of the most important things you can do is just what you did."

"What's that?" I questioned.

"You got right to the heart of what was bothering you and came clean about it. There's no reason you must hide any issue from me; it only makes it harder to fix. You swallowed your pride, explained exactly what you meant, and now we've put it to rest. Most folks can't do that; they hide their true feelings, misdirect their intent, and you don't know them at all. Don't forget that."

He followed me to the end of the street, and I walked into the woods a few yards and threw the untied bag into the brush.

"Why did you throw the remains out instead of leaving them in the trash?" he asked on the way back.

"They stink like hell for one thing, and I didn't want to put them in our garbage, raccoons scatter it everywhere."

"Why do you care about that?"

"I don't want anyone to see fresh garbage strewn across our yard; it would give away that we live here." I sat, feeling he already knew the answer.

"That's right. Being lazy or thoughtless can be very dangerous. Staying hidden is your biggest ally." He clapped me on the back quietly, and we headed into the back yard again. He ducked out of the shed, reached for his pack, and we entered the house again.

26 Maryn

When they returned, I heated some soup for Lew, and he sat and ate without saying a word. I feel like it's been a while since he's eaten anything warm, and it's soon gone, washed down with his now cold coffee.

"Show me the bathroom and where I can sleep tonight." He said, grabbing his rucksack and rifle. It looks like Mr. Davenport's AR-15.

"We have an extra bed in the basement if you want to sleep there."

Lew shook his head and said, "I'd rather sleep up here."

"Okay," I said and went back to the kitchen to clean up the dishes we left behind. Gid had already gone upstairs to that bathroom, and I assumed he was in the shower, so when I was finished, I headed back down to Jimmy. He was scratching his dog and had the monopoly board set up for us.

When Gid came down the stairs, he said Uncle Lew was already asleep on the couch, and we got settled right into a game of trying to bankrupt each other.

The next morning, I woke up and saw that Gid was already out of bed. I climbed the stairs and smelled cooking. I saw Lew standing over the stove and Gid sitting at the table, cleaning his pistol. After leaving the bathroom, I gave Gid a stern look over his lack of table manners, which he calmly ignored, and I sat down across from him.

"Ready for breakfast?" Lew asked, and I turned around to look back at him. I can't make out much in the predawn gloom, but he's shirtless, cooking something that would have made my mother screech, along with Gid cleaning his gun at the table. I nodded and saw Jimmy coming into the room, rubbing his eyes. He stopped halfway to me, then realized he had to pee and turned around and headed back to the bathroom.

Lew sets a plate in front of me with ham and eggs on it, and I'm in disbelief.

"Where did you get this food from?" I asked.

He grinned. "There's a house about four blocks from here on Crane Drive that has chickens in the backyard. They must have left the coop door open when they got sick, because the birds were still coming back there to roost and lay eggs. I saw them scratching around in the late afternoon, waited until they went home to sleep, and followed them. If I had known you were safe, we would be eating fried chicken right now instead of just the eggs. I found the ham in their freezer, and it was still cold from a whole-home generator that had run for a few days after the power went out."

"They can live wild like that without anyone feeding them?" Gid looked up from his cleaning.

"That's a granny question for when you see her. I'm not too familiar with them since leaving home."

"I'm glad you brought that up. Have you spoken to the old folks since this started?" Gid asked, rolling up his gear as Lew set a plate of eggs and ham before him.

"No, I spoke to your granny before I left Cleveland to come here. As I said, she warned me not to come home because of sickness and to come here instead for you. The only reason I covered so much country on the way here is that I rode a bike—

it was night and day. I only rested when I had to, and I was shot at several times. There are roving bandits and murderers on the main highways, and from here on out, traveling on these roads is tricky.

"Why didn't you call us?" I asked. "You could have let us know you were coming."

"I did call. Well, I called your mom at least. No answer. I suppose you two think I'm not cool enough to have your numbers. After speaking with your Granny, the line disconnected. Looting, murders, and general pandemonium, and I figured the best thing was to get here soonest. Charles sent me a text to "come a-runnin," and in our family, that's serious business. That was on Wednesday or Thursday, I don't remember which, and I've been on the go ever since.

He put a plate on the table in the empty spot for Jimmy just about the time he opened the door and walked in. Hair defying gravity and still half asleep, he never said a word, just stumbled over to the table and went to work on his food. Lew slipped on a tan shirt before sitting down, and we ate in silence for a few minutes.

"Why didn't you drive instead of riding a bike?" I asked, and he smiled before answering.

"The traffic around major cities is snarled, and where it's not, gangs have set up roadblocks to waylay people. A bike is quieter for sure, and I had started in my truck, but the engine was shot to hell and gone between Cleveland and Toledo by some highwaymen."

"Did you have to kill people?" Jimmy asked around a mouthful of eggs.

“It was touch and go,” he said, offhand, as if Jimmy asked him if it was going to rain today.

“Where were you when it went sideways?” Gid asked, setting down his oil rag.

“I heard on the news that a lot of people were getting sick, but I didn’t pay much attention since they hadn’t made us mask up as we did during COVID. I got to work and saw how many people were missing from the job, and since it hadn’t been payday the day before, I suspected something was wrong. I talked to your granny for a second, then got a text from Charles, and I’ve been making my way here ever since.

“What did he say? ” I asked him.

“As I said, he told me to ‘come a-runnin,’ and I did.” They shook their heads at the corny saying that has been handed down and unchanged, as far as I know, for a hundred years.

“It may seem silly to you now, and as boys we made mock of it, too, but it is serious. If anyone in your family gets this message, it’s your duty to drop what you are doing and get to their aid. It’s not something to be taken lightly,” he told us sternly.

“Did everyone you saw try to harm you?” I couldn’t conceive of every stranger wanting to hurt us just because they were afraid.

He shook his head and grunted, “No, but enough of them were to make me wary of strangers. Everyone is scared, and most people aren’t the most intelligent and rational beings in good times, so it’s spun out now. I won’t speak of what I saw, but it’s a horror show, and we are going to try to avoid all that we can.”

“Thanks for coming,” Gid said after wiping up his plate with a piece of bread.

“I know you’d do the same for me.” He said and started on his food.

After he set his plate in the sink, he started putting his gear on the couch and rummaging through his pack.

“Seems a good setup here, and you have been careful for the most part. I’m going to show you where the chickens are, and I want you to feed them and collect their eggs every day until I get back.”

“Back from where? Are you going to check on Granny?” I asked.

“I’m going to find Charles before we leave out of here for good. She specifically told me not to go there, so I have to assume she has that handled down there for right now, but I can’t face my mama without knowing what happened to her son while I’m this close. I almost want to take you with me so that you can have a practice run of what it's going to be like on the road, but all travel is risky, so y'all stay here until I get back.”

Gid started to protest, but Lew raised his hand to silence him. “If I knew for sure he was dead, it would be different. It’s senseless to put your life at risk for someone that no longer has theirs, but he’s my brother, and even though we don’t like each other, he’s still my family.”

I’m shocked by his sudden announcement —both that he's leaving and that he and my father didn’t get along.

“You don’t like him?” I asked, getting ready to defend my father.

"That's the wrong phrase; let's just say he wounded me once and I haven't gotten over it." I immediately look at the myriad of scars on his chest and shoulders. Small puncture marks, slashes across his chest and one shoulder, the opposite one slick from a burn.

"Not that kind of wound," he said, noticing me looking at his collection, and continued, "Anyway, that's our business and none of yours. Let's get dressed and head over to the chicken house. I'm not leaving until full dark tonight, so there are a few things I want to go over before I go. Grab your shit and let's be about it."

After the plates were all taken care of and we were dressed for the cool morning, Lew said, "Gideon told me about the old man who shot at him. Have any of you seen anyone else around here? Heard anything that may be people? Anything like that?"

Jimmy shook his head and said, "Just our dog." Lew raised an eyebrow and sat until we were ready.

27 Gideon

"First thing we need to do is go through some houses and find you better weapons." He looked down at my holstered pistol and asked if that was my father's gun. I nodded, and he asked, "Have you found anything else, but what I see here?"

"No. Everything so far has been empty or locked up in a gun safe." I told him.

"Let's start where you last stopped off, then, and see what we see." He turned and walked through the back door into the early morning light.

I led the way to the third house away from our "zombie" encounter, and we started there. Of course, the door is locked, but Lew just picked it. He scanned the room with his weapon, shifting to every angle that could be seen. As soon as the door opened, I could smell the death in here. We stood outside, hesitating to go inside. Lew cleared the room and motioned for us to come in. I saw Jimmy start to tremble when the smell hit him, and I rested my hand on his shoulder and said quietly, "Just stay here in the kitchen with Maryn until we've had a look everywhere, okay?" He nodded, and I took off toward my uncle. He's already up the stairs and searching for those rooms before I can catch up. I passed the first room, and it's thankfully empty, and he's already heading back to me.

"Go tell them to start checking all the rooms; we'll do the ones up here." He started back down the hallway to the last room. I head down and told them to check downstairs; they were clear of dead people. I went back up and started searching the first room on the left. Just a spare room that no one slept in regularly. No sheets on the bed and no clothes in the closet. It doesn't take but a few seconds, and as I left the room, I heard a muffled scream from Jimmy downstairs. I sprinted down the steps, pulling my pistol as I descended. I heard Lew right behind me as we turned the corner, and I saw Maryn and Jimmy tussling in a doorway leading into one of the rooms. She had her hand on his mouth, and he was trying to wriggle away from her while screaming.

"What the fuck?" Lew asked and pushed me aside and whirled Jimmy around by the shoulders, sending Maryn off balance and nearly falling on her ass. Jimmy, freed from Maryn, had tears running down his face and was taking a breath to start another scream. Lew put up his hand and said to him.

"Shut up and don't make another sound," Lew said as Jimmy shuddered with a sob but didn't let any noise escape. He's struggled against Lew to leave the doorway, and I walked over and looked inside to see what had set him off like this. A small body on the bed, and it looked as if it had melted into the bedding, like a rotten wax candle. I felt bile rise in my stomach, and I had to stamp it down so I wouldn't lose my breakfast. Maryn regained herself and ran to Jimmy, embracing him and giving Lew a look of anger. She soothed him, and she walked toward me, so I stepped out of the way, and they headed to the back door. The dog almost tripped them as he rubbed against Jimmy's trembling legs, trying to comfort him, I assumed. I looked at Lew, and he was glaring at me.

"Back to the house, everyone," he said after walking by me, heading in their direction. I closed the door, and we got home.

28 Maryn

In our basement, I finally got Jimmy calmed down, and Lew stormed down the steps. I could see his anger radiating off him like heat waves. No matter what Jimmy did, his behavior was unacceptable, and he could do with a little of my anger. He sat down on the unoccupied bunk and steepled his fingers under his chin.

"Okay, what happened back there, Jimmy?" He bored his blue eyes into the small boy, showing more patience in his voice than his face showed.

"He had a terrible experience the other day with a dead person. He's trying to deal with it but today didn't help at all. A heads up would be great before we enter a room that has someone who looks like a melted candle would have helped." I shot back at him, and Jimmy retched again. Gid walked him over to the sink and turned on the water, wetting a washcloth for him.

"Seeing bodies is the new reality, and everyone, and I do mean everyone, will have to learn to deal with it. You can't shield him from it, and Jimmy, we will have to survive next to death. The world has changed, and the folks who won't change will perish. It's really that simple. Now, when I ask him a question, I expect him to answer, not you." He turned his gaze to Jimmy and beckoned him over as my face flushed with heat from the reprimand.

"He's just a scared little boy who's had a hard time, so maybe cut him some slack. I'm starting to see why you and my dad didn't get along." I seethed at him.

He turned back to face me fully. “There are no such things as little boys anymore. There’s only the living and the dead, and if you want him to stay among the living, then help him get his head wrapped around that.” Lew kneeled in front of Jimmy and placed his hands on his shoulders, looking into his eyes. “I understand that you’re scared, but foolish and careless won’t do. It ain't the dead that are a danger to us.”

“Why did he look like that, though? I didn’t know people melted,” Jimmy asked piteously.

“Did you notice the electric heaters in the room? A generator kicked on after he died, or he died before most others, when the power was still on. Old folks like to have their home hot, so it was, ugh, well, it got hot in there, let’s say. That’s why the smell was so prevalent outside.” He explained, and Jimmy looked as if he just staggered off a spinning ride at the carnival.

He walked over to Gid and spoke to him so low that I couldn’t hear what he was saying. He nodded after, and Lew came back over to me.

“We are all going to the chicken house and sort those eggs out. I want to show everyone where that is and how to deal with them, so gird your loins, Jimmy, and let’s head back out.” Jimmy was planted in place, washcloth slowly dripping from his right hand, water glistening on his face. He still looked queasy, and Lew showed him mercy. “No more dead for you today, Jimmy, just egg collecting and then back here.”

He stood and looked at me. “Ready?” he asked me warmly.

I walked up with Jimmy in tow, and we all gathered at the back door again. “Remember to be quiet and to pay attention,” Lew said to Jimmy while ignoring me. Shouldering his rifle, we started off again.

29 Gideon

Collecting eggs used to be a mundane task for some people. Day in and day out with your livestock, and they mostly conformed to the same routine. Well, these hens weren't having it, and Lew just handed me the two-gallon bucket he had taken from my dad's work shed and pointed at the coop. It's still early morning, but only four chickens and a rooster are outside. Of the beds, I can see only two with no hens sitting. I collected these first and went to the live birds last. I nudged the first hen up, and she ran out flapping her wings, and I got her eggs with no issue. Next, some clucking, but no problem. She's got four eggs here, so I know Lew didn't collect her eggs from yesterday. The last hen raised hell before I even extended my hand. She squawked louder the closer I got, and when my fingers came into range, she started pecking; luckily, most of the damage was hampered by the bandage still in place. She flew upward when I snaked my hand under her, sending feathers and squawks careening and flapping past my head as she looked for the exit. She had six eggs warming up, and I grabbed them and added them to the others. We had a decent haul—enough for breakfast every day if we collected them regularly.

While I was dodging the mad hen, Lew searched the shed beside the coop. He came back out with a small bucket and threw the contents on the ground around the door.

“That should keep them coming back here every night. It's a wonder that a fox hasn't gotten to them yet; they must be roosting in these trees. They need to be fed every day, and the eggs gathered. It seems a good job for you, Jimmy.”

Jimmy was squatting down and petting one of the eight hens

that had come running to the coop, seeing Lew toss the feed on the ground. Our blue companion sunned in the grass, tongue bouncing, not concerned about the chickens one bit. Shaking his head, Lew went into the coop and inspected the feeder that was already installed. Of course, it was empty, so he refilled it from a sack from the shed and made sure the auto-waterer was working as well. Once he was satisfied with that, he waved us toward the house.

I don't feel as vulnerable walking around in daylight with Lew here, and we make it back home in a few minutes. "Maryn, Gideon, and I are going back to the house we were just at and finish checking it out. Sit tight, and we'll be back in a couple of hours. I want to make sure you are properly armed before I set off tonight." He turned his gaze to Jimmy, and I felt him wilt under his stony stare. "Help her out any way you can, Jimmy."

The house with the melted body held nothing except some canned goods, which I happily scooped up, and we went next door. We found the next house unlocked, and the stench was even worse. The smell felt like a physical blow when we stepped inside. The cause was a dead person fifteen feet away on a couch. Turning the corner from the kitchen to the living room, it was chaos. Three children and one adult were lying on the floor in front of the couch, where I found the first body upon entering. Sheets covered them, but not the one on the couch. Lew walked over and did a quick search and quickly left out into the hallway, motioning with his head for me to follow. After checking the downstairs room and finding nothing, we headed upstairs. It's the same here until we get to the main bedroom. The owners here had several pistols in different calibers in an open gun safe. A 20-gauge and a semi-auto Rossi .22 rounded out the collection. "Grab all the pistols, I'll get the shotgun and rifle," Lew said to me. He also crammed the ammo he found in there, along with some from a dresser drawer, into his kit.

Leaving out, I'm looking forward to breathing fresh air again, but Lew goes back to the couch and bends over for something. I can't make out what he's found, and he tucked it into his belt.

The next two houses are a bust on weapons, but we did get some more food and a brand-new backpack for Jimmy from a closet in the last house we checked. No more dead bodies, either—thankfully—but I did get some valuable information from Lew on how to clear rooms.

We left the last two houses we searched, their back doors broken, and headed for home. It was midafternoon, and I think he might be hungry. I was still queasy from the bodies in the living room, but it didn't seem to faze him at all. We set up all the gear we found in the hallway and got to cleaning the recovered guns. One of them, a nine-millimeter Glock, he scrubbed on for a while before I realized it was the one from the house with all the bodies in the living room. I wasn't superstitious, but it made me uneasy using a gun that had been used to take a life.

"What's your face all screwed up like that for?" He caught me looking at the pistol.

"It's not weird that a gun has killed someone?" I asked him.

"The gun didn't kill anyone; it's just a gun. When we leave this house, do you think these walls will remember you? Does the ground remember your shadow after you pass? That kind of thing lives only in the human mind, Gideon."

"Get me a large bowl, will you?" I grabbed one and brought it over, and he dropped the pistol in it, covered with some kind of liquid.

"Set it outside before your sister gets on us about the smell."

30 Maryn

I heard the back door open and Gid and Uncle Lew step inside. I was trying to help Jimmy wash the dog when I heard them talking in low voices below us, but couldn't make out what they were saying. The heeler wasn't barking, but he was not enjoying the water and soap. We managed to get most of the funk off of him, and then I had to scoop dark hair out of the drain. Jimmy made a face when he saw the wet fur in my hand, and I threatened to make him some shorts out of all the hair. He laughed and wrapped a towel around the dog before we let him out of the tub.

"Hungry?" I asked them at the table as Jimmy came out of the bathroom and headed over. Gid was smiling as he motioned him over. Jimmy stands beside him, and Gid swung the new backpack around with a flourish, holding it out to him.

"Found one that is your size." Jimmy reached for the bag, grinning like Christmas morning. He didn't wait to remove the tags; he slipped it on and turned to show it off to everyone. Lew had a scowl like always, but it delighted Gid and me to see him have a little happiness about something. He's less impressed with the small rifle that Lew tried to hand him. He hesitated and looked at me. I smiled at him and nodded my head, and he cautiously reached out for it.

"This is yours and your responsibility to take care of. While I'm gone, Gid and Maryn will show you how to care for it and any basics you need to know. Have you ever owned a gun before?" Lew squinted at him, looking for a lie.

"N-n-no, sir." Jimmy managed.

"It's not, sir, it's just plain Lew, just like everyone else calls me, okay. They will walk you through it over the next few days and make you familiar with it. You know what the most important rule about firearms is?" He leaned forward, getting closer to Jimmy and making him even more nervous.

Jimmy shook his head.

"Don't ever shoot me with it." Lew cracked a smile, and it got a chuckle from Gid. Lew reached out, rubbed his head gently, and got up and got a drink of water from the sink.

The only person who didn't eat much that afternoon was Gid. Not sure what was going on with him, but he ate only a couple of bites and looked like he was about to be sick. Maybe the canned foods we had been eating were starting to get to him, or something else was. He won't say, and I stop bothering him about it. If he wouldn't open up to you in the beginning about something, he never would.

Lew went over his plan for the trip to find our father, and we sat around, looking at a Rand McNally he had taken from someone's car. He explains that he will mostly travel at night, getting there and back as quickly as possible.

"If I find him and he's hurt or sick and can't travel fast, I want you to start heading here." He pointed at a small town outside of Council Bluffs.

"Iowa?" Gid asked.

"Yes, we need to go there first and get my friend. We served in the Army together, and we could get help there. It's not too far out of the way, and it's worth the trip. We can provision ourselves there and head south before winter sets in this year. "It's getting close to the end of March." He slides his finger along the dates and rests on the 25th, a Wednesday. "I will be back here in six days." On the first, if I'm not back here, this is the route I want you to take."

"Without you?" I asked, surprised.

"Yes, without me. I will catch up with you eventually, because there's no way you three can travel as fast as I can alone, so I will get with you as soon as possible. Let's go over the route, and I need all three of you to pay attention and listen closely."

He went over the details and instructed us to camp on the opposite side of the road each night we traveled and to cut a tree trunk with a knife every morning to mark our path. He explained in detail what to take and told us that if we made it to the address, we should remember that his friend Thomas would help us until he got there.

"It should take twenty days to reach Council Bluffs. The journey will be slow on this trip because I want you to travel at night and avoid the major roads. Cook your food after daylight and away from the road. Eat and then move down the road a bit to sleep that day. Always have someone awake and on watch. Take turns with it; it'll be hard at first, no way around that, just part of our new lives. Traveling at night is dangerous, but being seen in the daylight would be more so. Don't approach anyone you see; always keep your distance until you reach this address. Memorize it, all of you. The paper needs to be destroyed so no one finds it." He pointed to the instructions on a piece of paper he had unfolded from his pocket.
"The day you leave, go to the small bike shop in town, you know the one beside the Culver's on Main Street, and take your pick. I assume you all know how to ride a bike, right?" he scanned us, not expecting anyone to say no to that, but Jimmy was shaking his head.

He hung his head, muttered to himself, and looked back at me. "If you can't find bikes to ride, then walk. Find some hiking shoes and take off. It may be best to start looking for these things right now so you can avoid town." He looked at Gid. "The old man who lived behind you doesn't have any rifles we can take? I thought he was a hunter?"

Gid nodded his head. "In a safe. I took the shotgun he had out for protection, and this pistol, but everything else is locked up."

Lew mulled that for a second. "Okay, so outside of not being seen, the most important thing is to gather these things we need for traveling. Weapons, ammo, food, walking shoes, bicycles. If you happen upon some NVGs, get them."

"NVGs?" I asked.

"Night vision that fits over your head and face or may look like binoculars. It's a slim chance but be on the lookout."

He headed to the sink with his plate and ran water onto it. "I just thought of something. Your daddy may have had an accident on the way home, so I need to travel during the day to look for him. Is he still driving that beat-up Chevy?" He looked over at us.

"No, he has a new Mercedes now," Gid said.

"Figures, what color?" Lew asked.

"White," I said. Lew went and opened the garage door. I know he's seeing my dad's old Chevy and my mama's Tahoe in there. He turned back to us and said, "Being as your dad may not be able to travel, I'll take his truck. In the morning, Gid and I will push it to the end of the road, and I'll crank it away from the house. I don't want anyone to hear it and pinpoint the source of the noise. Any more gas cans around besides this one?" He looks at Gid.

"Not except the one-gallon one for two-cycle fuel." He gestured outside to the back yard shed.

"Where's the key?" he asked.

"Top of the fridge in a basket," I told him.

He headed inside and pulled the entire basket down. I can see he's lost for a few seconds in thought. He hasn't taken the key out, just staring at the basket.

"Everything okay?" I asked.

He nodded. "Your father and I stole two of these from the Woodville Dairy Queen on a fishing trip back from Pleasure Island with the old man one year. I'm not sure what happened to mine, but this one's his." He shook his head slightly, grabbed the key, and set the basket back in place.

Lew slid in the key and turned it to activate the gauges. I heard the fuel pump whine, and he checked the dashboard gas gauge. Satisfied, he switched it off and gently closed the door.

"Half a tank, really need to find another gas can just to make sure."

Mr. Davenport always kept one full in his garage." I said, and I saw Gid get jumpy. What's wrong with him? He's been weird since getting back this afternoon.

"Gideon, let's head over and get his, and with the one here, that should be plenty until we can scrouge more." Gid looked nervously around and shook his head.

They both head to the back door, sliding into their boots and jackets.

Once the back door closed, I made sure the shotgun was beside me, and I started the hot water for the dishes. Jimmy came over and asked if he could dry. We could just lay them in the rack, but I know he needed something to do, so I nodded and smiled at him, glad he's starting to come out of his shell some.

31 Gideon

"There's something I need to tell you," I told Lew once we were outside and away from Maryn.

"Tell me as we walk then." He waited for me to lead the way.

"Mr. Davenport doesn't have any more fuel. I know because I used it to burn that house down that you saw smoking," I admitted.

"That was probably the stupidest thing you could have done while trying to remain unnoticed. The goddamn flames had to be 75 feet high. Why?" he put his hands on his hips, giving me a bewildered look.

"That's where we placed Mama and Mr. Davenport, and after seeing the rat come out of the guy's body, which freaked out Jimmy, I couldn't bear the thought of them eating her, so I burned it down, and I'd do the same for you," I said stubbornly.

"You risked everything for someone who isn't even alive anymore. The dead can't see or know anything you do for them. You can visit their grave a thousand times; they can feed the crows, and it will mean nothing to them and won't make a single difference. The living is all that matters, and we don't put the living in unnecessary danger for the dead. You must understand that Gideon. Risking your life for a loved one is something that people must do sometimes, but if they are already dead, what's the point?" Shaking his head at what he's seen as my foolishness, he stomped off before turning back to the house and opening the back door. I heard him tell Maryn we'd be longer than we thought, and not to worry.

He walked back over to me and told me to lead off to Mr. Davenport's anyway. Standing outside his house, Lew reached down and unspooled about ten feet of his garden hose. Two quick cuts with his knife, the hose was hanging loose in his hands, both ends severed.

He looked at me, "To the garage."

After entering it, a thought occurred to me—something my grandfather had said to my granny that I hadn't paid much attention to at the time, but it came rushing back. Lew had pulled out some soldiers from burning vehicles, and some of them were dead. I asked him why that was okay and not what I had done.

"I was the only man there who could do it. Everyone else was hurt too badly. That is not the same thing as I am speaking of with your mother, though, if that's the point you're trying to make. First, I wasn't sure they were all dead yet, and in the heat of it, you try to save everyone you can. If I had died while pulling out dead comrades, how would that have affected you? It wouldn't have, but if you called down a desperate mob onto your location with that blaze, you would have endangered not just yourself but your sister as well. Thing is, I like your sister and don't want to see her harmed." I got the point and nodded with understanding. I don't like it, but he's right.

We were standing by the old Bronco, and he ran one end of the hose into the gas tank and placed a shop towel to seal it off.

"May as well learn the technique of siphoning gas." He placed the other end into an empty water bottle and sealed it off with his hand. He starts to squeeze the bottle, drawing gas from the tank into the water bottle. He moves the hose to fill up the gas can and holds it until it's topped off with five gallons.

"I thought you were supposed to suck on one end to get the gas out?" I said to him.

He arched his eyebrow at me, "You'd prefer to suck on the end? That's how you like it?" He smirked, and my face started to burn with embarrassment.

"No," I said, feeling foolish.

"I'll cut another piece of hose and bring it with us in case you get the urge later." He smiled at me, and my face got warmer still. I shook my head and smiled at his joke.

"Pick that up," he said and pointed his chin to the gas can. I tightened the spout back on, and we headed for home.

We entered our garage, and I filled the tank with the five gallons he had just siphoned. He then threw the hose and gas can into the back of the truck.

"Why don't you siphon the fuel out of her truck?" I asked him, and he stopped and looked back at me in the doorway.

"Newer vehicles have a mechanism to stop siphoning, not worth the aggravation."

"Don't mention that I burned the house down." I grabbed Lew's arm. He looked down at me and slightly nodded.

"Don't take them over that way when searching the neighborhood. I've shown you how to enter these homes. After you clear a few, maybe bring those two back to them and show them. That way, you will know they are clear, but remember that anyone alive could still have found shelter in them since you cleared them last time. Don't assume they are empty, but at least you will know there aren't any bodies that will send

Jimmy out of orbit again. Start teaching him mundane tasks that need to be done. Cooking, cleaning, using his gun safely, and caring for and cleaning it. I know you have spent time outdoors around weapons, but he sure hasn't."

He stopped at the door, turning back to me. "You wouldn't consider sending him back to his home, would you?" He looked at me, knowing the answer already. I shook my head.

"Scared of Maryn?" he teased.

"Some," I said, grinning back, and he clapped my shoulder and laughed

32 Llewelyn

"We have a new plan now that the truck is a factor. I'll get Gid to help me push it a few blocks over in the morning, and I will start right at daylight, so I don't have to use the headlights. I may be able to make it there and back today, but if I don't return, the 1st is still your start-off day. What I need you to do hasn't changed, so keep doing it until I get back or the leave day arrives. Everyone understands?" We all nodded.

"Let's eat and get some rest. Sleep in the basement again tonight, but when I leave tomorrow, move your bunks up here unless you can fix the outside door. The basement is a good spot to hide in because of the bolted door, but you don't want to be trapped here in case of looters or fire. Never stay where there's one way in and out. Just because you haven't seen any more people doesn't mean there aren't more here.

"Jimmy, come here and show me where the old man's camper is located?"

Jimmy jumped at being addressed directly by me. My face hardened at Jimmy's fear. I'm not letting him off the hook over this, as the silence stretched out, and Maryn jumped in to save Jimmy.

"I think I know where it is."

"I didn't ask you; Jimmy was there, so let's get to it, boy." Maryn was visibly angry and started to say something. I looked at her and shook my head. Jimmy crossed the other side of the table to look down at the city map Lew had spread out.

"It's by the park," Jimmy told me, and I moved his finger there.

“What street?” I asked.

“Rawhide, maybe. I didn’t pay attention.” I started to snap at him, but instead, I put my hand on his shoulder and told him. “It’s okay, just try to remember anything about the place.”

“There’s a large red barn in the front and a white metal shop. The place is surrounded by old cars and junk. There’s a large office building beside it, I think. I never saw the front of the place, just the side, so I’m not sure what it is.”

“Anything else? A church close by?” I asked.

“N-n-no.” Jimmy stammered. “But there is a railroad beside it and a place where they grow plants.”

“Plants? A farm?” We stared at the map.

“Like roses and stuff.”

“A nursery, you mean?”

“I-I-I guess so.” Jimmy’s nervousness was apparent, being so close to me.

“Rawhide? Hmm. Do you mean Rawson?” I pointed it out on the map.

Jimmy looked at me, on the brink of tears. “I think so.” His lip quivered, and I waved him back down; he did so in relief. Maryn wrapped her arm around his shoulders and told him he did a good job.

“Gid didn’t you use to take him cans and food Mama cooked?” Maryn asked him, and I looked up at him.

“Well?” I asked.

"Yeah, but that was his old place. The church bought him a new camper, and I don't know where it is. I didn't even know he was out of the hospital until he shot at me," Gideon admitted.

I slid my finger down the street and nodded my head. "Right here, I bet." I stood up and folded the map into my army fatigue pocket. I rummaged through the loot we had gathered and pulled out all the nine-millimeter ammo and placed it in my pack. With a fully loaded spare, I tucked the rest of the box into my pack and took out his cleaning kit.

"Reach out there and get me that bowl," I told Jimmy.

"Is that rust around the barrel?" Gideon asked because it shows dark spots in the kitchen's low light.

"No, blood," I said and broke it down for cleaning.

"Gather up, and I'll show you three how to clean it."

33 Gideon

I'm awakened by someone squeezing my shoulder. My eyes open immediately, and I reach for my pistol. Lew was standing by my rack and jerked his head back toward the stairs. Maryn and Jimmy were still asleep, and I used the nightlight's low light to get dressed and go upstairs. Closing the door, Lew is standing there drinking coffee with his pack on his back.

"Let's be about it." He said, and we went into the garage, and I opened the door as he slung his gear and rifle into the cab.

"Won't people be able to hear this engine?" I asked.

"This pawpaw truck has the small 305 in it. I don't imagine your daddy put glass packs on it so that it will be fine." Once the garage door was opened as quietly as I could, he whispered, "Get behind the wheel and keep it on the road." He reached over along the wall, got a shovel, put it in the bed, and what that signified hit me in the chest. He waved impatiently at the cab for me to get behind the wheel, and I slid in and gently closed the door. I rolled down the manual window on the old 1997 as we started forward. No power windows, doors, or locks, and the low, subtle old vehicle smell got in my nostrils as we rolled out of the driveway, and I cranked the wheel as much as I could. Lew closed the garage door, jogged over, caught up with the slowing truck, and pushed from the back, while I never touched the brakes. I started to get out to help, and he waved to me to stay behind the wheel. The only sound was the tires rolling over the pavement, and the cool air flooded in through the open window as we picked up speed. A couple of minutes later, we are at the end of Michigan at Pennsylvania Avenue. Lew slid his hand across his throat in the universal sign for "kill it" or stop what you're doing. I gently pressed the brakes, and we stopped. He came around and told me to put it in gear. I stepped on the clutch, shifted into first, and slid out from behind the wheel. Lew took my place, and the sun was turning the world gray.

"Be careful, and I'll be back as soon as possible. I'll give you a few minutes to get back to the house before I crank the truck. Take care of your sister and work on the things we've gone over."

I nodded my head and took off back home in the predawn light. That old truck was so quiet, or I'm so far away when he does take off, I don't hear the engine. I walked inside and started making breakfast for us. Yesterday's eggs and the last of the ham Lew brought with him would start our day. It's almost done when Maryn came up and sat at the table. Jimmy isn't entirely up, but he's ready to eat, and I'm heading to the sink with my empty plate. He started on the plate Maryn had made for him and was still going after it when I turned to talk to them.

"I'm heading out. You going to collect eggs with Jimmy this morning?" She nodded, and I stepped back into the chilly morning air. I went to close the door, and the dog darted out. I started to tell Maryn, but it won't hurt for him to be outside for a bit, and I closed it and took off.

34 Maryn

By the time Jimmy was ready, I had washed the dishes and set them out to dry. He was looking for his dog and calling quietly for him.

“I think he went outside with Gid,” I told him as we got our shoes on. The air was cool, and the sun was climbing over the trees as we took off for the chicken coop. The dog ran from Mr. Davenport’s yard to join us, and we were underway.

Jimmy handled the chickens that were still lying on their nests, four of them this time, like a pro. He talked to them quietly, and they only puffed out their feathers and clucked softly while he gathered the eggs. They don’t peck or flap their wings at all with him, and he came out of the coop with his bucket of eggs and a huge smile. The hens followed him while I checked the feed and water levels. Both are still good, so we head back to the house. He’s so happy with the job he’s done with the hens that he’s swinging the bucket a little too vigorously. I touched his arm to slow him down before any of the precious eggs got broken.

He's not discouraged too much by my gentle reprimand, and it doesn’t take the smile off his face. A blue streak took off in hot pursuit of squirrels that climbed up a tree, a safe distance, and chattered at him. The only thing about today that’s different from any early spring day is the lack of people and noise. There’s a slight smell of smoke in the air, but a complete lack of human sounds. No cars, kids playing, or radios blaring. An assortment of covered grills in backyards makes me involuntarily think of my father smoking brisket and how Mr. Davenport made a point of coming over when he smelled that smoke drifting on the breeze. The taste of the meat and the realization that none of those things would happen again with the same people caused my mouth to water and heart to ache at the same time.

Back home, we put the eggs away and began organizing our food. We had several boxes of Ramen, jars of peanut butter, sleeves of crackers, a stale loaf of bread, and a couple of jars of jelly. The beef jerky was half gone, but we have dozens of MREs that Gid collected. I found my mom's bread recipe, but I needed the ingredients. I decided today to look mainly for these.

I have some quiet time while Jimmy is occupied teaching the dog tricks to consider where we are now. My estranged uncle showing up here was something I would have never guessed. The last I heard, he was stationed in New York. New Jersey, maybe? I can't be sure, but we hadn't seen him in years. My father didn't speak of him much, and my grandfather was openly hostile toward him when he came up. My mother never mentioned him much except that time in the UP, and I wasn't sure what the contention was, but it didn't seem he was well-liked by anyone else except my granny. She wouldn't hear a bad word said about him, and she was fierce in his defense. Every few years, he would show up for Christmas or Easter, but usually he was gone, fighting in the desert or the mountains, Granny said. I never asked my father why they didn't get along, and I know he wouldn't have told me anyway. My mama's silence was strange because she usually made jokes about the problems people had with each other. Mr. Davenport didn't like his next-door neighbor over a property line dispute, and since the day she learned of it, she has referred to the neighbor as his "girlfriend" or "best friend." As in "Cliff, I saw your girlfriend out watering her roses today, or did you shovel the snow off your best friend's steps?" etc., etc.

She wouldn’t miss a chance to rile him over the riff, so it must have been something serious. I was too busy with my own life to worry about what old people were up to, so I didn't concern myself with it. The surprising part was that he talked about family and then risked his life for my dad, whom he clearly didn’t like. I decide that when he returns, I will get to the bottom of it. If he ever returns, that is.

Gid came home in the afternoon, and all three of us helped him unload his haul. He brought home another shotgun and more canned goods. Also, two more boxes of .22 for Jimmy’s rifle. He washed down a package of peanut butter crackers with room-temperature water, and we headed back out.

We cleared two houses quickly. The first was abandoned before the sickness and was almost empty, and the next is home to an elderly woman who must have either died right before or moved to a retirement home. The one after that, though, is different in every way. The sickly smell wafting from the open back door reveals death inside. Gid turned to Jimmy, “There are dead people in here. Do you want to stay out here and wait for me to get done?”

Jimmy took a moment and shook his head, gripping his little .22 in his hands. He inhaled a deep breath and followed Gid inside. The smell was much worse here, and I wasn’t sure how much more I could take. Jimmy squinted against the stench, and the scarf he wore around his nose and mouth wasn’t doing much to mask the foul odor, as mine didn’t either. I touched his arm and pointed to the pantry. Gid went down the hallway to check the bedrooms. Afterward, he walked upstairs while we went through the drawers and cabinets. Honey and yeast were the most significant finds for me, and while I secured them, Gid waved us upstairs.

"Any dead people up here?" I asked before taking the next step. He shook his head and followed him up. The first room on the left is full of quilting and tailoring supplies. I dug through the drawers until I found what I needed when I first met Jimmy. There it lay surrounded by various other scissors and thread. Embroidery scissors. Small, with golden handles and a mother-of-pearl sheath. I also tucked away all the threads and needles I could find. When I was satisfied that everything I could use was put away, I turned back to the hallway to find Gid and Jimmy.

They are standing in the middle of a room, the bed flipped up against the wall. The upended bed nearly obscures the windows, blocking most of the light. A rug was crumpled up against the bottom of the bed, and there was a door swinging out from the floor. Gid was on his knees, Jimmy holding the light down into the open space. He passed back two rifles to me, and I leaned them against the wall. Magazines and ammo are following, along with two matching pistols and two more boxes of ammo, presumably for them. He also fished out a belt and a vest. Not sure what use these are, but he put them down beside him, stood up, and closed the door. He gathered his find and put it into his bag. The same with the magazines and boxes of ammo. He handed me one rifle, grabbed the other, and we went downstairs.

We dropped our cache at home on the table, and I set the rifle aside and instead took up the shotgun again, as I'm more comfortable with it.

"You don't want to use the SKS?" He asked.

"No, I'm not familiar with it, and I don't want to need it and not be familiar." He nodded, and we went out again.

35 Llewelyn

I know it's a risk to head straight north through the city, but I couldn't skirt it this time. Charles may have been close and pulled over and died on the side of the road, and I would overshoot him while going around the city. I took a while to navigate the traffic jams, but I only had to push two cars aside enough to pass through. Only one gunshot was fired in my direction, and that was an hour into the trip. Fortunately, after I was through the city and could speed up, I was able to drive faster than a walk but not for long. The traffic was worse than what I had encountered so far. I had to stop several times, either to push vehicles off the road or to drive into the median to go around. It was frustrating work for a hundred-mile trip, I thought as I wiped the sweat from my forehead and pushed a tow truck out of the way.

I stopped twice to check on the white Mercedes cars I found on the side of the road. Neither of them was the one I was looking for, so when it got dark, I found a place to pull over and spent the night. I didn't want headlights shining and giving me away from a mile away, so I pulled over in Port Washington to get out and listen to the night for a bit. When I got tired, I took the keys and laid my bedroll on a hill beside the interstate, away from the vehicle, in case someone noticed it had just been parked. I also didn't need some jackasses driving by and using it as target practice while I slept inside, so this was the safer option.

The next morning, I started the truck up and headed north to continue the search. I had strange dreams about him and Jess all night and woke up in a sour mood. It got even worse as I turned a corner about ten miles up the road. I saw a white car, and when I got closer, I parked the truck and ran over to check. Sure enough, there lay my brother, and he had been dead for a few days at least. The car was crumpled against a concrete barrier separating northbound and southbound traffic. A rig truck was caught in the rear quarter panel, and looking at the driver of the truck, it looks like it killed them both on impact. I got back in his truck and retraced my way south to a Christmas tree farm I had seen, with equipment sitting outside a barn across the street. I kicked in the shop door and looked until I found a row of keys on the wall. Taking all the Deere keys, I cranked the excavator and drove it up the road to where his car had crashed on the shoulder. I grabbed it with a bucket, forcing it apart from the rig truck, and dragged it over to the northbound side of the road. Leaving it on the shoulder, I drove over the fence separating highway property from the tree farm and dug a hole big enough to hold the car and all.

Welding and soldiering hadn't given me much experience running the hoe, but I soon got the hang of it and dug a massive hole in the rich soil. I dropped the car over in it, using the bucket's thumb to lift it and set it in the hole. I covered it with dirt and packed it down by running the excavator over the top when I was done. I turned the machine off, took the keys out, and threw them into the high grass in case someone came along and tried to move it.

Having done my final duty with his remains, I wiped my tears, whether for him, Jess, his kids, or my mama, I couldn't say, and walked back to the farmer's shop where I left the truck. The sun was starting to set, so I needed to find somewhere to hide out for the night.

36 Gideon

Maryn had a point about the rifle, but since I didn't have one, I brought mine. It couldn't be too different from the AR we shot in the UP with Mr. Davenport. I'd go over it in detail tonight, but I have the basics covered if needed. I slid an extra thirty-round magazine into my back pocket and hung the rifle from the sling across my chest. The next two houses have dead people, and I steered Jimmy away from them in their rooms, but the last house was unescapable. The living room had two people huddled together in death, and they were staring at the door when I opened it. The scene wasn't awful except for their faces, but the smell was wretched. I warned Jimmy and Maryn about it, and they managed to keep it together as they searched for the kitchen. Nothing notable in the home besides the corpses, except that Maryn found something she needs for bread making.

Returning home late in the afternoon, we each start on things we find essential. I go over the SKS, Maryn was sorting through her newfound tailoring supplies, and Jimmy was entertaining himself with the dog. That reminded me that we must name him. I ran through normal ones while my hands are busy and can't land on anything. Hell, he's Jimmy's dog, so he should be the one to name him. Satisfied with that, I turned my focus to the operation of the rifle. It's straightforward, and the only thing I'm uncertain about is the recoil. It's chambered in 7.62, and I've never shot one before. The first time I would likely learn about it would be in a serious situation, and that was unsettling, but there was nothing I could do at the moment.

We spent the rest of the day taking care of minor things like laundry and a meal. Afterward, Maryn sent Jimmy and me to the poor house in Monopoly, and I took a shower and went to bed early. It has become easier for me to fall asleep at night since this all started. I think the adrenaline of entering people's homes and the possible danger of it all sapped me more throughout the day than anything that had come before. Not even football practice drained me like this. I lay down on my rack, my hands clasped above my head, and thought about how different life is now. Dead or missing family, no electricity, food shortages, and utilities were going to fail altogether soon. No more social media, hell, I don't even remember where I left my new iPhone. The constant worry and fear had replaced the need for the hottest Insta pics from girls in my high school. The only reason I wish it were still operational now is so survivors could contact each other. Besides old man Burns, Jimmy, and Lew, the only human presence had been burnt buildings in the distance, and I'm not sure those were deliberately set.

I imagined the stores had been thoroughly looted by now, and if not, only because there weren't enough left to loot. I don't know which scenario scared me the most, but there wouldn't be much point in worrying about that until I could check for myself. Lew had seen a lot more of the new world than I had, so I would ask him more about it if he managed to return.

I understood why he went to check on my father, since they are brothers, and I would do the same for Maryn and more. I tried to imagine my father doing the same for him, and I'm not sure he would. He was usually distant with me, and sometimes it seemed like he secretly didn't like me at all, but grownups were hard to understand, and maybe that's just the way fathers were? Many friends from school didn't even have their real father living in the home with them, so they wouldn't know.

Now they had extensive experience with stepfathers, and that was usually bad for other reasons. He was never cruel or abusive in any way, but he was always aloof and seemed to live a separate life away from us. He worked away from home a lot and was often in and out. We usually missed each other, and it didn't seem to bother him too much. I filled my life with things that made me happy and focused on the things I liked. My mama was the primary source of affection and love, and she filled our lives with it, so we weren't unloved or abused in any way. She was the opposite of him, showering us with her attention and happiness. I felt my eyes water as I remembered her, and I clawed the tears away and forced my mind elsewhere. I focused on tomorrow's activity and what I wanted to achieve, and soon I drifted off to sleep.

I stood barefoot at my mother's crypt in the gentle night rain. The street had flooded, and I could see rivulets cascading along the pavement, rushing toward the storm drains. Mr. Davenport was raking leaves with an old, dingy cast on his leg and turned to look at me when I shouted at him. His face was gone, and only a skull grinned back at me as he waved with his free hand. He dropped his wave and his rake, shuffled onto the small porch, and opened the door. Thousands of rats boiled out of the front door and scurried toward me. I stood there in my underwear trying to swing my new rifle up, and a figure walked after them, with his right hand in the air but covered from head to toe, striding toward me. I felt like my arms were trapped in amber, as if a physical force held them down because they moved so slowly. The first of them reached the street edge where I'm straining to bring my rifle to bear, and the cloaked figure dropped his hand, and the rats and Mr. Davenport fell over and stopped moving. I'm still lifting the rifle when his pale hand dropped to clench my throat and squeezed. Golden eyes shone from behind something resembling a bronze, bearded mask, but I couldn't make out any further details because I was struggling to breathe. A storm battered me, whipping my clothes as the wind howled, causing my shirt to snap and pop like a sail caught in a strong gust.

"So strong. A fighter?" The figure said with a voice like a thunderclap. A woman's voice cut through the tempest, but I can't make out her words, just the repetitive chanting. The golden eyes slid from me to something over my shoulder that I can't turn to see, and I heard her clearly now, just not understanding the language.

I've almost gotten the rifle up and flicked the safety off. The sound of it was loud as a branch snapping in a Wisconsin ice storm. I heard laughter behind the masks, like glass being ground together, and it made me squint and yell out; I felt my eardrums would burst. One last effort: the barrel finally came up. I squeezed the trigger, only to wake up in the dark basement. My breathing was still restricted, and I put my hand to my throat; It felt tender to the touch. I swung my feet to the floor and took a few deep breaths. I stood to get dressed and noticed my feet felt damp.

37 Maryn

The next day, when I woke up, Gid was already gone, and I got Jimmy up, and we got started on breakfast. Afterward, we got the eggs and checked on our new flock. I noticed that Jimmy is happiest when he interacts with animals, and tending to the chickens in the morning boosted his mood. The dog running around like a psycho made him laugh, and he was generally happy just him and me. I think the others made him feel less because he wasn't as tough as they were, and he was intimidated. He didn't feel he measured up, which compounded his nervousness around them, especially Lew.

Of course, Llewelyn was intimidating to say the least, towering well over 6ft tall, broad at the shoulders, and brusque in speech. The opposite of Jimmy, who was short, skinny, and timid. The only way you can tell that Lew and my father were brothers is the same black hair and blue eyes that Gid and I also shared. My father was rail-thin and not quite as tall. Gid had already gained on him this year, and he had a few years left to grow. Lew's face was darkened and had several small scars covering his left cheek. His left eyebrow also bore a slash, and his hair was rough and dirty. I had never seen my father with dirty hands; he always wore gloves, and outside of the fence he and Gid put up late last summer, he didn't work outside much—almost completely different men from the same parents. My father was often distant, especially toward Gid, but he gave off a steady, gentle aura. Llewelyn, on the other hand, was like being around a wild animal in a zoo that might not have been fenced high enough to contain it. I don't know how much gentleness he has, but it wasn't apparent. He always seemed ready to do violence and wouldn't think too much about it afterward.

Just before I entered our yard, I saw some movement off to my left and across the street. Looking back, I waved to Jimmy to hurry to me. He didn't see me and ran over to the dog, bending over and scratching his belly as the dog wriggled in the grass. I snapped my fingers, and he looked over his shoulder at me. Motioning him to come, he sprinted over, and the dog followed along nipping his heels. When they reached our back gate, the dog sent him tumbling by biting his heels. He hit the ground; the bucket of eggs went flying, and I heard the wind go out of him. The dog piled on, playfully biting him. I push him away and pull Jimmy up. His eyes are wild with panic, and I showed him how to put his arms up over his head to help catch his breath. His gasping seemed so loud to me that I'm sure it can be heard a block over. He fell to one knee and bent over, but I could hear some of his breath coming back. He continued to gasp as I tried to hold the dog off; fortunately, we were hidden from view by our fence, except for Mr. Davenport's house or the upper stories of our neighbor to the east.

Jimmy regained himself, and we went inside. He's complaining about his left elbow, and by the time I get his shirt off, and he's sitting at the table, it's already swollen like a baseball. We have ice packs, but they have long since thawed, so I used cold washcloths and wrapped them around his arm with an Ace bandage. I know it won't do much, but it's all we have for sprains.

When Gid opened the door, he had his rifle at the ready.

"What's happened?" Gid asks, walking over to the table, looking down at us. Jimmy's arm has turned deep purple and is tender to the touch. I constantly change the washcloths to keep them as cold as possible, but it doesn't work.

“The dog tripped him when they were playing, and his elbow is hurt. How did you know something was wrong?” I asked him.

“There are eggs scattered across the back yard. I’ll get them, just wanted to make sure of what was going on before walking into danger with eggs in my hand instead of my rifle. Jimmy, is it going to be alright, or do we need to cut it off?” Gid winked at him. Jimmy sniffed and looked up at him with a tear-streaked, dirty face and gave him a thumbs up with his unhurt hand.

“It's okay now,” he sniffled.

“I’ll be right back. I got something that will make you feel better.” Gid left his rifle and went back out. He returned with two buckets: one we used for eggs, and the other was larger and black. He set them down and kicked his boots off at the door. Picking them up, he brought them both into the kitchen. He took the eggs out and put them by the stove.

The black bucket was square and tall, and he smiled at me and said, “It’s a survival kit for food. I found several buckets like this in the basement, and I’ll get them too. The best thing is this one has chocolate pudding in it.” He smiled at Jimmy.

“I like pudding,” Jimmy said, starting to perk up at the info.

“I know you like putting it in the back of your underwear when you see dead folks,” Gid teased, and I swatted his arm, but he and Jimmy both laughed at the joke.

“I thought I saw someone across the street when we were coming home from the chicken coop.”

His head snapped towards me. “You don’t think that’s

important enough to lead with?" His eyes flashed at me, all trace of humor gone.

"I had a lot going on, and I'm not 100 percent sure it was someone. It could have been a bird or animal." I told him defensively, understanding that I should have checked this out myself as soon as I got Jimmy home.

"I'm going to go next door to the woods and keep watch, don't expect me until dark." He stepped back into his boots, grabbed up his rifle, and was gone in an instant.

I went through the bucket of food he'd brought and set aside what I intended to make for us tonight. I continued to monitor Jimmy's arm, but it looks like it's done swelling. I switched out the cold cloths, though, and gave him an ibuprofen for the pain.

"We're done outside today, let's get your bath out of the way and start doing our laundry." He walked out of the dining room and asked over his shoulder if I would get him a pair of underwear. "Yes, just make sure you're clean when you come out this time," I told him as he shut the door.

38 Gideon

I carefully slipped into the woods beside our home, by the back fence, and tried to circle back toward the road as quietly as possible. The rain helped soften the limbs and leaves, and once I could get a clear view of the houses across the way, I settled in. The minutes dragged by, and this is the hardest part of doing any hunting. It's not terrifying like when I was hiding in that culvert, head bleeding, but it was boring. I'm warmly dressed, the weather was clear, so the tedium was the only thing to deal with. An hour dragged by, then another, and I saw something moving behind the house adjacent to ours. Just movement, but I can't tell what it is for sure. Probably a stray dog, but I can't make it out, not even a color. I sat, unmoving, for perhaps another two hours, seeing no further movement. The light breeze had died down, and the shadows were growing long. I wanted to go check out what I've been seeing, but I won't cross the street in full daylight.

With twilight here, I moved on slowly through the woods as best as I could. The house across from us had a couple in their thirties that I really didn't know. The man I'd only met once and had seen three times was named Dale, and I'd never spoken to his wife or whatever she was. He told me that, the one time we met, he was a boilermaker and traveled a lot for work. It didn't seem to bother his girl too much, as there was a steady run of guys in and out while Dale was away this last time. The day I met him, he was backing an old Lund Boat in his yard when he called me over and asked me to stand by the culvert so he could see where it was in the mirror. I was practicing free throws across the street at my house, and my old Papa always said that if a man asked you for help, you helped him. I backed him into a spot by his garage, and he got out and introduced himself. That was a few days after we moved in, and the boat hadn't moved since then. It had been full of wet leaves, soaked, life jackets, and beer cans then.

Standing at the back of said boat, I peered around the back of his house, not seeing anything moving—no noise except a few birds. I stepped through the wet grass to the next house, and I saw the movement again. By the bike path that ran behind all the houses on this street, there is a large maple, and a slight drop off to let rain run off toward the creek. Standing up, I could see something shuffling around close to the ground. That's why, sitting in the woods, I couldn't see it clearly because it had been below my line of sight until I was standing. Relief flooded my body because it's some animal, not a person. The light was fading, and I don't have binoculars —another thing that needs to be on my list, so I squatted down and watched for a second. A light breeze from behind me cooled the back of my neck. A few seconds later, a small head pops up and looks around, sniffing the air. Too late, I realized the animal was smelling me on the wind. It snarled and stepped a few feet toward me. I'm only thirty yards away, but I can't quite make out what it is because of the light. Maybe a medium-sized dog? A groundhog? Do groundhogs snarl? I don't know, but I quietly step backward to Dale's house, and the small dark animal came running toward me with a clicking sound.

I turned and bolted for the old boat, launching myself into it as the animal bore down on me. I looked down, and there was a small bear clawing its way into the old boat with me on the fender well of the trailer. A few seconds, and it would be inside with me, and it'll be hand-to-hand combat. From the teeth and claws, I could see it would be one-sided, so I looked around for an escape. The roof was about four feet above where I'm standing, so I slung my rifle over my shoulder and jumped. My fingers slide on the wet shingles, not finding any purchase, and I almost fell to the ground. A snarl from behind and below motivated me to regain my handhold and get my forearms up. I scrabbled my way up, wrenching the gutter off, burning the skin off my forearms on the shingles, and my heart pounding in my ears, but not loud enough to cover the sound of claws on aluminum as the animal tried to get in the boat. I managed to toss my right foot over and pull myself up since the gutter was no longer in the way. Lying on my back, lungs pumped, fingers screamed, and scabs bled from the rough dragging, but I made it. Rolling over to my side, I saw the wild monster gnashing its teeth and foaming at the mouth. Standing up and keeping a closer eye on this thing, I warily walked to the back of the garage that I'm on top of. The animal dropped down from the boat's side and followed me to the back. I squatted down and tried to get a better look since I'm no longer in danger. Flicking on my light, I shine it down into its face. Teeth and claws are the biggest attention-getters, but they are low to the ground and cinnamon-colored. Rising on its back feet, I see a lighter band of fur on its chest, almost like the patch on our blue heeler. I don't know what this is, but it reeks and was ferocious as hell, so I intended to sit here until it's far gone. I thought I was going to have to apologize to Jimmy as I almost filled my pants with pudding. I smiled in the dark and wiped the sweat from my brow.

After getting bored with me, I watched it slink away back to where I spotted it earlier. Probably eating something over there and thought I was here to take it. I can't imagine anything in the wild that would take anything from that little mad bastard, smaller than a grizzly but as mean. I switched off my light, gave it a few minutes to resume its business, and walked to the front of the garage. The moon was almost full this evening, but it's hit-or-miss with the clouds scuttling overhead.

I looked out over my neighborhood with no artificial lights, and it's a strange sight. The solar streetlights hadn't made it here yet, so the world was bathed in moonlight only. The cars and homes that would sit abandoned, I wondered what this place would look like in twenty years, with grass grown over, roofs caved in from snow, and all vehicles sitting on rims after the weathered tires gave way.

39 Maryn

I told Jimmy to stay put while I checked on Gid. Something must have happened for him to be out late past sundown. Turning the corner off the house, I saw him running across the street back to us. He waved me off, and I went inside. He stepped in right after, closed it, and ran the locks. He kicked off his boots and brought his rifle to the table, setting it against the wall.

"What took you so long?" I asked him as he slipped off his gun belt, looped it over the back of a chair, and started looking through the books on the shelf in the living room.

"Have you seen that book about animals?" he asked without answering my question.

"Book?" I'm surprised, as he's not an avid reader.

"The Reader's Digest one about animals." He said while searching through novels and law books on the shelf.

"The last time I saw it, you had it in your room.

He whirled around and said, "That's right, thanks," and bounded up the stairs. After a few seconds, he's back and carrying the book. He tossed it on the table and asked about supper. Jimmy and his dog came over, sat down, and I started supper back up.

"Are we having pudding again?" Jimmy looked hopefully at the meal I brought to the table.

"Yes, but it's the last of it unless Gid has found more." We both looked at him as he scanned the wildlife book, ignoring his food.

“Ha, a wolverine!” he spun the book around for us to see, pointing at the small brown animal.

“That’s what you saw in the neighbor's yard that also tried to eat me this evening.” He grinned like a maniac as he recounted today's action.

I’m not sure how he’s survived this long with his love of danger and sheer carelessness. Both of those would have to change to survive in these new times.

“If that thing had rabies and bit you, there’s nothing we can do to save you. You realize that, right?”

He looked up at me, smiling, “I wasn’t going to let it bite me, rabies or not.” He smiled at Jimmy, scratching the dog's ears.

“Jimmy, have you ever seen any of these in the wild before?”

“I’ve never seen anything in the wild before,” and went back to playing with the dog.

Shaking his head, Gid got back to his book. I started to get up and take the dishes to the sink. Gid put out his hand and got up himself.

“Jimmy, let’s wash these dishes since Maryn’s been nice enough to cook three days in a row.” They took the dishes over and got to work on them. I have all our laundry out to dry and nothing else to do tomorrow. Maybe I’ll go with Gid and help bring in the buckets.

I run some bath water and wonder where Lew and my father are. Hopefully, he’s been found, and they're both headed back here. It made me nervous to think about going all the way to

Iowa without Lew. We need to start searching for bikes and retrieve the cache Gid found. Gid cleared the basement door as Lew instructed, so we could sleep there as usual, and tomorrow we could help him search for more weapons. I didn't like the bread from the survival kits he'd found, so I wanted to look for more yeast anyway. I climbed into the tub, placed a hot washcloth over my face, and enjoyed the soak.

40 Gideon

I heard something, light tapping on the door down here. With the weird dreams I've had, I'm not too sure it was real until I heard the dog growl low in his throat. There's no way to see out from the basement, so I went to the back door. Slipping on my boots and grabbing my rifle, I went out the back door and to the side of the house where the basement door led out. The full moon was bright, and I could see a man standing at the door. The wind has picked up through the night, and the cool wind pebbled my skin. Cold or fear, I can't say, but over the din, I easily sneak up on the silhouette.

"Turn around slowly," I said just loud enough for the wind not to catch my words. The man didn't jerk in fear, only extended his hands, and turned.

"Your turn to sneak up on me?" Llewelyn teased, his face hidden in shadow from his hoodie.

Sliding it back, I could see he's grinning, and I jerked my head toward the back of the house. He picked up his pack and followed.

Once inside, I asked about my father.

"Best go wake your sister; I don't want to tell this tale more than once." He went to the stove and began filling the percolator with water. I went to get Maryn, and she and the dog followed me upstairs.

"Well?" I questioned. "We're all here, let's hear it."

"Have a seat, it's hard news, I'm afraid." He motioned to the dining chairs.

"I'm going to go through the entire thing, so listen up. If you have any questions, wait until I'm done, and I'll do my best to answer them," He nodded, and we do likewise.

"Let me start by saying that I found your father, and he was heading back this way in his car. He was in an accident, and I'm sorry to say he's gone. It looked instant and painless, and that's the best any of us can hope for."

Maryn stood up, sobbing, and headed to the bathroom. "There's more," Lew said stonily.

"Give her a second," I told him angrily, but he ignored my plea and pushed on.

"Have a seat and let's get through this. You can grieve after."

She wiped her face and sat back down. He continued.

"I put your father to rest in a nice spot and did all I could for him. He's gone, and we need to prepare ourselves, or we will end up the same. I was shot at on the way there, but I didn't see anyone. The point is that travel is perilous. If we didn't have to, we would stay here, but we all realize that's not possible. It's risky but necessary. Tomorrow, the focus will be on finding bicycles and on ways to transport water or water-purifying supplies. It may take a few days, and I am going to brace that old man and make sure he isn't a problem while we prep to leave."

He walked over to the coffee pot and poured a cup. Taking a test sip and grimacing, he looked back at us. "Any questions?"

"Why don't we just take the truck instead of worrying about bikes?" I asked.

"We're taking the truck, too, but we need backup transportation in case the roads are bad. I had two vehicles shot out from under me on the way to you, remember?"

"Have you ever had to tell someone that their daddy is dead before?" Maryn asked, catching Lew by surprise, I thought.

He shook his head slowly. "I can tell because you're terrible at it." She stood and headed for the bathroom again.

"Anything else from you?" he looked at me.

"Where is he?"

"About fifty miles north of here, in a small town called Belgium. I buried him in a Christmas tree farm there." He showed me on the map and then asked about old man Burns.

"You aren't going to kill that old man?" I asked.

"Depends." He stared at me.

"He's crazy, don't forget," I added.

"By 'crazy,' what exactly do you mean?" He gave me his full attention and set his cup down.

"He talks to himself and doesn't regularly bathe. I've only seen him a few times riding his beach cruiser with sheepskin mudflaps, going around digging through store trash for aluminum cans." I told him.

"Just because a man lives differently than you don't make him crazy. Talking to himself doesn't either. I often do it when I need expert advice on things." He smirked. "I'll not hurt any man that is not trying to harm me or mine, but he DID shoot at you, remember?"

“I was there, and I remember,” I said.

He asked, “Anything else?” Picking up his cup again and taking a sip before hurriedly setting it back down again.

“No.”

“Nothing about your dad?” he looked in my eyes, seeming to dare me to challenge him over his description of events.

“No,” I repeated.

“Tend to your sister, she needs you,” and sipped his cup again.

“She’s right, you know, about you delivering bad news.” I walked to the bathroom and softly knocked on the door. Maryn opened it, and I embraced her as she was racked with grief.

41 Maryn

My head hurt from crying and lack of sleep as I went up the stairs to start breakfast. We don't have as many eggs because some were broken in Jimmy's tumble, but I'll scramble what we do have and make some pancakes from the survival kit. Gid must have had the same idea because they were already on the table when I came into the kitchen. He and Lew were gone, though, and I saw their plates in the sink, and the coffee pot was still hot.

Waking Jimmy up, he complained as he rolled onto his hurt elbow. It's still swollen, but the worst is over, and it will soon be back to normal. He and his dog headed upstairs while I made up his bed. He was coming out of the bathroom when I got upstairs, and I noticed his shirt was wet from the sink, but even after waterboarding his hair, it still wouldn't lie down. I grinned at him, and he sat down and poured syrup over his pancakes.

We cleaned up and went to gather the eggs again. The morning was foggy, and you couldn't really see more than fifty yards in any direction. The grass we walked through drenched our boots and our pant legs up to our ankles—no birds this morning, just the soft drip of water from tree leaves onto the ground.

We wait until a little after sunrise every morning to give the hens time to clear out. We opened the small back gate to the yard with the coop, and it seemed clear. Jimmy went in with the bucket, and I could hear the soft clucking from the hens that decided to sit on their eggs as he made his rounds.

"I think something attacked this hen," Jimmy said near the

back of the coop, and I peered inside to get a better look in the dim. An explosion happened near my head, and I felt wind buffeting my hair. Something grabbed it, twisted it up, and I heard the dog barking. My skin above my ear was pierced as I threw my hands up to ward off whatever the hell this is attacking me. One solid smack and my hair was released, and the rooster hit the ground, feathers floating in the morning air. He stood back up and opened his wings to jump back on me, but the growling dog grabbed him by the head and shook him around in circles. Between my surprise yelp, the rooster and hens squawking, and the dog growling, it's mayhem. A few turns and the rooster was limp, and the feathers blanketed the ground around them. The dog looked up at me, red feathers still stuck in his mouth, tongue lolling out, breathing hard.

"What's going on?" Jimmy stepped past me through the door. Seeing the site, he looked at me.

"What happened?" he asked again.

"I wasn't paying attention and let the rooster sneak up on me," I told him, rubbing the back of my head and feeling damp in my hair. Gid had wanted to kill and eat the rooster the first day we came to the coop, but Lew stopped him.

"We don't need a rooster for eggs," Gid said.

"He will help protect the hens from predators because they're mean and he's too old to eat, probably tough as hell," Lew explained.

"Like you?" Jimmy questioned, looking at Lew. After realizing what he had said, he looked at us with horror.

Lew smiled and said. "Just like me, kid."

We started back home with wet feet, bloody scalp, banged up arm, and the dog sneezing out feathers. I carried the rooster back with us to clean and eat later. I'd never cleaned one alone, but I had seen my granny do it a couple of times. Jimmy put the eggs on the counter, and we started over to the woods on the other side of our house.

We crossed the road so I could clean the rooster, and it took me a lot longer than it did for her. It wasn't pretty, but I was satisfied; it was the best I could do. We headed back home. That's when I realized the chicken offal might attract the wolverine that attacked Gid. Too late now, I would have to warn him of what I had done so he could be more alert. With the egg bucket filled with cut-up chicken, I tossed in the filet knife I used, and we headed back. Jimmy got the door for me, though he stayed his distance while I was butchering the rooster. After washing up, I put the old bird in the sink to soak, and Gid and Lew were back with the first haul from the survival cache. They made two more trips, cleaning it out and storing it in our place so we had plenty of food for weeks. We had peanut butter crackers and sweet tea for dinner, except for Gid and Lew, who don't like tea and drank warm sodas. Then we all went over the supplies again.

42 Gideon

Finding bicycles was more complicated than I thought since Maryn and I already had bikes and thought most everyone else did too. That's not the case. We went through a dozen garages and homes until we found something suitable for Jimmy. Lew, of course, still had the one he rode in on. Finding one that would do, we got to work showing him how to ride it.

His tender elbow didn't help, and by the end of the first afternoon, Lew was completely frustrated, throwing up his hands in exasperation. Of course, Maryn was the most patient with him, and I just stood lookout while they tried to get him used to not having training wheels. Lew finally judged he would have to keep them until he got used to it on the way. He wanted us to go over our gear, and we still had to figure out how to arrange our packs for travel and what was essential for the trip.

The next day, we packed, repacked, and put the final touches on our kits. Lew emptied most of Jimmy's and told him only to carry a sleeping bag and fire-starting kit. With his hurt arm and lack of riding skill, he knew too much of him would make it worse.

Lew returned late, not finding the old man, so we were ready to hit the road. I was relieved that he hadn't hurt him. He left the truck at a store so no one would see him driving to our house. We walked to it, refueled it, and packed it with more food, leaving enough room for our bikes. We would take the truck as far as possible, so it could take only a day or two if the road conditions were good. Lew figured we could get eighteen miles a day once we all got used to riding if we were forced to bike.

On a cold, foggy morning, we left our home in Wisconsin for the last time. Turning north onto Pennsylvania Ave, I looked back to see the place once more, but the curve in E Montana hid it now. Jimmy was wobbly at first but soon began to improve. We come to the intersection where Lew had left my father's truck in the auto parts store's parking lot. We crossed County Rd BB and entered his parking lot. Lew parked his bike beside the truck, and we pulled up alongside him. He put his bag in the back seat, and I set ours in the bed while he fiddled with a jug of water. I set the tailgate down, loaded up the dog, and saw a flask of yellow and heard shouting and gunfire from the front of the truck.

43 Maryn

I heard the yell “VC!” and then gunshots. Turning around, a frail figure in a yellow slicker was firing a rifle toward us. Lew was out of sight, and Gid was ducking down behind the passenger side of the truck. Jimmy stood still, frozen with fear, and I pushed him to the ground, the shots ringing out loud. I heard the dog barking, then a boom from Lew’s side of the truck, and then silence. I peeked around Gid’s side of the truck and saw him at the front with his arm extended, holding his pistol. I heard gravel crunch, and Lew said something unintelligible. I duckwalked around behind Jimmy, who was squatting down, holding his ears and his eyes clamped shut. Lew was lying on the ground and had his rifle pointed at the front of the truck. I wasn’t sure who had done the firing, and I could see a red spot on Lew’s jacket. He scrambled up from the pavement and tried to stand, but fell into the driver’s seat of the open door. I ran to him, and he tried to hand me his rifle, and I saw Gid walking in front of the truck with his pistol still pointing in front of him.

“Gideon is he down?” Lew managed through gasping breaths. Gid didn't say anything, kept walking toward the dumpsters by the store. I let go of Lew and slid around the door to see what Gid was doing. An old man was stretched out on the ground, his rifle lying beside him. I stepped closer and saw his open mouth full of dirty and broken teeth, blood pooling around his head on the pavement. Gid put his hand on my arm and stopped me from going forward, but not before I could see that the top of his head was missing.

I ran back to the truck, grabbed the bed rail, and sent my breakfast to the ground between my boots. My body was shaking, and I was on my tiptoes, retching. I heaved until I saw Jimmy walk toward the man through my tear-blurred eyes. Reaching out, I grabbed a handful of his jacket and hauled him back toward me so he couldn't see. I got him too close to my vomit, and he joined in. What kind of survivors are we? Half of our team was trembling and vomiting, one was shot, and the other was standing there watching a dead man twitch on the ground. I could hear my mama laughing and saying, "The circus must be in town because I found all the clowns!" Gid came to his senses first and ran over to the driver's side, took Lew's rifle, and set it on the floorboard. He picked Lew up and sat him in the driver's seat and started to strip his jacket as Lew grimaced from the wound.

"Get the first aid kit," Gid said and continued to undress him.

"Get the kit," Gid said again, snapping me into action. By the time I have it out and back to the driver's side, Gid has him almost down to his t-shirt. Lew's arms are caught in the sleeves of his jacket and outer shirt, stuck. "Go around to the other side and help me get his shirts off." He barked at me.

I grabbed the sleeves and rolled them off from the passenger side, one at a time. I thought Lew was surely about to faint, but once he's free of the bloody clothes, he's alert and moving to help us get his t-shirt off.

"Did it go all the way through?" he asked through gritted teeth. I told him yes as I saw the hole leaking blood from the right side of his upper back. "Do you see any material from my clothing in the wound?" I peered into the bleeding hole and shook my head. "Put a compress on both sides and put pressure on it." He growled.

Holding it for a few moments, he instructed us to wind the

bandage around to keep the compresses in place, and we taped it off. I thought we used too much, but I didn't want it to fall off. After wrapping it up, he said he needed his sleeping bag. I got it from the truck bed, and Gid helped him slide over to the passenger side. We wrapped him up, and Gid stepped out of the truck, telling Jimmy to get in the back seat. He stood there shaking the whole time. He doesn't move, so I grabbed his arms and told him again. He nodded, winced at me holding his hurt arm, and climbed over the driver's seat into the back seat. This model doesn't have a third door, so the only way to get in was to climb over the seat or slide the seat forward.

Gid waved me over to get in after Jimmy threw down his small bag on the back seat, reached back, and opened the sliding glass door to pet the dog and hopefully calm him down.

"Maryn, get in the back seat and let's get out of here." He said to me, and I closed the passenger door softly, making sure Lew wasn't hit by it. I slid the driver's seat forward and motioned Jimmy to slide over behind Lew. I settled in, grabbed the seat, and pulled it back into place.

Gid took his seat, and Lew turned to him and asked, "Did you see him before he started shooting?"

"Yes, just before." He replied.

"Why didn't you shoot him then?" and Gid shook his head.

"I don't know," he admitted.

"You don't hesitate ever again. When it's killing time, you get to it, or people you care about can die." He stared at Gid and then looked at us in the back seat. "That goes for you two as well. It's dog-eat-dog out here, and there's no room for monkeying around when you should be shooting."

“What are we going to do with the old man?” Gid asked.

“He made his choice, and he can feed the coyotes and buzzards.” Lew glared at him.

“If you don’t start the truck and get us underway, there may be some more people who show up here and put new holes in all of us, or I may bleed out, and you’ll have to deal with my body.”

Gid started the truck and shifted into reverse. I could see that the old man had stopped twitching on the ground, and the puddle had gotten large enough to run out past his feet. I felt the bile rise in my throat, but I held it down with sheer will. Besides, I’ve emptied myself on the pavement already, so there can’t be too much left. We turned left out of the store and headed back up Pennsylvania. Gid smoothly shifted the gears on the floor, and we turned onto Layton. There aren't many abandoned vehicles here, and Gid speeds up to about 60 mph.

“Try to avoid the interstate,” Lew mumbled from the passenger seat.

Gid shook his head and said, “No, we’re going the fastest way possible; we have to get you some help, or you will die in this truck.” Lew didn’t say another word and seemed to sleep. Gid reached onto the dashboard and handed the atlas back to me.

“Find us the fastest route. If we run into a blockage, we’ll turn around, but until then, let’s gain as much ground as possible. He reached down and passed me Lew’s rifle as well. “If we get into any trouble, dump the entire mag.” He said over his shoulder as he sped up the truck.

“Jimmy, if we start firing in this truck, cover your ears, do you hear me?” He looked in the rearview at us. Jimmy nodded, still in a daze.

The cold metal from the rifle comforted my flushed face. The air was cloying in here, smelling of blood and the sick on my boots and breath. Partnered with the backseat motion of the vehicle, I thought for sure I was going to lose it again. My mouth filled with saliva, and I tried to smile at Jimmy to give him some comfort. He's looking out at the back glass at his dog, and I don't bother him. Whatever small comfort he can find, I won't begrudge him. I finally defeat the queasy sensation, though I think it mostly has to do with having nothing else to let go of. I'm drained, and my nerves feel frazzled. I placed my head against the cool barrel and closed my eyes.

I snapped them open, remembering I had a job to do, and opened the atlas to direct him to the highway. Jimmy kept his arm out the back window, petting his dog until the cold wind forced the pup to lie down on the cover we brought for him. I put down the atlas and picked up the calendar to give him something to let his mind escape what he's seen today. Each month features a different animal, with a breakdown of its habitat, diet, and importance to the environment. We have it creased open to March since looking at it the other day, and as Jimmy read off the information about wolves that's written on the top half. I do the math in my head from when Lew left and see that today is March 30, 2026—our eighteenth birthday. I looked down at Lew's AR-15, racked the charging handle to confirm a round was chambered, dumped the magazine to reseat the round I had just ejected, and added another to replace the one he had fired earlier.

44 Gideon

I didn't feel guilty about Lew getting shot because I knew I didn't have enough time to fire on the man before he shot Lew, and I would have had to shoot through the truck windows to hit him, even if I had time. I put the gas down on the old truck and let the gently rocking vehicle eat up the miles. I did take his advice to heart about not hesitating, though.

We passed by Madison, and it's a mess. Wrecked and abandoned vehicles littered the highway on both sides. My biggest worry was getting stopped on an overpass or bridge, but we managed to navigate the traffic without slowing down too much. After that, the small cities and towns of Wisconsin flew by without any trouble. I stopped on our side of the Mississippi River to check out the scene ahead before crossing the bridge into Dubuque. I petted the dog as I climbed into the bed and made the metal protest as I stepped onto the cab and put Lew's binoculars into my eyes. No movement: little congestion on the other side, but it was on a side road, not on the bridge itself.

I dropped down and gave the dog some water in a bowl Jimmy had made sure to bring in his little bag from the cab.

"Anyone got to pee, now's your chance." I put my head in the window to check. Maryn and Jimmy both nodded, so I pulled the seat forward, and they headed to the side of the road. I reach into the bed, pull out one of the five-gallon cans, and pour it into the tank while waiting for them to get back. Sitting the can back into the bed and scratching the dog's head, I looked around and only saw Jimmy coming back.

"Where's Maryn?" I asked him.

Shrugging his shoulders, he said, “She didn’t go on the same side with me.”

“Get back in the truck, we’re about to take off,” I told him.

“How much further is it?” He looked up at me.

“Four, five hours.”

“Can I ride in the back with the dog?” He pleaded with me.

“No, it's too dangerous, too cold, you’ll get pneumonia, go on and get in the truck like I told you.” His shoulders slumped, and he shuffled off to the backseat. A minute ticked by, then another. What the hell is she doing, I wondered

“Gid,” I heard her before she emerged from the trees. I looked, and there’s a man with her, his hand on her arm. He was short and fat, with an unshaven brown beard and dirty brown hair poking out from under a trucker hat that I couldn’t really make out the color of. He had a knife pointed at her side, and they slowly walked down the embankment onto the shoulder.

“Hands up or I’ll stab this bitch. I don’t want to hurt anyone. I need something to eat. Give me that, and you can go on your way. I’m just hungry.” He stepped closer, and I slowly raised my hands. They walked within five yards of me.

“Nice and slow, get me some food out of that truck, and don’t let that dog out or I’ll stick her. you understand?” he licked his chapped and cracking lips.

I nodded my head, still holding my hands up. He had his eyes on the truck bed, and I wondered if I could draw my gun fast enough without him stabbing her, but I decided my hand was too far away.

He jerked his head to the truck. “Go on now.” I felt hornets sting my neck, and a shot exploded from the cab as the dirty, stained t-shirt jumped once, twice. He flew backward from the impact and landed on his back, knife flung out and not even moving. I looked back and saw Lew pointing his rifle through the back window, which was no longer there. Maryn ran to the tailgate, and the dog was barking like hell. The knife-wielder was looking at the sky with a surprised look on his face.

“You... shot....” His mouth worked like a fish out of water. Blood ran from his shirt front down to his belt and from his mouth, flowed over his yellowed teeth, down his sunburned lips. I left him dying there and went to Maryn, expecting her to be crying and shaken up. She waved me off and went to the truck, where Jimmy was holding his hands over his ears, screaming. Blood pounded in my ears, and I could hear Jimmy’s screams or the dog barking over the ringing. Maryn slipped into the back seat and embraced Jimmy, rocking him back and forth while his mouth formed a circle and the whites of his eyes shone bright. Another man ran from the same side Maryn had come out of, and he was shouldering a rifle, pointed at the truck or me, I couldn’t be sure, but I felt my pistol buck in my palm, once, twice, and his shirt splashed with red as he fell to the ground, and I ran over and sat back down behind the wheel. Lew set his rifle barrel down on the floorboard and looked at me, and then at my hands that weren’t shaking, and nodded. I saw his lips moving, but he sounded like he was shouting from a football field away. He flicked his hand at the ignition, and I broke out of my fog. The sounds were overbearing now in the cab: Jimmy’s screams, the barking, the ringing from gunshots pushed my skull inward, and the stinging on my neck ramped up. I turned pushed in the clutch and turned the ignition.

45 Maryn

Jimmy finally cried himself to sleep, and his tears drenched the front of my shirt. We drove across the Mississippi with Illinois to the southeast and Iowa ahead of us. Dubuque was the worst traffic so far, with hundreds of abandoned cars strewn across the highways, and it took us an hour to get through the tangle. Twice, Gid had to push vehicles off the road so we could pass, and once it was so tight the paint on the passenger side was scratched, but he didn't let up. Lew was cycling in and out of consciousness, often out for only moments at a time. Once Jimmy stopped sobbing, he too fell asleep, and Gid handed me Lew's rifle again, and we continued to swerve and jerk through the vehicles.

"Help me look for tunnels because we have to avoid them even more so than bridges," Gid said, looking at me in the rearview. I nodded and looked at the back of his head. That's when I saw his shirt collar was bloody.

"Your neck is hurt," I told him.

"You're telling me?" he grinned at me in the mirror. I took out the first aid kit, and the alcohol wipe damn near made him run off the road. I smiled at his grimace in the mirror and carried on. He's got something stuck in one of the minor cuts, and I dug it out while he squirmed in the front seat.

"Damn, that's enough." He growled as I held up the small piece of glass with the tweezers.

"I need you to man up some," I said, smiling at him in the mirror, wiping at the cuts, then looking for more glass. It's clean, and the bleeding has stopped, so I spray his neck with antiseptic and leave him alone.

"Did you kill that man in the woods?" I asked him, and he looked up at me in the mirror before answering.

"Yes, are you okay with that?"

"Hand me your pistol, and I'll reload it for you." He did so, and I returned it to him. I didn't see that he had a choice, so of course, I was okay with it.

Once we were out of the city, we picked up speed again, and the scenery glided past.

Before Gid can get carried away, I told him, "I still need to pee."

He flashed his eyes up at me, and I returned his stare.

"I didn't get the chance earlier, and now it's an emergency."

He turned off on the shoulder and stopped. Stepping out, he pulled the seat forward for me, and I got out. He was climbing on the truck again to look ahead and said over his shoulder.

"Don't go off in the woods again, squat down and hold onto the hitch, and go right here."

That's fair, I thought, and when I pulled my pants up, he was still looking down the road with the binoculars.

"You see something?"

"Yeah, it looks like a burning car on the road." He got down and watered the dog again while rubbing his neck.

"What are we going to do? Can we go around?"

"No need, I don't see anyone, just the smoke. The car — or whatever — is burning and is hidden from my line of sight here. Let's wake Lew up just in case and be watchful as we pass through here." He shook Lew awake, and I slid his rifle back to him with its fresh magazine.

"Wake Jimmy up in case there's any shooting, so he doesn't wake up screaming."

I gently shook him until his blurry eyes rolled to me. "Jimmy, wake up for a minute, we have a situation." His eyes flew open then, and fear was sketched across his face.

"It's okay, I just want you to be awake in case. I'll be right here with you."

Gid filled in Lew, and we slowly started toward the smoke. The burning car was off the road, so there is no concern about blocking the way, but it's still a problem that it's on fire. Of course, we had seen several fires on the way here, especially in the major cities, but the single-car way out here was odd. The "car" turned out to be one of those new electric trucks, and the fire was in the cab. Didn't these have a problem catching fire? I thought I saw something about that online, but I didn't pay much attention. Anyway, Gid stopped about fifty yards before getting to it and stepped out of the truck, this time taking his rifle.

"I'm going to check it out and see what's happened here, be right back." He left the truck door open and walked to the other side of the highway, where there was an old truck flipped over. I felt like something was wrong and looked over at Lew, who had his rifle pointed out the passenger window, down range toward the burning truck. Once Gid reached the overturned truck, he slowly started back to us.

Getting back in, he said, "There are dead bodies around both of those vehicles; someone must be ambushing cars here."

He put the truck in reverse and backed up. A roaring sound from behind us, and I heard tires spinning on the blacktop. I whipped my head around, and Gid gunned the truck – not backward, but forward. There's an old Ford behind that, about 70 yards away, and it's barreling toward us. It looked like two people were in it as the distance closed. Lew swung his rifle over our heads in the back seat, and I told Jimmy to cover his ears. I did likewise just before the rifle boomed. He pulled his gun back, stuck it out the passenger window, and I looked ahead to see two guys on ATVs sitting in the middle of the road, rifles pointing our way.

Lew sent rounds at them, and one guy flipped off the back of his and hit the highway. The other got scared and rushed off the side of the road behind the overturned truck and kept heading off the road, enough for him, I supposed.

"Keep your ears covered," I yelled at Jimmy, and he slithered into the back floorboard, hands tightly squeezing his ears. The rifle in the cab sounds like a cannon to me, and we sped up, getting up to the ATV and its dead rider. He swerved to miss it, and Lew looked behind us. I followed his gaze and saw the truck closing again.

Spinning around, putting his left knee into the seat, swinging his rifle over the front seat so the barrel danced in front of my face as he tried to get a clean shot at the truck.

"Duck down!" he yelled at me, and I'm already heading down with Jimmy when the firing resumes. I can't see what's going on, but I heard Lew ram another magazine home and fire some more. I felt the truck speed up, and I heard Gid tell Lew to shoot the guys in the truck.

"I'm trying not to kill your idiot dog," he said, looking out the back with fevered, red-rimmed eyes. I could hear him barking and raising hell in the bed.

He fired four more quick shots, and I heard Gideon yell out from the front seat.

"I think I'm shot," and Lew said, "Who ain't, keep driving." Lew emptied that magazine too, and I guessed that was enough for the Ford truck. When Lew turned around and reloaded his rifle, I sat up and looked back and saw it careening onto the shoulder and into the grass, the distance between us growing.

46 Gideon

Lew was looking me over for wounds as I kept driving. "Where are you hit?" he asked me frantically, searching.

"My neck," I pulled my shirt down. He ripped my shirt back and laughed.

"A bullet didn't wound you, just the brass." He said, grinning like an idiot.

"Hot brass going down your shirt hurts like a pig bite, don't it? That's show business, baby," he mumbled, a slight grin on his face as his eyes half closed.

I looked over at him to tell him how I felt about his joke, but the sight of him stopped me. He was bleeding again, and his color was pasty. The only thing that looked like he still had enough blood in him was his eyes. He was slumped into the seat, dead, I feared.

Pulling the truck over, I got out and told Maryn to rewrap his bandage, and I went up to the slight rise we had just dropped below, checking behind us for the ambushers. I sat here for a few moments, waiting until she was done.

"It's the best I can do, but we need to get him some real help soon, or he will die." She told me as I was walking back to them. This time, when we set out, we drove without interruption until late afternoon, and we pulled in front of a two-door metal shop in the middle of farmland. The old mailbox outside had the address that Lew made us memorize. I walked around to the small side door and wondered how this could be the right place. No vehicles, livestock, or anything around. Just farrow fields laid out in the last hour of sunlight.

I knocked and then knocked again. Nothing. I walked around and looked for another door, but outside of the roll-up doors, there aren't any. I go back to the main door, knocked again, and press the button I see mounted to the doorframe. A crackling sound and then a static voice.

"Can I help you?" I heard an old man's voice over the intercom.

"Yes, sir, my uncle gave me this address and said one of his army friends lives here, and you would help us," I told the intercom, not sure if my voice was getting through.

"Who is your uncle?" he asked.

"Llewelyn, Llewelyn Spears." I told the box.

"Where is this Llewelyn?" the box asked.

"He's in the truck and in a bad way. He needs medical attention, or he will die."

"Next time, start with that, stop monkeying about, and get him in here. Oh, and leave your guns outside, all of them." I ran back to the truck, and between us, we got Lew to the door, which stood open, with an old man in the doorway. He waved us over and dipped out to make way for us to come inside.

"Not that dog, you aren't bringing him in here." He said, looking at Jimmy.

I nodded, and Jimmy commanded him to stay. We walked in, and an old truck sat on one side of the shop. Tools were scattered across the shelves on the wall, and it reeked of oil, grease, and diesel.

"Down here." He said, then pulled up a rug that looked like artificial grass, with a door attached to it. He pointed and motioned for us to head down into what I assumed was a storm shelter. Being as we were so far away from any houses that I could see, I thought the old man had built this in case a storm showed up while he was miles away from his home working the fields, and would run here in case of danger. I couldn't have been more wrong.

We had to slowly carry Lew down so he wouldn't fall, and we still almost managed to do that. At the bottom of the stairs was a door that led to a room with doors on each wall. The old man closed the door above us and waved us on into the door behind the steps.

"We have a makeshift hospital room down here." We followed him inside and through a door into a room with beds and rows of medical supplies on the walls. A shower in one corner, separated by a pony wall, the other beds, three of them, separated by pull screens like a hospital. We lay Lew down, and the man started removing all his clothes.

"What's your name?" the old man looked up from his labor, asking me.

"Gideon," I told him.

"Well, Gideon, why don't you and the boy step out and get out of our way. Young lady, who are you?"

"Maryn. He's my uncle." She looked at him defiantly, daring him to toss her out.

"Maryn, stay here and help me get him cleaned of the blood and filth so I can see what we're dealing with. When did he get shot?"

Maryn told him that morning, and he shook his head, at a loss to explain why he was running a fever so quickly. He looked back at me and jerked his head back to the door we've come from. I turned and ran into an IV, making it clatter as it hit the floor.

"Out!" he barked behind me, and I turned to look at Maryn to make sure she was comfortable being alone. She nodded at me and got back to work, bringing towels to bed.

Jimmy and I sat on the cold floor, waiting. He snuggled up to me and stared off into space. I feared he may never recover from the trauma that he's suffered, but outside of not adding to it, I don't know how to help him.

Several minutes later, the old man walked through the door, wiping his hands with a towel and motioning for me to stand.

"Is he going to be alright?" I asked before reaching my feet.

"We're days away from knowing that, but I've done all I can for now." He threw the towel over his shoulder and said, "Let's go back up top and get your truck put away."

I nodded, thinking he meant to drive it into the shop, but realized that it would block the door. Curious, we went out the same small door we entered, and he told me to pull the truck around back. I did, and it's almost entirely dark by the time I get everything unloaded, especially with the dog darting around getting underfoot. I don't think he fully understood the old man's rules yet, but there wasn't much I could do.

I stashed everything that could get wet inside the shop, and he insisted we leave our firearms up here. He took us back down the shelter stairs, but we went to the right instead of behind, to the infirmary. He opened the door, and I saw a long hallway with four doors on the right, three on the left, and one door at the end.

“Pick a room for each of you and the showers at the end of the hallway. We got plenty of hot water and soap, so make sure you put it to use.” He sniffed and closed the main door, leaving us alone. I opened the first door, and it’s a small bedroom with a little table-and-chair combo and a mattress on a steel rack. A standing clothes locker at the foot of the bed. It reminded me of a prison cell you saw in a movie, only with a large bed and no toilet or sink.

“Let's check them all so you can pick which room you want, okay?” I told Jimmy, and we went to the next. It’s the same, and so are the next five. The room closest to the shower had boxes piled in it, but otherwise it's all the same. The bathroom had stainless-steel toilets and sinks, and the shower was in one corner, just like the other one. No curtain, just a drain in the floor and two shower heads mounted on the walls, facing inward, with a single handle that regulated the water pressure and temperature under each.

Closing that door, I turned to Jimmy and said, “Well, they look the same, so you choose.”

“I’ll wait for Maryn to pick her room first.” He said, and I stepped into the first room we checked out.

“Fine, I’ll take this one, check that locker for bed sheets,” I told him, and he set his pack down and opened the door.

“Sheets and pillows in here.” He said, pulling them out and handing them to me. I already set my pack down and took the sheets and pillow, sitting them on the bed.

“We’ll shower before making the beds, but let's check on Lew and let Maryn shower first, okay?” We walked down the hallway and into the infirmary.

The doors opened at my touch, a relief, because the dread of being locked in here by this old man was on my mind. We were at his mercy for now, and it was truly uncomfortable. I'm not sure how my uncle served this old guy because he looked like a Vietnam veteran. May have to wait until Lew recovers to figure out that mystery.

Maryn was carrying a basket of towels down the hallway, past the infirmary shower.

I went to grab the basket, and she shook her head, saying, "Get the other one beside the bed and bring it." Turning, I saw the one she meant, and I grabbed it up and followed her.

47 Maryn

Dumping the bandages and towels into the washer, I heard Gid let out a "whoa" as he saw the room for the first time. The same as I had when I entered. Three washing machines for regular clothes and two industrial washers, one of which I was using to wash the towels and sheets. Five washers, four dryers, and racks of white towels, laundry detergent, and bleach. There were also gallon jugs of peroxide on the shelves, metal clothes hangers, and one shelf full of white bed linens and pillows sealed in vacuumed plastic. Extra towels and washcloths were on the shelves, but most were also sealed and labeled. Rows of dehydrated foods took up the remainder of the wall space. Buckets like the ones Gid had brought home were stacked to the ceiling, and a small four-foot ladder was folded and leaning against the buckets.

"This isn't the coolest thing." I walked past Gid as he still tried to take everything in, then went to the end of the hallway, past the entrance door, and through the door directly across from the infirmary, left of the stairs that led up top. It's a long hallway with three doors. Two on the right and one at the end. The two on the right were locked, but the end door opened to a cinderblock room about fifty yards long and ten wide: on the far end were human-shaped paper targets set up for practice, and on the wall next to the door was a locked case of about twenty rifles that looked similar to the ones my uncle Lew carries. AR-15, AR-10? I couldn't tell, and before Gid could inspect them more closely, I closed the door. He was crestfallen, but I told him we didn't have permission to be here, so let's go back.

As we entered the "bedroom wing," I chose the room third

down on the right and told Jimmy that if he took the room between us, he would always have one of us close to him. He liked that idea but didn't seem convinced yet. With nothing to be done for the sleeping Lew, I went to shower and sent Jimmy in next. I made up my bed while he was showering, and I went and made his up, too. Plenty of warm blankets, and I marveled at the cost this older man had spent on this place.

Once Gid headed off to the shower, I went to the only door we hadn't explored yet and knocked on it. A few seconds later, the old man swung the door open and welcomed us in. I could smell cooking, and I looked around the living room, with two chairs and a couch along one wall and a big TV mounted on the opposite wall. He waved us on through, and Jimmy and I followed him to a dining room/kitchen combination. A large wooden table with eight chairs dominated the room, and in the center sat a vase of flowers, which I thought was odd—a galley-style kitchen with another door leading out the back.

"Sit down, sit down, I've almost got supper ready," he told us, and we sat. "Where's the other one?" he looked back suspiciously.

"Showering, and his name is Gideon," I told him, still trying to be polite, after all, he probably saved Llewelyn's life, so that a bit of his thorniness can be tolerated.

"Sir, what's your name, and how do you know my uncle?" I asked, and he waved me off.

"When we have a full house, I'll go over everything, so I don't have to do it twice." He said gruffly, then returned to work at the stove. There are two bowls set at four spots around the table, along with three Pepsis that are sweating on the sides.

Jimmy and I sat here awkwardly, waiting for Gid. When he knocked, I went to the door to let him in. He looked at me questioningly, but I shrugged my shoulders and waved him into the kitchen.

"Ah, thanks for joining us."

The old man sets down a steaming pot in the center of the table, with a ladle inside. The smell started my stomach growling, and I saw that Jimmy's eyes wouldn't leave the pot. He next brought over a steaming pot of rice and set it down. The last thing was a pre-sliced loaf of bread. He went back for a ceramic cup that he set at his place.

"Any of you need to say a prayer before we start?" he asked, looking at each of us.

Jimmy surprised us by bowing his head and saying, "Good food, good meat, good God, let's eat," unfolding his hands.

The old man thought that was funny and chuckled to himself as he stood and filled bowl after bowl with rice. He took up the ladle, scooped the hot, thick stew over the rice, and handed it down. The bread was passed around last, and we all started eating without another word.

Jimmy dipped the remainder of his bread around the inside of the bowl and cleaned it all out before popping it into his mouth.

"Need some more?" the man asked Jimmy. Jimmy nodded eagerly, and the old man looked at me. "Does he know how to speak?"

"His name is Jimmy, and yes, he knows how to speak," I answered sweetly, and I got another bowl of rice for him and myself. Gid also got another bowl, and we sat on to this round as well.

Afterward, the old man said, “Let's get down to business then. I usually go smoke my pipe after supper up top.”

“My uncle says he served with you in the desert and that you may have a place for us to stopover at on our way home, maybe get better weapons and food if you have it to spare. Of course, that was before he got shot this morning, so I don’t know what to do now.”

The old man cackled at that. He had changed out of his bloody clothing earlier, but he was still wearing the same thing when we showed up. A white T-shirt with overalls. No boots this time, just sock feet—so this must be his everyday wear. His white mustache twitched into a smile.

“Well, as far as serving with your uncle, that wasn’t me, but I know who he is, and that’s the only reason you are sitting here in my home bellies full of my food. I will shelter you for a bit because your uncle did me a great turn one time. My name is Erskin Smith, but most people call me “Doc”. They have for the last fifty years anyway, so that will do.” He scratched his white hair with his gnarled hand and looked at us in turn.

“There are rules that must be followed, or I will insist you take yourselves down the road. There is enough water and electricity capacity here to support 20 to 30 people for about 5 years. I don’t want anything wasted, though. Don’t take overlong showers, don’t leave lights on, and don’t waste food. I’m expecting more people to show up, so don’t take up too much room.” He stood up, scooping up his old straw hat and heading to the door.

“Don’t put that food up. I’ll deal with it after you clear out of here, but those dishes need washing. Gideon, follow me.” He looked at him, and they went through the door. Jimmy helped me pick up the bowls, and I brought the stew and rice pots back to the stove. The canned Pepsis he had for us to drink, I wasn’t sure what to do with, but everything else we washed and left in the strainer to dry. I went to check the closed door at the back of the kitchen, but it was locked.

“Well, I guess it's off to bed for us,” I said, smiling down at Jimmy. He looked nervous, but he followed me into my bedroom.

48 Gideon

I followed Doc upstairs and into the shop. He gave me a mean look when he saw the dog lying inside the shop under the parked International Scout truck next to the hidden door.

"I thought I said to let that dog stay outside." He grunted

"He must have slipped in when I was bringing in our gear from the truck. I'll grab him up."

"Never mind that for now, let's get outside." He looked through the peephole and checked it before opening the door, slipping his boots on, and walking through. Around back, he had an old bench that was almost bleached the same color as his hair and just as rough-looking. He sat down and packed his pipe, and I looked around and found an old five-gallon bucket to flip over and sit on. The air felt warmer here than back in Wisconsin, and there were no lights visible in any direction. Already the stars were bright in the sky with the full moon, and there was not a cloud in sight. You can see fifty yards easily at night here, and Doc's hair seemed to glow in the eerie light, and I watched him strike a match and put it to his pipe. A few puffs later, he appeared to be content with it, and he set it down by his side, looking at me.

"You smoke?" he asked, pulling on his pipe again, and his face became obscured by smoke.

"No, sir," I told him, slightly recoiling from the sweet stench of the pipe.

"That's good, smoking is bad for you." He picked it up and pulled on his pipe again and launched a spume of smoke into the air.

"You aren't worried about anyone smelling that and finding your place?" I asked him.

Shaking his head, he relit the pipe and pulled on it a couple of times. "This isn't my place. Well, technically, I own all this as far as you can see, but this isn't my homestead. It's a ways from here, and my closet neighbor is a mile from there. I've checked all the nearby homesteads, and they are empty, so there are no neighbors to worry about.

"How much land do you farm?" I asked, thinking about how far we were from anyone.

"Two sections, but I don't farm them all. One of my sons is a famous heart surgeon in St. Louis, and he and his wife are the ones who poured all their money into this shelter. You look like a learned young man; maybe you've heard of him? Named after me and he's been published several times in the New England Journal of Medicine," he said, but I thought he was only half serious. He smiled, his pipe between his teeth, and for a second, he reminded me of my old Papa.

"No, sir, it's not likely. I stopped reading medical journals when I turned five; they started to bore me." I shot back.

Doc hooted with laughter and slapped his knee over that. The pipe smoke caught him wrong, and his laughter turned into a hacking cough.

Great, I think I just killed our savior with my sarcasm, but he recovered, eyes filled with tears, from the coughing.

"Thank you, young man. I do miss laughter." He tapped his pipe out on the bench arm. Nodding to himself, he said softly, "That's enough of that for tonight."

"Smoking a pipe isn't as hazardous as cigarettes, they've always told us, but combined with your sense of humor, pipe smoke could lay a man low." He grinned at me.

"Why do you smoke? I never thought to ask my papa." I wondered aloud.

"It makes old men seem wise, I suppose." He reached for an old, thorny nail into the bowl, cleaned it out, and set the pipe down on the bench beside him. "You never tried his pipe when he was away?"

"No, sir, I suppose my balls aren't saggy enough to be curious about that sickly stink it gives off."

The old man's eyebrows shot up, and he stared at me open-mouthed, and I thought I had gone too far. He tilted back his head and guffawed with laughter. "Boy, you always push for the edge, don't you? I bet you've pushed it your whole life." He wiped his eyes and regained himself.

"You ever kill a man?" I thought he was testing me to slap me back in my place as inexperienced, but his face changed when I told him the truth.

"Yes, sir. One today and saw at least three more killed." I leveled with him.

He took a second to figure out his next move. "Goddamn son, you killed a man today? How old are you?"

"We turned eighteen today," I told him.

"You've looked around a bit, you're thinking of killing me and taking over this place? A salty lad like you could take an old man like me if you wanted to, surely?" he leaned forward, and his eyes became shadowed, and the moonlight framed his face like a bearded skull. A shiver ran down my back, and I felt the danger come from this old man somehow.

"No, sir. I wouldn't harm a man who saved my family."

He sat back, and I could see the wariness on his face. "No? Why not? You could have everything here if so. That's the way this new world works, boy."

"Any man that would help me and mine will get no harm from me. You may have saved my uncle's life, and I'm running short on family, so I appreciate it. You've been kind to us, and I won't repay that with betrayal. Despite the gruff attitude you've put on with us, you've been extremely helpful, and I won't ever forget that. I'm not sure how much longer Maryn will put up with your attitude, but you will have to learn that on your own, like everyone else does. You brought me out here because you think I am maybe a danger, but it's her you need to look out for. She'll tomahawk you over table manners, so save your caution for her. She's sensitive about Jimmy, too, so be warned."

Doc chuckled at that. "How long are you planning on staying?"

"If you would allow it until Lew is back on his feet again. You would have a better time frame for that than I, but I won't stay here if you don't want us to." I stood up from the bucket.

"Your uncle shares the same philosophy about being a house guest?"

"You act as if you don't know him. He told us you served together, so you would know him better than I do." I'm surprised to learn he's worried about Lew's behavior. Strange, I thought.

"The first time I saw your uncle was this afternoon. You're mistaken about our relationship, so forgive me if I'm not 100% sure you are who you say you are."

He stood up as well and put his pipe in his chest pocket of his overalls. "Trying to assess the risk I'm at by letting you stay here is all, don't take it personally, young man."

"I don't understand the systems you have in place here to operate them. Locked doors, guns, electricity, and plumbing. Until I figure these out, I'd say you aren't in any danger from me."

That made him chortle, and he slapped me on the back as we walked back inside.

As we entered the door, he said to me, "Over my lifetime, I've met a lot of good, honest people, but very few I genuinely like from the get. You remind me of a boy I used to know when I was a younger man."

With that, he pointed me to the dorm wing of the shelter, and he headed back to the kitchen area.

49 Maryn

The door opened, and I saw Gid silhouetted against the low light in the hallway.

"Everything okay? He asked.

"Yes, Jimmy's in here, so be quiet." I slipped from the bed and looked back in the dim light. Jimmy is up against the wall with his back to me, sucking his thumb, peacefully sleeping.

I was almost asleep when Gid opened my door and startled me.

"What is it? "I asked a bit too irritably.

"I think things will be fine here with Doc. He doesn't seem to be likely to murder us in our sleep, but I'll take the first watch tonight anyway. I'll wake you about two and then get myself back up at six, okay. I don't want all of us to be asleep here until we know for sure," I nodded to him, and he closed the door back. The warmth of Jimmy was comforting, and I closed my eyes.

I woke up shaken. My mind was in a whirl, and I don't remember where I was for a second. I swung my arm out and connected with someone.

"It's me, Gideon." I heard him say, exasperated. "Your turn for watch." He said from what seems like a mile away.

"Give me another minute, okay?" I pleaded, and the next time I woke up, Jimmy was crawling over me.

"What are you doing, Jimmy?" I asked, still foggy with fatigue.

“I got to pee.” He said, and I heard his bare feet slapping the floor as he ran to the door. “Come with me?” he looked back at me with the door open.

“Yeah, I’m coming,” and rolled out of bed. Did I dream Gid shaking me awake last night? Oh, shit, I was supposed to take watch from him but instead went back to sleep. I followed Jimmy to the bathroom and went in after him. I called him back in to clean up his mess on the floor in front of the toilet. I then used it and went to Gid’s room. He was doing push-ups when I opened the door to let him know we were up.

“Thanks for getting up.” He stood and grabbed some shorts and shower supplies, brushing past to get to the shower. He closed the door, and I got dressed and went to help Jimmy get ready for breakfast. I’m nervous about our new life and not sure what our new routine will be. Jimmy and I head over to check on Lew. He’s sleeping, and I readjusted his covers, making sure his IV isn’t tangled in the blankets, and we stepped out without a sound. Next stop was the living room, and I’m not sure whether to knock or go right in. I looked down at Jimmy, and he shrugged his shoulders like I had all the answers. I suppose you can’t go wrong knocking, so I did. Doc opened the door, wearing the same old overalls and white shirt from last night. He turned and waved us in, and I saw he was wearing house shoes. No chance he has any more of those, I thought, as we followed him into the kitchen and he motioned for us to sit down at the table again.

“Good morning, Mr. Smith,” I said, trying to start things off on the right foot with this prickly old man.

“It's Doc, I told you, and it's past breakfast time.” He groused. “Youngsters need to be up and at it early, not lying about waiting for room service. I generally close the kitchen at this hour, and anyone not here before then is left out." I looked at my watch, and it read five thirty.

"Well, we have some food that we brought with us, so I'll just build us something from that. It wouldn't be asking too much to use a camp stove outside on your property, would it? Gid and I can do without breakfast, but I WILL make something for Jimmy." I felt my neck getting hot and my patience slipping with this man. He's hit me in one sensitive spot, and that's making sure Jimmy is fed when possible.

"It's a busy day around here, and it starts early, so we all have to get on it early." He growled at me, along the same lines as before, and my defiance ratcheted up to another level.

"We'll take the truck to town, and I'll cook him something there. I'll check while there and see if some more suitable arrangements can be made for us. I appreciate what you've done for my uncle, but it seems your kindness extends only to him, and that's acceptable. I won't have this disagreement again with you, so thank you for the hospitality so far, but we'll change our living situation." I flashed back at him, my anger still building.

The old man looked past me and grinned widely. "She is quick to show her claws just like you said."

I turned and saw Gid standing in the kitchen doorway.

"We eat breakfast here or in town somewhere?" he asked Doc.

"Everyone, simmer down and take a breather. I was only needling her to see her grit, and now I've seen it, let's all back down a bit and hit the reset. I need to know the folks that are living with me and what they're about." He turned to me, as I was still fuming. "Please, Maryn, have a seat, and I'll get some breakfast started for everyone. Truce. You guys are my guest." He said, putting up his hands.

Gid sat next to me and motioned me to take a seat. I do, and Jimmy looked around at us, confused.

"Mr. Smith, would you be so kind as to lay out your expectations for us, while we're your guests? What time are meals, what chores would be like from us, that sort of thing. Maybe things that are off limits to us while we're here?" I ask if my face is still hot with aggravation.

"It's Doc, not Mr. Smith. I would prefer you to use that in the future when addressing me. As far as chores, what can you do? Let me know your skills, and I'll find something for you. There's scouting to do, clothes to wash, food to prepare, shelter to clean, and hunting to do. Farming, tending to a bullet wound, dressing changes, his messes to clean up, and about a hundred other things around here. Which would you like to do?" he shot back at me.

"I can do any of those except tend to bullet wounds. I didn't have any experience with that until yesterday, but I can stitch better than you. If you want to check Gid's scalp, you can see that yourself. Other than farming, I've done other things regularly. Gid's a better hunter than me, but I have killed and butchered animals with my Papa, same as him. So, if there are any of these things you would like us to do, please don't hesitate—we'll get on with it. It's the least we can do for you, taking us in and caring for my uncle." I flashed back at him, daring him to test my skills in any area he listed.

"You can certainly get your back up quick, that's for sure." He chuckled to himself. "I could use a hand around here with the housework. I fall behind because the everyday chores here always need attention. They can be skipped for three days in a row, but then it takes a week to catch back up. I've never really been much of a hand at cooking either, so if you're capable of that, it would help me out immensely." I don't understand what he means.

"The stew you made yesterday was excellent. I don't think you give yourself enough credit," I said to try to calm the waters, and it was true.

"That's because he didn't make it; I did." I spun around, and a young woman with long blonde hair stood at the kitchen entrance. She's wearing jeans, an old Ely work shirt that my Papa will wear to town, and old cowboy boots. She had a gun belt strapped around her thin waist and a red bandana over her hair.

We are all stunned into silence at her sudden appearance, and Doc cleared his throat and said, "Please meet my granddaughter, Becca. Becca, this is Jimmy, Gideon, and this spitfire here is Maryn."

"Hello," I said, extending my hand and standing. She took it.

"Hi," she said, giving a little wave to the boys when she released my hand. She then walked over and sat down in an empty seat. Jimmy was in shock at the sight of her, and Gid looked as if someone had punched him in the solar plexus.

"Doc is just giving you a hard time and stalling breakfast this morning because he doesn't want anyone to figure out that there's something he can't do. He's kind of like the guy behind the curtain in the Wizard of Oz." She giggled and looked back at me. "If you are any good in the kitchen, please save us from his breakfast," she winked at me, and I instantly liked her.

Catching a glimpse of Doc's face turning red with embarrassment boosted my mood, and I'm more than happy to make the meal.

It took me a few minutes to find everything in the kitchen, and then I opened the fridge, and I'm astounded. Butter, cheese, eggs, bacon, and milk are stuffed in the refrigerator. Link and pan sausage, lunch meat, mustard, mayo, and of course, cold Pepsis.

"Any particular thing you guys want for breakfast?"

"It's the dealer's choice when you're cooking." Doc huffed back at me after he found his seat and got his coffee.

"Omelets it is then. I don't see any peppers. Do you have any?"

"Pickled jalapenos in this pantry," Becca pointed to a large door to my right, and, opening it, I am amazed again at how they have gathered so many resources—canned and dehydrated vegetables and fruits, dry cereals, vacuum-sealed packages, and cases of evaporated milk. I fished out a jar of peppers and went to work.

"Jimmy, do you want peppers on yours?" I asked sweetly

"Not if they're too hot." I popped one of the slices into my mouth, and he smiled and nodded.

Doc looked around at me, "You didn't ask me." He huffed.

"I know a strong, tough man like you could handle a few peppers."

"Yeah, I believe anything a Texan can eat, I can too." He smirked lightly at me. I smiled at him, and I could see it on his face. I'll never have trouble with him again. I may not have been able to defeat him with vinegar, but the sugar was too much for him. I smiled inwardly at the foolishness of men. Speaking of Gid, he was staring at Becca like he had drunk a love potion, and even Jimmy seemed at ease in her presence. I felt a niggle of jealousy for a second, then brushed it away, thinking how foolish I was being.

Setting the last plate down, we all go to eat without any talk. This was the best breakfast we had in two weeks, and everyone seemed to enjoy it. Becca wanted to know our story, of course, and how we came to be here, so we took turns laying it all out again. As soon as I was done, she immediately got up and asked me to follow her to where my uncle lay.

"Doc, you should have told me about him first thing." She flashed her annoyance at him, and he fired back with, "I checked on him this morning, and there's been no change. You need breakfast before tending to him."

Lew was still in the same condition as before breakfast, and Becca took off the clothes she had been wearing. She hung her gun belt up on the back of a chair against the wall and stepped into the shower, turning it on. It had an overhead outlet, and water sprayed down on her naked skin. It shocked me how casual she was about getting undressed in front of a stranger, but she turned to me, washing her hair and leaning her head back, and I caught a glimpse of the dark blonde hair between her legs, then looked away, embarrassed.

"There are some disposable surgeon hand scrubs in the laundry room. Will you get a couple? There's also scrubs in there, please grab a couple of pairs." I looked around in here until I found what she meant, the scrub tops and bottoms come in one size, and that's XL. I gathered two of each, the hand wash, and returned to the room. She's toweling off, and I caught another glimpse of her. I averted my gaze and handed the scrubs to her. She threw them on without underwear or a bra, unpacked the hand sanitizer brush, and moved to the sink to wash her hands. She looked back at me. "Shower and change, I need you to help me hold him still if he needs bullet fragments removed or stitches.

I blushed with the thought of getting naked in front of this stranger, but there really isn't much choice, and I do so. It's not like I haven't showered in front of girls at school or even in front of my mama before, but those were girls I knew and were my age, and those showers were semi-private. Becca was older and much more confident than any teenage girl I've been around, and there's no hiding in this shower. The wall bordering it was built to retain water, not privacy. I pushed through it and repeated the steps she had taken, and when I was dressed, she had already pulled the blankets back and was checking Lew's bandages. She pointed at a box of latex gloves on the wall, and as I slipped a pair on, Becca unwrapped the bandage and brought it up to her face to sniff it. She holds it out to me to smell, and it's rancid.

"Infected?" I asked.

"Very, we need to start another penicillin drip in his IV. He's probably got a piece of cloth in the wound we need to fish out. That's usually what causes infection this fast." She pointed to a drawer of instruments, and when I slid it open, she pointed to what she wanted.

I then searched through the bags of saline and other supplies until I found one, and she handed it back to me to hang. She connected it and started the drip.

"He's got another hour of pain medicine, and then I'll change it out. Since there are two of us, let's clean the wound and then resew it. The front is fine with glue."

I helped hold Lew down while she dug into the wound, pulled out a scrap of his shirt, and laid it and the tweezers in a stainless-steel dish. We rolled him on his side while she worked on the needle and thread through the wound.

"Going to leave this open at the bottom to drain, don't forget that it's important." She flashed a smile at me.

Once she was done, we rolled him back down gently, and I'm picking up the plastic from the suture kit.

I heard Lew mumble something. "Jess, is that...you?" I snapped my head down, looking at him. "S-sorry, thought you were Je-...." and he slipped back into unconsciousness.

I looked at Becca, and she asked, "Who's Jess?"

"My mama," I told her. "He's delirious," she said, throwing the gloves into the trash.

"Do I look like her?" she asked.

"No."

"A beautiful lady, then. Shuck those gloves and let's go check on those boys; they probably didn't have the decency to clean the kitchen before slipping off to do something fun." She laughed lightly.

50 Gideon

I was wiping off the table when Maryn and Becca came back in. The dishes were drying in the rack, and Jimmy was upstairs feeding his dog with Doc. I looked up when I heard them come in, and seeing Becca almost took my breath away. She was wearing hospital clothes, and I could tell she didn't have a bra on as the points in her shirt revealed. I groaned inwardly. My mama and sister were both beauties; don't misunderstand, and even years of age hadn't blunted my granny's looks too much, so there was no scarcity of womanly beauty in my life, but this woman made me feel a way the girls from school didn't, and certainly not the feeling you have for your kin. Her golden hair, flared hips, and tight pants made my skin feel hot and dulled my senses. My breath seemed to catch, and it was hard to find the right thing to say around here, so I stayed quiet.

"Well, not all men are worthless, it seems." Becca beamed at me, and I felt the flush rise to my scalp. I brought the cloth back to the sink and rested it on the edge before trying to make a quick exit, as the women moved past me into the kitchen, started poring through the pantry contents, and making plans for future meals. I turned to leave, caught my knee on a chair, and made a screeching sound across the floor. I heard them giggle behind me, and I darted out without a backward glance, embarrassed over my clumsiness following me up the stairs. The shop was empty, and when I opened the outside door, I saw Jimmy and his dog running around like lunatics, and the old man smiling at them. He glanced at me and waved me over.

"Every time you step out of shelter, you need to be wearing your gun."

“Where’s yours?” I asked, feeling salty about my earlier mishap.

“I don’t need to carry a short gun if you are so get yours. You’re probably a better shot with it than I am anyway, and besides, I’m no Cullen Baker gun hand like you. Don’t forget your rifle either.”

Returning to them, the old man took up his bolt-action 30-06 and pointed over to the east.

“See those trees over there?” I shaded my eyes against the morning rays and nodded. “That’s where we’re headed.”

He took off with a long limbering walk that belied his age, and I waved at Jimmy to come on. He grabbed the frisbee he was throwing for the dog and ran after us. He seemed at ease in Doc’s company; maybe it was daylight and a full belly that helped spur it. He darted, trying to keep the dog from tripping him, and when he did, he would roll up, laughing. The morning was beautiful; you couldn’t tell it in the clean air I’m breathing that so many people were dead and something tragic had happened across the world.

The dog ran in circles around us, daring Jimmy to throw the frisbee, which he did, and the dog caught it in the air when the throw was decent. It didn’t seem like a problem in the world until I heard the dog crash into Doc, and the old man fell like a bowling pin. He hit the tilled earth and looked back up at me like I pushed him down. I stuck my hand out, and he took it, and I swung him back up to his feet.

“What’s that damned dog’s name?” he asked me.

“We haven’t named him yet.” I shrugged at him.

"Boy, take that fat bastard away from us." He said to Jimmy, and they both took off chasing each other. "You see the way he ninja'd me to the ground, you should name him Chuck Norris." He grinned. "Better yet, since he's so fat, name him Chunk Norris." He smiled at his joke, and I thought it was clever.

"Chunk Norris it is."

It took us three minutes to walk to the tree line, which surprised me because it looked so much closer.

"Trees in a row in this part of Iowa usually mean one of two things. Property line or water. In this case, it's a branch. Across the road is my actual homestead."

He thumbed back over his shoulder to the north as we crossed a wooden bridge that he told me he had built himself twenty years ago. A small path wound through the trees to a cluster of buildings on the other side. I could smell animal shit the closer we got, and I heard chickens clucking when they saw us.

"You have chickens?" Jimmy asks excitedly.

"You bet, cows and pigs too. Even got some riding stock around if you want to ride." Doc said to him, as Jimmy was trying to take it all in.

"Horses? I never rode a horse before." He said nervously

"Well, you won't be able to say that tomorrow," Doc told him.

He jerked his head in the direction of the first barn. He opened the door, and the smell of animals was overpowering. Hay, sweat, and shit flooded my nose. Horses on one side, and chickens scatter before us as we walk inside.

"I'm turning out the horses today with the cows, and I found a couple of my neighbors' donkeys wandering around and penned them in the field with my cattle." He opened the first stall door, and a beautiful buckskin gelding came out looking for a treat, which Doc produced from his front pocket. A dried apple before it disappears into its maw. He swung his head over and nuzzled me, and I reached up to rub his neck slowly.

“You know horses?” I nodded; my grandparents have a few back home.

“That’ll help.”

He walked to the next ones: a black mare, a blue roan filly, and three chestnut mares, which round out the lineup. Jimmy was wary of the horses, but he did take notice of the roan.

“Hey, he’s blue like Chunk Norris,” he said excitedly as they milled around the old man looking for treats.

“She. Not he.” Doc said as one of the chestnuts nipped at his jacket arm impatiently. “That’s Alice, and she’s mean as the devil, so don’t turn your back on her or she’ll take a piece of your scalp.” He told Jimmy, pointing out the mare biting his jacket.

Something my papa says came to me when I see her, “Four white stockings and a white nose, tear off the hide and feed it to the crows.” Doc laughed out loud about that.

“I know you learned that from an old man.” He chuckled and continued. “Well, in this case, that’s accurate. The other ones I named “One” and “Two” for their stockings, and they won’t give you any problems. The roan isn’t broken yet, and old Buck here and Bucephalus are great horses all the way around.” He walked over to a door, opened it, and went inside. He came out carrying three blankets.

"Go get those first two saddles and set them on Buck and One. I got a smaller saddle for Jimmy, but it's put up, and we'll give him Two."

I saddled the three horses and noticed that Jimmy's saddle was won by Becca for barrel racing in 2017. The old man watched me to make sure I did it right, and we walked the horses out, and Doc and I climbed on. I got on Buck, then turned around and dismounted to adjust Jimmy's stirrups, and he settled into the saddle, looking at me scared.

"Don't be scared, the horse doesn't want to hurt you, she just wants to take you where you want to go and be treated well. Pet her neck and talk to her gently. I'm going to get on and show you how to move, okay."

Swinging back in the saddle, I turned back to him. "Hold the reins like so." I showed him. "No with your left hand. Your right hand is for a rope or a gun, always." He switched hands, and I nodded to him. "Yes, and to choose which direction you want to go in, you pull the reins like so." I showed him by walking around my horse.

"To go, give her a little gig with your heels. Not hard, just a gentle touch. If you need more speed, give her another light kick. To stop, pull straight back on the reins like this." I demonstrated it for him and asked if he had it.

"I think so, Gideon."

"Let's be about it then and give it a try." The other horses were milling around, getting bored with everything, when Alice tried to bite Chunk Norris. He's too fast for her, though, and she turned to send a kick his way. The kick hit the roan filly, who kicked back, hitting Two. She started to crow hop and buck, and Jimmy's eyes were as large as eggs as he grabbed the reins with both hands and flailed around in the saddle until I could get close enough to him to calm Two down. She trotted around the yard, but soon settled down, and I could see Jimmy was rattled. I assured him he was fine and everything was okay. He's pale and terrified but doesn't try to get off. I'm proud of him for not giving up.

"That goddamn dog is a pain in the ass," Doc grumbled, and I must agree. "Let's put these other horses out before a brawl breaks out and we all end up in the dirt." Chunk was darting all over the yard, antagonizing Alice. I suppose it's a mutual hatred now, and as I watched them, I wasn't sure animals didn't know how to hold a grudge against one another.

Alice wasn't the only animal that didn't appreciate Chunk. The donkeys curled their lips and commenced to holler like idiots when they got sight of him. I closed the gate before they reached it, though, after running the other three horses into the pasture. The cacophony grates on my nerves, but Jimmy seemed to love it. He grinned from his horse and watched their antics with amusement.

Doc said, "Well, I got them for that reason, so they know their job."

"What job?" I couldn't see any use of these bellowing animals.

"They hate canines of any type and will keep coyotes away from my cows. That damn dog is going to cause more problems than a barrel of monkeys. Let's go check out the chickens." He nodded toward another structure, and we walked the horses over.

The chicken coop was rigged with a battery-operated drop

door set to a timer. It ran on solar and activated like a streetlight. Once it got so dark it closed at night, and once it got so light, it opened the switch and pulled the door open. Ingenious, I thought, and told him so.

“Can’t take credit for it, I was vaccinating a guy’s herd over in Red Oak, and he designed it. I just copied it and haven’t had any trouble with it so far. Of course, in the winter, they must be in the barn for warmth, but for several months, they prefer to use this one. Let’s get these eggs and then come back for them because I want to show you two other tasks, I would like for you to do.”

“You aren’t a doctor, you’re a veterinarian?” I asked with horror, remembering him running the IV into Lew.

“Yes, and yes. Doctor is a doctor in these crazy times, wouldn’t you agree?” he asked with a smirk.

Jimmy slid off his horse, more than happy to deal with the chickens. Doc showed him a bucket and the chicken feed.

“Grab that up and put some feed out for them and collect those eggs when the bucket’s empty,” he said to Jimmy, and while he busied himself with that, Doc went into another old shed and came out with two fishing poles and a small tacklebox. He handed them up to me on my mount. We walked back to the coop, and Jimmy tried to get back into the stirrup, but the egg bucket was smacking against her, and she turned away from him, circling. Doc laughed, and it made me smile to watch him hopping on one foot and dancing around while Chunk bounced around them both, barking.

“Chunk, knock it off, Jimmy, stop.” The dog looked at me like I kicked him, and he sulked off. “Slowly put your foot in the saddle and pull yourself up with the horn on the saddle. If she starts walking before you get seated, it's okay, follow through with it. She doesn't like that bucket hitting her; it's something new."

He nodded and tried, keeping the bucket far up his arm this time, away from her. She stood still after a couple of attempts, and we followed Doc off to another stand of trees, mainly running east to west.

"The north-south creek over there, called Graybill, he told us, "and this one coming into it is Farm Creek. After the confluence, it's just Farm Creek," he explained.

Probably named by the same person who named horses One and Two, I mentioned, and he just glared at me without saying anything. Cresting Farm Creek, I saw it was deeper and broader than Graybill, and according to Doc, it had more fish.

Fishing was another area where Jimmy excelled, and soon we had a stringer of brook trout and perch. Remembering the earlier lesson on where to clean fish, he asks for a knife to clean his own. Doc scolded him gently for being so old without his own pocketknife, but took his out and gladly handed it to him. He took his time, and it's not bad. We threw the fillets into a basket Doc had draped over his saddle horn, then headed back to the shelter.

This ride was a little different because of the uneven rows; the horses had an abnormal gait that seemed to cause Jimmy considerable displeasure. Reaching the back of the shop, Doc and Jimmy dismounted, and Doc told him to remount and take his horse back to the barn, unsaddle and brush her.

"After that, turn her loose in the same pasture as the others."

He said over his shoulder as he carried the fish basket and his old bolt action inside, leaving us with work. Fair enough, I thought, the old man had given us refuge, and a little work was well worth it. I told Jimmy to set the bucket of eggs by the door before we head back to the barn.

Jimmy remounted, and we rode back to the wooden bridge and into the barn. I showed him how to unsaddle, unbridle, and brush them when turning them out. We walked them over to the pasture gate and slipped them in before the donkeys got too close, but they did start raising hell again after spotting the dog. We walked back to the coop, grabbed the eggs, and headed back on foot.

51 Maryn

Doc stuck his head in the kitchen. “Anyone here?” I was kneading some bread, and Becca was checking on Lew.

“I’m in here, Mr....Doc.”

He stepped full into the room and asked, “Could you cut up some potatoes into French fries? The boys caught a mess of fish, and I’m going to fry them up. Where’s Becca?” realizing I’m here alone.

“She’s with Lew, pop in and check on them,” I told him.

“Hell no, you know what she would do to me if she caught me in there dirty like this? By the way, don’t mention that we were dirty when we dressed him yesterday, either, okay. I’m too used to working on animals, and she would have my hide for not scrubbing in. Our secret?”

I crossed my heart, and he smiled at that, turned, and left the room. I covered the bread to rest and pulled out a vacuumed bag of potatoes.

The whole crew was upstairs when I checked. The bread was in the oven, and I had a few minutes. Gid was sitting on a bucket, mooning over Becca as she sat across from him on the bench beside Doc. Jimmy was running around with his dog, and when he saw me, he ran over, his cheeks flushed and in the best spirits I’ve seen.

“Maryn, you should have seen me ride a horse today, like a cowboy with her bucking and everything. I caught a lot of fish and even saw two donkeys, though they don’t like Chunk Norris much.” He poured out breathlessly. It made me happy to see him so cheerful and full of life. He didn't seem like the timid boy that I had held a pair of clothing shears to his throat in Mr. Davenport's. Of course, thinking of him reminded me of my mama and daddy, and that almost ruined the day. I stamped that down; there's no time for tears during this outing, and for a second, we looked like we were having a regular family gathering at a cookout. My worries about the present slipped away for a bit, and I felt lighthearted for the first time in weeks.

"Chunk Norris?" I asked, already guessing who that moniker was for.

"The dog, since he's a chunky boy and knows kung fu." He peeled off back to his play without explaining the latter part, and I let him be a carefree boy. I brought the bowl of cut potatoes to the table set up against the back of the shop, and Doc sprang up and shuffled over to the fryer. It was loud like the one my Papa boiled crawfish in back home, or fried fish. That was the only similarity, though. I didn't see any of the same seasonings set out here except salt and pepper, which we used back home. My papa told me once that my granny was from the state shaped like a boot, and that she put everything that grew in the swamp and the field into her cooking. Her daddy was a coonass he told me once, and I thought that was the strangest thing I'd ever heard. I told him my granny was a granny, not a coon's behind, and he roared with laughter.

The fish were under a towel in a stainless bowl, covered in flour, not cornmeal. I shrugged my shoulders and minded my business. As Doc said, if you were doing the cooking, it was dealer's choice, so I kept quiet and went to check on my bread.

"Sit a minute and visit," Doc said, but I brushed past them.

"I have bread in the oven," I told him, heading for the door.

"We don't eat bread with fish," he said back.

"No, but I bet you'll be slathering butter on it in the morning, though, won't you?" He grinned at me and gave me half a salute, and I arrived just a few seconds before it's ready to come out. I set it on the stove top to cool, and I go back to join the fish fry. When the bread cooled, I'd put it into an airtight Tupperware that was probably older than Becca, which she set aside for me.

The fish were frying by the time I got back to the party, and Doc was pawing through the hot fries while watching the fryer. Becca was telling Gid something, and he was lost in her eyes. Jimmy threw a ball into the air, hoping Chunk would catch it on the bounce. At this rate, he won't be chunky for too long. I said as much to Doc, and he handed me a cold Pepsi from a cooler under the table, telling me that Chunk isn't fat, that he has heartworms, and that's what kept weight on him.

"That's fatal though, right? "I asked, alarmed at the thought of Jimmy losing his best friend with so much he's been through already.

"I'm a veterinarian, remember, I started him on his first treatment this morning while you were still drooling on your pillow. I care a lot more about animals than I do about most folks." He gave me a wink.

"Yes, I could tell that by your manners." He laughed into his beer as he took another swig from the unmistakable red and white can.

"I like your sauciness, girl. Want a beer instead of that pop can of sugar?"

“No thanks, I don’t care for the taste of piss.” He hooted with laughter and danced a little jig with his feet. I couldn’t help but smile at his foolishness.

“More for me,” and turned it up.

Gid went into the shop at Doc's direction and brought out a white plastic table. He unfolded it and set it up by the bench, brought me a couple of buckets to sit on, and we had our first outdoor picnic here. Doc had Jimmy jammed between him and Becca on the bench, a French fry black hole hiding under the table, with food being slipped to him from both Doc and Jimmy. I sat beside Gid, and we fell to it.

The shadows started to deepen, and the fish was completely devoured, though Chunk got more than his fair share. Doc sat back with his pipe, and Jimmy took off with the dog. He noticed small bats flying around and tried to throw the ball up and hit one. Of course, Chunk doesn’t understand the game; he’s just happy to chase the ball and bring it back.

Gid moved his plate aside, looking at Doc. “Becca says she was doing residency in Iowa City when this all started, and she’s too young to have served with my uncle. The years she spent at school wouldn’t allow for that, and you told me yourself that you don’t know him. Can you tell me about your connection with him? Something is missing, I don’t understand.”

Doc pulled on his pipe and shrouded his face in smoke before answering. “You could fill a tome with what you don’t understand, but it’s not my story to tell. I will tell you this much: your uncle saved my son’s life in Iraq in 2010. My son, Thomas, Becca’s father, was in command of Llewelyn’s unit, and they were ambushed. Six men died that day, and it would have been more if it weren’t for your uncle. He carried my wounded son out of danger and several more, as I understand it. I'm not clear on the details, as I wasn't there, and my son, Thomas, wouldn't elaborate much. His missing arm and burn wounds spoke to how awful that day must have been. When they got them out, everyone was shot, burned, killed, or all three. Lew has my eternal gratitude for what he did; it's hard to find other men who will bleed for you, but Llewelyn bled for my son, so he will always have a place here. I wrote to his mom after looking her up online. I missed him a couple of times at Walter Reed while he was visiting Thomas, and he was redeployed often after his wounds healed. I wrote to him as well, but never heard anything back, but no matter because you are here now and I can return the favor."

He cracked open another beer and took a long pull, and I said, "Your son must have been considerably older than my uncle if Becca is 25. I think Uncle Lew is thirty-six." I said, not understanding the timeline.

'Yes, Thomas was born in 1980, and Becca was born in a hospital in Germany in 2001, while he was serving his first overseas deployment. Of course, he was sent to the desert a couple of times, and on the last one, it was when your uncle saved him. He was a Captain before that day in 2010, and of course, he was older than most of his men. Becca and her mom were living here with my wife and me when we got the notification that he had been wounded in combat. He stayed in Germany for months, then was sent to Maryland for treatment. That's where we first learned how badly he was hurt." Becca shifted uncomfortably, and the dusk couldn't hide the tears in her eyes. My heart broke for her, seeing her daddy at that age in that kind of condition. "I stayed there as much as the farm would allow, and soon after, I made my wife come home for treatment herself because she had cancer. She met Llywelyn a couple of times, and she stayed as long as she could. Too long, really; it killed her in the end. She put off getting checked so she could stay with Thomas, and the window for treatment came and went, unknown by any of us." Doc's voice got hoarse, and I could tell he was fighting off the terrible sadness of losing a wife and having his son in that condition at the same time.

"Anyway, we buried my Rose a couple of weeks before they released Thomas. Once home, his wife decided this life wasn't for her and took off." I heard Becca sob and knew this must be excruciating for her too. "Understand that your uncle saved my son, but he was never the same again. It wasn't just a missing arm and burnt skin that had changed either. Something inside him died in that sand and never made it home. He was happy to see the farm again, but the light had gone out of him. I got to make peace, and Becca got the chance to say goodbye to him before his seared lungs gave up and he was gone. I got to tell my son how sorry I was for being the kind of father I was, and he forgave me. You can't put a price tag on that, so I'm in debt to your uncle, and until it's paid, it won't sit right with me." He switched the beer out for a bottle. Once he took a shot, he continued. "Anyways, my oldest boy and his wife are missing. I went to St Louis and checked myself, and I may never know what became of them. Instead, I must do all I can to keep Becca safe and try to make some life out of this madness." He drained his beer and crushed the can with one thorny old hand and tamped out his pipe with the other. "Going to bed, I've had enough of people for one day." He grunted and headed into the shop, leaving the bottle of Tennessee whiskey on the bench.

I moved it, sat by Becca, and told her, "I'm so sorry about bringing that up in front of you."

"It's a story I can't change, so I understand you wanting to know the details of this strange situation. I think most situations from here on will be very different from before. The old man has never gotten over his boys, so don't take him being ornery personally. He's down a wife, two sons, and a daughter-in-law. My aunt and uncle never had children and focused on their careers as surgeons rather than family, and I think that hurt him too. They are the reason this place exists, though. They poured over two million dollars into this setup, and they weren't conspiracy theorists or anything; they treated it like a hobby. Lucky for us, too." She stood up and announced it was shower time for her, and we all gathered up the plates and empty cans and went back inside.

I was last to shower, and I saw Jimmy rolling up his blankets when I walked past his room. "You moving out?" I teased.

He shook his head and said, "I'm going to sleep in the shop with my friend." He pouted.

"I thought we were friends?" I smiled at him.

"You are Maryn, but Chunk is lonely by himself up there."

I nodded to him, "Okay, just don't unlock the door for any reason. You mustn't go outside the shop, okay?" he agreed, and I grabbed his pillow for him, and we headed up.

Our sleeping bags are still up top, so he unrolled his bag into the bed of the old International truck. He patted his leg, and Chunk Norris jumped up beside him, and they snuggled in. There are banks of batteries with charging lights up here, but nothing else to see me until I open the underground door. I look back at him, and he's murmuring to Chunk Norris. By the time I got down, I checked on Lew, and he was sitting up and talking to Becca. She was giggling when I walked in, and they both turned to look at me. “Here’s the main reason you didn’t bleed out in a truck cab right here.” She smiled at me.

“Our very own Florence Nightingale.” Lew stared at me. “Did you patch up Gideon?’ he asked.

For a second, I forget what he meant, then I remember the burns on his neck and shoulders from the hot brass going down his shirt. I put aloe on that right after getting Lew situated in bed, and it had completely slipped my mind. When I saw him doing push-ups this morning, the burn side was away from me, and I had a lot on my mind since then.

“One of them will scar, but he’s fine,” I said with a smile.

“How are you?” I asked, and he grinned at Becca.

“Honestly, I thought I was dead when I woke up seeing this angel here.” Becca blushed at his corny joke, and I slipped my hand into his.

“Glad you’re alive, there’s plenty of work to do here, and the owner is not likely to put up with layabouts like you.” He smiled at me and said, “Go get the Colonel, I need to thank him for saving my family.”

Becca looked at him and said, “Sorry, my daddy died a year ago from pneumonia.”

“Your daddy?” he asked, confused. “The little girl he carried a picture of in his helmet?” He sat up more.

“The same,” Becca said as a tear ran down her cheek. “I’ll get my grandpa, and he can fill you in on what’s happened to our family. I really don’t want to go through it twice in one day,” she walked over to the shower and started to change out of her scrubs.

“Mr. Smith is here?” he asked. I started to warn him about the “Mr. Smith” moniker but decided to let him find it on his own. He deserved that for the flirting that was going on with Doc’s granddaughter, and I smiled at the thought of the old man bracing him over that, too.

“Can I get you anything?” I ask him.

“There’s a book in my bag you could bring since I’m going to be sitting here for a few more hours.” He said, stretching his arms up as much as possible.

“A few more days, you mean?” Becca said sweetly to him and playfully swatted him on the leg as she walked out of the infirmary.

When the door closed, I turned back to him. “Thank you for getting us here. What is the name of the book you want me to bring you?” He shifted to get more comfortable in bed.

“There are only two in there, bring me one called 'Outlaw' by Warren Keifer, please.” I nodded and asked if there was anything else he needed, and he shook his head, patted, and squeezed my hand. His color wasn’t bad, and it makes me feel better since he’s awake.

Opening his bag, I grabbed the first book I saw, but it was poetry by someone named Lord Tennyson, so I put it back and got the right one. Bringing his book in, he was rolled over with his back to the door and fast asleep. I set the book down, softly closed the door, and went to my bedroom. Gideon was stretched out in his bed, reading a hunting magazine.

“Are we putting on a guard tonight?” I asked.

He looks over his magazine at me and says, “We. Who is we? You mean, am I?” He sat up, and I apologized for last night. He shook it off, “Smear some of that grease on my burns again, and we’ll call it even.” I got the tube of cream from my room and applied some to the three burns that start at his neck and slide down to his ribs.

“It’s not grease either, you neanderthal, it's cream from a plant.”

He grinned stupidly at my jibe, and when I stood up, he said, “I think the old man is genuine. What do you think?”

I snapped the lid shut and asked, “You want my opinion? A silly little girl like me?” I affected an exaggerated southern accent. He threw his pillow, which I slapped out of the way easily, and sat back down. “Yes, I think he’s genuine and has no intention of hurting us. The opposite. Is there something about him that bothers you?” I looked at him searchingly.

“No, nothing like that.” He shook his head and asked me to throw his pillow back.

I bent down and retrieved it, and with the accent again, say,” Here’s your pillow, good sir, nice and fluffed for you, just like you like it.” he rolled his eyes, and I threw it into the corner where he’ll have to get up and get it and stepped out fast and shut the door behind me. I giggled as I closed the door, while he playfully yelled at me. After showering, I was asleep as soon as I hit the pillow—dreamless and refreshed.

52 Gideon

The next few days were much the same, except for fishing. We visit Doc's actual home, and it is quite plain. Except for rows of solar panels in the back field, it looks much like any other farmhouse in this area. You would never guess the amount of money spent here from the unassuming home. He explained that his son had sent him money and drawings, and Doc spent it on the things he wanted done. After all, the places would be his one day, and Doc didn't care how his son spent his money. Doc also made almost a million dollars a year from his crops, leases, natural gas, and equipment rentals on his place. He stored diesel underground for his tractors and had the tanks treated every year to reduce the risk of it going bad. The extensive farming was usually gearing up this time of year but would be reduced to about four acres. Sweet corn, tomatoes, beans, squash, melons, potatoes, and okra instead of acres of soybeans and feed corn. Just a household garden now, really, and whatever he had going on in his greenhouse. I mentioned why he hasn't planted corn yet, and he said he usually waits until mid-April or so. I asked if that was late, as my old papa usually put his in mid-March.

He replied, "Well, we don't grow that trash corn here like you Southron folk do; here it only has to be knee high by the fourth of July." He never missed a chance to rib me about Texas, but I didn't mind. I started to like the old crusty bastard. Lew was getting stronger every day and was soon out of bed most of the day. He took his meals with us, which Maryn mostly cooked, since Becca was in deep water except for that tasty stew we ate at our first meal here.

Maryn asked about stores in the area that might carry the

spices she wanted, so Doc and I rode into Oakland and checked the one grocery store there. A small store called Rubacks was untouched, and it gave me some hope. The old man fiddled with the door and, after a few minutes, had it open. I swung off Buck and walked to the door. The stench of rotting meat and produce lingered in the air here. I pull a neckerchief up over my face to mask the smell. The spice aisle isn't much, and I only got the dried stuff: no barbecue sauce, nothing like that. I just emptied the shelf into a leather pack and headed to the canned goods aisle, grabbing a new can opener along the way. I opened a can of peaches and ate them. Finishing them, I drained the can while Doc was doing something in the back. I raked the canned goods into my bag, and Doc was heading toward me with a huge grin.

"Got these." He held up a leather-wrapped bag. "Got what you needed?" he asked.

"I got what they had, so I'm ready when you are. Are those adult diapers?" He ignored me and walked out to the horses.

I slipped the bag over my saddle horn, and Doc closed the door behind us.

"We need to bring the truck next time and get this charcoal loaded up and brough home. I'll show you Texans what real barbecue tastes like then." He mounted up on One, and I held my hand up to silence anything he may be about to say. I heard something north of us.

"Is that dogs barking?" Doc spun his horse around and listened. Shaking his head, I swung around and looked at my horse. Buck heard it, too, and I pointed north. I could hear a dog—maybe two—barking, and it sounded like someone yelling. It's a street over and a few blocks from us by the sound.

We cut through the parking lot of a Chevrolet dealership and past a Dairy Queen, and there's a red building that the noise seems to be coming from around back.

I went the long way around on foot, and Doc stepped down to walk on our near side. He nodded at me when I was at my corner, and I took off down the side of the store with my rifle shouldered. Turning the corner, I heard Doc yelling something over the din. It was dogs barking, and when I turned the corner, the boom of Doc's gun once, twice added to the din. Fear rose in me then, and I raised my brand-new rifle from Doc's inventory toward the direction of a dumpster. A dog lay on its side, and another ran off, dragging its hind legs. I saw Doc swing his rifle around like Davy Crockett at the Alamo, and a mangy yellow dog gnashing his teeth at him just out of range of his arc. I shot the dog with one of Doc's brand new 5.56s from his armory, and he fell over without another sound. I ran to Doc to check on him. His sleeve was dripping blood, and he was bent over, wheezing from the struggle, but seemed otherwise unhurt.

"The dumpster," he croaked, and I turned to see a face looking back at me from it. I lifted my rifle from its strap around my neck and pointed it at him, and two hands accompanied the face.

"Get out of there," I said.

He clumsily climbed over the side of the dumpster, dropping down to the ground. A young man around my age, just a shade taller and skinnier. His dark blonde hair was so dirty it almost hid its true color, and his green eyes looked desperate. Carefully, I watched him, and it appeared like he didn't have a gun, which was crazy to me.

“You armed?” I asked him, and he shook his head. “Come over here and get this first aid pack from my horse.” I let him pass me, then I followed to our ground hitched horses, which I’m happy to see didn’t run off from the shooting.

“It’s in the saddlebag,” I pointed with my left hand, leaving my gun aimed at him. He warily approached One and dug into the bag, removing the rigid plastic box. I jerked my head back in Doc’s direction.

“You could have walked over to the horses; your legs didn’t get chewed on,” I grumbled to Doc as we got back to him—the boy from the dumpster shakily handed Doc the first-aid kit.

“Open it up and let’s get out what we need,” I told the dumpster boy. Doc looked at the grease and filth on his hands and arms and stopped him.

“To hell with that,” Doc says, “give me your pistol, and you get the supplies out and bandage this. That boy looks like he may have a slew of diseases on him from being in that trash.” I handed him the pistol, slung my rifle across my back, and bent to clean and bind his chewed-on wrist.

“The bite marks are deep,” I said as he winced as I cleaned them.

“Maryn will have to sew this up. The good news is that you probably gave the dog rabies, as mean as you are, and not the other way around. All whiskey in your blood probably killed off anything that may have been in dog slobber.” He grunted as he handed me back the pistol, and I used my left hand to help him up, keeping an eye on our guest.

“Who the hell are you?” Doc asked sourly, probably pissed about my joke at his expense.

"My name is Finn, sir." I walked around to give him another look for weapons.

"What kind of name is Finnsir?" the old man groused.

"No, sir, not Finnsir, just Finn. Finn Sutherland."

"So, Finn Sutherland and not 'Just Finn?' The old man could get wound up with his bullshit, even bleeding and with us in real danger, he couldn't help himself with the tomfoolery.

"Doc, maybe we should talk about this somewhere else, maybe away from a parking lot full of dead dogs we've shot and alerted everyone in a mile?" I said, starting to get uncomfortable with how long we've been here after the shooting.

He walked over, swung up onto his horse, and I told Finn to collect Doc's rifle. It's empty so that it will do two things for me: tell if he'll try to harm us with it and keep my hands free to shoot if anyone or anything else shows up before we can escape. Doc handed me back my pistol and swung up on One, and I told Finn to slide the rifle into the scabbard. When he did, I got up on Buck, still watching him, using only one hand.

"Which way, Doc?" I asked, and he spun One and walked down the street in front of the building, where I could only make out the letter "R" on the door. We turned off that road onto another, and a block later, we were on gravel, surrounded by corn.

"Here's far enough," Doc stopped his horse and turned to the boy. "Time for some answers, first off, where are you from, and how have you stayed alive so long? Especially walking around with no gun?" Doc queried.

"My name is Finn, and I live here in Oakland on Oak Street. I have been hiding for as long as I could. Several men came to my neighborhood, riding horses like you, and kidnapped my neighbor. I didn't even know he was alive because I hadn't left my house then. My mother and sister have gone to Lincoln to visit my sick aunt, and I've been alone since. That was a day before people started dying on the news. I stayed inside after hearing gunshots for a couple of days and seeing smoke all around. The men who showed up were ransacking homes and taking prisoners of anyone they caught. I ran to my grandma's house, which was out back of ours, and hid under her bed while they searched. When they left, I looked out the window and saw a couple of people being dragged away with their hands bound and ropes around their necks tied to saddles. They looked beaten and bloody, but the only person I knew was the little girl who lived three houses down." He seemed to be on edge, darting his eyes back and forth.

Doc guessed his intent and said, "We aren't with those men, and we mean you no harm, just want some information, and then you can be on your way. First off, how many men were here on horseback and when was this, exactly?"

Finn thought for a few seconds. "The men came about ten days after my parents left, and I saw at least four men. I have seen people twice, and both times, a man on a white horse was there. They didn't see me, and I just now have run completely out of food, so I had to go further to find some."

"Where have you been getting food from?" I asked him, and he looked ashamed to say it.

"There are no wrong answers," Doc assured him at his hesitation.

I'm not so sure, and he looks at the old man and says, "I've stolen from people. I went into their homes and took food from them. I'm ashamed of it, but I'm hungry." His eyes showed his embarrassment, but Doc barked out with laughter.

"Is that all? Goddamn son, nothing wrong with that, it's survival. I was worried you were going to say you were eating dead people." Finn looked horrified, and Doc laughed again, then dismounted and walked over to him. "It's okay, son, we got a spot for you if you want. We live about nine or ten miles from here if you want to come with us. The only thing is you must pull your own weight; we don't need any slackers." Finn looked confused, and Doc plowed on, "You can work, can't you, aren't any kind of a degenerate?" Finn shook his head. "No, you can't work, or no, you aren't a degenerate?" Doc smiled.

"I'm Irish, not degenerate, and yes, I can work." Doc found that hilarious and pointed over to the road ditch.

"Go wash that funk off of you and climb up here behind Gideon, and let's get from here."

I turned to Doc and said, "Damn, you're quick to invite him in, considering how you treated me when I showed up."

"Well, he doesn't look like he eats as much as you, and he seems to have better manners." He would joke, I thought irritably. Finn came back from the bar ditch, reeking of stale water, but it was better than the grease and dirt from the dumpster. Doc looked down at him and turned serious.

"Don't take it personally, but we are going to blindfold you. Until we become better friends, I don't want to risk our little sanctuary. Agree to that, or you can go back to running from wild dogs in dumpsters." Finn agreed, and Doc looked at me and nodded. I moved my left boot out of the stirrup so he could climb up with it and my extended hand. Once seated, I reached and untied the empty leather bag from my saddle horn.

"What in the hell were you doing in a dumpster when we found you?" I asked him.

"I was trying to kill a squirrel with a stick, and the dogs caught me, and it's the first place I thought to get," he said sheepishly. Having been attacked by a wild animal myself, I sympathized. I handed him the bag, and he set it over his head.

Doc laughed his ass off over him trying to kill squirrels with a stick. "I wish I could have seen you hotfooting it into that dumpster," he chuckled as we headed for home.

53 Llewelyn

I made my way around the structure to see what kind of operation the old man was running here, and I was surprised by the accommodations. The water and electricity systems were high-tech and rugged, the living quarters neatly arranged, and the kitchen and storerooms expansive. The shooting range was the cherry on top, though. He had sandbags set up at the back end for rounds and mats rolled up against the walls for wrestling and grappling. The extensive collection of rifles and pistols was a small fortune just in themselves, and the rows of ammo for them were staggering.

Doc explained that his son wanted to sink money into this place, and looking around, I see he's put a considerable amount of his own money into it as well. This setup had to be north of four million dollars, I guessed, with storage tanks for diesel and gasoline, as well as solar and filtration systems.

I walked around outside while Gideon and Doc were in town for Maryn, taking everything in. The farming equipment was put under lean-to sheds and full barns for what I deemed the truly expensive equipment. His red Dodge dually stood in the backyard beside Charles's old shot-up Chevrolet, and I wondered why they hadn't taken it. It's quiet, but maybe the old man just wanted a ride.

Jimmy showed me the barn and chickens. He blabbered while sending his dog back and forth with a tennis ball.

"Thank you for letting me come with you here. I like it," he said, throwing the ball.

"Wasn't up to me, thank Maryn for that. If it had been up to me, I would have tossed you in the Mississippi River," I teased, and he turned to me with a serious look.

"Good men wouldn't do that, so I know you wouldn't have, silly." Well, he's got me there. I'm not too sure about the good part, but I wouldn't have discarded him.

"You know I've heard you do a lot of bragging about catching these fish, why don't you show where you get them from?" He grinned and rocketed on past the chicken coop and the barn where Doc stored the fishing poles, toward the creek. I walked toward him, swinging my arm, trying to get the stiffness out of it without causing it to bleed. I wasn't sure where Becca is today, but if I busted these stitches, I would catch hell.

Thinking of her, she appeared near the creek bank, book in hand, and leaning against an old cottonwood. Jimmy pointed out his favorite fishing hole and then threw the ball into the water, which Chunk was more than happy to go get.

"Sorry to disturb your peace. Are you reading or writing poetry?" I asked, squatting down close to her in the shade. She had been smiling at Jimmy and turned her head to me, flashing me with its glow. What a beauty, I thought.

"Reading it today, did you want to recite with me?" She asked with a smile.

"Afraid I'm not big on it."

"Strange, I thought you would be a 'Cannon to the right of them and Cannon to the left of them' type of guy." So, she's seen the book in my bag. I shook my head and sat all the way down.

"No, I'm more a 'Clowns to the left of me and jokers to the

right' type." She burst out laughing at that, and the sound was so alluring that it made me look at her. We chatted for a few minutes until Jimmy and Chunk were covered in mud, and they decided to head home for lunch. Becca and I followed. She described their life after the illness and asked about mine.

"Not much to it. I was born in the mud of the Neches and will probably die in mud somewhere. I joined the Army, they sent me on a world tour, shot at some folks, had some folks shoot at me, and now I'm here."

"That's the sum of it?" She asked, smiling devilishly, if she was flirting with me? Of course not, I'm a shade old for her, I remembered and nodded my head.

"I think there's more to it than that," she said, swinging her hand over the tall grass on the other side of the wooden bridge. "You ever been in love, Llewelyn? You seem like a heartbreaker," she grinned.

"More of a bone breaker, really. I was in love one time, and now it's as dead as everything else in the world." We stopped in the garden, and Jimmy waved to us. She looked up at me, still wearing the impish smile.

"Is it really dead, Llewelyn?"

54 Maryn

Kneading bread, I heard Doc's booming voice from the living room, "Maryn, we are having a guest for dinner tonight. Just wanted to let you know so you don't claw me later."

"A dinner guest or a new member of the Doc Mafia?" I asked, thinking he meant a pet raccoon or some other foolishness. He was the most unserious person I've ever been around, so you could never tell with him.

"We'll put him through the paces at dinner, and I'll let you decide if he can stay or not. How fair is that?" he smiled at me. "But for the nonce, can you come and put some thread in my wrist? A dog scratched the paint off me this morning." He flashed his bandaged arm.

"Sure, let me wash up, and I'll be right in there. Where's Gid?" I asked anxiously.

"Don't worry, he's fine, just sorting our guests and making sure he's properly cleaned up before he has to meet the best cook in Iowa," he winked.

"You mean in America, right?"

"Agreed!" he chortled and headed to the infirmary. I know Lew and Becca have gone off to check the garden and look in on the animals. Jimmy was supposed to be washing Chunk Norris, since they had been at the creek earlier with Lew and got muddy. Probably slipped off to fish, though.

He and the dog were inseparable, and Doc had grumped about Jimmy sleeping upstairs with the dog.

“You could always let him bring the dog down here,” I told him one morning, when he was raising hell about it.

“I’ve been a vet for most of my life, and I’ve never had an inside dog, and I don’t intend to now,” he huffed.

“Well, you can change your mind, you know. I changed mine about you after all. When I first met you, I thought you were genuinely kind and caring, but soon you won me over to realizing that none of that is true and that you are just a grouch that only takes pleasure in tormenting people and drinking beer.” I smiled at him.

“I like to drink whiskey now and again, too, and smoke my pipe,” he snorted.

He hadn’t budged on the dog yet, but he would. Becca and I ran things here, and he wanted it that way. He liked to complain and act ornery about everything, but in the end, he rolled over and showed his soft belly. I think he was happy to have people around—the more, the merrier —but he kept up his brusque façade; no one was fooled by it anymore. He had worked his way into my heart, and I looked forward to his banter and grumpiness every day. Now that Lew was getting around more and Jimmy was starting to run wild, I was able to focus more on Doc. Becca loathed any housework and preferred to be outside when possible, so I took on the inside chores, and everyone helped, so it was usually light work.

When Doc wasn’t busy showing the boys how the electrical or plumbing systems worked, going over the cattle business, or any of the other little things he had time for, he would sit in the kitchen with me and regale me with his tales. When I cooked, he would sneak food, and he built me a little area where the fish fry was set up so I could cook outside when the weather was nice. He preferred that, I know, because he could smoke his pipe and whittle while jabbering like a magpie. He went out of his way to get me anything I needed; he grumped about it, but I knew it made him secretly happy to be useful.

His demeanor toward me and Becca was different, and he secretly doted on us. He didn't try to force Becca into something she wasn't, and he let her do whatever she felt like doing. Don't misunderstand me about her because she worked her ass off around here. Feeding cows, hogs, and horses; checking fences, helping me with the cooking and cleaning, and even helping Jimmy catch fish occasionally. Just like Gid, Jimmy was half in love with her and enjoyed her company. She and I fixed each other's hair, but neither of us wore makeup, of course, but she didn't need to. I think my showing up here made her happier than Doc because she got to spend more time outside doing things she liked.

Lew had been spending most of his days in the armory with the boys until he was well enough to ride. They shot rifles and pistols, and I usually joined them. Jimmy was improving significantly, and we all became decent marksmen, with them all topping me, but I didn't mind. I had no intention of ever shooting anyone, but if I had to, I wanted to be good enough, and I was. The hunting fell to Becca and Gid until Lew started to get around enough to go, which was approaching. We had plenty of fresh venison and wild pork, and we ate it instead of stored food unless it was about to expire.

One evening, while Doc was knee-deep in Maker's Mark and we were outside with the grill going, he told me that, along with his son and daughter-in-law spending a massive fortune on this place, he had started buying things himself for the shelter. From the food, water, and electrical systems alone, that must have cost several hundred thousand dollars. The shelter cost had to be staggering as well. They had thought of just about everything and had plenty of it. Ammo, rifles, and pistols, and the inventory was mind-blowing; the only things they didn't have in quantity were the seasonings I liked to use and our clothing. House slippers were the direst need for me, as my feet had been cold since we got here. We would have to go and find those or start making them. There were racks of coveralls in the gun room, but that would be a last resort. Coats, jackets, thermals, hospital scrubs, they had thought of all that.

"Hell, I didn't really have anything else to spend my money on. My wife was gone, Becca was at school, and I thought it would make my oldest boy happy." He admitted that night.

I didn't press Doc too much on his family because he would get moody. I know he's dealt with a lot of tragedy, and not knowing about his oldest son must be awful, so I avoided any subject involving them. He whittled away, and I let him enjoy the small happiness he could find now. I was sensitive to that, and I felt like that's one of the reasons he liked to spend time with me. He made it a ritual to come in early, when possible, to sit with me before the others showed up for meals, and I got used to seeing him and hearing him yarn away. The trip today had only happened because I wanted more seasoning, and Gid was restless, stuck around the house for so many days.

An hour after getting back from town, a freshly showered and clothed young man trooped in with Gid and Jimmy, followed closely by Doc and Lew. They walked him over to the table and introduced him to me. I heard Doc tell him Becca would be here in a few minutes, and he saw her coming across the field. Lew stayed behind today to look around, sharpen knives, and had the entire lot from the kitchen outside in the shop.

'Hello," I said to him, and he nervously grinned back at me.

"This here is DC," Doc said, the devil in him showing from his eyes while holding his freshly stitched wrist with his other hand.

"DC?" I asked curiously.

"Yeah, Dumpster Cat." He said through a grin and dropped his wrist and shot his hand out for a slice of bread, laughing to himself.

"Finn," he said to me.

"I'm Maryn. Sit down, Finn, it's ready."

Doc would joke about something embarrassing. I flashed Doc with a look of annoyance, brought the platter of pork chops over, and set them on the table. Gid helped me with the mashed potatoes, and I grabbed the black-eyed peas and bread and set them down. After taking my seat, I saw Finn staring at the heap of food, and my heart went out to him because it's probably been days since he's had a good meal. We were making our plates when Becca and Lew came in and met Finn. We then ate without a word, and Finn finished his entire plate and another.

We all went upstairs and gathered around to hear his tale. None of us felt better after hearing what Finn had to say. Dangerous men riding around looting, burning homes, and kidnapping people was some of the worst news.

"These men will have to be dealt with," Doc said, looking at Lew, in the dark with only a fingernail moon in the sky.

‘How many and where they come from needs to be our focus. We shouldn’t fire any weapons outside anymore until we know for sure how close these people are. I’ll go into Oakland tomorrow and see if I can track them back to where they live.”

Gid stood and said, “I’ll go instead so you can get over your gunshot wound.” Lew poured out his coffee on the ground. I could tell he was about to say no, but he surprised me.

“You can come with me, but not instead of, time to learn, I suppose. Seems we have an extra hand here now with Finn, so get your gear stowed. Besides your weapons and ammo. Bring two canteens of water and food for a few days. We’ll be traveling fast, so we don’t need much weight.”

“I’m going with you,” Becca said.

Finn stood up, “I can come too, I’m the only one that can recognize any of them.”

Lew asked, “Can you ride a horse or shoot?”

“I never have, no, but I can help.”

“Help by staying here and doing whatever Doc tells you to do. I can’t use you this time with me.” Lew said coldly.

Doc said, “I need you here with me; these Texans aren’t very good at conversation, and they don’t know anything about farming.” I’m so proud of him for trying to soothe Finn’s pride, but it blew up in his face.

“I don’t know anything about farming either,” Finns said in a sulk.

“Well, you won’t be able to say that after tomorrow. A man born to this land is equipped with an advantage over our southern cousins. We learn the art of farming early because we are born with a superior intellect," the old man said, and he relit his pipe.

"I wasn't born in this land, either," Finn said dismally to everyone's delight except Doc's.

Later, while Doc was smoking, I came up after Lew had shared his plans with him. The sounds of the night lulled the senses, warmer now, and insects were starting to ramp up their cacophony. A light breeze of warm air promised hotter weather ahead, but it was hard to appreciate while our people were in danger. The last several days of peace and routine had mesmerized me and kept the outside problems from my mind. Danger isn't that far away after all, though, it hid just beyond your peripheral vision, close enough to prick the hair on the back of your neck but just at the edge of your other senses. Even their leaving in the morning felt like a detachment to me, as if they were riding off to do their daily chores. Of course, keeping murderers and kidnappers at bay was a chore now.

I wanted to ask if they would be okay, but Doc knew just as much as I did about the future, so I kept my silence and just listened, just as he did.

55 Gideon

Maryn had breakfast ready for us when we met in the kitchen this morning at five. Doc was already there drinking coffee and looking cross. We breakfasted in silence, and Maryn gave us hugs all around, wishing us a safe journey. She packed our food for us to take and handed it over.

Doc announced, "I've lost enough people in this life, can't stand to lose another." He shook Lew's hand and hugged his granddaughter.

As he turned to me, I said, "You consider me your people?"

He squeezed his nose with two fingers and cleared his throat, "Ah, in truth I meant those two, but sure you too," he put out his hand to me, and I took it in mine. Surprisingly, he pulled me close with an embrace. I could swear he was about to cry when we left out, but of course, he covered it with his usual banter. "I suppose I need to get these other lazybones up around here or they will sleep all damn day," he complained behind us from the kitchen.

Jimmy was up and swinging his legs over the tailgate when we came up. His hair stuck up everywhere, and he was mid-yawn when I opened the door. He dropped off the tailgate and came over to Becca and hugged her.

"Don't get hurt or stay too long, okay?" he looked up at her, and she smiled down at him.

"You tend your business here and don't aggravate the old man too much, alright?" She ruffled his unruly hair with one hand and kissed his cheek. For an instant, I burned with jealousy. Jimmy also hugged me and told me to hurry back, and the second surprise of the morning was his embracing Lew. His head reached the lower part of his chest, and for a second, Lew looked completely bewildered by the gesture. His scarred and hulking body towering over the boy and the brief, confused look on his face almost made me laugh out loud. Lew awkwardly patted his head and told him to get down to breakfast before Doc took a belt to him, which, of course, was absurd.

"Take care of them, Lew, like you took care of us coming here." Lew nodded to him.

"I will squirt. Now unhand me and go eat." Jimmy stepped back, and Doc opened the door.

I heard Jimmy behind us, "Do you want to take Chunk Norris with you? He is a great guard dog."

I turned to him, saying, "If we needed a biscuit guarded, we would, but he aggravates the horses, so keep him here with you and protect my sister, okay?" He nodded, relieved really that we weren't taking his friend, and went downstairs with Chunk circling our feet looking for pats. I rubbed his thick blue coat and held him inside with my foot until I could close the door with him still indoors.

We got to the spot where we stopped to talk to Finn outside of town at daybreak. Lew was on Alice, Becca rode the black mare, Bucephalus, which Jimmy shortened to Boo, and of course, I had saddled Buck for myself. We had to be careful of getting too close to Alice; she would bite our horses or us and was happiest when she could kick something, so letting Lew lead out was prudent. She wouldn't bite him, but would try to get any of us, except Jimmy. She followed him around like a lamb when feeding or brushing, but only Llewelyn rode her.

As soon as we could see well, Lew kicked her into a walk, and we started at the place Finn lived. Burned-out homes and tracks everywhere were easy enough to find, as he described. We searched for an hour before finding tracks along Highway 6 east of town. We stayed on the shoulder as much as possible to avoid leaving tracks of our own. Lew took the north side, and Becca and I rode south, looking for signs that they had left the main road. Shortly before noon, as we crossed the bridge, Becca saw tracks on our side of the road. She waved Lew over, and we studied them. He got down and handed me his reins. I put my foot out to keep Alice far enough away from Buck so she couldn't bite him, but she ignored us. Lew walked along the shoulder and counted the tracks. He came back, and I handed him his reins, and he remounted.

"Let's go down the same place and water the horses." The bank was lined with trees and foliage, starting to green out. "East Nishnabota River," I read on the sign before we passed it and entered the wooded riverbank. The deer here may be bigger, but the name "River" is really a misnomer for most bodies of water here; this would be a creek back home. Rocks protruded from the middle, and the water split in two on either side. Beautiful spot and serene considering the tragedy that's probably happened along the banks to those trafficked people. I thought about what Lew had told me back in Wisconsin about a place not remembering, and I hoped that was true.

"I need the ladies' room," Becca says and heads south along the riverbank.

"Don't go too far," he warned her.

"Just enough for you boys not to blush, I promise," she smiled at him, and he shook his head. I took a swig from my canteen as Buck drank from the river.

"See all these tracks?" Lew pointed, and I nodded. "Six horses, heavy with a rider and two sets of shoe tracks, so these must be the ones Finn saw with two captives." I stepped back in time to miss Alice's teeth flash by my shoulder, and he reined her around straight. Buck was looking at me like "you know better than to get that close to her," and I stepped back away from her as Becca came from the woods and drank from her canteen before remounting. I'm standing as long as possible because this much riding is more than I'm accustomed to, and my ass was starting to hurt. Lew swung back up and asked Becca about the town ahead.

"Lewis," she told him.

"How big? Any jails or airports, anything with high fences?" He wanted to know.

"No, that won't be until we get to Atlantic, it has a county jail and a small airport. We must cross this river again and then pass Lewis to the south, and it's maybe six miles further." She opened her saddle bags and took out an Iowa map, which they studied together for a few minutes. It gave me time to move around and work out the kinks in my legs.

"We'll head north before crossing the river again and get on these gravel roads that head north. I don't want to use any main roads; we can avoid them."

She agreed, and they turned their horses and rode away. I got on Buck and caught them on the bridge crossing the river. A couple of miles later, we see another bridge ahead. Here, there's a gravel road on the left, and Lew points us that way.

Becca looked over at the blue sign on the road and said, "I'm surprised you don't want to ride this road all the way down,

Lew."

He looked at her in confusion. She pointed to the sign that reads "White Pole Rd," and I couldn't help but laugh at the look on his face. He shook his head in mock disgust at her. Her laughter floated in the air like a cool breeze on a hot summer day. It fired my blood, and I went from laughing to blushing with the thoughts that filled my head with her. Lew trotted off, leaving us, and she laughed even harder at his irritation.

Miles later, we crossed the river again, this time on Lansing Rd, and then turned north again onto another gravel road and followed it up until it split. We crossed back over the river on a bridge with steel trusses, the road painted with graffiti. This time, there are no roads, so we walk along the riverbank north until we reach another. There's only about an hour of daylight left, so Lew told us to camp by the river and settle in for the night. I unsaddled and brushed the horses; even Alice was tired enough to cooperate. Becca and Lew set off on foot to get a better look at the town. They aren't gone for half an hour and come back to camp.

"Well?" I asked.

"I saw a man on horseback, but I'm not sure where he was heading. Tonight, I'll slip into town and get a better look around. We won't do anything until I get back, and we'll form a plan. Make sure you get plenty of rest and don't start a fire or make any noise. It's cold camps until we get out of enemy country." Camps, not camp. I wondered how long he planned to be here, but I was the one who volunteered, and honestly, the thought of not being horseback for a day sounded like heaven.

We ate the meal Maryn made for us that morning, biscuit

sandwiches with sausage and eggs. Becca had a bag of oats on her saddle, and we split those for the horses and left them hitched close to water. Lew told me to move them away from the water before it was fully dark, in case a storm came up, and the water rose. I thought that was complete nonsense, but I did what he asked. He came over to my sleeping bag and squatted down beside me with his rifle resting on his thighs and a pair of Doc's NVGs on his head. He smelled like horses and sweat, as I'm sure we did, too.

"I'm heading out, but I'll be back before daylight. If you hear any shooting, head west on this road until you are past the airport, then start making your way south until you get home. I'll catch up, so don't wait for me. I've told Becca the same thing. She's taking first watch and will wake you after midnight. Be watching the road and bridge. If anyone crosses, silence them. I'll call out before crossing the bridge, so don't worry, it's me. The moon was a fingernail tonight, so you can easily see across the bridge even without the glasses once your eyes are adjusted. I've gone over this with Becca, so she knows what to do as well. She's going to follow me to the bridge and then stay there until it's your shift, got it?" I nodded my head. "Be back for breakfast," he slipped into the dark and made no sound. For the first time, I'm glad he's not out hunting me at night.

A hand on my shoulder woke me, and I heard the wind rustling through the leaves, and I'm confused about where I am.

"Your watch, sleepy head," Becca whispers almost silently, and I got up, pushing off my sleeping bag and turning my boots over and shaking them in case some critter crawled in there during the night. I stopped to pee on the way, slinging my rifle over my shoulder and listening to the night. Frogs and insects have quieted down with the chill, and the night was as silent as Lew. I settled at the woods' edge and started letting my eyes get adjusted to the dark—all the hours I spent doing this, and it never got any easier. I would rather take an ass-whipping than watch, but it was my duty, and I didn't have any choice. The monotony of it was soul-crushing, and I never found a way to overcome it except for sheer stubbornness not to let boredom defeat me. I buttoned my coat to ward off the low-fifties temperature and fought to stay alert, watching the aluminum side rails on the ridge glow in the moon's weak light.

I was still battling with it about three hours later when I heard a low whistle, then a voice from the dark. Lew was mistaken about the light being enough because I couldn't see anything to distinguish him. I picked up my NVGs and saw him standing on the bridge waving his arm over his head. I dropped them back into their belt pouch and waved back, and he walked toward me. I sat for a few seconds watching him materialize right beside me. It was damn unsettling how quiet he moved, I thought.

"I'll get some sleep and brief y'all in a couple of hours, wake me at dawn," he said, and headed back to camp, leaving me at my post on the bridge.

The gray light sent me in search of him, and he's already up eating a sandwich and a can of peaches. Lew hands me a sandwich and my choice of peaches or raisins. I've finished my bacon sandwich and am halfway through the can of peaches when Becca walks into camp carrying a rolled-up bundle.

"Had to bathe even if it's in the river," she reached over and squeezed water from her hair, and the thought of her bathing this close to me sends my mind reeling.

"A bit cold for a bath, isn't it?" Lew asked her.

"I'm not used to smelling like a goat, I'd rather be a little cold than smell like you," she shot back, and they both smiled at each other.

"You want something to eat?" He rested his back against a beech tree, sitting on his heels.

Shaking her head, she said, "I ate when you were getting your rest. I guess this country is just too tough for some people," she teased, but Lew didn't go for it and instead got to the business at hand. Using a stick, he drew in the dirt the jail and where he spotted people.

"The jail is here, and there are clear fields of fire for the entrance and exit," he pointed his stick to show us where. "We are going to watch them today and find out how many there are and plan on taking them outside of the jail, though. I don't want to be in a concrete-and-steel building with rounds flying if I can avoid it. Gideon, that tree over there will help you see any movements on this side of town. Becca and I are going to check north and south. We'll meet here an hour before dark to share info." He stood up and added, "If you are seen and must shoot, make sure to kill. Avoid that as much as possible, though, because it will alert everyone within three miles of here. These men don't deserve our pity, and we aren't in the prisoner-taking business, understand, but I don't want to lose the element of surprise," he looked at both of us.

"Today is just about observing, so stay hidden and observe until we know what we're dealing with." Becca and I nodded our understanding, and I followed him over to the tree he pointed out. He cupped his hand and boosted me up with just a pair of binoculars, a canteen, and my pistol.

56 Maryn

Doc took the boys out to the garden with him after the others left, leaving me alone with worry. Gid wasn't a hard killer like Llewelyn, and Becca probably wasn't either. Against several rough men, I didn't feel good about their chances. I overheard Lew and Doc talking the night before about possible outcomes, and Doc demanded that Lew bring anyone being held against their will back here, but Lew refused. "If we force them to come here, they may feel it will be changing one master for another. I will do all I can to set them free, but I won't force them here. I will invite them here, but that's it. They want to return to their homes or run off into the woods and start a blood cult, I won't interfere. I won't see innocent people held captive or any potential danger to us here."

Doc disagreed with Lew, "These people may have been mistreated and aren't thinking clearly when you show up, coupled with the violence they will see you visit on these men, and what's already happened to them, they may not be thinking enough to see the wisdom in coming here."

Lew grunted, "I'm bringing Becca to help soothe any of these folks that may have been misused and to prove we aren't just going to continue their mistreatment, and that's all I can do for them. The choice will be theirs, completely, and that's beyond discussion." He left, and Doc came back into the kitchen.

"Oh, I didn't know you were still up. I'm hunting something to drink," he says to me. A stiff shot or two, I imagined after that conversation.

"I'm just finishing up, so help yourself, and I'll see you for breakfast," I hugged Doc because I knew his disagreement with

Lew was frustrating, and I wanted to give him what small comfort I could.

"That uncle of yours is a hard son of a bitch, Maryn."

I stopped at the door and turned to face him. 'It's a good thing, too."

At dinner the next night, I finally got to pay attention to our new guest. Finn was wearing the surplus coveralls I mentioned earlier, as he had no spare clothes at all. Now that he was clean and had been fed a few times, I could see how handsome he was. He smiled at me from his rice and gravy, and I felt something inside of me grow warm. Doc droned on about something or other, and afterward, Doc and Jimmy went up top, and Finn volunteered to stay and help me clean up. We didn't speak until the dishes were done, and he sat down next to me with a cold glass of lemonade.

"This is the best I've eaten, thank you." He said, bringing the glass to his lips.

"Well, I expect it's been hard for you to find quality food since this has all happened." He set his glass back down.

"No, I mean the best I've ever had in my life, you're a great cook." Finn smiled, and the heat rose in my face.

"Thanks, I had a lot of practice. A homely girl like me must win a man with something other than her looks. Didn't your mother cook?" I asked, and he shook his head.

"Not too much, and she's from Ireland, and they like mutton. I don't care for it, but my big sister did, so she made that a lot, but mostly we ate out." his eyes turn sad, mentioning them.

“What does homely mean?” He asked.

“You know, plain, boring, ugly even.” He frowned and shook his head.

“Well, I’m glad you’re so homely, because you really can sing on the cook stove,” he joked, laughing.

“Tell me how you come to be here, Finn.” I saw his face change when I said his name, and I knew I had to be careful; the line between teasing and flirting would get blurred.

“My mom moved here right after I was born and worked at the Nebraska Medical Center. We lived here because her parents already owned the house and had moved to Florida. We got citizenship, and she decided never to return to Ireland or to my dad. They fought on the phone a lot and then for years didn’t speak at all, so I’m not sure what happened with that.” He sipped the drink again. “He’s a doctor there in Galway, they both were, and he only flew in at Christmas, and then it was every other year and none at all for the last four years....”

“Do you know what happened to your family? Any word from any of them after this sickness happened?”

“My sister was killed in a car accident last year; her boyfriend was drunk and drove them into a river after prom. I haven’t spoken to my mom since the phones went down. She called and said she was at the hospital because she got sick, and well, you know. I don’t even have a number to reach my father if the phones still worked,” he dropped his head, and I could tell he was trying to hold back his tears. It didn’t work, and they fell onto his lap.

The sadness and vulnerability in him called out to me in a strange way. I was used to being around men who hid their feelings well and would probably rather be burned at the stake than cry in front of a stranger. His openness touched me, and I felt my heart break for him at that table.

"Sorry about that," he said and abruptly stood and walked out. I'm bewildered by his sudden departure. Jimmy and Doc were around the back of the shop, and the old man was trying to teach the boy how to whittle a whistle from cottonwood. These were simple ones with just a solid cylinder, but I had seen Doc making one that was fish-shaped when Jimmy wasn't around. I suspected it would be a gift for him. Their strange dynamic was one of the odd things that had come to pass in our new lives, the gruff old man and the sweet, skittish young boy. Jimmy was obedient and listened to Doc with rapt attention about everything from fishing to caring for animals, but he wouldn't budge on the fact that Chunk Norris couldn't sleep inside. It was a divide that they couldn't breach, and the mere mention of one or the other giving in would send them both off in a sulk. People are so weird, I thought as I watched them work together, knowing that mentioning the dog would ruin the evening.

Looking for Finn, I found he's not up here with them, and before I can get away, Doc called me to have a seat and rest a bit. So as not to arouse suspicion of my real reason for being up here, I sat and listened to them banter back and forth about fishing for an hour before heading to bed.

At breakfast the next morning, Finn was subdued and wouldn't look me in the eye. He stayed out after I went to bed, so I didn't see him come in last night. The other two didn't seem to notice, and Jimmy was pelting Doc with questions about Gid and Becca getting back. Subconsciously, he understood there isn't as much reason to worry about Lew as the others, and doesn't mention him when going on and on about how he wants to fish with Becca or ride horses with Gid. Doc fielded all his questions with the same defense of "I don't know, Jimmy" a half dozen times. We don't know when they will be back, but I DO know if they stay out any longer than tomorrow, they will be out of food since I'm the one who packed it. I was determined not to worry until the next day, so I was relieved when they left to go about their business, and I was alone again. I said a silent prayer for all of them and hoped they would return as they had left.

57 Gideon

From where I sat, I could make out the front of the jail. I couldn't distinguish faces, but I could tell men from women. Soon after daybreak, a man walked two women across the street to a van and opened its side door. He stepped aside, and they grabbed some boxes and turned to carry them back inside. Before they got back, another man came out with a man and a little boy, and they stayed out front while he walked around to the side and out of sight from me. A few minutes later, he rode up on a pinto and brought two more roans with him already saddled. Four more men came out, and two of them climbed onto the roans. They separated: two men walked with one rider, and the man and boy with the other. They headed into neighborhoods where I couldn't see them. The solo rider rode out of town, heading straight toward the bridge where we are camped.

My pulse quickened, and I carefully lowered myself to the ground. He was crossing the bridge by the time I hit the ground, and, snatching up my rifle from the tree trunk, I went to meet him on the road. I moved as quickly as I could and remained relatively quiet. My biggest fear was that he's a decent tracker, saw where we were posted last night, or my horse whinnies, and he sends up the alarm. Soon, as I thought it, I heard Buck behind me and to my left. The horse on the pavement stopped and whinnied back. Damn, I froze, but I'm still five yards away from the road, but lower down against the embankment. The brush is thick because of the season; it hasn't leafed out fully yet, but enough for cover. I'm looking at him, seeing only the top of his hat, but he's peering back to where Buck is, and not where I am. If he left the road, he would see him in the trees, and the game would be up. If he turned around and rode back for help, I'd have to leave in a hurry, so I don't get caught alone. He stopped and looked into the brush past where I'm hunkered down and sat there for a minute. Eventually, he started to move forward, and I could see from the bill of his hat that he was still searching the woods where my horse and camp were. He slowly walked his pinto until he was past the guardrail, then veered off the shoulder to where Buck was. He saw my horse standing there and looked all around to see if anyone was still in the vicinity. Fortunately, he doesn't turn around and look back behind him to see me. He was holding a pump shotgun, stolen from the police station, probably, and wearing a pistol. When he stepped down from the saddle with his back to me, I stepped out with my rifle pointed at him. Strangely, I felt calm, and when his horse turned to look at me, he still had one foot in the stirrup.

"Stop right there, mister," I said to him softly. He jerked, startled, still holding the horn in his left hand and the shotgun in his right.

"Toss that shotgun," I told him, and he did. His horse shied away from the gun, hitting the ground, and his foot slipped from the stirrup, causing him to lose his balance and land on his knees.

"Stand, and put your hands up," I told him, and he did instantly. I walked quickly to him, reached out, and pulled the Glock from its holster. Tossing it behind me, I asked, "Got any more weapons on you?"

"N-no, I don't," he stammered.

"Get out of those clothes, down to your underwear," and he skinned out of them fast. He must have been cosplaying as a police officer because he had the whole uniform, including a belt with a spray and cuffs. "Shake those cuffs loose and put them on your wrists," he bent down in his filthy underwear and complied. As soon as he locked them both down and was standing in only his underwear and boots, I told him to turn around and saw him clearly for the first time. Dirty, unshaven, with shaggy hair. The left side of his face was scarred from a deep cut, which caused his lip to point up at the corner like a permanent sneer. I could see his yellow teeth peeking from the upturned lip and healthy plug of Levi Garrett in his jaw.

"What's your name?" I asked him, pulling my pistol, and slung the rifle over my shoulder. I waved the gun to get him to move away from his pile of clothes, guns, and horse.

He shuffled away and said, "Tommy."

"Well, Tommy, one shout from you and I'll give you every round in this pistol, you understand me?"

He nodded, and I walked him over to a large cottonwood. "Put your back to that tree and slide down," I heard the bark scrape as he did so, causing him to wince from the pain. I reached up and took his reins and tied his horse up before he could run off. I released the rope he had secured to the saddle horn — presumably to tie prisoners together, according to Finn — and wrapped it around him, tying it at the back. When I was finishing, Lew appeared next to him, setting his rifle down against a small willow tree.

"I see you got it handled," he breathed hard. I don't know if it's from finding me still alive or from the exertion of getting here. "I had to wait for a work detail to pass before I could pass and get here." He explained, still panting.

Lew kneeled on one knee in front of the tied man. "Name?"

Lew asked.

"Tommy," he repeated, and Lew dragged his knife from the upside-down sheath he carried on his chest. "We're going to play twenty questions; have you ever played that before?" Tommy eyed the blade and shook his head no.

"It's easy, I ask a question, and if you lie, you get cut. Lie enough, and you can bleed out here beside this river, and I'll throw your rotten corpse to the turtles. Now do you understand the rules?" Tommy nodded, eyes widening at the thought of being eaten.

"What the hell are y'all doing with these people you've captured?" Lew asked.

"They work for us. The women wash and cook, mostly the men and boys we send out to garden, mostly, sometimes to fish for our supper."

"How many people are prisoners?"

Tommy took a second to figure this out in his head. "Three women, one of them mute, two men, and a boy." He nodded to himself, proud to have gotten the correct tally.

"You sure?" Lew asked.

"S-s-sorry, sir, I'm not good with numbers," he said, "b-but I think yes."

"This is the most important question, so take a second to get it right. How many men are with you holding them prisoner?" Tommy, who we can see, is on the slow side, closed his eyes, and took his time.

"M-my brothers and Clint," he said.

“How many brothers you got?” Lew pressed.

“Three b-brothers,” Tommy says, “Travis, Timothy, Trevor.” So, all “T” boys, I thought. Lew puts the knife close to Tommy’s face.

“So, five of you, I thought there were six?” Lew looked up at me, and I nodded. He looked back down at Tommy and flicked the knife point across his nose, causing him to buck and jerk in the rope.

“You didn’t forget someone?” The blood welled on the tip of his nose and fell onto his dirty underwear.

“No, no, no,” he pleaded. “Travis, Timothy, Trevor, Tanner, Clint, Kyle, and me,” he whimpers.

“What’s the last name of this familial trash pile?” Lew glared at him, fury standing out on his face.

“What?” He asked.

“Your last name. What is it?” Lew stood up.

“Hodges, m-my brothers are Hodges,” Tommy whines.

“Repeat those names,” I said, and he went through them again, counting them out on his fingers this time to make sure it’s right.

“Who is Kyle? You didn’t mention him.” Lew moved the knife close again. Tommy eyed it with fear and said they'd brought him from Anita, and that he was a cousin. “So, there are seven of you down there?” Lew edged closer.

“No, I’m here, and my older brother Travis went off to Des Moines to check on another of our cousins there. He left yesterday."

"Any of your brothers or cousins been in the military?" I asked, wondering how much experience we were up against.

"Trevor went, but the Army sent him home for being a drunkard," Tommy explained, not taking his eyes off the knife in Lew's hand.

Lew walked away and waved me over to him out of earshot of Tommy. "I hate to leave one of them alive, but we have to do something today since we have this lump of shit out here tied up," Lew whispered grimly.

"I didn't know what else to do with him," I said defensively, bewildered at his reaction.

He surprised me by not berating, but instead he clapped my shoulder and said, "No, you did the best possible thing. Shooting would have brought them down on you, and knifing him would be tricky business with a guy that big, and your inexperience. Besides, we wouldn't have gotten the info we needed. You did a fine job." My chest filled with pride at that.

"When Becca gets back, we're going in. Hell, as green as these boys are, I should let you take them out, and I could sit here and enjoy a nice picnic with Tommy." He chuckled.

"What are we going to do with him?" I asked without turning around.

"He's mentally challenged, so I figure we could just leave him tied up and let him work himself free. I'd hate to kill a man like that if he's innocent and is only going along with his brothers like he probably has his whole life." I agreed with that, relieved we won't be doing murder.

Becca rode in twenty minutes later, and we shared our information. There were two guys at the jail with the women and one each with the pair of workers in separate gardens. Lew told me to grab Tommy's clothes and shotgun.

"There's one missing we haven't seen," Lew shook his head.

"How many of you lie about in the jail all day, Tommy?"

"I dunno, they send me out to work while they stay there doing nothing but having fun with the girls," his unintentional sneer almost caused me to club him with my rifle butt.

"So probably three at the jail, then." Lew looked at us, and we nodded our understanding.

"Put your rifle on his horse, but carry his shotgun. I think we can trick one of them into believing you are Tommy. There's a crew at the end of this bridge working in the backyard, running a tiller for rows. Walk to the end of the bridge and wave him over to you. Once he sees you trot back here, and I'll grab him from behind these trees here," he pointed at the opposite side of the bridge.

"It's simple, and that's what usually works. Come with me and bring your rifle in case something happens, and if he gets away from me, kill him before he can run off. Got it?" he looked at us, nodding.

We understood and got into action. His clothes were disgusting and reeked like hell. His hat and clothes were too big, but they would do for the trick, I thought. We walked to the end of the road, and they melted into the trees. I gave them a few seconds to get ready, and I rode out about forty more yards into the open and looked to my right for guard and workers. I saw them instantly, and the boy was leaning on his hoe, taking a break, seeing me first. I waved, and he turned to the man sitting on a roan guarding them. He looked in my direction, and I waved him over. They're one hundred fifty yards away, so little chance of him making out anything without a scope or glasses, except clothes and the horse. He gigged his horse forward, and I turned and did the same to the camp side of the river. I got there about the time he crested the embankment and got onto the road, passing the trees where Lew was hiding. Lew stepped out and grabbed the guy's right arm and wrenched him out of the saddle, sending his knife into the man's throat. Becca held the horse's reins and walked it over to me. Lew dragged the body into the bushes on the roadside and rolled it into the ditch.

He came up to us and told me to take off those clothes and to bring my rifle. He escorted Alice out. "I'm going to cut off these two working in this garden so that they won't panic and alarm the others. Look at your watch and give me five minutes, then come to the yard where they are working."

We mounted, and he took off. Flies droned by, and the river played over the rocks, gurgling slowly here. This quiet place was about to erupt in violence, and it seemed almost impossible that a man was lying in the brush with his life's blood staining the grass just a few feet ahead.

The five minutes burned down, and we started. Turning to the same place I waved from earlier, I saw Lew setting his horse and talking to the man and boy. We trotted up, and I saw the man and boy clearly for the first time—dark-complexioned skin and hair, and no doubt father and son.

"Mr. Jagneaux here tells me the three middle brothers are the ones who lie in jail all day, too lazy even to make other people work for them. Let's visit them." He looks to the man on foot.

"If you want to wait at our camp, we'll bring the others there when we're done."

The dark man's head bobbed his affirmation and said, "We'll wait across the bridge. C'mon, boy," he tugged his son's shirt, and they ran out of here. I heard the French lilt to his voice and looked over at Lew.

"The hell are two Cajuns doing up here?" He turned to look at me and asked the same thing about a couple of Texans.

"According to the man, the other field they tend is southeast of the jail. Becca, I want you to be on top of this Matco truck that's parked across the street beside that church. We are going to have to go inside, even though it's the last thing I want to do. When we start shooting in the jail, he will come flying back this way," he dragged his finger down 8th street on the map. "Make sure the horse has an empty saddle before he can shoot at us or cut off our retreat from the door. Mr. Jagneaux has given me the layout of the jail, and he said they keep the back doors locked. Leave our horses here in this shade and walk in. Once I see you settled on the truck, we'll enter the jail. Switch rifles with Gideon, too. We'll be in a tight spot, and the Mini-14 will serve us better inside." He handed me a semiauto pistol. "Use this inside, don't shoot that carbine in there unless you have no choice, use the .22 instead. A ricochet in there could just as easily kill you as the person you are shooting at."

"Understood," I told him and checked the magazine and chamber, making sure I was familiar with the safety.

"Ready, Becca?" She nodded while stuffing her hair under some kind of wrap. Once she was done, we switched and took off. Both of us are checking the magazines and chambers to ensure they are ready.

By the time we reached the jail, I was sweating and winded. It's not overly hot, just turned off warmer, but I know when we go in here, I may have to shoot someone, and my nerves were humming. Becca had the short route, so she was in place before us.

"Catch your breath, and then we'll go in. Don't ask any questions here. You see a bad guy, you put him down, no hesitation." I nodded, catching my breath. I wiped sweat from my face and adjusted the carbine to make it more comfortable on my back. He unholstered his 9mm and raised his eyebrows at me.

I nodded to him, and he squeezed my shoulder. We sprinted to the door, which I swung open, and he stepped inside, peeling off to the right. I went left and around the desk in the center of the hallway. The first two rooms were empty, and I heard clinking dishes down the middle hallway. The last door I opened revealed something that didn't register at first. I heard a grunting noise and saw a man's dirty ass cheeks clenching and thrusting with someone underneath him. For the first time, an indescribable rage blew through me like lightning, but all the nerves in my body were calm. Pointing my pistol, I sent the .22 through the back of his skull, and the blast nearly deafened me in the close room. He pitched forward and then, incredibly, stood up and turned to look at me. I tried to fire again, and an empty round was jammed in the slide. He lunged forward, and I dropped that pistol and pulled mine from the holster and put a round through his forehead. I didn't even hear the .22 clatter on the floor before my shot, and this time he fell backward with gore painting the wall and the woman underneath him. He rolled off and onto the floor, jerking like a landed fish, and I saw the first round had only grazed his head. I reached down with my left hand to help the woman up from the dingy mattress and couldn't tell who she was beneath the blood and filth.

"Let's go," I said and held out my hand to her. She was trying to wipe the blood out of her eyes, so I took her hand and pulled her toward me, and noticed her other hand was cuffed to the bars. I dug through the jeans pocket of the dead man, which were pooled on the floor of the cell, and fished out the key ring to unlock her. I heard two shots from the other end of the jail while I singled out the key, stepped over to her, and sent it home to release the cuff on her wrist.

"I'm here to help," I told her, but I'm not sure it registered. A close gunshot, and I knew Lew was done on his end. I dragged the hapless girl from the room, and she dropped her hand on the metal table and picked up a pistol. I inspected her by the doorway, where the light was better, and ran my bandana over her face to help clear her vision. She gasped but didn't make another sound. She turned the pistol to the man on the floor and sent another two rounds into him before I could stop her. The pistol slide locked, and she tossed it on his body as I pulled her arm down, looked into her gray eyes, and motioned with my head to follow, sure I would never be able to hear again. I understood how a flashbang was so effective now, as I felt discombobulated just from the loud noises from the gunshots, even without the flash.

Lew was looking down at the hall at me with a thumbs up, and I nodded to him. He turned and said something to the people at the end of the jail. I still couldn't hear anything, but I could see his mouth moving. He hustled a couple of older women out of that side and toward the door. I saw Becca looking down the street we expected the other kidnapper to emerge from, and the rifle barked once, twice. Lew gave her the thumbs up, and she gave it back, so we exited the foul-smelling jail with the women in tow. Becca slid off the truck and ran over to us. Lew told us to get our horses and head back to camp; he would bring the two men left in the fields.

I reached down, pulled the girl up, and put her in front of me. She only had a ragged nightgown to cover her nakedness. Her hair was tangled and dirty from blood, gore, and unwashed, the color indiscernible, but it was light-colored; that's all I could tell. Red, maybe, or dark blonde? I was never good at guessing girls' ages, but I think she's probably seventeen or eighteen. She hadn't hesitated when I put my hand for her, and she gripped mine firmly with her dirt-encrusted fingers and swung up. The other women refused to get on with Becca and decided to walk instead.

Entering the clearing, my passenger kept silent, and I thought I may have hurt her eardrums as well as my own in the jail cell, or she was afraid she was just being traded from one group of monsters to another.

Tommy was still tied up at our camp, and his horse watched as I came up into the clearing with a mouthful of grass. She shied away from Buck when I got close, and I realized the smell of blood made her eyes go wild with fear. I helped the young lady down, and she slipped out of her gown, walked past the Jagneaux father and son, waded into the river, and washed the gore from her hair. The water was cold, but it was worth it for her to get cleaned off, I supposed. I got a bar of Ivory soap out of my saddle bag and tossed it to her, and she started scrubbing herself. She squatted down in the water to wash her privates, and I turned away, embarrassed and enraged at what she's had to go through. After scooping several mouthfuls of water, she walked from the shallow river and made the motion as if she were hungry by putting her fingers to her mouth. I dug into my saddlebag for the last biscuit Maryn had sent with me and handed it to her. She ate it in three bites and washed it down with my canteen while standing there nude, welts and bruises visible all over her.

I staked Buck out and gave her my blanket roll to warm and dry herself with, and my spare jeans and shirt to wear. She was dressed by the time Becca and the other women joined the Jagneauxs, who had watched all of this open-mouthed, but silently, and the women embraced the man and the boy. They are all crying when Lew showed up with two men, one young and the other, probably as old as Doc.

They made introductions all around and told their sad tale. Lew informed them that we have a good shelter within fifty miles of here; he's being vague on purpose and invites them all to stay if they want. Of course, the Jagneauxs had already decided they were heading south, and the women weren't interested either. They didn't seem trusting, so they decided to head over to Council Bluffs. Mattie and Deb were their names. The younger man, Wayne, decided he would go with them, but the older fella wanted to try his luck with us. I asked the girl I had brought out, and she covered her mouth. She took up a stick and drew the words 'Gwen Stark' on the ground and pointed at herself.

"You're mute," I said, and she nodded, "but you can hear?" She nodded again. Understanding, I asked her if she wanted to come with us, and she took up her stick again and scratched on the ground. I read it and was surprised. "What about him?" she had written, pointing at Tommy. She brushed the writing away with her bare foot and walked over to Tommy. She pointed at him and turned her hands up to ask me what, like what's going to happen to him. Becca told her our plan to leave him to untie himself, and she nodded.

Gwen nodded and walked off—I assumed to pee or be alone for a minute—and I heard one of the women say, "Oh dear." I looked up at her and then to where she was looking. The blast was so close that it jolted me. I turned, and Tommy's head was leaking from both sides, and Gwen was standing over him with his service pistol taken from his gun belt I left looped over his saddle horn. She pointed at his horse, then back to herself, and I nodded. She wrote on the ground again, and I walked over to read it. 'Go with you,' and I looked in her eyes and smiled. She saddled the pinto and swung up in the saddle with my clothes hanging on her like a scarecrow. Gwen slid the Glock back into what is now her pistol belt, wrapped it over her head, and rested it on her shoulder, waiting for the party to break up.

"They raped us," Mattie explained, "but they mostly abused her. They all did." Lew nodded, and the older man, Nate, caught up a sorrel and got in the saddle. Lew told the Jagneauxs that there were three more horses in town somewhere, and the older man thanked us for saving their lives.

"I'll get them before we leave if you don't want them." The older man said.

Lew shook both of their hands and told him to take anything he wanted from that town. "If you don't take them or any other animals that may be there, at least let them out so they don't starve."

"Thank you for rescuing us. If you're ever down our way, stop in." I didn't catch where he said they hailed from, and we said our goodbyes right in the dark, and I never saw the Jagneauxs again.

“We were told that a little girl was caught and brought in, too. Where is she?” Lew asked, and the woman, Mattie, sobbed.

“She died beside the river on the way here,” she said, and more tears from both women now.

Our party left the clearing in the moonlight without a backward look at Tommy, and I handed Gwen my extra pair of socks to at least add some warmth to her feet, as she had crammed her little feet into Tommy’s boots without the benefit of any. She took them and handed me one boot after another until her feet were covered and rebooted. We headed home, heavy three horses and two people.

58 Llewelyn

The ride home was long and onerous. Even though the trip wasn't as far as I had let on to the newly released people, you didn't want to tell folks exactly where you lived anymore; it was still going to be a trek for us. The old man, Nate, was blown after a few miles, and honestly, the horses were worn down as well, so we would have to camp again.

I found a small farmhouse along Walnut Creek about ten miles away from the town, and we bedded down there for the night. Becca and Gwen found some more suitable clothes. She dressed and walked outside to stand beside Gideon.

When they returned inside, I split all the jerky I had in my saddlebags, and everyone found somewhere to sleep for the night. I told Gideon I would wake him for his shift later, so he and Gwen went outside to get some rest while Nate and Becca made do in the living room in front of a cold fireplace.

I sat out away from the little house and watched lightning dance across the sky from where we just left. Hopefully, rain was falling on the town and would erase our tracks from the place. I thought of the rain falling into Tommy's dead eyes as he rested against the elm tree and was disturbed by his death. I didn't really know how I felt about Gwen killing the man; on one hand, he was mentally ill and was probably set to evil by his kin, and I'm not sure how responsible he was for his actions, on the other hand, he had raped her, so I understood her reasoning in killing him. It must have been that I didn't know her that gave me pause, because when I put Becca or Maryn in her place, I would absolutely have killed him, so it left me pondering how fair and impartial I could be with the people I encountered. Hopefully, this didn't bleed into that and cloud my judgment too much, but it was impossible to know what seemed fair and reasonable anymore.

The killing in the jail didn't seem to bother Gideon at all, and that troubled me somewhat as well. That's the second time I've seen him kill with no aftereffects, and I wondered if it was something he pondered over later. Did he wrestle with his conscience? Did he blame himself for doing something so terrible? Blame me? I'd have to speak with him about it when we were alone and get his take. I didn't want him to find it too easy to take life, but also didn't want him struggling to sleep at night over what we had to do.

Turned out I didn't need to worry about it keeping him up because when I woke him for his watch, he and Gwen were piled together in his bedroll. They both rolled out and went on watch together. Another issue I would discuss with him later, perhaps.

59 Maryn

Near lunchtime the next day, Jimmy ran into the kitchen, yelling that they were back, and we all went upstairs to greet them. I have never seen a more miserable-looking bunch in my life. Rain started before daylight this morning and continued throughout the day. The only reason Jimmy had spotted them was that he kept checking on it to slack off, so he could go out and play with Chunk. He thought it was completely unfair to put on a slicker to do chores, like feeding the animals and gathering eggs, but not be able to play in the rain without a shirt.

In the break, I saw right off three extra horses and two riders, as they trooped up and dismounted. The older man was stiff as he got down, looking completely used up. The slim girl in clothes that were too large for her barely had her eyes open and didn't get down. Her face was bruised and dirty. Doc and Finn helped the older gentleman, and Lew and Becca followed them in, handing their reins to Gid. He flashed his smile at me, and I felt tears forming in my eyes at the sight of him. Jimmy volunteered to take the horses, but Gid told him to help me get some food ready; there was no sense in him getting soaked, too. Alice tried to kick Chunk, but she was so tired that it was only half-hearted. He easily ran to safety back in the shop, grinning over having riled her. I asked the young lady if she wanted to get down, and I'd get her cleaned up and put on some new clothes. She just shook her head; rain-bedraggled hair and oversized clothes made her look much smaller than she was. Gid asked her as well, and she refused again, pointing at herself and then back at Gid. Strange, I thought, but I had work to do to get more food going. I saw them walking the horses to the barn, the rain starting to fall in sheets again, baptizing them on the way.

Thirty minutes later, the hugs and handshakes all done, the older man sat at the supper table in fresh coveralls, and introductions were made all around. His name was Nathan Reynolds from a small town outside of Des Moines, where he'd been a college professor at Marshalltown Community College for thirty years. He went by the name Nate and was a lean, spare man with white hair and a mustache.

When Doc asked him what he taught, Lew interrupted and said, "Philosophy, I hoped you could have someone to talk to, so the rest of us aren't bored to tears."

The sour look on Doc's face made us all laugh, and Nate said, "Alas, no, I taught history."

Doc rubbed his hands together in glee and said, "That's great, you can regale us with how we whipped the hell out of these Southrons a few years back." He crowed with laughter, relieved they were back home, safe.

Gid and the mystery girl came in last, and I caught them in his room, gathering towels and soap for the shower. He stepped out into the hallway and hugged me, asking if I had any clothes she could wear. He smelled like a goat, and when I told him that, he grabbed me again and rubbed his wet clothes into me again.

"Aargh, I hate you," I swatted him playfully, which he easily dodged out of the way of. "Yes, I'll get her some clothes. Do you know what size she wears?" His look gave me the answer, and he waited while I got her some scrubs from the infirmary.

She sat naked on the bed in Jimmy's old room with only a blanket wrapped around her. I brought her the scrubs and underwear, hoping they fit. Gid told me her name was Gwen, and I went up to her and introduced myself. I asked if I could look her over for injuries, and without any modesty, she stood, and the blanket fell away, and I got a glimpse of her battered body. She's a little taller than me and leaner with dark blonde hair and gray eyes. Marks covered her body, her nipples were bruised and swollen, and her arms were crisscrossed with purple and green welts. Her left hand had fingers smashed and swollen, and her right had a dark red circle on her wrists from being bound. There were bruises around her throat, and one eye was bloodshot. The clothes fit well enough, and she hugged me, her hot tears against my cheek. No telling what she's gone through, I thought, and told her to come and eat. I had plenty ready for them. She wouldn't leave until Gid showered and changed, though, and they came into the dining room together. They both ate with gusto but didn't add much to the conversation. Once they were done eating and had been fawned over by Doc, they retreated to their bunks.

I showed Nate where his room was again. I know being somewhere unfamiliar can be disorienting, which was right across the hall from Gid, and he went straight to bed. Soon, everyone followed suit, and Doc told me on his way out of the kitchen that as soon as the rain stopped, we would have a big barbecue outside.

The rain, which had held off for most of the spring, decided to catch up, and it wasn't until the next day that we had a break in the weather. Everyone got plenty of rest, and we went through a lot of food. Doc wasn't worried about that, though. He had a plan that would help with that, he said, so don't worry, he assured me. Becca helped with the cooking and cleaning, and everyone spent the day and night cleaning weapons, mending gear, eating, or sleeping. Doc brought out a pen and a yellow notebook for Gwen to communicate with us, but she mostly only conversed with Gid. She came to me that afternoon with her pad and showed it to me. I was shocked by what she had written, and I wasn't sure we had what she wanted, so we asked Becca. She told Gwen we didn't have any here, but when we went to town for clothes, we would be sure to pick them up. She nodded at that and disappeared back with Gid.

"When are we going to town?" I asked Becca, while Gwen waited.

"Looks like tomorrow. Gwen needs clothes, medicine, and you've been saying you need some slippers for the cold floor."

"Kinda dangerous for some slippers, though, isn't it?" I asked.

"Honey, there ain't many more dangerous than your uncle out there, and little Gwen here is mighty fierce her own self," she smiled to the new girl who returned it.

60 Gideon

They planned a trip that night to find clothes, but Doc and Nate said their shopping days were over, and they had no reason to leave home. They would hold down the fort if it had plenty of pipe tobacco and sipping whiskey. They studied a map showing that Target, Walmart, and JCPenney were all within three blocks of each other in Council Bluffs. This trip, Gwen and I demurred and told them we had a top-secret mission to do for Doc, so everyone else, including Chunk Norris, loaded up in our '97 and headed out. I told Doc we would be back in four days and not worry until it was eight. He nodded and warned about going close to Atlantic again.

"They are around Lewis, so there's no reason to have to go all the way to Atlantic again. Ever." He squinted at me, and I swear he knew. Anyway, we headed out on One, and a dun mare that showed up here trying to get in the pasture with the other horses, that Doc named Godiva, and had a good ride, he swore. We camped that first night under the stars with our sleeping bags beside each other. I was getting used to her being this close without it feeling weird. The night before last, our first night back, I woke up to her whimpering on my floor and flailing her hands in front of her. I shook her awake, and she wanted to be in my bed where she slept through the night without a sound. Out here, she seemed so much happier and more upbeat. She grew anxious whenever we were apart for more than a few minutes, and I didn't mind being close to her. Some of her bruises were starting to fade, while others were still at their darkest. The swelling on her face was almost gone, and she seemed to be improving daily.

Gwen started showing me how to sign, and I picked it up

quickly. For her story, though, she had to write it down and let me read it. Her parents had been farmers in a small community called Wiota , east of where we found her in Atlantic. She had lost her ability to speak when she was four years old due to a bicycle accident. The town was so small that they were bused to Anita for school. She graduated last year and was going to Iowa State for ag science. She could hear perfectly, learned to sign so quickly that they let her stay in regular school. Her mama had taken over the farm duties since her father was killed by lightning the year before last, and they both worked as much as possible to keep the place going. Her mother died of the sickness, and she was left alone in her community. The Hodges brothers had caught her about a week ago while she was fishing in the little creek that ran by her house. They had abused her and kept her prisoner in jail until the day we showed up.

She cleaned weapons with me, breaking them down and reassembling them faster than I could sign. Our bond was strange, and it drove away my sexual thoughts of Becca. The burned image of Gwen being victimized in my brain killed my libido and filled me with disgust, and I could hold onto her without my bodily cravings, and not because she's not attractive; she was the most beautiful woman I had ever seen. Her tragedy touched me, and I wanted to give her sanctuary in my company. We lay side by side, watching the bright stars, with only the night noises. She slid her hand into mine, and a minute later, I heard her breathing steadily. The moon was waxing, we hadn't built a fire, horses would warn us of any danger around, and we didn't worry much about that out here.

The next morning, I asked her where the little girl died. Since she had been taken from the other direction, we had to rely on what the other women told her; she walked us down to the creek bottom. I found her small bones scattered across the mud from carrion animals and gathered them up. I dug a small hole for her and dropped them in.

We took ten beefs from the ones we had seen when we first came through here and started them on their way home. I don't know if you've ever tried to drive unbroken cows, but it's not simple. Cattle were dumber than a squirrel, stronger than pigs, and craftier than a cat. The overalls she borrowed from Doc did little to stop the saddle burn from zigzagging in the saddle after the strays. At night, she stripped down, and I applied the anti-chafing cream Doc sent. I know she was miserable, but for our plan to work, we had to lay the groundwork.

It took us two days to get them back, and we added them to the small herd of three cows Doc already had. The horses and cows were left loose on about forty acres, and there was no need to move them except to the next forty-acre pasture beside it when it got tired.

Everyone was happy to see us, and we had a big feed that night from the grill Lew had loaded up with bags of charcoal for Doc. They had found no people, and most of the stores were looted. Luckily, jeans weren't on the steal list, and they brought back dozens of pairs and yards of denim for Maryn to make more and to patch holes. New sewing machine, plenty of thread, and rolls of butcher paper and tape per Doc's request. They also found only the weapons and ammo taken from the sporting goods section and grabbed jackets, ponchos, underwear of all sizes and designs, and, of course, Jimmy loaded up on dog toys and fishing supplies. Lew found an untouched Boot Barn and returned the next day, loading the truck with hats, caps, jeans, shirts, belts, and boots. You got the choice of hats and shirts in your size, and we all looked like the rodeo was in town. He also found a wood smoker on a trailer and dragged it home.

We ate grilled burgers that night with homemade buns that Maryn made, and they were the best I've ever had. Gwen and I ate our dinner together and sat with everyone else, cutting up with Doc, teasing us about not being real cowboys because a handful of Iowan beeves had worked us for a couple of days.

“Well, we took it slow. I didn’t want to run the fat off of them. Like most things Iowan, they are extra plump and lazy.” The old man roared at that, and everyone laughed. Except for Gwen, who thanked them for the jeans and underwear they brought; unlike the others, she didn’t join in the joviality. Sensing her need, I excused myself to bed early. We worked on sign language for a bit until she was bent over with laughter at my clumsy attempts.

She picked up her new nightgown that Maryn brought back and showed me her flat stomach underneath, still rife with yellow marks, and asked me if I thought she was fat. Bewildered, I didn’t understand what she meant. She signed so fast I only caught part of Iowa, and then it registered about the cow joke. I explained I was ribbing Doc, and it was only a joke and not real. We laughed together about the misunderstanding, and when she was ready for bed, she once again snuggled her back against me and went to sleep.

61 Maryn

The next morning, I found Gwen coming out of the bathroom and called her into my room. I handed her the box she'd asked for, and she hugged me with thanks. One less worry off her mind, I supposed. She seemed more chipper at breakfast, though she didn't talk with anyone except Gid.

Becca has to slip off to a clinic in town to find the pills, and I wasn't sure how they worked, but she seemed confident in their ability to effectively stop an unwanted pregnancy. She was sworn to secrecy and brought back enough to supply our shelter in case anyone else needs them.

I passed it off to Gwen, relayed the instructions I got from Becca, and she hugged me for it, immediately opening the bottle to get at the contents. Leaving her there with her business, I went up top where everyone else was gathered just in time to hear Doc send out a request for me.

"Lew, I need your help today and maybe tomorrow. I remember there's an old woman who lives outside Red Oak and sells crafts every year at the festival —mostly Louisiana-themed stuff. Crocheted crawfish and alligators, things of that nature. Well, she also made some disgusting sausage-and-rice combo called boo dan or something like that and sold it, too. She gave me a card when Becca and I stopped by her booth last year, and it has her home address printed on it. Let me see if I can find..." He trailed off, digging through a cabinet drawer that seemed to collect every miscellaneous thing in the shelter, as I smiled at his pronunciation of boudin.

He rummaged through a rubber-banded stack of cards until he said, "Got it!" like he won a prize.

"You think I need a quilted nutria rat?" I ask him incredulously, after laughing at his pronunciation of boudin.

"No, no, no, the point is she cooked food, and she told me her son brought her loads of Louisiana supplies for her to sell out of her home. She had nothing official, mind you, but the law didn't bother her about it because she offered something you couldn't get around here. Authentic Cajun food, and it grew on a lot of folks. It's not for me, mind you, but she stayed busy with cracklings, sausages, gumbos, and whatnot."

"She has spices then," his point dawned on me.

"Yes, and something to cook these things in, too. I didn't set this place up for you. I never expected people like you to live here."

"What kind of people would that be?" I asked innocently.

"Folks around here generally drink fire, we don't eat it," He chuckled over that.

"Yeah, sure, we can head over after breakfast, you know where the house is?" Lew asked, and they sat at the table, looking over a map and talking to themselves. Nate decided he wanted to go as well, and after eating, they gathered up and left. Finn, Jimmy, and Becca take off to check the garden, cows, and horses. Doc nodded to Gid, and Gid announced that he and Gwen were going to bring in some more strays. Lew looked at Doc and then shrugged. Gwen stayed behind to help me clean up, and I asked if she had taken the pill I had given her. She told me yes with a nod of her head, and I let her know that severe bleeding can be a side effect, and she shrugged it off.

"You shouldn't be out bouncing around on a horse for a few days," I told her, exasperated. She smiled at me, gave me a hug with soapy hands, and went back to cleaning.

Gid came in and let us know the horses are saddled and ready. Outfitted in her new jeans and chaps, this time, Gwen looked prepared. She put the food in a bag for them, and I slipped off to the infirmary and packed her another bag. I handed it to her in the hallway as they were heading up.

"What's all this?" Gid asked.

"I wanted to make sure Gwen has extra clothes to change into in case it rains again," I said, surprised at how easily the lie came.

"A coconut pie would have been nice," he growled and took the stairs. I followed up, and Jimmy and Chunk were standing by the horses Boo and Two. They also have One with a pack saddle on her. Gid wants to rest the horses they had ridden lately, so they took these instead.

"I want to come with you, Gid," Jimmy begged, and Gid shook his head.

"Not this time, there may be other dangerous men around." Not quite a lie, but something in his answer was false. Why? It wasn't that they wanted to be alone for romance; the pills Gwen took negated that scenario, so why the subterfuge?

"We'll turkey hunt when I get back, and I'll teach you how to call," Gid handed him something from his bag. "Be practicing until I return." Jimmy held up the turkey call and ran off with it screeching from between his lips, Chunk raising hell at the odd noise. Gid laughed at them and swung up onto the black mare, Boo.

"How long are you going to be gone?" I ask them.

"Hard to say, but depending on the weather, a week or so. Any longer than two weeks, come look for my bones," he smiled, and I wanted to punch him. He has changed since the Atlantic raid and seems even saltier. He didn't show any outward signs of distress over killing a man. Becca confided in me that she had bad dreams about it, but it didn't bother her too much either. They deserved it and had I been there, I would have agreed, she assured me. Maybe so, I thought, but I was still worried about Gid. He didn't treat any of us differently, but I could see the world was reshaping him. It had to change all of us, I suppose, or we wouldn't adapt.

Wearing some of the clothing Lew brought back, they at least looked the part of cowpunchers, I thought to myself with a smile. Gwen wore a short-brimmed black Stetson, and Gid had chosen a dark gray one with a full brim.

"Coconut pie when I get back?" he asked from under his hat brim, grinning down at me.

"I promise." He winked at me, and they started off.

He turned back and said, "Make sure that pie is here or else." He flashed his smile again, and they turned onto the gravel road and trotted off. They had all switched to boots, except Jimmy and me. I preferred my sneakers unless I was working around the cattle or in the garden, and Jimmy shunned shoes altogether. As soon as the weather started to warm up enough for him, he also didn't feel the need for a shirt, and he seemed to think early May was soon enough. His skinny form began to fill out a bit and darken under the Iowa sun.

Finn seldom wore a shirt outside, either. I must admit, seeing him like that gave me a strange feeling in my stomach. He was extremely shy around me and even Becca, but he seemed especially uncomfortable when we were alone, which, with so many people, doesn't happen often. A brush in the hallway, a shy glance, and the unintentional touch while putting the dishes away together would send me reeling, flushing my face. He was a year and a half older than us and had started filling out his frame more. Gid was just as tall, but Finn was leaner. When we were against each other in self-defense, I found that we held onto each other a little longer than was necessary, or he would get reprimanded by Lew for going too easy with me.

His blonde hair had gotten lighter the more he spent time in the sun, and his skin had also tanned. Seeing him shirtless beside the barn with Jimmy now reminded me of the first time he had spent all day outside like that; he came in that evening with a sunburn. He was lying face down in the infirmary bed, and Becca was going to cover him with shaving cream to take out some of the heat.

She asked what I had left for supper, and I told her it was already made except that Doc was cooking pork chops on the pit. "I'll go start bringing the food up then if you'll spread this on for me." The thought of rubbing my hands on him started my heart beating like a bass drum.

"S-sure," I said, stammering a bit. She smiled and winked at me and left.

Left alone with him shirtless in the room made me the most nervous I had ever been in my life. I'm not sure what the emotion was called, but I did feel something I had never experienced before. My hands touching his hot skin and his stiff muscles while I gently rubbed his back down was the most erotic thing I had done, well, until I told him to turn over so I could get his chest and shoulders, and I saw the bulge under the cover when he flipped over. He saw me look at it, and we both blushed. I quickly, and probably too roughly, finished up and hastily left the room so he could get dressed and come up. My whole body trembled remembering that, and I forced it down so Becca wouldn't see and tease me about him. She loved needling me about Finn, but none of the men seemed to notice except her, with a smile when I came up top. Strange how men and women see different things in the same situations.

I hadn't been alone with Finn since that day, and I ached to touch him again. Becca and I were fast friends, and talking to her about it didn't help. When I told her about my feelings, she said, "His room is like all of ours, no locks and right across from yours, isn't it?" She giggled, and I moaned inwardly at her being flippant. She was a lot like her grandfather at times.

62 Gideon

Gwen and I made it to Atlantic that next morning. We could have pushed on and made the nearly thirty-mile trek in one day, but we were in no hurry, and Gwen seemed sick. She looked pale and ran off to any thick stand of trees at every opportunity. She carried the small bag that Maryn had packed for her, and I assumed it was feminine products for her time of the month. I told her we could wait, or I could go alone, but she wouldn't have it. After the fourth time she ran for the bushes, I asked her if she was okay, and she smiled and nodded.

"I am now," she signed as her dark blonde hair flowed from under the black hat, and her skin looked more pale than usual. I told her we probably needed to camp early so she could recover, and she agreed.

We cut across to Lewis and found a house close to the water tower that would do. There were no human tracks around the town coming in, but I wanted to watch for a little while just in case. She cooked us a little meal over their gas stove, and I sat on the roof overlooking the town. Once the sun began to set, I climbed down and made sure the horses were fine and had plenty of feed.

Inside, Gwen waved me over to the bathroom. The tub was full of water, and she pointed at it and signed for me to get in. The water was warm, so she must have heated it on the stove. I stripped down and climbed inside. She brought me another pot and dumped it in. I tried to hide myself in the shallow water when she reentered, but I shouldn't have wasted the effort, as she then undressed herself and sat down in the tub, pushing me back with her foot to make room. I was shocked speechless by her sudden nudity and didn't move. She pushed harder with her hands this time until I moved my legs apart for her to sit. Her light-colored pubic hair flashed by my face and disappeared into the water. The water level rose, but not enough for her breasts to be covered, and I gawked at them. She smiled and splashed my face with water, bringing me out of my shock. I hadn't been in a bath with a girl since I was a little boy bathing with Maryn, and my expression made her giggle.

We bathed together, and when she stood and turned around, I was relieved that she wouldn't see my arousal jutting from the water. My relief was short-lived, though, as she handed me shampoo and a cup to wash her hair and sat back down, my erection jabbing into her back. I dowsed her hair while she arched her neck back to keep the water from her face, and her back pressed against me. I rubbed her scalp with shampoo, and she closed her eyes and relaxed. I rinsed her off, and she stood again and dried herself, and she set down her damp towel on the toilet lid and used another to wrap around her hair. It was getting too dark to see in here with no outside window, so she motioned me out. I stood, and she handed me her towel, which she'd dried off with. She stepped out, and I followed her to our packs. She handed me a pair of boxers, and she slipped on a pair of panties and an undershirt that she likes to sleep in. I laid the sleeping bags on the carpeted floor, and she grabbed the bag Maryn had given her and went back into the bathroom with it. I made sure my rifle was within reach, and my pistol belt was near my head, and she came out and slid into the cover beside me. A bed or a couch was our first choice, but both smelled musty, so we settled for the floor.

Her heat against me dragged me to sleep, and that night I dreamt of water dripping down pink, silver dollar-sized nipples and wet pubic hair that was the color of hay. She was somehow cloaked in shadow when she turned to face me. Even though her body was wet, we were in bed back in my room in Wisconsin. She impaled herself on me and gasp, and I looked upon her face, and it was my ex-girlfriend, Lana. The sex had been awkward since we were both new to it, and afterward, when I noticed the blood, it freaked me out. We had been together twice more after that, but she soon grew tired of my interest in football and other activities and moved on. The only person I talked to about it was Maryn, and I had sworn her to secrecy to ask about the bleeding. Once she explained, I felt foolish but relieved. The woman who mounted me now isn't the inexperienced Lana; she is a seductress who has me in her thrall. Her face changed, but not her body. She's Lana, Becca, and then Gwen. When I'm about to peak, she turns into a cowl with golden eyes, the same ones with the rats and Mr. Davenport. I pushed away with revulsion and heard laughter, not with my ears but from within my head somehow.

I was shaken awake, and my eyes flew open into the wide-eyed look of Gwen. I must have pushed her in my sleep. I apologized and looked at my watch. Four ten. I heated some biscuits Maryn sent in the gas, and after we ate, we saddled the horses and slowly head out to Atlantic.

Seeing the buildings in the gray light of daybreak was a relief. The golden eyes lingered in my brain, and I don't understand what that signifies. Shaking it off, I pointed to the southern end of the town, and we walked our horses through there and turned them out in the baseball field. I unsaddled them, stashed the gear in the visitor's side dugout, and we shouldered our packs and walked three blocks to the jail, the one place we know Travis will show up after his Des Moines trip. Buzzards and crows competed over the man Becca had shot, and within a block of the jail, we could smell the bodies. Gwen, seeing the top of the jail, started to shake, and I grabbed her hand and smiled. She smiled back, set her shoulders, and we walked wide of the jail and the body in the street. There was a two-story house on the northwest corner of the jail, and across the street stood a park, another street, and the church. Perfect, I thought, and pointed to the steeple on the church roof, and she agreed. We opened a window, climbed into the house, and went upstairs to check the view. Acceptable for one to see from here and one in the church, I thought, as I looked down the street and saw a truck heading up the street.

I dashed down the stairs and motioned for Gwen to get her rifle. The truck slowly drove past between the park and us, heading for the jail—an old blue Ford with a rusty red passenger door, and two men. We were standing at the corner of the house, and Gwen used binoculars to watch the truck pass. She set them down and shrugged her shoulders. Gritting my teeth in frustration, we watched the truck pull into a service station across the street from us, and both doors opened, and they got out. Seeing the buzzards, they reached back into the cab and fetched their rifles.

Gwen glassed the driver and nodded to me. "Get him," I told her, "And I'll get the other one." She rested behind her scope, and I counted off barely a whispered, "One, two...fire." The shots rang out together, and they both hit the ground. My guy was splayed out on the pavement, and Gwen's was writhing around on the ground. We ran across the street and kicked the injured man's gun away from his reach, and I saw his lower stomach was covered in blood. I checked the guy I shot, and he's done, and I picked up the rifle he was carrying and found it to be a rusty lever-action 30.30. I jacked the rounds out, busted the stock against the truck, and threw it on top of the store, where it clattered and scared off carrion birds waiting their turn at this new buffet.

Rounding to the driver's side, I squatted beside the gut shot man.

He looked at me and said, "Why the hell did you shoot me? I didn't do anything to you." I stood up, and Gwen moved over to look down at him, blocking the sun, so he didn't have to squint to look up at us.

"I didn't shoot you, she did." He looked at her as the sunlight made her hair blaze from behind.

"I know you, you're that dumb slut who likes taking us two at a time," he tried to laugh, but groaned instead, his teeth coated with blood. His hand moved, and ropes of him spilled onto the concrete. "You've killed me, you dumb bitch, but my brothers will get you. They'll cut your tits off for this," he whined at the last. The pain must have been excruciating. She bent over him and moved her hand with a flicking motion forward under her throat to say, 'fuck you,' and she shouldered her rifle again. I pushed it down and asked who the other guy was. "That's my cousin, and if you've killed him, there will be hell to pay." No need to walk to the passenger side to check on the man I shot because I knew he was dead. I looked in the truck bed for anything we might need, and I heard two shots from Gwen. I looked over, and she has shot both of his elbows. She pulled out her knife, and I thought she was going to cut his throat.

"Gwen, don't." She turned to me, her eyes blazing with fury. "Don't kill him, let him see what the crows and coyotes are having for dinner." I pulled her arm away, sheathed her knife, and we left him there and sprinted off to the horses. That was the last time I ever thought of her as a victim, and I saw her for what she really was, a lioness.

63 Maryn

Lew, Doc, and Nate returned that afternoon with good news. The old lady was missing, but she left behind a massive supply of seasonings and pans. They had loaded them all up, along with her crafting supplies—yarn, threads, and quilting frames. They also have a trailer with several fuel tanks.

“What do you need all that fuel for?” I asked Lew when they pull the trailer back around the back of the shop.

“We’ll go over it at supper tonight,” he told me, and went back to talking with Doc. “It doesn’t make a goddamn bit of sense to take them there instead of bringing....” Doc’s voice trailed off, and I left Lew, Doc, and Nate to talk.

Jimmy proudly announced that four new chicks had hatched at the coop, and I told him what a fine job he had done caring for them. Becca and Finn were changing the horses' shoes and would come in when they finished. I handed Jimmy a slice of bread and one for his dog as the men came in. He darted past them and headed upstairs.

“I swear you spoil that boy worse than I ever saw, young lady,” Doc grumbled, sitting at his usual place. He reached over for a piece of bread himself, and I lightly slapped his hand with a dishcloth. He withdrew his hand, looking at me sulkily. “The older gentlemen here are treated with no respect,” he grumbled, and when I turned back to the stove, he stole a slice anyway, and I pretended, as always, that I didn’t see.

“You’re just grumpy that I got a full day's work out of you today instead of sitting in the kitchen yarning as you do,” Lew put in, and Doc spluttered as I laughed at that.

"A full day, by God, we had to pull over on the side of the road and let you get an hour-long nap in a field of Prairie Violets because you were so worn out from carrying a couple of pots," Doc said, red-faced.

The idea of Lew getting tired and having to lie in a field of wildflowers made me laugh out loud. Lew looked at me, smiled, and nodded. Doc was all huffed out, and like usual, Nate just sat there silently, grinning at the exchange. In truth, they had only been gone till lunch, I had enough time to sort everything and make dinner that night from the ingredients. Well, sort of, we didn't have any tasso, so smoked sausage and chicken would have to do it alone until I could convince Doc to make some.

Jimmy stuck his head in and yelled, "Becca and Finn are coming." He then closed the door and went to wash up.

After everyone made it to the table, I served gumbo, rice, and potato salad. Finn smiled at me, and I spilled the sweet tea I was pouring for Jimmy. He cried out as it ran down the side of his glass, and I caught myself, embarrassed because Lew had caught me looking at Finn.

Lew shunned tea like Gid; he thought the colonists had the right idea with it in the harbor, and Doc drank coffee and whiskey only unless he was on a health streak, then it was beer. Everyone else liked tea, so I made gallons of it. Nate claimed my sweet tea was the first he'd ever had, and he loved it.

"I'm leaving for Texas tomorrow." The announcement from Lew stunned me as everyone sat around the table; Finn and I were putting away the dishes.

"I don't understand. Gid won't be back by then, and we aren't ready." Leaving Finn disturbed me deeply. Lew held up his hand to stop me.

"I'm not bringing you or Gideon, I'm going alone, and I intend on bringing your grandparents back if they're alive." I looked up at him.

"Her and Papa, right?" I ask suspiciously.

"I'll do what I can, I promise." I knew he didn't get along with my grandpa, but he surely wouldn't leave him behind. That's what all the whispered conversations between him and Doc must have been about, and they must have hatched this on the way to get the spices and pots for me.

The next morning, I cooked several soft tacos for him to take on the road. They spent the morning before dawn filling Doc's Dodge dually with diesel from his storage tanks. The cans and the 60-gallon tank were topped off as they figured out how much he would need for there and back. Of course, that's with clear roads and no mechanical or human issues. He borrowed a rifle from Doc and took it and a sidearm and stacked them in the truck with another AR and hundreds of rounds of 5.56. He left his .308 behind so that he could shoot the same ammo out of either rifle.

"How far is it?" I asked him as he hugged me before leaving.

"1600 miles there and back, I reckon. Three days with no trouble. Don't come looking for me for three weeks, though, and bring a sack for my bones if it's been that long." He smiled at me. That's where Gid got that dumb saying from.

He pulled me to the side to speak alone. "I trust Doc, or I wouldn't leave you here with him, but tell Gid no more overnight trips away from home until I get back. I will feel better with him here instead of doing side projects for Doc. Could be plenty of dangerous people still around." I agreed with him, understanding. "Keep working on your shooting, and I'll be back as fast as I can." He started walking away, then came back and hugged me again. Straightening his arms, he looked down at me, "Do you love that boy?" I'm speechless and completely taken by surprise.

"Um, ah, I don't know." I stammered out.

"Okay, just be sure before you end up naked underneath him." I'm so embarrassed by this unexpected talk that I want the earth to swallow me. He put his hand under my chin, raising my eyes to his, so blue like mine, and said, "It's hard when you're young, I know, but be careful. If I get back to your Granny and you're in a family way, she will switch the hide off of both of us. Probably throw in one for Gideon, too, for not protecting your virtue." We both laughed, thinking of different times in our lives when we faced her wrath and switch.

"Please come back," I said, doing all I could to hold the tears back and failing.

"Dry those tears, I said I promise." He embraced me again and, without a backward glance, he was in the truck and heading south down the gravel.

I wiped my face with my hand and headed back in, and I heard a voice from the dark. "I never met a more capable man; he'll be back when he can." A struck match lit up his face before it was stuffed into a pipe. "I convinced him to go get them instead of going to Texas with all of you. It's not just that I would be lonely; I truly believe we can live a fuller life here. We have had enough food and fuel for years, and we are never running out of ammunition. I feel like the last few years of your grandparents' lives would be more fulfilling at this place." He patted the bench beside him, and I sat down, feeling the cool wood through my nightgown.

"My granny is only around sixty, so she's got twenty good years left," I told him, and he chuckled, drawing on his pipe and sending pungent smoke out.

"Honey, the days of old people regularly making it to eighty are probably gone for a few generations. A sickness that we used to bitch about taking antibiotics over because it gives us constipation could very well be deadly now. Any accident that would send you to the emergency room is likely a death sentence. You, youngsters, need to enjoy your lives, but you also need to be careful. Women will die in childbirth more often, and there will be no more smallpox vaccines. It's a new world and will be for some years. Now, before I catch typhus or die from consumption, can you get on the cookstove for an old man?" He grinned in the dark, and I saw his teeth flash and smiled back.

"Why do you think you'd be lonely if Gid and I went to Texas? Wouldn't you come with us?"

He stood up groaning, "No, my traveling days are done, I got one long trip in me, and that's to the hereafter. To be honest, I'm starting to look forward to it. I know there won't be one Texan accent there, and I'll never have to eat that bowl of fire you made the other night for supper again," he joked.

"Well, the food is not Texan, it's from our neighbors right across the river, and the place you're going in the afterlife may not sound like Texas, but you can bet it's going to be as hot," I told him as he shook with laughter, and we headed in.

Once Doc had a cup of coffee with him, I thought about something else he said. About being alone, and I asked him what he meant. "Well, I think everyone else would pack in and go with you." I'm surprised he would think Becca would leave him.

"Becca wouldn't leave you no matter what happened, silly." I slapped him playfully on his wandering hand, going to the biscuit platter.

"I lost Becca the night she saw your uncle lying in that hospital bed. Strange that she's nowhere to be seen this morning, isn't it?" He drained his cup and mumbled that he was going to wake the boy up, meaning Jimmy.

What did he mean by that? Were they lovers? What did Doc see that I didn't? They both surprised me this morning about what they perceived and what I didn't. I would ask Becca about this after breakfast.

64 Gideon

We pushed fifteen more of these hardheaded cows into the pasture and stripped down the horses in the barn. The dark cloud over Gwen seemed to have lifted when we left Atlantic. The closer we got home, though, the more she fell into a funk. It was midday on the fourth day we had left, so no one was expecting us back, and everyone was gone except Maryn.

She hugged us, then sent us to the showers to clean up. She said everyone else was looking at a new pasture to plant next year, maybe. We tossed our weapons in our rooms, stripped down, and went to the shower together. We walked to the showers together like that's the way it's always been done, and if she was comfortable with it, I sure as hell wasn't going to complain. We both stood under the hot water for a few minutes, letting the road wash off—Gwen, with her arms out on the wall opposite me, mirroring my actions under the showerhead. The water covered our faces and seemed to isolate us from the rest of the world. Her closeness made me happy, and we lost ourselves for a few minutes.

After showering and brushing our teeth, we got dressed, not expecting to see anyone; neither of us had brought clothes to the shower. Seeing Maryn's standing in the hallway and her face go from confusion to realization to embarrassment jolted me back to our reality, though. She spun around and left the living quarters after getting a full frontal of both of us walking down the hallway in only shower slides. Gwen turned to me with a worried look, and I smiled at her, letting her know it was okay.

Sitting at the table, I could feel the tension in Maryn. She had barely glanced our way since we came into the dining room.

“Maryn, sit down and talk to me,” I said, and she sat and poured herself a glass of tea.

“Sorry about that, earlier,” I told her, flipping up the cheesecloth she had covering biscuits left over from breakfast and snatching one.

“I didn’t know you two were...” she trailed off, and I looked at Gwen.

“You didn’t know that we took showers?” I asked her as I tasted the delicious bread. I grabbed a cold Dr Pepper from the fridge and opened it after Gwen stood and poured herself a glass of tea.

“No, ugh, I mean about you two, well, ugh....” She trailed off and hurriedly put in, “If you are, it's none of my business, and I’m sorry for walking in on you, but you were in a public place.” She reddened.

“True, and I’m sorry for that. I need to know something, though.” She looked up at me.

“What?” I leaned forward, “What was more shocking to you? Gwen’s tits or my enormous hog?” Gwen snorted at that, and Maryn turned beet-red.

I laughed, and she stood up and said, “I hate you!” That got me going.

“Since you don’t have a pie ready for me, let’s call it even.”

“I built you a pie,” she claimed.

“Yeah? Where is it, pray tell?” I asked her.

“We ate it,” she admitted with a grin. I went to chase her, and she shrieked and pretended to run around the counter. Just for that, I had one on standby.

“Don’t pretend you haven’t seen Finn naked in that same hallway.” I grinned at her discomfort, and as my words sank in, she got more flustered, and I’m worried she forgot how to breathe. She stared down at me after getting her composure.

“I haven’t seen any man naked, even after today,” Gwen chortled at that, and Maryn plowed on, “and I’m only sorry that I surprised Gwen. It was really like walking into the gym showers and seeing two girls naked, to be honest.” Gwen was in hysterics now, and Maryn was building steam, about to continue, but I stopped her.

“Why are there truck tracks leaving the yard around back?”

She explained where and why Lew has taken off.

“How long has he been gone?” I ask, trying to calculate where he might be.

“Today is the third day, so he should already be on his way back and maybe getting here tonight or tomorrow,” Maryn said hopefully.

“Hmm,” I replied, thinking the roads wouldn’t be clear that far, most likely.

“Also, he wanted me to tell you not to go off overnight until he gets back,” she said, then went to the fridge to start getting food ready for supper.

“Want some help with supper?” I asked.

“Why don’t you go nap for an hour or so? I’ll wake you before everyone is supposed to be back, and if they come back early, oh well, you two can have some privacy," she left that hanging and didn't seem to believe me about us not having sex. Understandable, I supposed.

"Better be some coconut pie here at supper or else...." I let that hang as she shooed us out of the kitchen. We left her to it and settled into the bed, and both were asleep almost instantly.

65 Maryn

After supper that night, Becca asked if I needed any help with cleaning up. I nodded, and she told the boys she would be up in a few minutes. They rushed out, and she looked at me.

I asked her, “Are you involved with my uncle?” Her eyes widened and then narrowed.

“What did he tell you?” She asked, surprised.

“Nothing but your grandpa suspects,” I said.

“Ah, what did he say?” I told her.

“He’s crafty, and he’s right. I do have feelings for Llewellyn, but we haven’t told a soul. I wasn’t sure how you would feel about it.”

“I just want him to be happy, and I’m not sure why you think I would have a problem with it? I know he’s a pain in the ass to Gid and me sometimes, but if you two are happy, I’m happy.”

“Well, he’s a few years older than me, but we have something. Is the age difference a big deal?” She asked me anxiously.

“Beats me, I’ve never had a relationship, inappropriate or otherwise,” I teased, and it was her turn to flush red.

“Your grandpa told me this morning that young people need to get busy living, and he already knows about you, and he knows about me, too, with Finn.” I confided. “He has plenty of time to figure things out while he works the hell out of the rest of us, so maybe he does know something we don’t,” she giggled at my assessment.

"Why didn't you see him off that morning?" I'm horrified that he spent what little time he had that morning with me instead of Becca.

"Oh, I saw him." She admitted softly, "I waited for him at the end of the road on his way out." So the old man had been right about that as well.

Hours later, I went to bed. I noticed Gwen was gone, and I knocked on her door, and she answered with her hair pulled back with one hand and a brush in the other. She smiled at me and waved me inside. Stepping in, she put her hair up in a twist, secured it with a tie, and reached for her pack. Reaching inside, she pulled out the bag I gave her with the pads before she left and opened it. She handed it to me, and there were a dozen packages inside, each like a stuffed envelope. I looked at her, confused, and she nodded, then gave them to me. I pulled one out, and it was a dress pattern. I looked at her, and she smiled with her warm, grey eyes, hugged me, and mouthed, thank you' to me. I hugged her back, glad I had helped her while she was gone, and promised myself I would make her a dress first. I took the leather bag into my room, then took out the patterns and laid them on my bed. I took the remaining pads back to the infirmary.

Supper that next night had Doc in high spirits. He had big plans, and he began to unveil them to us, a little at a time, for our long-term survival. Cutting trees for fuel, both to keep us warm in years to come when the fuel and solar fail, as they eventually would, and to cook with. He wanted to construct a smokehouse to cure meat and a viable slaughterhouse. The wood we could get started on right away and get the lumber, too, but the actual design he wanted to get Lew's and, if possible, my grandfather's advice on, since he had one in

Texas.

"Living here will be great for five, six years maybe, but you young people will most likely want to consider how to survive with no power, fuel, or canned foods except what you grow and can yourselves. The MREs and survival foods may say they last 25 years, but I wouldn't count on anything past 5. My son expected more people to live here in case something happened, so there's plenty of room and resources for now. What he didn't foresee was something that was so...permanent. My point is, we must take steps now to ensure our group's survival for many years. I won't always be here to give you my sage advice and counsel or to make the best food that's ever been on a grill, so pay attention while we have this opportunity. Maryn, like always, thank you for preparing the food today, and I hope it's something tangy like that sticky chicken you made last week.

"It's a TexMex dish tonight," I said as I set the Taco Shepherd's Pie on the table. Doc gave it a doubtful look, and Nate looked like he already had heartburn. These Iowa men are going to have to get tougher, I thought to myself.

"Does this have hot seasonings in it?" Doc asks suspiciously.

"No, just some mild taco seasoning I made and some homemade salsa," I sat down and dished a helping on his plate.

"It smells spicy, so that's good. It's been a while since I spent two days in a row with flames coming out of my ass."

Jimmy looked at him, "You won't be able to say that tomorrow." Throwing one of Doc's favorite sayings back at him. Everyone roared with laughter at Jimmy's crack, and Doc looked crestfallen. I can't help but laugh, seeing him squirm at being the butt of a joke. He ate two helpings of the food, and even Nate seemed to like the dish. The last bit, Jimmy hustled off to Chunk as we went up top to sit around in the dusk for a bit.

Doc pointed out that a couple of other benches needed to be built and that it had been an oversight on his part not to have done so long ago. "Good thing you didn't, because you can now teach everyone else how to do it. Carpentry, electrical, plumbing, and farming are all things we need to learn, as you said earlier. Maybe after you've taught everyone those things, you can teach us how to smoke a pipe and drink whiskey?" I teased him.

Nate smiled around his pipe, "He's already taught me a lot about that," and raised his glass, and both the old men laughed.

Gwen signed something to Gid, then got up from the truck tailgate and headed up the gravel road. Jimmy asked if he and Chunk could go with her, and she hesitated for a second, as if she was about to say no, but she nodded and petted the dog. They walked off in the darkening evening, with Jimmy throwing a ball in the air, trying to catch a bat, and only catching Chunk.

Gid got up and said he's going to clean up the kitchen, and I followed him in. It's the first time we've been alone in days, and I want to talk to him. We left Nate, Becca, and the old men laughing in our wake.

I ran the water in the huge sink and added a little Dawn. Chunk had already consumed all the excess food, so the plates were ready for soapy water. After washing them and handing them off to Gid, I ask him what happened when they found Gwen.

"Some men had her and some others captive." He said without elaborating.

"Captive for what?" He rinsed the plates off and looked at me without saying anything.

He glared at me, "No, I mean what else, I know what men do to women when they can get away with it," I told him.

"Well, they had the women washing their clothes and cooking, the men they sent out to start farming, and whatever task they were too lazy to do themselves. Hell, maybe they even raped the men, too. I don't know and didn't ask. They didn't get away with it, though."

"You killed them?" I know the answer.

"We'll never have to deal with them again."

"She's in love with you?" I asked, knowing this answer too, but he shook his head. Surprising me.

"It's not like that. I bring her peace somehow, and she does the same for me, so we're just close. It's not sexual, I told you."

"Only because she turned you down, you mean?"

"Finn told me he was shy around you because he didn't really have that much experience around girls, but I told him not to worry because you had been with the entire basketball team and had plenty of experience." He smirked, and I looked at him in horror.

He reached into the sink, cupped his hand, and splashed dirty dishwasher water on my face. Wiping my face and trying to slap him at the same time, he darted off laughing. I couldn't tell whether he was serious because that's the kind of stunt he would pull. Sometimes I really could stick a knife in him. He ran through the door laughing and was gone, leaving me to wonder why I didn't devour him in the womb.

66 Llewelyn

It took me three days to get here, but I turned off the Dodge about half a mile from the house. I want to walk in and check things out before anyone around here could hear me. The old road heading in was filled with more than dust. I had only been here a handful of times since the Army sent me to South Carolina. My father and I didn't get on, and I wasn't sure why exactly. He held something against me but would never come out and say it. He had issues with Charles, too, so I know it wasn't just me, but then again, I didn't get on with Charles much in the end either, so maybe it was all three of us that were the problem.

It took me only a few minutes for the old home place to come into view. It was the middle of the afternoon, and chickens were scratching around in the yard. She always had a goose or two around as well, and they were mean as hell for the most part, I remembered. Chickens scattered as I walked up to the front porch and called out through the screen.

"Mama? Mama, are you here?" I heard rustling noises and footsteps on the old floor.

I saw her outline appear on the screen, and the guilt flooded me for not coming home sooner. I stepped back as she swung open the door, and I saw the years on her face. Sixty or so, and she had changed, but I would have recognized her anywhere. She still had warm brown eyes, but she had lines around them, and her honey-colored hair was threaded with gray. She hadn't gained a pound and was still a beautiful woman.

"Llewelyn? Baby, is that you?"

I would be lying if I told you I didn't tear up a bit with her arms around me. There is no pain like hurting your mama, and it hammered me. She broke her embrace and looked at me, tears streaming down her face, so happy to see me.

"C'mon out here so I can see you better," she pulled me onto the porch, then out into the May sunshine.

"My handsome boy, I knew you were too tough for it to get you," she hugged me again and sobbed.

She made us coffee, or I should say 'built' some coffee, because that's what she called it and always had. 'Sit a while, I'll build us some coffee' was something I heard her tell grownups all my young life. She looked at me over her cup and wiped her eyes again.

"I knew you'd come. I told the old man that if anyone would get back home, it would be you, but I fully expected you to bring all the family with you."

"Where is he?" I asked, dreading her answer either way. I had already seen the fresh pile of dirt in the family cemetery as it came in.

"Buried a month ago. Had a heart attack and died. He was sawing trees over at Mr. Bean's, helping them out, and they brought him home in the bed of his truck. I know you didn't get on with him, but he's gone now, and that's the end of it." I nodded, knowing she had loved the old man and feeling terrible for her loss.

"Now, how come you to show up here alone? Where are the others?"

"Charles is buried on the side of the highway outside of

Milwaukee, and Jess was cremated in a suburban house in Oak Creek. The twins are in Iowa." She had sobbed again at the news of Charles and Jess, but it didn't seem to shock her too much.

"Take me to them right now."

"We'll leave first thing, but I have to get some sleep first; I've spent the better part of three days getting here." I drank the coffee and set the cup in the sink.

"How's the river?" I ask her as she bustles in the kitchen, getting a skillet out of the oven.

"Low so far, go for a swim, and I'll get us some supper going." I nodded and told her I had to get the truck and bring it down first.

I grabbed a pair of shorts out of my bag, along with my rifle, and headed down to the Neches. The bend was familiar, and I saw the old rope that had been up since I could remember was still swinging in the slight breeze. I wouldn't trust my weight in it now, but Charles and I had swung it into the water hundreds of times. Just down the river, where the old Mexican fort had been. I slipped into the cool, muddy water, and the memories flooded me. My first love, how we'd made love on the sandbars, argued over our future, and finally, how it had all blown apart by different dreams. Her father wanted her to marry a church-going man, and in the end, she didn't; she married someone else. Neither I nor her father ever really got over it. Too late for amends now, or a chance to rekindle, it was all gone.

I walked back in my mostly dry shorts, and Mama saw me without a shirt. The burns had healed, but they splashed across my side and part of my back like smooth and twisted glass. The bullet holes were healed over, except the latest one, which was still pink and stitched.

Mama looked at the exit and asked who stitched it.

"Maryn, she's good at this, like you. She did some fine work with Gideon's head."

She stepped back around me and glared, "What do you mean?"

I laughed and patted her arm, "He's fine, just scratched from being clumsy."

I packed her clothes and everything else she considered necessary into the truck bed. She turned her chickens out and left a note on the kitchen table in case someone stopped by to check on her. I grabbed several jars of her honey, and we set off, blowing dust behind the truck, and the trailer rattled on the bumpy road, threatening to launch my tied-down fuel cans into orbit.

"Want to stop in and see Mr. Bean before we leave?" I asked her.

"He's not home; everyone is hiding from a roving band of outlaws that call themselves the law down here now. They have a big nest over in Lufkin. I hope we don't run into them." We didn't, and the first person we did meet wasn't even in Angelina County; it was our neighbors to the north.

The loop in Nacogdoches had an old Civic on the shoulder, hood up, with someone standing by it, checking under the hood. A woman I could see as we got closer, waving her arms at me to stop.

"Mama, don't get out of this truck no matter what. I'm going to check this out." We just passed the highway patrol station, and there wasn't anything else around here but pushed-out trucks and cars.

I grabbed my rifle, and she said, "You ain't gonna shoot her, are you?"

"No ma'am, unless she tries to do me harm. People are desperate," I opened the door and stepped into the already hot, humid air. Waves of heat danced in the distance, front and back. Not seeing anyone else, I flipped the safety off and walked over to the lady circling wide in case she was hiding a gun; she wouldn't be shooting in the direction of the truck, trying to hit me.

Her straggly brown hair was blowing in the breeze, and it was blowing the wrong way. Her scent hit my nostrils like a wave, and I could smell that she wasn't friends with a bathtub.

"Need some help, ma'am?" I said, trying not to gag over her stink.

"Thank you for stopping, mister. My car won't start." She smiled, and her teeth looked like burnt-off stumps.

"Go try to start it and let me take a look for you." She nodded, and I stepped back, forcing her to walk in front of me, and she crossed, thankfully taking that smell with her. It made my skin crawl to think of what her car smelled like inside.

I watched her slide behind the wheel and turn the car over. It started up, and I sprang out of the way as she gunned it forward, trying to hit me with the front bumper.

"Llewelyn!" I heard my mama yell and saw a man lurch from

behind the concrete barrier and come running toward her with a pistol in his hand. He's going to cross between her and me, so I pulled up the rifle on him, and he skidded on the road trying to stop. I gave him two rounds center mass from forty yards, and he and the pistol clattered on the ground.

The woman in the car yelled at me, "You killed Kevin, you bastard!" and tried to stab me with a steak knife from the car seat. I'm just out of range of it, and she opened the door, screaming the entire time, and I turned the rifle and put one round into her rotten mouth. She flew back in the seat, and I took off for the truck. Sliding behind the wheel, I dropped it into gear and took off. Her ragged car slowly crossed the road and crashed into the guardrail on the other side after crossing the grassy median. About a mile down the road, Mama looked over at me, and I expected a lecture or worse recrimination about killing.

Instead, she reached her hand over to mine and squeezed it and said, "Thank you for coming to get me."

She went into the ammo box on the floor between us, opened it, retrieved a fresh magazine, dropped the old one out of my rifle, and slammed the fresh one home. "Did you bring me one, too?" she asked, and I smiled at her. Tough, I thought as I jerked my head to the back seat.

The drive back was easier for two reasons. I cleared the traffic heading down, and the other was that no one ever fled north during a crisis. It took me almost three days to get here because I had to clear the road and the bridges along the way. I made a mental note to tease Doc about people not rushing to the land of bland food and testicle festivals when shit hit the fan. Mama commented on the clear freeway in disbelief.

"I cleared some of it off the road to get through, especially around Kansas City and Tulsa."

"Funny that people don't go north when the world ends, isn't it?" She asked, and I laughed. Great minds think alike and all that. We drove, and she asked about my life since she last saw me, about six years ago.

"I went where they sent me and didn't care much where. Stayed at Walter Reed for a spell via Germany to heal the new plastic look I got on my skin. Sent me back, then brought me back for a medal ceremony, and I've been stateside since then. I was welding at a powerhouse when all this started outside of Cleveland, and I've been with the kids as soon as I could get to them." I left out the part about going to look for Charles or the raid on the sheriff's office. There would be hell to pay when she learned of that, but for now, I left it unsaid.

The next day, I told her we would probably get there about four o'clock in the afternoon. Right past Hastings, she told me to pull into a little roadside park with a tree in the center and white poles driven in the ground. It was drizzling rain, and I said, "We're almost there."

She turned to me and said, "I know, but I want to talk to you about this before we get around anyone else."

I turned the ignition off, and she started, "First off, I didn't know all these years, I only came across this because I was looking for your father's apron to bury him in. In his Masonic box, he kept a notebook and a letter to Charles, I assume he intended to mail before this mess all happened, stashed with his Bible. I need you to read it." She reached into her sewing bag, retrieved the notebook, and handed it to me. I opened it and flipped through his various accounts and ramblings, business details with his partner, Luther Dunn: a mean bastard and Jess's father. There's a note still attached but written like a letter addressed to Charles. As I read it, I couldn't believe what he put in here, and I had to read it twice before closing the notebook and handing it back.

"You didn't know this the whole time?" I always suspected Charles, but the news about Jess really made my stomach sink. "How? Why?"

She looked at me sternly and said, "I admit I suspected about the children, but when I asked Charles about it, he assured me it wasn't true and that they were in love and had been seeing each other even while you two were dating. I also must admit I'm ashamed of how I behaved toward him. Hearing this broke my heart, because you know how I feel about Jess. The truth is, they did it for two reasons: one to keep her from losing her daddy in every sense, the other to help hide his real identity. You know how close they were. All through school, always at our house. The old man hated you and would have put her out over an unplanned pregnancy. She and Charles cooked this up and somehow slipped it by all of us except your father. I never guessed it was an arrangement, but that's what they did."

"All those years...." I felt sick inside.

"Yesterday's gone, and nothing can be done about it. I wish it were different, but it never will be, so we need to fix this as best as possible," she pointed out sadly.

"You think I should tell them?" I asked her.

"You mean to keep lying to them?" She asked, and I stared dumbly ahead, not sure what to do. "I think you should look at this as the gift it is. It's not every day a man finds himself rich like you have today."

The thought took me aback. She hardened her voice and told me, "No more lying and hiding this. Families get torn apart by these kinds of secrets, and it's up to you to make sure this doesn't blow up. I won't have any part of a cover-up with them, so figure out how you want to tell them, or I will." A velvet glove but a steel fist inside.

67 Gideon

The last two days thundered and stormed with a mix of light and heavy rain. Doc grumbled about the weather, though he claimed the crops needed it, and he didn't have to feed the chickens or horses in it. It did put a halt to his outside pipe smoking, though. We shot in the mornings; I worked on perfecting my quick draw with my pistol under Doc's scorn, exercised, and read some books the old man dug out about homesteading and carpentry. He laid out what he wanted to build before winter set in this year, and he added a lean-to over his bench and wood smoker to the list.

I talked with Gwen and had the time and opportunity to have a candid talk with her about us. I explained that she wasn't beholden to me in any way and that I didn't want her to feel pressured to spend so much time with me.

"Do you like being with me?" she asked.

"I do."

"What's the problem then?"

"I won't bring this up again, but I want to know how you feel and why you believe we are so close." She looked confused for a second and then replied.

"I never had peace before. I feel safe with you, but if you are uncomfortable, I will stay in another room."

"No, it's not that. I just want you to understand that you don't owe me anything for getting you out of Atlantic. I like you being close, and it brings me peace as well, but you aren't obligated," I think I've made her understand. She stood up, walked to the door, and suddenly turned around.

"I like the way it is. If you do too, let's keep it this way. I intend on living my life the way I want, and being near you makes me happy. If you aren't in the same place, then we can make a change," she waited for my answer.

"I like it the way it is. No need to change anything. If you're happy, I'm happy." I tell her, and she walks over and kisses my cheek.

"Let's be happy, then."

When the storm seemed to pass to the south in the afternoon, I was outside with Doc and Jimmy when I heard the clatter of a diesel. I looked down the road, but, of course, there was no dust from the rain. I saw the red flash between the fallow fields, then the entire truck. I told Jimmy to get Maryn, and he darted off. As they turned in, I watched Lew and another passenger, but I couldn't make them out in the low light as Chunk bounced and danced by the driver's door. He pulled around back, and I walked back, and he shut the engine down and stepped out. The other door opened, and it's my granny. She beamed when she saw me, and I ran to hug her.

"Oh, baby, I was so worried. Look at you, you're grown!" She squeezed me with surprising strength. Maryn called from behind me, "Granny!" and ran up to us, and I wrapped my arms around both.

Lew said from the back of the truck, "Boys, help me get this truck unloaded," and I heard them walk past us. Releasing Granny, I saw Doc standing by his bench with water dripping from the shop behind him. "Are you going to introduce me to your aunt?" he slyly asked me.

The supper that night was a mix of good and bad news. I was sad to hear about Papa, but seeing my granny here really made me happy. It was strange at first because I always associated her with her warm kitchen or, mostly, her garden. Picking tomatoes, pruning roses, and cooking were things that most of my memories were built on. Her homemade dress and this commercial stainless-steel kitchen seemed out of sorts, like two cultures clashing, which I supposed is what it was, in a sense. She was introduced to everyone and never had to be told a name again, forever remembering them. Maryn made spaghetti that night, and Granny complimented her, and she beamed at the high praise. After supper, she ushered us outside and out of her hair. Gwen came with me, but Becca and Maryn stayed behind, and I assumed they would fill her in on the living situation around here. When they came up, there were big smiles all around, and I wondered what was afoot with them.

The next morning, after we finished eating, Granny asked Doc. “Have you assigned everyone chores to do every day?”

He shrugged, “Not anything set in stone. The boy gathers eggs and- “she cut him off there,

“His name is Jimmy.”

“Yes, ma’am, Jimmy gathers eggs, and Gideon usually feeds the horses and tends to them. We all just kind of do what we want.”

“Well, it’s been my experience that if you let men do whatever they want with no direction, they’ll be neck deep in trouble or won’t do anything at all. Please stay and let’s talk for a bit, Mr. Smith.”

She looked at Lew, "Llewelyn, I believe there's something you need to discuss with the twins, isn't there?" Lew looked like a trapped animal. That was our cue to go away because, from the look on her face, Doc was about to feel her claws, not the tender scratches from Maryn. I was the last one out, and as I closed the door, I heard her say, "First thing, you have Jimmy sleeping in your truck?" I'm thankful it's him in there and not me. She had a world of patience for children, but not for much else.

The sky was clear, and the overnight moon was still visible when we poured out into the backyard. We all took off for the barn, and Jimmy held up his hand to stop us at the beginning of the field.

"Let's race to the barn," he exclaimed, and I turned to him and pointed back at the shop.

"First, you need to get that," I said, pointing behind him. When he turned to look, I bolted, and I heard him screaming behind me, "CHEATER!" It made me laugh, and I almost lost my footing. By the time I got to the barn, only Lew was almost able to catch me. I hit the barn door gasping, and when Jimmy got here with his disappointment, I had almost recovered.

"Not fair, Gideon, you cheated." He pouted. Everyone piled on about how much of a low-life scoundrel I was for the dirty trick. They all wrestled me to the ground, and I mean all of them except Gwen, who looked on with bewilderment and not a little anxiety. Lew grabbed my waist; Maryn grabbed my left arm; then Becca, Finn, and Jimmy got on. Once they had me on the ground, Jimmy called Chunk over, and he licked my face while I squirmed under his hot tongue.

"First place is dog kisses!" Jimmy chanted repeatedly to

everyone's hilarity. Once they started to get off, I stood up, wiping my face, glaring at Chunk Norris and at them. This made them laugh even more, and I walked into the barn, leaving them in stitches.

After feeding was done, we checked on the animals, we watched the donkeys try to murder Chunk, and saw Alice flash her teeth at Becca, trying to nip her on the shoulder. We went to look over the chickens. Jimmy went in, spoke to them in a low voice, as he did, and gathered their eggs. He made sure his biddies were fine, the feeder was working correctly, and the water level was right. Satisfied, he came over to us with the bucket.

"Okay, Gideon, this time no cheating, and since you did last time, you have to carry the eggs while we race."

I took the bucket and said, "Even with these eggs, I think I can-" I took off mid-sentence, leaving them in the dust again. I'm in full flight, and I hear Jimmy hollering behind me. I assumed, distraught over being tricked again, but a second later, something hit me in the back of my legs. I fell into the muddy rows, dropping the bucket, and landed on the ground. After rolling over, I saw mud and eggs scattered around, with Chunk Norris chasing the rolling eggs like tennis balls and crunching them in his jaws. I had the breath knocked out of me, and instead of getting the eggs, Jimmy ran past me, laughing like an idiot, and then everyone came. No one helped me to my feet as they streamed past, and it took me a few moments to regain my wind. Standing and seeing them all laughing by the shop, I vowed to make everyone pay for today's indignity. Gwen rubbed my back while I got control of myself, helped me pick up the overturned bucket, and took the five eggs; the rest were broken on the dark soil or down Chunk's gullet.

Doc and Granny were standing by the door when I got down to the shop. She looked at me, disheveled with mud everywhere, and then in the bucket. “Five eggs about what you turn out every morning from two dozen Iowa hens?” She looked over at Doc.

“Well, maybe the rain turned them off?” He tried.

She rolled her eyes and looked at me sternly. “This is exactly what I was talking about with youngsters with no direction.”

68 Llewelyn

The old lady's appearance had shaken the foundations around here already. She already cowed Doc, and he left her to organize the work and help him lay out what needed to be done and in what order. He handed the day-to-day to her. After this morning's debacle, I pulled the twins aside. I told Gid to go saddle horses for the three of us. When he came trailing horses, he had four saddled. Gwen mounted on the pinto she named Mix. I looked up at her, about to say something, then shook my head and changed my mind. I climbed onto Alice, and they followed me.

I took them to a little spot on the confluence of Jordan and Farm Creeks. It's a spot Jimmy and Maryn had shown me one day when I was out checking on the cattle and came upon them fishing. They had dragged a couple of downed pin oaks closer to the water to make makeshift fishing benches. I walked my horse to the edge and dismounted.

Looking at Gwen, I asked, "Gwen, do you mind watching the horses for a bit? I want to share this news with the twins alone." She took the reins he handed to her and gathered ours as well.

She looked down at Gid nervously, but he smiled at her and said, "I'll be right back." She smiled back, and I turned to Maryn, as he was walking to the water's edge. The rain made it slick, and he nearly lost his footing, falling into the mud for the second time today.

"Have a seat," I waved to the smaller tree, and they did. "I'm going to tell this straight through, and I know you will have questions. Keep in mind it's been a while ago, and I'm only one of three involved in this, so I don't know how exactly everything played out." I sighed and sat on the bigger tree trunk.

"Your mama married Charles right after we got out of school because she got pregnant. Your grandfather Luther would have disowned her and you two as well if he found out she got pregnant out of wedlock. He was religious, as you know, and she was his only child left alive. His property, money, and even what passed for love for him would have been forfeit. I can't make you understand his mindset because it's from a different time, and I never understood him anyway. If your grandmother hadn't died early, maybe she could have tempered him, but who knows? He hated me, and always did, for some reason, so my opinion of him is tainted. I want you to understand that, too. The only reason that he would let his daughter around us was that he partnered with your Papa on timber contracts. I don't know the details, because I avoided both men whenever I could, and I sure as hell didn't ask them anything that would make me stay in their company a second longer than I needed to. Those are hard truths, and everyone in this story shares some blame. Me, most of all."

"I want you to understand the situation your mother found herself in, so you don't judge her too harshly for her decisions and maybe understand why she did the things she did. A daughter's love for her daddy is special. Hell, I've seen women dote on their daddies who were complete trash and had mistreated them their whole lives, abandoning them, mentally and sexually abusing them, even, and they still love him. Boys and their mamas are similar, but the point is, she was devoted to her no-account daddy, and she wouldn't want to break his heart. Also, keep in mind that Luther didn't like Charles either, but it was nothing like what he felt toward me. In all fairness, I was a wild boy, and it gave my father fits, so I can't expect a man with a daughter my age to be happy about her being in the same county as me, let alone at our house all the time. She rode the school bus home with us, and we played together until her daddy thought she was getting too old to be hanging around boys, especially boys like me. By then, it was too late, and she was sneaking out to come over on the regular."

"In the end, she defied her father and kept meeting the man she loved, and risked it all, and they married and ran off together? That sounds like a romance novel to me." Maryn seemed happy about that. I knew that happiness wouldn't last.

"Not exactly," I said, feeling uncomfortable. Being like this was new to me; I was usually confident in most things, but this was unfamiliar.

"She was sneaking out to see the man she loved, but it wasn't Charles she was meeting with secretly. It was me."

Her eyes went wide with surprise, but Gideon said, "For a minute there, I thought you were going to tell us something scandalous like she was having an affair with Papa or some such."

"There's more to it than that, if you two will keep your teeth together, we'll soldier through." My face darkened at his quip. "Jess and I were in love our last year of school. I wanted to leave and join the service to escape our fathers, but she wouldn't leave him on his own, even though he was a complete bastard. I pleaded with her, but she wouldn't budge and told me that if he found out about us, it would kill him, so we could never be together. Keep in mind your grandfather had lost his wife and two other children in a car accident when Jess was thirteen, so she didn't want to cause him any more distress.

Really didn't have much to do with his land or money, as my daddy thought. Anyway, I left for the Army, thinking she would change her mind when I got back from boot camp. I came home, we reconciled and then fell out again when I pushed her to leave and come with me after I was stationed somewhere. She refused, and when I was out of AIT, I got a letter from Mama telling me that Jess and Charles had married, and that the following spring, you two were born. Imagine my surprise and heartbreak over that. I thought they must have been carrying on in secret behind my back, and her daddy was furious about her marrying someone not from the church, but she did brace him about that, and he learned to somewhat get over it. I was in a black rage about it and held it against both until yesterday. Your granny found a letter Papa had written to Charles, telling him that everything was forgiven and that he should come back home. Unfortunately, he never mailed the letter, and soon after he wrote it, the world fell apart. In that letter, your Papa mentioned he knew Charles wasn't your father."

"You?" She asked, tears streaming down her face. "It's you, isn't it? She got pregnant, and you were gone, and she got married to hide it, didn't she?" I nodded without looking at her.

I felt like someone punched me in my stomach. "She never told you?" Maryn asked, and I shook my head.

"She never told anyone?"

"No," I said.

"She strained her relationship with your Granny, the woman she was closest to, over this secret. Of course, after Luther died, they hid it not to hurt you, so in a way, she did something that she felt was right to protect her family, and I want you to look at it like that. She loved you two more than anything, so it's understandable. I was tempted to bury it myself, but I knew your Granny would tell you, and maybe she's right. Anyway, that's the broad strokes of it."

"There's something else, isn't there? Something isn't quite fitting in my mind. How did Papa know for sure that he wasn't our father? There's no way to know that for sure," Gideon wondered.

I looked at him and said, "Charles didn't have sex with women." Maryn looked faint, not with disgust but with surprise.

"He's gay?" Gideon asked.

"I suspected early on. The only difference between the other boys we lived around, and him was that he didn't seem too interested in girls. Ever. I was fishing one day and saw him kissing what I now know to have been an older boy from school, who was openly gay. I'm sorry I never told him he's still my brother; it wouldn't have changed how I feel about him. I didn't, though, and now that's never going to happen." Gideon stood up and walked to the water's edge. "We all made mistakes and decisions that affected each other's lives. The right thing to do isn't still clear to me, but you know now. I don't expect you to feel any different about me, or to change what you call me. I only ask that you not hold it against us for doing what we thought was right at the time, especially your mother, but Charles, too. I love you two, and I will spend the rest of my life trying to protect you. I'm fond of Becca, and that may develop into something down the road, but you two are the only children I will ever have." I walked back up the bank and waved Gwen over with the horses.

"If he was gay, why did you think he got my mama pregnant and married her behind your back?" she asked.

"I wasn't sure of his sexuality, only suspected. When I asked, he denied it all and started dating girls regularly. I believed I made a mistake by misidentifying the person he was kissing that day, and after I thought they had cuckolded me while I was off in the Army, I was furious at both for a long time after, and the deception was ironclad then. When I'd see you at the house for the holidays, they would never answer any of my questions about it, so I had no closure or understanding of the situation. The point is I know the truth now, and you do, too."

69 Maryn

When I went into the shelter, Granny rushed over to hug me. My eyes were red and swollen, and her embrace comforted me. Of course, the first person I turned to for comfort was Gid down by the creek, but having her here really helped. No one said anything about our mystery ride, and we went about our day without anyone asking about the small meeting we had.

Granny took a room behind the kitchen where Becca and Doc's rooms were. This was the first time I'd been here, and it's identical to our side, except that another door opened to the right before the showers. Surprisingly, she goes to this door and opens it, and there's another shower on the left and a mirror image wing to the other living quarters. Only one room on the left was empty, and her things were in there. Doc had put her in a wing by herself. Granny sat on her bed and patted a spot beside her for me to sit.

"Honey, I'm sorry that things are the way they are, but that can't be changed. I know you may resent me for pressuring Llewelyn to tell you the truth, but you need to always understand how things ARE, not just how they seem. Knowing the truth about situations, we can make better decisions and choices, even when the reality is a bitter pill to swallow." Of course, I wasn't angry with her, but it would have felt better if I hadn't known. I didn't see the upside in knowing this was just the pain.

"I don't feel better knowing." She took my hand and looked in my eyes.

"We don't make decisions on how we feel, do we? We make them based on facts and reality. Leave the rashness to Gideon and focus on your ability to ponder problems and situations. You two are the heirs to our places in Texas, and I fully expect you to return one day and make it your home. For three hundred years, there's been a Spears at that homestead, and it will continue."

"We aren't staying here?" I asked her.

"Honey, this isn't our home. Now, let's switch gears and talk about this Iowan lad you have a fever for," she smirked.

I blushed at that, and I'm starting to understand that there were no secrets in our small community. "He's sweet," I say, caught flat-footed by her even suggesting my feelings toward Finn.

"Sweet is one thing, but men and women now need to have the bark on, as my daddy used to say. Your father, your real father, is so rough he wears out his clothes from the inside first, and that's the type of man this new world needs. You and your children will one day manage our home, and you need a steady partner who shares your goals." She stood and ushered me up. She hugged me and whispered, "Keep the talk of returning to Texas just between us girls for right now, okay?"

Supper that night was so good that even Doc was smiling all through the meal. I think the great weight of running this operation had started to fray him, and now, after he and Granny had spent hours today plotting and planning, a burden seemed to have been lifted off him. I was worried at first about Granny taking over the plans for and management of the shelter, but Doc and Becca seemed pleased by it. For the first time, everyone seemed able to relax and enjoy being alive. She was a far better cook than I was, and that instantly improved the mood.

The first thing she insisted on was a barn and corral for milk cows. Lew, Gid, Gwen, and Doc went on the first run for lumber. I went with them, as we often didn't get a chance for a town trip. The world's silence was eerie, and we didn't see a soul. We drove to a hardware store with both trucks, Doc's Dodge and our old '97, trailers on both, and loaded in all the lumber and hardware we could carry off.

The next day, it was the same. On the third day, Granny asked Becca, Finn, and me to look for some suitable milk cows; Jersey or Holstein would be perfect, she told us. Becca and Doc knew of a Jersey farm not too far from Mineola, and we rode over on horseback to take a look. He told us to find them only, then he would drive over and load them onto the trailer instead of walking them this far, since they were for milking.

"You could have done that for Gid, you know," I reminded him, and he grinned.

"Have to find things for him to do so he stays out of trouble. Now just go find them, make sure they're in the loading pen, and come home. No heroics. I don't want you to be driving around this noise machine attracting attention across half of Iowa, so you will have to do the scouting the hard way." his smile told me he wasn't too upset about that, and we set off to search.

We got to the place in the early afternoon; Finn was the first to spot one, and we rode over. She acted like a puppy, with a two-week-old calf in tow. We gathered up two more, but the barn smelled like nightmare fuel as we got closer to it.

I told Finn," Let's get away from here," but he insisted on going to check and make sure nothing was alive in there. The door had claw marks on the left side, and the right side lay on its side, the hinges ripped from the wood.

"Anything that was in there is out now or dead," I said, and he agreed as the smell became so overpowering. We turned to leave when a loud growl came from behind Finn. I looked past him and saw dogs running towards us, snapping their jaws, barking, teeth bared. I reached into my saddlebag and pulled out my pistol. Finn's horse, one of the gelding roans Lew had brought back from Atlantic that we named Stepper, was bucking and trying to get the dogs away from his back legs. I fired into the din, and they scattered except for the two that I hit. A large yellow dog jumped on the back of Stepper, but before I can shoot it, Finn swung his fist around, crunched against the dog's skull, and he went over her back, landing hard on the ground. Finn reached for his gun while I ejected the magazine I had run through and put a fresh one in, thumbing the slide. I put two rounds in the yellow dog before he recovered and looked around for more. Four were streaking away from us, cutting across a winter wheat field.

Becca ran over to us when she heard the firing, her rifle out and scanning for targets. "What the-?" she started and saw the dog carcasses strewn on the ground. "Too bad we don't eat dog here, I bet Miss Ruth could really fry these up into something tasty," she smiled at me. "Either of you hurt?" I shook my head and looked at Finn.

He's checking his horse and said, "Stepper got some blood here." Becca rode over and looked down at his hock.

"Scratched the hell out of him. We'd better get camped, and that attended to."

We drove the cows ahead of us, walked them about half a mile, and loaded them into a neighbor's pen. We hobbled Stepper and doctored the gash with antiseptic and purple spray. "Luckily, it's not going to affect how he rides, but once he stands around and it gets sore, you won't be able to ride him for days. We'll leave the cows here and ride for home tonight, grab the truck and come back and get them tomorrow," Becca said, and we mounted back up.

When we pulled into the barn that night and unsaddled the horses, I was dead tired and sore. The wound on Stepper was bleeding again, and Doc chewed our asses for riding him back that night instead of walking him. Becca tried to explain her reasoning, but he wouldn't hear it.

"I won't have these horses misused in any way, even if it means you have to walk twenty miles back home. From now on, when you are out in Indian country, and there may be dangerous creatures or people, have your fucking guns out and ready." He looked at Finn and me and stomped off to treat Stepper. It was the first time he had been angry with me, and I felt terrible.

Doc and Lew rode out with us to the site the next day and examined the dogs' bodies while we gathered up the cows. After studying them for signs of rabies, Doc asked again what happened. I didn't want to embarrass Finn, so I said he'd killed the yellow dog and that we'd both been firing at the pack. The front of the barn was mostly concrete, and Lew collected the spent casings and threw them into a ditch of high grass. He asked Finn to see his firearm, drew it from his hip holster like Gid carried, and handed it over. He dropped the magazine into his hand and examined it. Slamming it back home, he handed the weapon to Finn, who holstered it. Without a word, he saddled back up and waited for Doc to finish his business.

Doc backed up the cattle trailer to the neighbor's pen we used, and we loaded the cows. They got into the truck, and Lew pulled me aside as I walked to the cab. While we were loading them up, two bay horses ran in from the pasture, nickering and snorting. Doc called Lew over and asked him to catch them up and bring them back to the house.

"These horses are riders, so get saddles out of their barn and bring them back with you." He said, pointing over to the livery.

"Can't just load them into the trailer with the cows?" Lew asked, reasonably.

"Yeah, and they may not ride and kick the hell out of my trailer or worse, your mama's milch cows. You want to tell her that the only milk producers in the county got kicked to hell because you were too lazy to ride a horse fifteen miles?" He didn't even wait for an answer and climbed up and closed the trailer gate.

"Thought you said they were riders?" Lew asked.

"Yeah, I've seen them saddled, but never in a trailer. You want to risk it?" Lew shook his head, and we got the tack from the barn and set it on the loading pen fence. Once Doc pulled away a bit, Lew called them in with a bucket of feed, and we saddled them. Seeing them saddled, Doc waved from the truck and laughed like hell, yelling out the window.

"I'll tell your mama you'll be late for supper!"

"Twelve-year-old grandpa," he said, laughing to himself as he led one over to me. I mounted, and the horse seemed a bit skittish but soon settled down. Once we both got the mares out of the pen and were walking toward home, he turned to me.

"Protecting people you care about is an important virtue, and I appreciate how much you care for that boy. Having said that, I know you are the one who shot all those dogs, and I want to know exactly why."

I went through it; this time, the real version, and he nodded along. "First thing, great shooting, but most importantly, you didn't freeze when needed, and you didn't shoot near the horse or Finn. It's a big deal to have the sense to get into action when everyone else around you is panicking. That really can't be taught, so you have the grit for this. Your shooting needs improvement, though," he winked at me. "The old man is right about having your firearm handy out here, too." I nodded, and we started for the truck when he stopped again and looked at me.

"It's my first full day as your father, and you are already lying to me, tsk, tsk," he added, smiling.

About two hours later, I asked him about my mama. "Did Mama always like you, like love at first sight kind of thing?"

He took a deep breath and said, "In a way, I suppose yes, we met as youngsters, you know, before the powerful pull of puberty and all that, but we always were easy around each other. All three of us, honestly. In school, people mistakenly thought we were siblings; we were so close. In a fashion, yes, I've loved her from the beginning."

"You loved her even after she married your brother?" I asked incredulously.

"It's our secret, but I still do." He looked behind us and stopped his horse, putting his binoculars up to his eyes.

"What about Becca? How do you feel about her?" I asked, not sure how or if you can love different people at the same time.

"It's different, but there are feelings." He kept the binoculars up to his eyes while answering.

"You don't feel the same for her as you did for my mama?"

"That young man and woman are gone like the sandbar we fell in love on. It will never be the same again, and that's a fact. I think you can love again after that, but never like that. Does that make sense?" He dropped the glasses and looked over at me.

"No," I replied, honestly.

He smiled and nodded. "It's hard to figure, but life will sort you out of that. Or you may fall in love with a man and stay with him for sixty years, who knows how it will play out?"

"So, you're saying you won't or can't ever love another woman like my mama?" I considered how scary that is to lose it all so young and never to find it again.

"Yes," he glassed off to our right now that we were both turned completely around looking at our back trail.

"That sounds like a Greek tragedy to me," I admit, and he dropped them again and looked at me and smiled.

"I suppose."

"What are you looking at?"

He scanned the direction we just came from, not saying anything for a moment.

"Maybe some coyotes?" He looked over at me. "Let's cut across this field and shave some time off. We'll have to cross a little river, you ain't scared, are you?" He smiled, and I returned it, shaking my head.

"Why didn't you ever fight for her, and why would she keep us a secret from you?" He stopped his horse and turned to look me in the eyes.

"She knew that if I found that out, I would have forced my way into her life and destroyed her father with the knowledge, and I would have pursued her because that's what would have made me happy. I wasn't mature enough to consider the best for her, our parents, or even you kids. As bitter as it is, she probably made the right choice. That's hard to admit, but a man must know himself. I know what I can do, what I can't, and what I can only achieve with a miracle. I face my faults every day and try to work through them, so they don't surround me and cut me off from my sanity. She was right to do what she did, and I'm not faulting her. You remember how bright she shone, and I would've smothered her with my resentments and broken her with loneliness. If you stare at your problems long enough, you will find most of the fault lies within, and it took me years to learn that, luckily, you're smarter than I am, so you have the inside track."

70 Gideon

Granny enlisted Jimmy with the milking chores, and he was, like with other animals, a natural. He still slept in the truck bed, and she still raised hell about it to Doc, but the weather was mild, and she didn't push too much. Jimmy liked to slip out when Doc came up to smoke and drink coffee in the mornings, and if he were downstairs, he wouldn't hear him. They talked every morning about animal care, medicines, diseases, cures, treatments, and the like. He helped Doc fix up Stepper, tended the chickens, did most of the cattle rotations himself, and fell in love with the milch cows, treating them like pets.

He gently broke the blue roan after asking Doc how. He walked him with a halter every day, giving him dehydrated apples as treats. When he wasn't doing his chores, he worked with Ozone or Oz, as he called her. Two weeks after he started leading her around with him, we went down to Farm Creek and into a particularly deep spot Doc knew. Jimmy walked her into the water like he did every day, except it went up to her chest. She stood there trembling, and Doc and Jimmy both brushed her and spoke to her in low, gentle tones. Jimmy slowly eased into the saddle, and Doc let go of the reins. Oz bunched her back, and crow hopped a couple of times and then splashed out of the water. Once she cleared the bank, she stood there snorting and trying to look back at this new weight on her back. Jimmy let one hand go of the reins and stroked her neck. She decided that was enough and started hopping again. Doc told Jimmy to put her back in the water, but she sped away from us and soon reached a full gallop. I heard Doc swear to himself, told me to stop laughing, and get them as we ran for the horses in the barn.

Before I had Buck saddled, Jimmy and Oz rocketed into the barn, upsetting Buck and causing chickens to scatter. She slid through the doors and almost slammed into Doc, who tripped over his own feet into some chicken shit. Between the dust, Doc cussing, and Jimmy yelling, it was mayhem. I grabbed Oz's reins and calmed her down while Jimmy jumped off and went to help Doc back to his feet. Gwen finally regained control of her mount, Mix, in the fray, and she, too, was smiling at the old man who was spilled on the ground.

"Unhand me goddammit," he growled sourly, and awkwardly got his feet, looking down at his hands, covered in shit. I did all I could not to laugh but couldn't hide the smile. He glowered at me and took off to the door, turned and looked at Jimmy, "If I ever see you run a horse to the barn again, I'll take a quirt to you!" He stomped off muttering to himself, and the three of us shared a laugh.

That night after supper, Granny and Maryn ran us out of the kitchen, and we went upstairs to sit around for a few minutes. Lew braced me about Gwen staying in my room off to the side, away from everyone else.

"Something you want to tell that grown woman she can or can't do, be my guest and tell her yourself," I dared him. He looked over at her and decided it wasn't something he was ready to delve into. Shaking his head, he went off to the barn, and Gwen and I back to the freshly made benches, to listen to Doc drone on.

She came and stood close to me while Doc bitched about the barn not being cleaned out properly and the doors being left open so chickens could get in. I told him the chickens would eat mice they found since we didn't have a cat here. "Well, no more. If we come across a cat, bring it home, but no more chickens shitting all over the floor in there." Gwen and I smiled at each other after seeing what happened today and understanding why he was pissed. Jimmy looked crestfallen with the rebuke, knowing it was one of his tasks to keep the barn clean. I looked over at him, and he brightened when he saw me smiling. I winked at him, and he hid his smile behind his hand, not wanting to anger the old man any further.

"A mean old barn cat may eat my biddies," Jimmy protested, and Doc got flustered with us sniggering and stood up, pissed off, and walked to the door.

'Figure something out, but no more chickenshit in the barn," he shot over his shoulder.

The next day, Granny pulled me to the side, and it was her turn to ask me about Gwen. So, Lew had passed the tough job over to her. "What is going on with you and that young lady?" I explained what she had been through and how it made her feel safe around me.

"She's a fool if she thinks she's safe from a young boy and his sex drive." She rolled her eyes, throwing her dish towel over her shoulder.

"Especially mine, it's a full-grown and insatiable," I said, in derision, and she whirled the towel at me. She made a big show of being frustrated with my antics, but I thought she secretly enjoyed my shenanigans.

"Boy, you aren't too old for me to bend over my knee," the anger creased between her eyes, a sign she's aggravated.

I laughed at that and said, "Gwen does that all the time, and it doesn't work."

Her face flushed at that, and her eyes grew dark. “Jokes are one thing, but that girl has been traumatized, and I won’t have it taken advantage of, and I need you to know I’m serious about that.”

I put my hands up once I was out of range of her dish towel. “We aren’t playing house if that’s what you are worried about. She needs comfort, and for some reason, she’s settled on me for it, and honestly, I’ve grown attached to her. She’s selfless and kind, and I would never take advantage of her. If she decides she wants something more with me, it will be her choice. You are more than welcome to speak to her yourself about this,” I assured her. Now was as good a time as any to put this to rest. “She can sleep in my bed for as long as she needs. I love you, but the days of someone telling me what to do with my life are over. I respect what you say, but I need you to know that if you, Doc, or Lew don’t like the arrangement we have, we will make our own way. I will be taught, counseled, and given advice, but no one will push me.” It shamed me that I might have hurt her feelings, but we needed to set some boundaries.

“I will never stop loving you or caring about what is going on in your life until you throw dirt over me. I’ll make time for Gwen and start a better relationship with her if she’s that important to you.”

“She is,” I hugged her.

“Tell your son I know it's his first week of being a dad, but he needs to pick something a little less thorny to deal with than this. He’s a shade old to be running to his mama for help.” She sent me off with a wave of her hand, half smiling and rolling her eyes.

What can I say of Gwen in those summer months besides that she bloomed? We spent so much time together that everyone else in our lives seemed like background characters. We hunted, fished, bathed, and scouted together. She learned to sew and cook from Granny, and she was interested in animal medicine like Jimmy. She spent time with him and Doc when they talked about that, but mostly, she and I were within sight of each other. She worked with me and the others in sign language, and I got good at it. She taught me bird whistles and the uses of native plants. I taught her shooting, and we all learned tactics from Lew: entering and clearing buildings, slicing the pie, ambushes, and how to defilade positions. When his shoulder is healed enough, he started us in jiu-jitsu and boxing. The shooting range turned into a fight school for us when we weren't burning through brass. We had to learn to reload rounds, break down, and clean every gun we had available. I still worked on my drawing every day, and soon I was efficient at it. The fast draw with the pistol wasn't the important thing, Lew explained, hitting your target first was. Slow is smooth, smooth is fast, he cautioned, and I took his advice and practiced with the pistol as much as the rifle.

The most challenging task for everyone, except for Lew and me, was butchering cattle and hogs. Understand, killing the animal was something I could barely bring myself to do, but a mishap with Becca stuck me with that duty after she had to shoot a yearling twice to get it down. It's not like shooting a deer or wild hogs; these animals we fed and cared for every day. Hell, I had to get onto Jimmy for naming the animals; it was hard enough for me to walk past them daily, knowing where they were headed, without knowing a pig's name.

Doc has silos with feed corn and grains that we feed them every day. Jimmy complained about carrying it to the troughs, but Doc insisted.

"If you are asking a horse to carry your sorry bones forty miles in a day, they need to be well fed and cared for," he warned us, and he was right. Feeding calves and hogs every day that you knew were meant for the table wasn't the same thing as feeding horses, though. It didn't seem to bother Lew too much, but even I didn't like this task. The actual butchering process was new to all of us except Lew, Doc, and Granny with her chickens. Doc showed us how to cut meat, remove the hide by fleshing, and wrap and store the meat properly. This part didn't bother me so much as the actual killing did. None of the others were ever as efficient at it as we were, so we mainly did all of it except chickens. Granny handled those once we had enough to start eating, and she showed all of us how to do that efficiently. It finally got to the point where Doc deemed we were as good as we would likely ever be, so he turned it all over to us. He claimed we would never be good enough to pass for Midwesterners at it, but that we were sufficient for him to go back to doing his chores, which mainly involved sitting around jawing.

I did take Jimmy on his first turkey hunt, as I promised, but it was weeks before we had any luck. Of course, the season didn't start until October, but he enjoyed going anyway, and besides, he learned all kinds of other things while out with us. The camp set up, building a fire, navigating by the stars, and Lew even showed him how to knap his own arrowheads and knife in an emergency.

When we stumbled on a bird, he missed his first shot, and I thought he would give up, but the weeks of living out here had changed him, and he became more determined. He got the next bird, and he never looked back after that. Though he never liked killing animals, he understood why it was necessary and often went with me on hunts. He was one of the few people I met in life who enjoyed the hunt, with or without bringing in game. The wildness of it, pitting yourself against prey, was enjoyable to him, no matter if he got something or not.

We had two large freezers full of meat, but we kept a close eye on them because ten people ate a lot. Once Granny determined we had enough eggs for everyone each day, she helped Jimmy raise biddies. She sent us to town to stock up on all the sugar and honey we could find, along with any seeds for vegetables, melons, and cantaloupes. She planted those, along with peppers, squash, and okra she brought from home, in the greenhouse.

Jimmy started camping outside near the garden to help keep animals out with Chunk Norris. Granny spoiled them both with treats and always made sure to compliment them on their fine work.

After Granny spoke with Gwen alone, she treated her more warmly. They laughed together while working and seemed to get along well. The women now spent most of their time outside since Granny oversaw the inside. She wanted things cleaned her way and folded a certain way and considered most of us underfoot in the way of her doing it the RIGHT way. If she wasn't giving instructions or lessons, she wanted everyone out.

We worked through the early summer until late July without letting up. We sent people out in pairs to scout two to three miles around, but mostly we were concerned about the west, where Council Bluffs and Omaha were. Lew taught us tracking, and I was reasonably good at it, but Gwen was exceptional. She and Becca were better trackers even than Lew, and he readily admitted it.

Finn spent a lot of time on the range and was usually my sparring partner when we grappled or boxed, unless he was trying to hold onto my sister, which was happening more often. I began to suspect he and Maryn were more than friends, but it was none of my business. She would tell me if she wanted me to know, but I saw them staring at each other and sometimes touching longer than necessary when they were partners on the mat. Finn and I got on well, and he did his part around here; if Maryn was interested in him, that was her decision. I can't have someone hurting her, but I can't control who she wants or doesn't. I wasn't going to do to her the same thing that Lew and Granny tried with Gwen and me; she had to make her own choices.

71 Llewelyn

Sheds went up through the heat of summer, and Doc even got his lean-to over his 'smoking' bench.' We built three more benches and chairs, enough to accommodate everyone. We all got a hand in the carpentry work, and Doc worked closely with us to make sure it was right. He and Jimmy were usually together, piddling, talking about animals, or he was with Granny while she milked or gardened. The three of them did most of the animal work here, outside of the horses, which Gideon did.

We foraged churns, sugar, and cheesecloths for Mama. She also needed gallon jugs, which we found in the basement of a farm about two miles away. Canning jars with lids, stored vegetable seeds, and, in the barn, we found a metal T-post and hog wire. We loaded all that up, and she soon had a fence around her garden, with Doc spending three days carving her gate. He carved swirls and patterns into the wood and then stained it. Beautiful work, and I told him so. His chest puffed out, and he allowed that it was not a big deal that most folks born in the Midwest were natural woodworkers.

He brought us to a map of his property and pointed out where he wanted to plant feed corn, soybeans, and winter wheat next season. We need more food for our livestock, he claimed, and went through the layouts, crop rotations, and other boring stuff with us. Jimmy was interested and seemed to pick it up, but the rest of us were almost in tears with the tedium. When he was satisfied that he had explained every detail of his grand plans, he broke up the meeting, and we went our separate ways.

"Going to farm with me this winter?" Becca asked me when we

were alone outside.

"Sure, I never knew a farmer's daughter liked plowing so much," I teased, and she laughed brightly.

"Soldier's daughter, you mean. Just like every daughter born now will be in some fashion or another." True, I thought. The race for survival was brutal, and as we had already thinned humanity since it began, I thought of how fragile the future was. Could we make it without taking any more lives? Doubtful, a sickness wouldn't change human nature to dominate and take from others as we've already seen.

She must have read my thoughts as she said," Be a cosmic joke if humans died out now because we just kept on killing each other, wouldn't it?"

"That's nothing new; we've tried to do that all of human history. I don't want to kill anyone, ever again. I think we both know that's not probable, though." I just wanted to joke about plowing, and the conversation turned serious.

"Nate says that we can go too far. Mankind has a tipping point, and if we reach it, extinction." She wrapped her left arm around the small of my back as we gazed at the stars while walking down the gravel road.

"Did he say how many?" I asked.

"How many what?"

"How many rapists, slavers, and murderers are the cut off? When do they need to be left alone to do what they want so we don't disappear from the earth?" I asked glumly.

"How many are too many for you?" She looked up at me

instead of the cosmos.

"Those types of humans deserve to be killed, and if our existence is left up to them, maybe our run should be over. A new species could take over from us. One who likes to walk down gravel roads and look at the stars? A species that doesn't focus on destroying?"

"It's getting a little too deep for me tonight. Maybe you should only focus on destroying my inhibitions tonight, instead?" She smiled in the dark.

"You have those?" She laughed and put her hand in mine.

72 Gideon

Doc and Lew hatched a plan to separate us while out doing our duty. They paired Finn and me together and Maryn with Gwen. Gwen refused at first, but I explained the real plan to her, and she finally conceded, though she was furious about their meddling. We agreed to go out separately, and they both seemed relieved at my acceptance. I had already confided in Doc about needing an excuse for the trip to Atlantic, and he's the one who cooked up driving the cattle back, so we understood each other. Granny was behind this tomfoolery, I suspected, but no matter, we could put on a magic show for them.

Around the end of July, Maryn, Finn, Gwen, and I were sent off on the first of these experiments. Two days and back by the third day, Doc told us. Nate and Jimmy were in the garden with hoes when we marched our horses out and rode past. Jimmy waved, and Nate wiped sweat from his forehead and waved his bandana at us going by. We waved back and kicked off into a trot. About two hundred yards away, we stopped so Doc could still see us. Gwen asked me a question, and I asked Finn, knowing Maryn had never been there before.

"Finn, have you ever gone to the Lewis and Clark monument above Council Bluffs?" he shook his head, and I explained it to them. "We're splitting up, but we will meet up at the silos in Carson and ride over together." Finn and I went east, and the girls went west, close enough for Doc and Granny to see we separated if they were watching. I could see Doc was for sure, so we played our ruse until we were out of sight, then cut back northwest using the gravel roads to hide our tracks from Lew or Becca's sharp eyes to the assigned meeting place.

Gwen had her dazzling smile on when we trotted up, and I looked around for Maryn, who was nowhere in sight. Her horse, the other roan we'd gotten from Atlantic and named Caddy because of her easy gait, was standing ground hitched.

"Where's that nerd?" I asked Gwen, pointing at the empty saddle. She stuck out her thumb like she was hitching a ride, then reached with her other hand and grabbed it, pulling it up along the thumb. "She went to shit?" Gwen smiled, and I laughed, and Maryn rounded one of the silos, zipping her pants.

"No, I wasn't," she blushed, "just had to pee." Her face blazed red in front of Finn, and I laughed. Gwen asked if we were ready.

"Anyone else need to shit before we go?" I asked. Finn smiled. Maryn grew even more embarrassed, gave me the finger, and we took off.

The horses were well-conditioned and well-fed, so we covered nearly thirty-five miles that day. We rested for about two hours to give the horses a break, then moved on to the actual monument. The late afternoon was hazy with humidity, and the heat stifling. The views were amazing. I thought the Lewis and Clark monument overlooking the river was worth the ride.

I asked Gwen about another monument I was interested in, but she said we can't go because it's in the actual town. Disappointed in not seeing the golden spike, we gathered up the horses and looked for a campsite. Thick trees by the river provided plenty of cover as we rode down to the river's edge in search of a camping site.

We checked a few homes on the way, but a couple had been

ransacked or the doors kicked in. Maryn and Finn found a place on the river that was still closed and plenty big for our needs that night. I checked around for any recent activity, but didn't see anything other than animal tracks. We crossed the interstate and railroad tracks and cooked in the woods before going back to the house, so no light would give us away near the house where we planned on sleeping.

I tied the horse up on grass near a cutback from the river so they would have plenty of water before brushing them down. Maryn and Gwen went down to the river for a swim while I took care of the horses, and Finn checked out the house after dousing the campfire across the road. I saw him walking to the water and waved to let me know everything was clear, and we had what we needed, and I stowed our gear in a small shop with a basketball-sized red wasp nest on the back wall and a grumpy garter snake that took off when I opened the door. The wasps flared their wings, but I didn't get close enough to annoy them, and I knew we would be leaving before daylight, so not much to worry about from them.

I walked down to the water and stepped onto a deck with screwed-down chairs at the water's edge. I suppose they did that so they wouldn't be sent downriver when it flooded. One had already been twisted off; only the leftover screws and the sheen of the newer deck stain evidence that it had been here. Another had driftwood piled against it and wouldn't survive the next flood. The house was higher up than the deck and, more importantly, empty—likely a vacation home —according to Finn. Both Maryn and Finn were sore from the ride, since neither rode much, and I sat down in a chair while Gwen stood watch, and I smiled at her having her rifle so close to hand.

The water and lights were off, but we just needed a place to keep the mosquitoes off us for the night, and it would do.

When they'd had enough of the water, Maryn and Finn grabbed towels and headed back inside. I teased them about being responsible as they walked by, and they both blushed at that.

"Ya'll coming in?" Maryn asked, and I shook my head.

"We're going to swim for an hour or two." She looked at me knowingly, then turned and went to the house while I watched the sun sink lower.

Gwen set down her rifle, and I stripped down and waded in. The water was cool and comforting after the hot day, and we welcomed the respite. There was a concrete runner built into the bank against the porch, and I sat there luxuriating in the water while Gwen swam around. She stood and wrung out her hair after washing it, her hands squeezed the water from the dark blonde hair, sending it streaming down her pink nipples and full breasts, and a groan escaped me. She looked at me, and I looked off pretending to have been watching the darkening river, and when I looked back at her, the water came right below her navel to the tops of her flared hips. My body responded to her, and she walked over to me, her breasts swinging with her steps, and I didn't even pretend to look away. I couldn't. She splashed water on my face and shook her head slightly, a small smile playing on her lips, her slim throat and chest jumping with her silent laughter. I had lost myself and forgotten for a moment about her past, only seeing her for what she appeared, and that was the most beautiful woman I'd ever seen. The guilt I felt about my lust embarrassed me, but I didn't see her as a victim anymore, only as the woman that I feared I was falling in love with. She smiled and lay against my chest, ignoring my evident arousal. Hell, at least she didn't hold it against me and understood it wasn't something I could control, and she didn't let it interfere with us being close or trusting each other.

An hour later, the summer sun finally dipped below the horizon, and she leaned forward and turned to me. I had my eyes closed and my chin on the top of her head, wondering how long we could stay just like this, not moving, and she seemed to hear my thoughts and slipped slowly away from me. When she turned to look back, her lips were parted and her eyes dilated, and as she came closer, I knew that it would take everything I had not to kiss her. She smiled, and I knew for sure I was in love with her. As she came back into my embrace, two gunshots from the house echoed across the yard to us, and we sprang naked from the pool, reaching for weapons in the wolf light of dusk.

73 Maryn

We were undressed and lying on the bedroom floor. Finn was on his side, looking at me on my back, both of us nude. The lovemaking had been awkward and uncomfortable at first. I didn't know what it would feel like, and the pain surprised me. The second time was a pleasure; I then understood the drive for it, and I went from timid to enthusiastic. Afterward, he lay behind me on the floor, running his hand around on my stomach, when he stopped, and I turned to look back at him. He put his finger on his lips to silence me, stood up naked in the dying sunlight streaming in from the top of the window, grabbed his boxers, and quickly slid them on. I rolled over to my elbows, thinking it's just Gid or Gwen coming back.

Finn grabbed his pistol and stepped out into the doorway. The two shots barely register in my brain before Finn fell backward onto me, and I saw his pistol bounce on the floor. The only thing I could hear was ringing in my ears from the noise, and I'm not sure what's happened until I tried to move Finn and saw his eyes were open and unblinking, and felt his blood running down my stomach to my right hip. I heard someone say something, but I can't make it out. All I could think of was why did Gid shoot Finn? We have to take him home to the infirmary so Becca can patch him up.

I saw movement in the doorway, and I reached over and grabbed his .40. A woman's face appeared in the room, and she must not have been able to see me on the floor beneath him because of the low light and shadows. She's perfectly outlined in the dusk, and I sent a round into her face. My hearing was gone for sure now, but I slid out from under Finn and saw the woman down in the door frame. I squeezed another one into her, and then the living room was washed in light from the opened back door. I staggered over Finn, trying to reach the door myself, and by the time I got to it, a man was standing just below the porch on the grass, his hands up.

Gwen aimed her pistol at him with one hand and held her clothes with the other, while Gid left his piled on the ground at her feet and was running toward the door I'm standing in. Gid was yelling at me, but I couldn't hear what he was saying. He walked past me, into the house, looked down at the floor, and then back at me. He knelt beside Finn, then back up on his feet and out to the yard, where Gwen and the man were. He walked to the man, grabbed a handful of his hair, and screamed in his face. Gid cuffed the man across the head with his pistol, and he crumpled to the ground.

He spoke to Gwen, and she came and got me and took me to the river and helped me clean up, washing my face and hair, sending my lover's lifeblood downriver on the current. I gave no thought to our nakedness; as a matter of fact, nothing really seemed to register through my numbness. She washed me like a baby and helped me get to the bank, using their towels to dry me off.

We walked back to the house. By then, Gid was dressed, carrying her clothes, and he took me around to the side where the road came onto the property. He brought me to our horses and told me to stay there. He left us there and came back carrying Finn over his shoulder and my clothes in one hand. Giving them to me, I dressed while he set Finn on the ground and saddled the horse. I stood there in a fog until he shook me to help him get Finn on the saddle. He walked around, tied his hands and ankles to each stirrup. I tried to shake off the numbness I felt and thought of Lew telling me about shock and how to defend against it. Instead, rage and grief I felt threatened to drag me into a black hole. Seeing him tying Finn over the saddle was when my resolve broke, and I fell to my knees crying. He left me to my wailing and went over to Gwen and covered the guy on the ground while she got dressed. When she was ready to go, Gid went back in, got our rifles, stripped whatever the woman inside had, and rolled the items up in his sleeping bag. They threw the man over the packhorse's withers and tied him hand to leg under her belly.

"Maryn, we must get away from here. I know you're hurting, but it's too dangerous to grieve here." Gid helped me into the saddle, and when he went for my reins, I held them back from him.

I just nodded with a sob.

We rode out of the city and kept going until near midnight. I know we passed our cookfire on the way out, and the flames were still visible. Gid looked at it, then at me. I realized Finn hadn't put it completely out when we left.

Past the interstate, through the hills, and then a small church, I didn't catch the name, only getting a glimpse of the steeple through my tears. It set in with me that he was dead, and Becca wouldn't be able to save this sweet boy, just like Granny warned. We came into a clearing, sheltered by a thicket of trees to the north and west, and stopped there.

"Do you know if he had any requests for a funeral? We should take him home, right?" Gid asked me. I shook my head.

"He mentioned once that he wanted to be cremated," I told him, remembering him saying he wanted his ashes to reach Ireland.

"You two watch this guy until I get back, and we'll send him off then." He turned to look at Gwen. "Make sure he's still alive when I get back, yeah?" She nodded, and he helped me down and unsaddled my horse. He put my bedroll down and eased me down on it, grabbed my legs and swung them over the saddle, propped them in the air, and told me to stay like that until he returned.

When he left, I got up, and I untied Finn, and he slid to the ground. I covered him with his sleeping bag and wept until I thought there couldn't be another tear coming out of my body again. I went back and got on my bedroll while Gwen untied the prisoner, and he fell groaning without the benefit of her even pretending to break his fall. She moved the pack horse away from him and left him stretched out in the clearing. A few minutes later, he groaned and rolled over to his stomach. Crawling up to his knees, he looked at me and then saw Gwen standing there with her rifle pointed at his head.

"Sit against that tree," I told him from my back, pointing to a small oak tree. He tried to stand but couldn't; he stayed on his hands and knees, crawled over, and sat down with his back to the rough bark. Gwen got my rope out, wound it around him, and tied it in the back. He seemed to hold onto consciousness barely, and he turned his head to the side and vomited once. I think Gid hit him too hard and damaged his skull, but it was well deserved, I thought.

Half an hour later, Gid came into the clearing so quietly it even startled the horses, except Buck, who was looking in his direction. He was pushing a wheelbarrow loaded with a shovel, two five-gallon gas can, and some split wood. He went over, woke the man, and talked to him briefly. I didn't make out what he said, but he untied him and handed him the shovel.

The man started to dig, and the realization hit him.

"I'm not digging my own grave; I'd just assume you shoot me now." Gid squatted down on his heels and looked up at the man knee deep in the hold.

"Mister, that isn't your grave," Gid told him, and the man looked at the body of Finn and nodded.

"Give me your word you aren't going to put me in this hole."

Gid stood and looked at him sternly, "I give you my word I won't, now get to digging, we have a lot of ground to cover tonight." That seemed to set his mind at ease, and he resumed. When the hole was chest-high on the man, Gid looked down into it and said, "Climb on out of there." He threw the shovel out and did so. Gid had gathered a pile of limbs while the digging was going on, and now he threw them into the grave. Satisfied with it, he added the firewood he had brought, then poured the contents of the jugs onto the wood, struck a match, and dropped it in. The expected rush of air and whoosh of noise didn't happen, and I understood he must have found diesel somewhere. The fire slowly caught, and it was small enough to make our faces clear to each other when we stood on the lip of the grave. I finally got a good look at the guy. His dark skin was hidden beneath a scraggly beard, and his long hair was braided and twisted like a Rastafarian. His nails and teeth were dirty, and his clothes were ragged. The smell of his exertions rolled off him, and his filth revolted me.

"Do you live with other people?" Gid asked.

He nodded.

"How many?" The guy shrugged his shoulders, and Gid walked around the hole and grabbed his ear and, with a quick flick of his knife, severed it and threw it into the woods. The man fell forward and screeched while Gid walked back around to where he was before. “That’s just to let you know I’m not fucking around. Now, how many?” The blood poured over his left shoulder and pattered to the leaves on the ground.

“People come and go, so it changes. There’s up to eight usually, but people come in and out.” I saw a tear roll down his cheek, and Gid pushed on.

“Where?”

“The jail,” he moaned. The Atlantic jail? I thought we cleaned that place out.

“Which one?” There are several between Omaha and Council Bluffs.

“The boys' prison in Omaha,” he said, still gasping in pain.

“What street is it on?” I asked.

“North 20th across from the Omaha Box Company.”

“What exactly is going on at this prison?” Gid slid the knife up under his chin.

The man dropped his hand and said, “People come to trade mostly and to take showers since they have electricity and running water. They take weapons and ammo for food and showers. They run it like a hotel.”

Gid looked at him hard. “You don’t look like you’ve been enjoying a hotel.”

“I was there this morning but didn’t have anything to trade, so I got up with Tandy, and we went prowling. You can’t stay there unless you pay. I'm not one of the regulars, and I needed your supplies to afford to stay there for a few days. We started to steal your horses, but she wanted it all, so we went inside to rob you."

"How did you find us?" Gid asked.

"Found your campfire and looked until we found your horses," he admitted.

Oh shit, I thought.

"You steal things from people and sell them for women and food, is that it?"

"Yeah," he nodded.

"Most of our gear was with the horses." A terrible realization came to me. "What did you really want from us tonight?"

"Any food you had. We weren't there to kill anyone," he explained.

"You did kill someone, though, didn't you?" I said with venom.

"That was Tandy. I don't want to kill anyone, I swear."

"What gets the highest price at this jail trading post?"

"Guns," he said, looking over to me for the first time.

"Not women?" I asked, dreading the answer.

He doesn't answer, and Gid starts toward him. "Women. We wanted to take any women we could find. You get the most for women at the prison. They can rent a woman along with a bed for the night."

Gid stopped midstride and looked down at him. “You mean to tell me they have women there against their will as prostitutes?”

He nodded. “A few stay because they want to; it’s the only way they survive. They have them cooking, too, and doing the laundry.”

“How many women are there?” he rolled his eyes up in thought.

“Ten or so.”

“Who’s the boss of this place?”

“A guy named Thu-“ he fell over into the hole onto the fire with a loud gunshot report. Gwen was standing there with her pistol pointed at his head, crying and trembling.

“GODDAMNIT!” Gid yelled. “Gwen, not again. He was about to tell us some more information.”

She signed to Gid, something I didn’t understand, and then she put her fingers to her throat and flicked them forward under her chin, then spit on the ground. She rapidly signed to him again.

“I wasn’t going to let him live, but I had more questions. You got blood all over me with your carelessness.” She shrugged at that and went to her horse.

Gid nodded. “Gwen, I’m not upset he’s dead, but I wasn’t done with him, and I have to drag this dead burning scum out of the fire.” Gid jumped into the grave and stomped the fire out, scooping the guy up and tossing him out of the hole. Gwen signed something to Gid, and I didn’t catch it all because she was so animated, and the light was nearly put out from the body being on it.

"I promised him this wasn't his grave, and by God, it isn't. I wouldn't bury him with my friend," Gwen stomped off in a rage, and Gid pulled Finn over when the flames caught again and eased him over on them, wrapped in his sleeping bag. I pulled it away from his face and kissed his cold lips for the last time and vowed I would never forget how fast life can change again. Despite the warm air, I felt chilled, and it seemed blasphemous that the heat from his body on the pyre warmed me and brought me comfort after Gid put him to rest on it.

74 Gideon

We rode into the yard the next day, right after noon. The horses were blown, and the only thing that saved them was me stopping and resting around six o'clock this morning for a few hours. Maryn was distraught and hadn't spoken a word since I covered up Finn's grave, and we saddled up. We hadn't slept except in the saddle and had nothing to eat since our early supper the day before. Doc and Jimmy were carving something when we rode in. He took one look at the horses and called Jimmy over to take them to the barn. I helped Maryn down, and Doc got her inside. Gwen slid down into my arms, and we staggered over to the benches.

Granny handed me a glass of lemonade, and I took a large pull. "Where's Finn, and what happened?"

I recounted it to them. I told them it was my idea to sneak off, see the monument, and go to the river for the night. The stern looks I got from Doc and Lew didn't dissuade me from admitting my part in all of this. I explained how the two caught Finn unaware inside, and that Maryn shot the woman who had killed Finn. Granny was silently crying at this point, and when I told them about putting Finn on the pyre, I could see they were disgusted —not just with me, but with what I was telling them was going on across the river.

"Where's the guy that you captured?" Doc asked, and I looked him in the eyes.

"Dead."

Granny got up and went inside after I told them about burning and burying Finn. She didn't even look at me, and I don't blame her for that. This whole thing happened because of my carelessness. After showering, Gwen's closeness and exhaustion dragged me into sleep.

Supper that night was a solemn affair. Granny looked at me sternly, and I braced myself for the tempest.

"Gideon, in these circumstances, life is vastly different from what it was for all of us here who are no longer young. We all took chances doing foolish things in the past, but the margin of error for mistakes has shrunk considerably. It's more dangerous to be somewhere you're not supposed to be, and I believe you see the consequence of that now. That sweet boy dying isn't your fault; it's just bad luck all around for him, and could have easily been you, your sister, or Gwen here. Some growing up needs to be done by you, and it needs to happen quickly. You left us unprotected, and that can never happen again. If we needed you here and I sent Jimmy to fetch you, it wouldn't do any good if you misled us. Do I have your word on that?"

I nodded my head and looked around the table, understanding the enormous error I had made. "You have my word on it."

She nodded, and I got up, followed by Gwen, and went to check on Maryn. She was still asleep, and I learned later that Granny had given her something to help her sleep. That night, I got into bed with Gwen; she apologized. I shook my head and smiled at her. "It's not your fault." She signed, reminding me it was her idea to see the monument and that she was the one who put us in danger.

"Hush that kind of talk," I told her. "I wanted to see it with you. More importantly, I want you to feel safe with me, and the way I behaved right before the shooting was inexcusable.

You're a beautiful woman, and I forgot myself. Please accept my apology."

She looks at me strangely and then signs, "There's nothing to forgive." She looked at me and didn't understand how I felt. Disgusted with myself for the lust I felt, I explained to her so there's nothing secret between us.

"I will never put you in that situation again. You are my friend, and I want you to always feel safe with me," I said.

She nodded and sighed, "Sex has only been used against me as a weapon. I don't understand the appeal of it. Being near you makes me happy, and I need to be close to you, but I understand men have needs. If you need to-" she started taking her top off, and I stopped her there by grabbing her arms and gently putting them to her side.

"Let's speak no more of my needs. Let's get some rest, I'm beat." She smiled and nodded.

The next morning, I hugged Maryn in the hallway by her doorway. Her face was puffy, and her eyes red-rimmed. "Did you tell them everything?" she asked.

"What they needed." She nodded, and we headed to breakfast. Instead of going in, Maryn went up the stairs. Gwen and I entered the kitchen, no Jimmy again, but Becca hugged us. Granny fretted over Gwen's hair, said she wanted to try a style with it later, and then hugged us both. Lew and Doc ate their food in silence, but Nate nodded to us, and we sat down and ate.

I found Jimmy at the milking barn and stopped to pet Chunk. "You're mad at me." It wasn't a question. Jimmy looked at the ground and then back at me.

"No, I miss Finn, though. Why'd he have to die, Gid?"

"Yeah, we all miss him, and he died because I made a terrible mistake. It's okay to be upset with me about it."

Jimmy shook his head again and said, "Gid, it's not your fault, I could never be mad at you."

"It was, though. I was doing something I wasn't supposed to be doing, and he died for it, and that's the truth."

I fought to get myself under control before I lost it in front of him.

"Did you get the people who killed him?" I nodded, and he went back to his chores. Chunk didn't bother the milk cows, so Granny let him wander around here, and he was happy to follow Jimmy. Of course, Jimmy squirting milk from an udder into his mouth when the old lady wasn't watching had a lot to do with his good behavior.

Lew came to talk to me in the barn with Doc. I was brushing Buck and checking his feet. "We're going to Omaha," Lew said behind me, almost making me jump. I turned, and he and Doc were standing there at the barn door.

"When you are done in here, come back to the kitchen and let's talk," Doc said.

"Okay," I told him, and they headed back to the house.

When I'm finished with the horses, I walked back past the milk pen. No Jimmy. I thought that was odd; he's always out here doing something. Maybe he slipped off to fish like he would do if Doc or Granny turned their backs for a few minutes. He was starting to go feral, having changed from the scared little boy we found back in Wisconsin.

Past the living room and into the dining room, I see everyone except Jimmy around the table. “Where’s Jimmy?” I asked.

“Fishing,” Doc said, “this isn’t boy talk.”

I sat down and looked over the map spread on the table. Doc pointed at a spot and said, “Here’s the jail.” I looked at the end of his finger.

“Tell us everything the man said about it again.”

I did, and then Lew says, “Eight full-time men, you say?” I nodded.

“That’s what he told me, but hell, he could have been lying about the entire thing. He looked like he hadn’t been near a bath in a while, so maybe the jail is all bullshit?”

“We’re going to see, it’s worth checking out,” Doc said.

“To what end?” I asked.

“To kill them, of course,” my old Granny said from the kitchen.

The next evening, we are tucked away in the trees by the pedestrian bridge that crosses Missouri into Nebraska. Doc stayed with the horses, and Gwen, Lew, and I walked across at full dark. Three miles there. We would observe all night and all day tomorrow to gather information on people coming and going.

No one was out when we arrived at the jail, and the parking lot was empty save for two tanker trucks idling. The lights were on, the yellow kind that provided just enough light to see anything close, but no way anyone could see us without night vision from the red warehouse as we walked in front of it. There's a two-story house just north of the jail. We passed it on our left, jogged through a set of apartments, and turned back to the prison and the home. We observed them both, and nothing moved for a while. Lew whispered to us.

"I'm going to check out the house. Instead of waiting out in the weather, we may be able to stay there and have a look at the place."

Lew took off quietly as a shadow, and I watched him cross the street with my goggles on. He tried the door and, finding it locked, he knocked. What the hell? Even more surprising, someone opened it.

Lew sprang into the house, and I braced for gunshots. After a solid minute, I started to think he's been killed or captured. I looked over to Gwen and pointed to the house. We crossed the road and flanked the open front door. I told her to go around back, and I'd check the front. She slipped around the side and stalked to the back door. I'm about to enter the open door when Lew stuck his head out, looking across the road for us.

"Here," I whispered, and he looked to his left at me. Waving me inside, I dipped to the back of the house to get Gwen. She was trying the knob when I whispered to her, and we both went to the front and entered the house. A guy was sitting in a chair with blood running down the front of his undershirt, eyes glaring at nothing. On a couch, a woman was silently crying with her hands tied in front and tape on her mouth.

"Is she a hostage or collaborator?" I whispered to him out of earshot. He shrugged and took her upstairs.

Sitting her on the bed, he said, "I'm going to remove this tape, but don't make a sound above a whisper, do you understand?" She nodded, and he ripped the tear-stained tape from her mouth.

"What's your name?" he asked her.

"Tammy," she sobbed, asking if Little Tom was dead.

"Who the fuck is Little Tom?" Lew asked.

"The man who was downstairs with me," she looked distraught over Little Tom.

"Yeah, he went for his pistol, so I had to kill him."

She sobbed again, and Lew tried to get her to focus on the information we needed.

"Why are you two in this house away from the prison?" Lew sits down beside her.

"W-we live here together. Thurman gave this house to Little Tom; he's Thurman's foreman and runs the day-to-day at the outpost."

"By outpost, you mean the jail, right?" Lew asked, and she nodded.

"How many armed men or women are in the outpost? How many prisoners are there?" he prodded.

"There are four guys there, including Thurman. He was the warden of the place before everyone got sick." She silently counted on her fingers, rolling each one out while mouthing the name of each, and declared, "There are a few that stay full-time. Four, I think. Two stay locked up mostly because they won't act right, but Mary and Denise have been here longer than I have."

"So, two women are being abused and caged in there?" his hardened look makes her cautious.

"All women get abused now, some just understand that and get a little better treatment, that's all."

"They keep this place locked up, I assume?"

"For sure, there are all kinds of trashy elements around out here. Someone is always on guard duty at the front, and they come to wake Little Tom up around two for his shift."

"They leave the gate and come here?" He asked her.

She nodded and explained. "Whoever is on the midnight shift comes and brings the keys to Little Tom, and then they walk back together. I don't see him again unless I go to the outpost around ten in the morning. He doesn't do any work, though, sleeps in the guard shack mostly." Lew looked at his watch—a little after ten.

"When we're done here, you can come and live with us if you want. No more trading your body for existence." He told her and stood. Gwen frowned at that. Lew told her, "Sit here until we're ready to go, and don't cause any trouble. We'll come back for you."

She sobbed again, "Please don't forget to come for me, I don't want to live like this anymore."

Downstairs, Lew laid out his plan. "When the relief comes, we'll kill him and take the keys and sack the jail before daylight. Only three or four guys are inside, and we'll catch them sleeping. I'm going to sit outside and intercept him before he gets here and do it quietly. I'll come back and get you two before I go inside. Set?" We both nodded, and he stepped out into the dark. Before he let go of the door, I heard a thud and a woman screaming out back.

"THEY KILLED TOM, THEY KILLED TOM!" Lew ran to the back, trying to catch Tammy before she alerted the jail. Lew streaked after her into the tall grass behind the house, and the night engulfed both in seconds. I didn't hear her scream again, but there was a light shining from the guard shack by the front gate, as the guard searched the grass. We both ducked down and waited what seemed like two minutes until he gave up and started walking to the house, waving the light back and forth. He's walked down the road, shining the light toward the back of the house where the scream came from. The closer he got to us, the more I knew one of us was going to have to kill him if we didn't want to be discovered. I'm at the corner lying behind a tree, and I'm not sure where Gwen is hiding. He turned to walk to the front door, and I'm out of time. I prepared to leap on him, and then he straightens his back, and a small hand goes across his mouth to stop him from making noise. Gwen stabbed him again and then dropped him on the front lawn by the ditch.

I'm staring at this lethal woman in admiration when Lew appeared at my shoulder and told her,

"Good work, Gwen. You saved Gideon a pair of underwear." I saw her teeth flash in the dark, and I can't tell if it's a grimace or a smile. Lew bent to the man's pockets searching for his keys. He tossed me his sidearm, a Sig 322. He also hands me a tube of some kind. I looked at it and realized it's a silencer for the pistol. I dropped the magazine, and it's full. One in the pipe, so I put the mag back in and screw the silencer on. I handed it back to Lew, and he said, “No, you use it. I won’t shoot in there unless we must, but I don’t want you knife-fighting if it can be avoided.”

“It better work better than the last one you gave me,” I grinned at him, and he just nodded and kept rifling the man’s pockets.

Lew walked through the open gate and into the front doors while we covered him from the shadows. He monkeyed with the keys for a few seconds, then swung them in and waved us on. The dim light inside felt almost like daylight after being outside in the dark for so long. Unlike the previous jail we went to, this one was spotless. The low light in the corridors was speeding us along until we came to the cells. Turned out the open ones had people in them; the closed ones were empty — the opposite of an actual jail. The first person I saw was a woman sleeping, and I almost ran into the cell door. I recognized her. Slowly walking in, I placed my hand over her mouth, and her eyes flew open.

“Mattie, it’s Gideon. Do you remember me?” I put the pistol to my lips to warn her to be silent. After a few seconds, she recognized me. Staring past me, she saw Gwen and nodded her head. I moved my hand and asked her, “How many men are here?

“Six, I think. They come and go a lot, except Thurman, he’s here almost every day.” She hugged me and almost choked off my breath.

“Where’s Thurman sleeping?” I asked her. She pointed to the end of the hallway.

“Okay, anyone else here that will give me trouble on this

side?"

"Yes, but I'm not sure who is all here. I came in late from the laundry, and I didn't see anyone." She walked to the cell door.

"Are all the men here woman abusers?" She looked at me and nodded her head.

"Wait here, I'm going to sort these boys out, okay?" She nodded again, and we're off. Lew was stepping out of a cell on the left with his knife wet and waved me ahead of him. Two cells down, I saw a guy in a bunk, and Lew looked at me and drew his hand under his throat. I put the gun to his head and pulled the trigger. Even in these small confines, it makes little noise and probably not enough to wake anyone. The rest of the cells are empty until the last one, where Mattie said Thurman was holed up. I saw his shape by the dim light and silently entered the cell. I nudged the sleeping figure with my boot because something looked odd in the bed. He rolled over with a groan, a fat brute, and when he saw the pistol, he put his hands in the air. I waved him out of the rack, and when he stood, a young boy who was in bed with him turned and looked at me frightfully.

"Over here, kid," I pointed with my left hand at the corner of the cell away from us, where he won't cross in front of me, and he shakily climbed out and stood by the bars. Turning back to the fat man, I asked, "How many men do you have here?" Even with the electricity and AC on, it's stifling. His heavy face jiggled and sweat began to bead on his forehead. The hot, still air inside here is like breathing through a ski mask.

"Answer me," I swung the gun up to point at his head.

"F-f-five is all that's here. If you're coming to trade, let's talk, okay? I got food, liquor, pussy, or anything you could want. Just tell me what you like. Hell, I'll let you sample my boy there if you want a taste." The soft pop of the pistol, his head rocked back, and after he hit the floor, I put another one in his skull just because. The boy watched the fat man quiver on the ground, and I told him to find some clothes as he stood there naked, and he pulled a pair of jeans from under the bed and slid into them. He stepped into some kind of shoes, and Gwen wrapped her arm around the small, naked shoulders, and we went back to where I'd left Mattie.

"Luke, we're going to be alright now, I know these people, and they are here to help," but the boy didn't say a word. "Another girl is on the other side, let me go get her so she doesn't get scared when you show up." I assumed she meant the lady, Deb, whom we rescued from the other jail.

Mattie took off down the hall, and I went to grab her, but she's off and rounding the central desk, and then stopped. I couldn't see where she's hit, but I heard the shot from outside the main doors. Someone came through the front and shot her, probably thinking she was escaping. Mattie stood still without moving for a few seconds and then dropped like a marionette with the strings cut. Gwen let go of the boy and got in front of him with her rifle out as we approached the main doors. She looked at me, counted down to three, and we both turned the corner, and a man was standing there, shocked by our sudden appearance in his boxer shorts. Gwen firing rounds into him made the boy behind her slam his hands over his ears and jump in shock. The man was on the ground, boxers wet with blood, the bolt action he shot Mattie with flung away from his dead grasp. Seconds later, I heard two more shots from a hallway that led behind the desk. Going down it, I pushed open a chow hall door and saw the stainless-steel tables and stool combos —the serving line — and Lew standing over two bodies.

The girl Mattie was running to was holding her body when I came out with Lew, and it's not Deb after all. Gwen and Luke were standing away from the front door until we all got ready to leave. We crossed to her, and Lew asked if she was okay. She nodded, and then he asked if there was anyone else in there. She pointed down the hallway she had come from and sat holding Mattie. I walked past and looked down and saw her head wound and blood spray on the wall where she had been standing. Stalking down the hallway and checking cells, expecting to be shot by everyone, was nerve-racking to say the least. Lew found one woman in a locked cell, had to dig through his stolen keys to open it, and when he swung the door open, she ran out and fled through the main door so fast no one had time to think to catch her. The other was in the last cell, like Thurman on the opposite wing. She was on her knees with her hands on her head, nothing but a nightgown on, and facing the wall when I got to her cell.

"Step on out here, ma'am," I told her, and she stood and walked backward to the door.

"Turn around and put your hands down," she turned and looked at me.

"You kill all of them?"

"I hope so," I said, seeing her grimace at that. Hmm, that's strange, and I tell her we've got to go. She moved toward the central desk, where everyone else was standing around waiting for us. Lew walked a few paces ahead, and the young lady let go of Mattie and was now standing with blood all over her clothes. Lew told her to change because our horses wouldn't like that smell and to find the boy some clothes. She took off, and then he turned to the lady who had been brought up. She's considerably older, probably a few years older than Lew. "I assume you were here against your will, were you?"

"No," she answered defiantly.

He faced the woman from the cell again. "You watched these men rape and abuse these women and didn't do anything to help them?"

"Mister, I couldn't help them, I ain't no secret force commando like you. You either use or get used, especially if you're a woman and especially now. They made their choices just like I made mine."

Lew nodded and stood in front of Gwen, shaking his head at her and lowering her rifle.

"Gwen, will you watch out front? Supposed to be at least another man here, maybe two," he nodded to the entrance, and she looked at me, and I smiled. Turning, she skirted the dead man in the hallway and went out into the night.

"You're welcome to make your way in the world with anything left behind here. Stay or go, I don't care, but the setup here with human trafficking is over. I will occasionally check in, and I hope the new owner takes this opportunity to change the inventory because there isn't enough lamb's blood to save them from my next round over here. We understand each other?" She nodded, and the girl came back dressed in a handful of Luke's clothes.

"What's your name?" Lew asked the younger girl. "Sara, and this is Luke," she said, helping him get dressed.

"Sara, you and Luke coming with us?" Lew asked.

"Please," she said and turned back to Luke.

"Sara, are there any more women here? The lady from the house says there are several," I asked, and she shook her head.

"There were three others around back in a building," she says quietly, and I went and checked. The door was open, and the cinderblock building was empty. They must have heard the shooting and took off. Back inside, I saw Lew talking to the woman from the cell.

"What about a woman named Deb who would have come in with Mattie, most likely? Do you know her? She was with Mattie and a young man named Wayne." I asked.

"She died when I got here. Thurman beat her to death while this bitch watched," Sara spat into the face of the other woman. "I think they killed the man before bringing them here."

The woman wiped the spittle from her face and asked, "You watched too and didn't do anything about it, didn't you?" She turned to Lew and asked, "What about me, don't you want to know my name, or am I too old for you? Am I not invited?"

"No," he said, and she cackled at that.

"What's your name, cowboy?"

Lew spat on the floor and said, "My name is death, and Hell is where you're going if I ever have to come back here." She laughed again in our wake. We gathered up Gwen and headed out of the city back to our side of the river, Sara and Luke doing their best to keep up.

I thought Lew made some of Doc's hair turn even whiter when

he snuck up on him back at camp. “Damn, it’s not prudent to sneak up on a man like that, especially a hardened killer like me,” he groused. He was always grumpy, but being woken at three in the morning without warning soured him.

While everyone was breaking down camp to leave, the young boy I had found in the cell with Thurman waved me to the edge of our camp and spoke to me quietly.

“Please never tell anyone what he did to me.” His sad brown eyes were red-rimmed and puffy from crying.

“I’ll take it to my grave,” I assured him, and he walked over and took Sara’s hand in his and didn’t speak again while we broke camp and made ready to leave. Gwen let Sara and Luke ride her mare, Godiva, and she climbed onto Buck with me.

Lew walked us about double the miles out of the way to make sure no one could follow us straight home, and when we came into the yard that evening, I was beat. The only consolation I had was to be up against Gwen on the ride. Becca and Jimmy took care of the horses for us, and we introduced two new members to supper that evening.

75 Maryn

Sara and I spent hours with my Granny, learning to sew and make dresses, and she was a patient teacher, and their tenderness and friendship helped me through the pain of losing Finn. Granny was generous with her time, showing us tips and tricks; no matter how long it took, she never grew short-tempered, and Sara was always there to talk to about how I was feeling.

The boys running into the shelter with dirty feet was Granny's main cross to bear, a problem she would scold them about, though it was usually sweetened with a cookie or brownie. Lew and Gid would feel the sharpness of her tongue about minor things that she easily overlooked with us. She reserved her actual venom for the older men, though. It seemed next to sewing, riding them was her favorite pastime. She browbeat them into an unlikely coalition that worked together to avoid displeasing her. The unlikely pair became close friends and were often together, walking the property, checking on the animals, or even talking about poetry. I believe their shared fear of Miss Ruth was what welded their friendship.

I asked her one day why she lets the younger boys slide with something she would wear Gid to the nub about, and she confided, "Boys all have the devil in them, and there's not much you can do to deter them when they're young. As they get older, you need to really start putting up more guardrails, though, or they will turn out to be old men that like to sit around all day smoking a pipe and drinking Tennessee whiskey." We giggled at that, knowing full well who she meant.

"Men will do what you let them for the most part. You don't want to turn your son over to another woman, and she has to raise him still, but you can't crush the spirit in him that makes him a man, either. You think building fences is a hard job? Try raising good sons. I'm aggravated with your uncle over his relationship with Becca. I think he loves her, and I want him to tell her grandfather and me. Gideon was testing my patience with Gwen, too. It's plain they love each other, and love can be taken away in a heartbeat. It's not to be hidden and only found in secret rooms where lovers snatch a few minutes of pleasure," She looked at me when she said it, and I knew she knew. My face reddened, but how could she? Gideon and Gwen would never tell, so how had she guessed? I didn't ask because she may have just been trying to get me to open up about it, and I wasn't about to do that with her now.

The end of summer was nearing, and the barn had been expanded to accommodate the additional cattle brought in. Soon, Doc threatened to cut hay but wanted to wait until no rain was imminent. Meanwhile, Gid and Gwen were out scouting, or Lew and Becca were. They were nervous about Omaha for some reason, and a pair was pulled off work here to keep an eye out. I asked Sara about it, but she made out like everyone there had been killed except one woman named Denise.

"Was she forced to help?" Granny asked.

"No, I think she did it because it saved her skin," Sara pointed out.

"She was probably scared out of her mind to behave like that," Granny added.

"I don't know about her, but I sure was," Sara admitted.

Sara said they had caught her hanging out her laundry one

day. “A man and woman?” I asked before I could stop myself. “A Jamaican-looking guy and a skinny woman named Tina, Tonya, something like that,” she nodded.

“Tandy,” I said.

“Yes, you know them?” Shaking my head no, she continued. They told her they were taking her to a safe zone with a community of people, but of course, that was a lie. Luke and Mattie were already there, along with a woman named Deb, who was a friend of Mattie's. Three other women lived there, but they wanted to be there. I was there for a month when they brought in another girl. They beat her and kept her locked up, so I never got to talk to her. When Lew let her out of the cell, she ran off and didn’t say a word to anyone. I hope she’s doing okay. I think her name was Jane or Jan, but I’m not sure.”

“I have to tend to this milk, you girls all set in here?” Granny asked and left the room.

“Luke was there the whole time you were?” I asked Sara.

“Yes, they found him at an orphanage somewhere in the city. Thurman took a liking to him and kept him for his use.” Aghast at hearing this, my heart broke for the small boy. The suffering he must have endured must have been enormous.

“Did they kill the men responsible?” I felt they would have.

She nodded, “For some reason, they didn’t kill Denise.” Strange, I thought. Lew had told us repeatedly that women were just as lethal as men and not to ignore them in any situation.

“I wasn’t there, so I can’t say for sure why they let her go. Maybe they had had enough killing for one day? Our people aren't monsters, they're my family." Mistakenly thinking she was passing judgment on them.

"Knowing that we won't be in a situation like that again is enough for me to skip any more killing," she said as Lew came into the sewing room.

"Where's the old lady at?" he asks me.

"Straining milk, I think."

"I checked the kitchen first. The boys are looking for her, so when you see her, let her know." He turned to Sara. "We are still in danger here, and more killing may be necessary. The lion's share of the takers and users survived the sickness. I may need you to save my life one day or, more importantly, Maryn's, so I need you to start spending more time on the range." He left, still searching for Granny.

"He's right, Maryn. I'm not very good at shooting."

"I'll help you," I told her.

"Think you could get that handsome brother of yours to help me hold the rifle?" Her eyes sparkled.

"Careful with that, Gwen will scratch your eyes out over him." I laughed with her.

"She follows him around like a slave, but to be honest, if he were putting that thing in me, I'd be following him around like one, too." We fell into fits of giggles. She was closer to Becca in age than to me, far more experienced in life, and her sense of humor, though downright dirty, really hit the spot most of the time.

We went into the kitchen to get some tea. Granny was

standing there with a switch in her hand, and Jimmy and Luke were washing dishes. Her hair and one side of her dress were drenched, and she looked furious. The boys looked stony-faced ahead and didn't turn to us when we came in.

"Granny, is it raining?" I looked at the boys, but they weren't wet.

"Raining shenanigans and it's knee deep and rising." When she was vexed, she had a wrinkle that ran from the bridge of her nose to mid-forehead, and Gid often joked that it was deep enough to wade in. I don't know about that, but it was deep this morning, and she was livid. We set down to drink a glass, as the boys finished up. She marched them out of the kitchen and scolded them in the hallway. I couldn't make out what she was saying, but when she came back, her demeanor had changed, and she was grinning. Sitting down, she poured herself a glass of tea and drank half of it in one draught.

"Sometimes tea just isn't enough to make it through the day with boys." She emptied her glass, and I asked her what happened.

"Those two punks put a bucket of water on the door to the milk shed, and when I opened it, splash." She smiled at us; her hair still plastered to her skull from the drenching.

"I thought you were mad at them?" Sara asked.

"So do they, or the little devils will keep doing foolishness instead of chores. We can't let them get one of the animals or themselves hurt. I can wash a dress, but I can't unkick one of them in the head if a cow got startled by their antics."

"You whipped them with the switch?" Sara asked, looking at it resting on the tabletop.

Granny nodded and said, “Love doesn’t just come from a hug or a shared moment in the dark, you know. It’s not just a bouquet of flowers or teaching a skill; it’s also in a switch, a belt, and sometimes from the barrel of a gun. I switched them to make them understand the danger of pranks around animals because I love them and don’t want anything serious to happen. My boys killed those people who were abusing you because of their love for humanity. I don’t like to punish those boys no more than Llewelyn likes killing, but it’s done for the same reason, love.” She stood up and took her glass to the sink. “Now you girls go find something productive to do before I swing some more love around in this kitchen.”

We rushed outside to see what Doc was up to. Doc or Lew had to be present for us to use the range, but Doc was busy watching the boys dig a hole in the backyard, and Lew wasn’t in sight.

“What are you two up to? You could have brought me a cold drink; it's hot out here watching these boys work.” He pulled off his hat and wiped his forehead with a rag he kept in the back pocket of his overalls.

“We were looking for you to see if you had time to let us shoot,” I told him.

“Sure, these boys will be here all day on this, so why not?” He smiled at me, looking at the boys sweating shirtless under the sun.

“Granny set them to doing this?” He nodded, smiled, and we followed him inside.

76 Gideon

As the days went on, it seemed like Finn was here in two different people. The small Omaha boy bonded with Jimmy, and Sara with Maryn, and they gave each other comfort through their tragedies. They couldn't assuage the guilt I felt over him, though, but our lives carried on.

Lew smoked a brisket to celebrate our new arrivals. Sara told us she was from a suburb called Green Meadows, and Luke was born in a town called Rosalie. He didn't remember his parents at all; somehow, he ended up in an orphanage. When children from the Omaha reservation were sent elsewhere for lack of funds, he ended up on the city's northeast side. They had both been lured with the promise of community and hope, and both had been treated horribly. Luke barely spoke at first, and that was only to Jimmy or Sara.

Sara Turner had a different coping mechanism, and it was through sexuality. I suppose they convinced her that was her worth and the only thing she had to contribute to society. Gwen had playfully warned me that she and I could end up taking a dirt nap together if I weren't careful. I hoped it was playful, but I wouldn't risk it. Gwen would never hurt me, but she was capable of violence, so I reassured her that she was the only woman I wanted threatening me. She smiled and pushed me for that, but it calmed her down. She signed to me that it wasn't Sara's fault and that was how she dealt with trauma, so I talked to Granny about helping her deal with her issues, and she took it as a personal mission to go out of her way to praise her and help her be better and things. She slowly realized she just had to be herself and not be physically used to feel valued, and she turned the corner. She helped with the cooking and worked outside with us as well, even taking direction from Lew and learning how to shoot.

It took Luke a shorter time to readjust, probably because of his age, and he soon was chattering like a monkey and driving Doc to madness. Paired with Jimmy and Chunk, it was like having a cyclone circling the yard. They got into everything, and if they had a spare minute, they were up to no good. They both went without shirts and shoes, wild as the wind. I enjoyed seeing them running free across the fields, jumping headlong into the creek, or hiding Doc's pipe or stashing Nate's glasses. They never really crossed Granny until the bucket-of-water incident, and after all the work she had them doing, they steered clear of her. Becca was open game, though, and they constantly bedeviled her. They found a rubber snake from somewhere and hid it in places they knew she would be. The infirmary bed, her boots, or her saddle were targeted many times. I saw her run the boys down on more than one occasion, pushing them to the ground and wrestling with them in the dirt while Chunk circled, biting their heels and barking. She pushed them into the water and around the creek; she even untied the rope they liked to swing on, and we watched Jimmy land in the mud at the creekbank instead of the water when the rope gave way. We laughed so much, our stomachs hurt. Chunk also faced her wrath, and she would occasionally make him stand in the outdoor shower to be cleaned and brushed, and it was almost as bad as not feeding him. Weird how he would jump headlong into a stinking, fetid bog but hated bathing. Weird like everyone else here, I suppose.

The boys ran these fields and creeks, spending most of their time outside, darkening their skin and callousing their feet, and Granny made them build a brick path from the shop entrance to their tent after seeing them lying in their sleeping bags one morning with their feet dirty. Only so much wildness could she abide, I suppose. Jimmy turned out to be a fine horseman, and he soon had Luke riding along with him. Though new to it, he soon was racing around the place with a blue streak chasing behind them. Luke turned twelve the day after Jimmy turned thirteen, and we had a birthday party for both, and that's where we learned his last name was Blackbird. Jimmy finally had to wrest it out of him, so Granny could put his initials on the cake she made for each of them, which Doc grumbled about, but she shut that down quickly.

Doc whittled the boys out wooden whistles that they used to call to each other while stalking imaginary prey or having make-believe army battles, having to double up his fish-shaped whistles once he learned Luke's birthday was so close to Jimmy's.

We all went to the creek for the afternoon, and those two days were a well-earned break for everyone, the birthdays, and a week later, Labor Day. Doc groused about so many holidays that we would never get any work done around the place, while he made sure to cook for each occasion on his smoker. Some men like to complain, I suppose, and old ones were especially so inclined.

Nate taught us about history and wars, the politics of different eras, and how economies function. Doc continued his medicine and healing, along with the human version from Becca, while Lew drilled us in weapons and physical combat. Our granny, though, was the one who held it all together with her simple rules, traditions, and meals. She taught the girls about quilting, sewing, and crocheting, which I thought was silly —what the hell good was anything with those big holes in it? She was also adamant about her garden and the milk cows. She bored me to tears with the making of milk and cheese. Making butter got me and the boys an ass chewing when she caught them churning suggestively and accused me of showing them that, which was completely true, but I denied it all the same. She directed most of her wrath at me, laughing about it, and shut down our butter churning operation for good.

She was Granny to everyone under thirty and either Mama from Lew or Miss Ruth to the Doc and Nate. She made sure your birthday was special—not just for the boys—and if you needed comfort, she was there. If you have a special food or treat you like, she will go out of her way to make it for you when you need cheering up. Lew threatened her and Doc with pistols at dawn if she ever made liver and onions again inside the shelter, though. Doc loved it, but everyone else hated the dish. Lew got so sick from the smell of it cooking that he had to go outside. He claimed it was worse than the portable toilets that sat out in the Afghan sun all day.

For weeks after the Omaha shootout, we had peace and day-to-day chores to do. It stayed hot and dry, and September was scorching. Doc bailed hay, and we labored under the sun loading bales. Jimmy and Luke drove the truck, and Gwen, Lew, Becca, and I sweated under the smiling gaze of Doc and Nate sitting under a shade tree, drinking sweet tea Granny sent with them. Maryn and Sara worked the barn duty, arranging and stacking bales, and it was miserable work. On the second day, Doc got off his ass and drove his excavator down to Farm Creek, and he and Nate stayed there all day doing whatever old men do when everyone sweats through their jeans.

That evening at supper, they kept their plans secret but spread the good news that maybe two hay cuttings might be needed next summer, given our projected increase in cattle. Looking forward to two cuttings made everyone groan, at least the ones sweated down on the trailer or in the barn. The two drivers and observers thought it was an excellent idea. Luke even suggested trying three cuttings. I knew Becca would get him after supper for that, but he just beamed at her from his dark face, shining his white teeth in his happiness. She glared at him and jokingly drew her hand across her throat.

Once the hay was done for the year, Doc took us to the creek, where he and Nate had been using the excavator for the last couple of days. He had dug out the creek banks and deepened the water by dredging the bottom. We had a picnic at the new bank he created and christened our new-and-improved swimming hole.

A few days later, Gwen and I headed south, then turned west and crossed the ankle-deep East Nishmabotna River. Gwen seemed to know where she wanted to go, so she led off. We were in no hurry, stopping frequently to rest the horses in the heat as we crossed the Tarkio River and Little Tarkio Creek. We wouldn't get to our destination until late afternoon at our pace, but we were in no hurry.

Crossing a gravel road, I saw someone lying in the grass on the opposite side, in the ditch. I warned Gwen, and we split up. She went south, and I circled north. She stopped at the edge of the road and covered for me so I could cross, which I did just below the slight rise in the main road. I hitched Buck here and walked around in the low brush and bone-dry, knee-high grass. Spotting something, I stopped and looked through my binoculars. What the hell? I could see what looked like an arm extended toward the road, in the direction we had ridden before circling. I glassed over but couldn't locate Gwen, so I started back off working around behind what I suspected was a body. I got to where I determined the person was hiding in the ditch and headed toward the road. Slipping around a pin oak and some low, stunted trees, I saw a torso and an arm pointed out. Dead for sure, I thought, and recent since the crows weren't here and the flies were no thicker than usual. I walked up, flipped the person over, and she was wearing nothing but shorts. Her silicone face and naked torso were exposed to the blazing sun, and I understood immediately. Gwen rode up, looking down at the 'body', a sex doll someone had thrown out for some reason. I picked her up and grinned at Gwen.

"I've been looking for a girl like this," I said, and spun her around like we were on a dance floor. Gwen was cackling in the saddle and signed to me.

"I knew you would eventually find a girl who isn't smarter than you," and we both laughed.

"At least she has a better sense of humor than you do," I told her, and she hooked her index fingers into each corner of her mouth and pulled her lips down into a frown. Laughing, I threw the doll to the ground and headed back to my horse. We had performed as Lew taught us when stalking an enemy that we outnumbered, and I'm glad it turned out the way it did; it's too hot to be killing folks today.

We rode into Viking Lake Park about two hours later, and she took us to the roped-off swimming area. She wanted to swim, but I told her let's search the area first and make sure we're alone. She headed south to check the RV hookups, and I went north to see what we had up ahead on the road leading from the beach—an open area with a boat launch and pier. A pontoon boat had blown away from this side to land on the opposite bank and had been abandoned for some time. I got back before her, not realizing she had twice as much to cover as I did. I headed in the direction she went to catch up after a few minutes of waiting for her. I met her on the trail heading back to me with a smile on her face.

"No one's here," and I nodded to her.

"Good, let's swim." She nodded, her face flushed with heat.

We stripped the horses and picketed them in the shade after watering so that they could roll in the grass. We stripped ourselves down and went in. The shallow water was warm, and it gradually deepened and cooled. Once she ducked under the water and came back up, her hair went from fresh hay to honey colored. Her face had tiny freckles scattered across her nose like stardust, and her eyebrows were so light they were almost nonexistent. Her warm grey eyes shone against her sun-darkened face, and I knew I was lost in her. She put her hands on my head and raised herself out of the water, her full breasts in my face for a split second before dunking me under the surface. When I popped back up, she splashed water at me, laughing. I rushed to her, picked her up easily, and tossed her behind me. She came up with her hair on her face, and it was my turn to laugh. She darted my way, and I dunked her under.

When we left to stand on the beach, I asked her if it bothered her at all being nude around me. I understood if she felt uncomfortable around men while unclothed. She shook her head and smiled at me.

"Those bastards could never hurt me because they don't mean anything to me. We dealt with them, and I'm at peace with it. Once the bruises were gone, so were they. They aren't taking up another second of my life. I was only embarrassed by the condition you found me in, and I was worried you didn't think I fought them."

"I never thought that. You wouldn't blame a tree that gets blown over by the wind, and I would never blame you for monsters in the world. Put that from your mind."

We made camp for the night, and I lay awake while watching the stars. I made sure to feed and water the horses when Gwen woke me for guard duty. They cropped along without concern until daylight started to break.

We spent the whole day exploring the grounds in detail, getting to know each other through her recounting her past, swimming, and just spending time alone. I gathered some sticks from the nearby woods and used a park grill to cook the sausages Doc had made. The showers were cold-water only but refreshing. Deer were everywhere in the park, and squirrels zigzagged across the grounds, headed to trees if we got too close. The day was hot and sultry, and we lazed about and enjoyed the water, mostly.

That night, looking up at the stars and hearing the horses munching grass, I was the happiest I had been since leaving Mr. Davenport's cabin last year. Football, school, and girls had cut into my time and harmony. Instead of graduating and going on to college, we were out here, focused on survival. The spray of light in the sky, the occasional meteors burning past, and Gwen resting her head on my chest lulled me into a sense of calm and peace. The heat and humidity conspired to keep me awake, but I wanted to make sure she got plenty of rest. I wondered how she really felt about us and if this was leading to a sexual relationship. Trying to see her as a victim was impossible now that she smiled so easily, and her body didn't bear physical abuse. I tried to direct my mind away from such things, but sometimes, when she had smiled at me a certain way, or her eyes closed as she laughed, it came rushing to me how much I desired her, and I ached to show her that, but I didn't want her to feel guilty about avoiding sex because of her past. I was in a quagmire of what to do, so I did the next best thing: nothing.

We rode out the next day and followed the West Nodaway River north to bring home a couple of deer. We split up at the Tenville Canoe Access to hunt the woods to the east and decided to give it an hour; if we hadn't seen anything, we would move on. I hadn't heard her shoot, and when it got close to time, I walked out of the woods and right into the clearing beside the highway. I stopped, looked around, then walked my horse out into the road, where I was met by a man wearing a baseball cap and a camo long-sleeve shirt. He was sitting on his horse in the ditch and casually turned his rifle to point at me when I broke the cover of the woods. He had me, and there wasn't much I could do about it, and we knew it. His face broke into a grin as he looked my gear over.

"Hello, stranger," he said to me as I stared at the barrel of his shotgun, about ten yards from me. I could see his long, shaggy hair was brown from this distance. His right eye was milk white, and a long scar cut its way across the same eye and cheek.

"Hello, nice day for a ride," I said, and he smiled again.

"It was." He looked me over and moved his sorrel horse over to put me out of position, almost behind me to my right. My rifle was lying across my saddle, pointing down and to the left, so there was no chance I could get it around in time.

"What's your name, young man?" He asked.

"Gideon," I told him, and gently moved around so we were

almost facing each other.

“Jim Khan,” he said. “Live around here?” He asked.

“No, from over Shenandoah way. How about you?” I asked.

“Close by. What are you doing out this way?”

“Hunting and minding my own business.” He frowned at that.

He walked his horse a little closer, and I turned more to face him.

“No reason this can’t be friendly. Just curious how you are so well armed and fed, must have a nice setup somewhere?” He was getting a little too intrusive, and I thought he was going to shoot me out of the saddle and take my belongings. Probably not until he found out where I lived, though. He never got the chance, as Gwen came up behind him and didn’t point her rifle casually; she aimed it right at his back.

“Welcome to the party,” I said to her as he turned to see who I was talking to. His face went white when he realized he was the one in danger now.

“Awfully rude to point a gun at a man,” he grumbled.

“She’s cautious. Now, where do you live, Mr. Jim Khan?”

“You going to rob me?” He asked.

“No, I’m going to avoid your home in the future, so there’s no misunderstanding. Good fences make good neighbors, sort of thing.” I smiled at him, and he looked over my shoulder and said, “About twenty miles south of here. I usually stay to myself.”

I nodded to him. “We’ll, be on our way, we don’t want to crowd you.” I moved my horse out of the way and gave him a clear path south.

He took off, and Gwen looked at me and asked, “Why didn’t we kill him?”

“Hell, he didn’t do anything that we wouldn’t have. Let’s get home.”

Of course, running into him added several miles to our trip because we couldn’t just go straight home; we had to take a circuitous route to throw off anyone tracking us.

We spent another night out, and I pondered over Gwen and us. I thought she would be self-conscious about our relationship, even though we weren’t intimate; it looked that way. She didn’t give a damn about what anyone else thought about us, and to me, that made her the bravest person I've ever met. She did what made her happy and didn’t consider ruffled feathers or putting people’s noses out of joint. I smiled in the dark, and she caught me and asked what I was thinking about.

“I was thinking of how much better you smell after a good shower; you are getting kind of ripe.” I smiled at her, and she threw a stick at me playfully.

Granny made smothered pork chops the next night when we rode in, and they were delicious. As we ate, I explained our encounter with the man, Jim Khan, and where he said he lived, so everyone would be aware.

“You know this man, Erskin?” Granny asked.

“No, can’t say I do.”

“Anything else of note happen while you two were out alone?” She asked pointedly, still not getting a handle on our situation.

“Nothing that is PG-rated we can discuss at the dinner table,” I told her smugly, and she furrowed her brows and blessed me with a scowl. She gave us suspicious looks throughout dinner, but our riding out together for days at a time had become commonplace. She was going to have to get comfortable with it, as everyone else did.

77 Maryn

The next morning, after Gid and Gwen rode in, I was in the laundry room getting ready to start some washing when Granny, Doc, and Lew came into the infirmary.

“You don’t have an opinion on this at all, Erskin?” Granny was the only person who called him that, and only when vexed.

“I don’t, and I don’t know why you think you do. We live how we want to now. The world has changed, and by God, let them get every bit of life they can. I wish Lew would charge ahead with Becca instead of pussyfooting around. I am happy to live my life here and do all I can to help everyone else while I’m on this side of the dirt, but you run this place, and that’s the way I like it. I’ve always been a lazy man, and I’m happy you’re here to carry the burden of management, but we don’t manage people’s lives. We should work together to help one another and let everyone sort out their own issues and feelings. I’m proud that Lew seems to make Becca happy, and if Gid and Gwen are too, then that doesn’t take anything away from my life in any way. Hell, it enhances it, so good day to you, Ruth,” and with that, he went out the door. So, Lew had told him after all.

“Llewelyn, you feel the same as him?” she asked.

“I do. The best thing we can do is make them feel comfortable around us. I’m not sure why you’re upset about this.”

“I’m worried about that young woman’s state of mind and also a pregnancy. You realize how often women and children die without modern medicine? You know of a teenager who worried about pregnancy too much?”

"Okay, I know that was for me, and I'll let that one pass and only say this. These children must grow up as our predecessors did. Their life is in more danger out here on horseback protecting this place than ever in the birthing bed. Hell, Becca, Doc, and you, we're better suited than anyone else around here. Take the day off and get some rest. Go to the creek with the boys or something and get your mind right."

"Being around boys at a creek is the furthest you can get from rest. I got work to do," she sighed.

"I love you, Mama, but I can't stop you from worrying about us. How else are things ever going to get back to normal if people don't procreate? Maybe if you look at it like-"

They went through the door, and their voices trailed off. I waited a few minutes to make sure the hallway was clear before I left. I wondered what had caused this to come to a head. Did Gid say something other than his usual bull to Granny?

Gid was wrestling both Jimmy and Luke in the back when I came up. He must stay on his knees to make it fair, and the boys could walk around looking for their opening. Doesn't do them much good, and even though Doc and Nate cheer them on, they can't overcome him. Not even with Chunk Norris's help. They were tired of their game by the time I saw them, and all three ran off to the creek with Gwen laughing behind them, chasing the dog for a change.

Sara was in the garden, but I didn't see Lew or Becca. I grabbed a hoe and helped her finish the last two rows she's working on. By the time she and I are done with our labors and chatting, the boys come rushing back, dodging Chunk Norris and shouting at Doc. I couldn't understand what they were yelling until they passed me.

"STRANGERS, STRANGERS!" Luke yelled, the whites of his eyes showing fear. Doc and Nate sprinted as fast as they could to the creek that the boys were pointing at. I grabbed up my rifle and took off as well, with Sara hot on my heels, thinking the man who had braced Gid and Gwen had tracked them home. I expected to hear the gunshots that would be his death at any second as the wind rushed past my head and I pumped my arms, willing my legs to work harder. I couldn't bear to lose him, too, and I fully expected to see him bled out of the creek bank when I reached the trees.

When I got to the freshly dug out swimming hole, Gid and Gwen were in the water up to their waist, talking to someone on the opposite bank. A man sat there on a huge black gelding and was flanked by two boys who looked to be younger than Jimmy on smaller ponies beside him. When he saw me pointing the rifle at him, the man put his hands up.

"I'm not here looking for trouble, ma'am."

Doc and Nate were coming along, and by the time I got breath under control, they were here as well. Gid invited them to cross the creek and talk on our side, and the man nodded and spoke to the young boys.

"I would just assume to leave them over on this side if you don't mind."

He smiled to lessen the suggestion he didn't trust us and walked his black to our bank while Gid and Gwen made it up on the slippery bank and into the shade where we waited for him. He didn't make it obvious, but he never let the rifle barrel waver too far away from Gid.

"May I get down?"

Doc nodded to him, and he dismounted and hitched his horse to a skinny willow tree. He walked over to Doc and Nate and took off his straw Stetson, saying, "My name is Alberto De Leon Torres, and these are my boys. My oldest on our left is named after me, but we call him "Bet," and my youngest is Ernesto De Leon Torres, just Neto will do, though."

Doc introduced himself and Nate. Gid nodded his welcome when he was named, and Gwen didn't make a move when acknowledged. She just picked up her rifle and kept it to hand while Gid fastened on his gun belt. I smile at the tall man with the black mustache and soft brown hair threaded with gray. He has light-colored eyes that I can't quite make out, and that surprises me because he has a Mexican-sounding name.

"Where did you come from, Mr. Torres?" Doc asks suspiciously.

"Over from the east bit. I bought a place over near Griswold last year." He was being vague on purpose, and looking at his boys, I understood why. He didn't know our intentions.

"You folks live here?" he looked around, hanging his hat on his saddle horn.

"Not too far," Doc said. "Have a seat in the shade here and rest yourself." He pointed to the small cluster of trees I had come through.

He turned to his boys and said something in rapid-fire Spanish. They backed their horses up and dismounted in the shade on their side of the creek.

"Forgive our caution, Mr. Torres, we've had a spot of trouble with strangers as of late."

"I know the trouble you speak of. I saw them left for the carrion in Atlantic a while back." He didn't seem upset about that. "I didn't realize anyone lived over this way. We were out looking for one of our horses that got out last night. Have you seen any new horses around here?"

"Jimmy? You see any horses that aren't ours this morning when you were checking them?"

"No," Jimmy said. "I can help you look, though if you need me to, mister," he said helpfully, souring Doc's look.

"Call me Beto, young sir, and thank you, no, we can manage."

"What particular horse are you looking for?"

"A black mare, sister to my horse here," he thumbed back to his mount.

"You know the county barn over on 92?" Doc asked.

"I know it," Beto said, nodding.

"If we run across her, I'll drop her off there for you. There's enough grass there for a day or two, and a water barrel there that the workers had out for deer."

Beto nodded at this and stood up and said, "Thank you, Doc."

He never turned his back on any of us until he rode back in the creek again, having told his boys to mount up. They rode off to the northeast, and we all waited until they were gone through the trees and into an open field before we started to leave. Lew comes out to the trees with his rifle, where the man and his two boys had been. Good thing there wasn't any problem out here. I then wondered if Lew would have hurt those two boys. Surely not.

We waited until the trio was out of sight, and Lew, Gid, and Gwen saddled up to track them away from us. The rest of us went inside and got to work on chores. It chafed Jimmy and Luke to be stuck inside, but Doc told them that with strangers riding around, he wouldn't risk them being caught outside. Granny joined his cause and got the boys to sit still for haircuts. While she was at it, she cut Doc's and Nate's as well. Once they were groomed to her standards, they went to the shooting range and shot for a while. We cleaned the shop floor and the pile of hair she had shorn and headed down to the kitchen to see what she was preparing. We took out some ground beef, and she dropped a bag of vacuum-sealed frozen peppers from her garden into the sink. She waved us off to the sewing room, and she set about going over quilting with us.

Later, we came into the kitchen to get supper ready, and the boys were at the table with Doc and Nate. Nate was telling them about a Roman legion being destroyed by natives in Germania. Not the importance of numbers, but by the superiority of their tactics, using the terrain and weather to their advantage. Right when the battle was heating up, Lew came in and saved Publius Varus by sending the boys out to put up the horses. He sat down and drank some water Granny put before him, resting his hat on the back of his chair.

"Followed him to the county barn you mentioned, leaving the horse at, and saw them going into the barn at a place the next street over. 500th. He does have Andalusians there, so that part is true. I didn't see anyone else with him and the boys. They don't appear to have any electricity at the place, but it's hard to tell without going in; they may have the same tint on their windows as Charles did in Wisconsin. There was a small garden, about ten head of beautiful horses, and no other people there. The thing is, we need to be careful getting too close because the man is a tracker. He checked for tracks back to his home and stopped often to watch his back trail. He's a cautious man, and I don't expect him to do us any harm unless he were to get desperate. If you want to have any relations with him, I suggest having him meet us at your house instead of revealing this place until we know for sure what kind of folks we're dealing with."

Doc's house was across the street from the shop, about three hundred yards away. We seldom went there, but he kept it up and clean. Doc thought about that for a second and agreed. "If we have any more dealings with them, that's what I'll do. Maybe have Gid outside ready in case something bad happens?" Lew nodded at that and asked me to check on the boys and make sure they weren't monkeying around with the dog instead of doing what he told them about putting up the horses.

Sara walked up with me, and the first thing we saw was a pile of boots and shirts on the floor by the door. Gid was pouring a bucket of water over his head from the hand well out back in nothing but boxers, and Gwen was unloading her rifle. When she saw Sara staring at Gid with water pouring down his naked torso, she jammed the magazine back home and racked the charging handle while glaring at her. Sara caught her look and glanced away. I smiled inside, knowing Gid wasn't interested in Sara, but it irritated Gwen.

The boys were not only taking the horses to the barn; they were riding them around. I yelled at them that supper was almost ready, but I'm not sure they heard me. Jimmy was on

Buck, and Luke rode Stepper, with Alice being led by her reins. She was trying to kick Chunk, and Jimmy was trying to hold onto her. Meanwhile, Alice's shenanigans made Buck shy away, and she wanted to bite him, but he kicked her. Luke looked on, grinning, and between Jimmy shouting, Chunk barking, and the dust kicked up from their antics, it was a mess.

"Why'd you let them ride to the barn instead of walking them?" I asked Gid.

"They walked them away, then mounted. They have been around you too long and are hard-headed as hell."

"If Alice manages to get away from Jimmy, I'll catch her. She won't run far, she's too lazy, and her life wouldn't have meaning without people to torment," he shook his head at me.

"Jimmy could get bucked off and break his leg or his fool neck," I told him.

"Well, I suppose he wouldn't run off too far, then, and would be easy to collect. Becca would never part with Alice; she's had her since she was a teenager, don't even bother mentioning it because Lew already got pissed at me for suggesting it," he explained to me, sinking the bucket back into the well.

"What's that over there?" he pointed off toward the barn, but I couldn't see because of the shop corner. Sara and I walked over to see and were hit with a bucket of well water from behind. Before I could turn, I heard him laughing and running to the shop to head downstairs, the bucket spinning on the ground.

He smiled at Gwen from the doorway, and she shook her head at him. She followed him inside, presumably to the shower, and we stood there drenched and watched as Jimmy continued with the rodeo his dog had caused. Sure enough, when they got to the barn door, Buck kicked Alice and started to pitch when she and Chunk rubbed up against him, trying to avoid each other. He sailed Jimmy through the air, sending him to the ground with a thud. Luke was laughing from the saddle, and Jimmy was trying to regain his feet. Buck ran off a few feet, still crow hopping, and Alice was still trying to bite Chunk Norris. She had her ears laid back and her teeth bared to him, and he ran just out of distance and continued his incessant barking. I ran up to the barn and grabbed Buck's reins, and Jimmy got Alice's, and Sara grabbed Chunk and held him down until we got them unsaddled and turned loose in the field. We teased Jimmy for flying through the air like a superhero and landing like a turtle in the mud. Granny was at the door when we got back, and she looked pissed.

I could still hear her chewing on them when Sara and I were going down the stairs, while she raised hell about the mud all over them and had them run to the outdoor shower. Gid and Gwen were out of sight, and everyone else was in the kitchen. We changed into dry clothes, then joined them. The living room door opened, and I heard Granny telling them to get in the shower right now. One of them told her something to her, and she said, "Well, when they get done, get your butts in there. Everyone's ready to eat."

78 Gideon

I saw the boys heading to the showers as we got dressed. Luckily, Gwen just pulled her shirt down before they walked by, and they looked in. I told her to keep the door closed, or she would have little pervs walking by, gawking at her every time she got undressed. She didn't understand I was joking and tugged my arm angrily. I looked up at her from putting on my shoes in surprise.

"Maybe you can stop posing for Playgirl magazine photo shoots in the yard then?" Her glare made me smile. Hot or cold, she was stunning, and it was easy to forget just how dangerous this woman was.

"What are you talking about?" I asked innocently, and she gave me a sarcastic smile.

She closed the door and unbuttoned the top button of her jeans, pulled her t-shirt over her shoulders, threw it on the bed, and picked up an empty clothes basket. What the hell? I thought. She gave me a sultry look and mimed pouring the contents of the laundry basket, as if it were a bucket of water. She then rubbed her hands down her breast to her stomach, pretending to brush off excess water, and licked her lips seductively at me, and gave a slow, suggestive wink. She mock flexed her abs and raised her arms, kissing each bicep. I stared at her in amazement. Her over-the-top charade of me rinsing off earlier with the bucket made me double over with laughter. The more I laughed, the more aggravated she became.

"I'm not interested in her, I promise you."

"If you are, I won't interfere. I understand how it is meant to be between men and women. Just because I can't, that shouldn't stop you from satisfying your needs," she signed so fast I don't catch all of that.

"I am not interested in her. If I were, I would say so. No secrets between us, remember?" I looked at her seriously. "I like what we have, and I want it to continue. Stop trying to tell me what to do." She nodded, and I picked up her shirt, tossing it to her.

"Now put your shirt on before my old granny comes looking for us and sees your tits." She looked horrified at that prospect and threw it up above her head and slid it down her thin arms, shaking her shoulders to get it to fall in place, causing her breasts to sway seductively, and I closed my eyes to the lust that burned through me.

Once the plates were cleared away and everyone was ready to go outside, Granny caught Jimmy and made him take off his shirt so she could look at something she noticed on his back. Seeing a large bruise on his shoulder, she told him to get to the infirmary so she could rub some liniment on it. Doc and Becca followed, asking how he got it, and I knew he was in for a serious ass chewing about the dog. Luke came up with us and took off, throwing the ball to Chunk Norris. Lew and Nate were talking about windmills, and Maryn and Sara set up easels to paint the sunset. Neither was particularly good, but Granny stayed on them about it.

Something dawned on me out of the blue: we would be here with snow. The snow last year in Wisconsin was light, and most of it was cleared by the city. Here, it would be all of us doing the removal, and we would have animals to care for. I asked Gwen how much snow they usually get here, and she signed, "Every year is different. The Farmer's Almanac that

Doc has says there will be heavy snow this winter. Long winter too."

She shrugged and told me, "If you want to know, we can find a persimmon tree and check the seeds." My eyebrows shot up at this.

"Some magic power you have? Reading seeds, folding a fitted sheet, and predicting the weather would have gotten you burned at the stake a few hundred years ago for witchcraft." I joked.

"I'll show you the seed trick."

"What seed trick?" I am completely lost.

She turns me so no one else can see what she is signing and says, "Surely you have shown girls your seed before?"

I could feel my face heating up at that. Her eyes sparkled with mischief, and she gave me her dazzling smile. The broken and beaten woman we had brought back here months ago was long gone, and she claimed she had come to grips with her trauma. As long as we were together, it was easy to believe; apart, she was rattled and anxious. I tried to make myself available to her if she needed to vent, but our silence seemed to comfort her most. When around everyone else, she tolerated my boisterous nature, but when we were together, it was almost like we both were mute, and that seemed to make us happy. We could read each other's body language, and she couldn't nuance things with me with language. It was straightforward, and no emotions were hidden; I'd never met another woman like that before. They seemed to hide their real feelings and intentions behind subterfuge and humor. She told me I saw her at the lowest point in her life, and still accepted her, which made the feelings grow. We worked and hunted well together, we seemed to understand each other without speaking at length, and I have never been more comfortable around another person, not even Maryn.

"I'll ask my granny why you're trying to get my seed for some witchcraft," I mimed to walk away, and she grabbed me almost in a panic. I turned and laughed, and she saw I was joking.

"We'll do the seed trick soon," she said.

"I'll return the favor by showing you my seed trick whenever you want," I smiled, and she blushed at that, lightly touching my arm.

That evening, Nate had us looking up at the darkening sky, searching for the International Space Station, which shone brightly as it orbited Earth. He explained that it didn't appear in the same area, so it was impossible to track without a chart, which we didn't have. I asked him if there were people up there, and he looked sick.

"Yes, I never thought of that until you asked about it. I'm not sure how many are on board, but it must be terrifying to have no one communicate with them anymore. Those poor souls...."

He went on to tell us about the working and living conditions in space. The thing that stuck with me, besides the people stranded inside of it and never being able to return home, was when he talked about two similar metals: if they got too close, they would fuse, and you couldn't ever separate them again. Gwen and I weren't a couple of bolts floating around in space forever fused, but we were a couple of nuts down here forever joined.

Nate spied the space station, pointed it out to all of us, and was gleefully giving us the rundown when Doc and Lew showed up and put a stop to his education, wanting to discuss the Torres situation. The stargazing was over for the night, and Nate took the boys and continued their tracking across the sky as we discussed our newly discovered neighbors.

“What’s the plan? Surely, we aren’t going in there guns blazing because they *might* pose a danger and killing a possible innocent family?” I ask incredulously.

“No, we have something else in mind. Gonna cause you to put a lot of miles in the saddle though.” Lew said to me.

“Better a sore backside than murdering small boys,” I said.

“I thought you’d be sore about him pointing his gun at you the other day. I generally take that personally when it happens to me.” Lew smiled.

“It wasn’t personal. The man came up on me, almost naked. I was in the water, so when I stood up, I knew he could see that even though I wasn’t close to a firearm, that I was well armed.”

Doc teetered at that. Granny looked like she swallowed a bug, and Lew just smiled. Maryn and Sara stood open-mouthed, and Gwen nodded along. Granny recovered from her shock and looked around, and the worry line on her forehead told me it was probably for a switch.

“I want to go out and find his missing horse and return it,” Lew hurriedly put in to move the conversation into serious territory and away from my jibe, “that will give us a nonconfrontational way to reconnect with him. From there, I want to get him over to the house, and we can get a better sense of the man.” Lew looked at Doc, who nodded along.

"What do you need me to do?" I asked Lew, noticing Granny scowling behind him at me.

He drew in the dirt. "Start heading east toward Elliot and then turn north to Griswold. I'll start north, head toward Oakland, then east to Lewis. If you find the mare, bring her to the fenced-off county barn here, but swing wide around his place, which is here." He pointed out both locations. "Take Jimmy with you; he's competent, and I'll bring Luke and get him more practice at tracking. No matter what, be back here the day after tomorrow, no later than supper, or we will be out looking for you," he looked at me, and I nodded.

The next day, the cool morning air teased us with the promise of nice weather. Our trio took off east, and Lew's went north with Luke still rubbing sleep from his eyes and Becca riding beside him so if he went to sleep, he wouldn't fall out of the saddle. The shoulders of the roads were dried out, brittle grass, and the only green spots in the fields were escaped soybeans and corn from the year before that had taken hold. No storm clouds on the horizon, and in a hundred years this place could be covered with buffalo again, I thought as we walked under the brightening sun.

At Indian Creek, I had Jimmy identify the tracks in the mud, and he was dead on—raccoons, deer, and turkeys. A set of skunk tracks excited him because he had never seen them before. The hard one to discern was between coyotes and red foxes, and I must admit that if the coyote were young and smaller, it would be tough for me, too. No horse tracks, though, so we kept on east. By the time we reached the East Nishnabotna River, the sun had risen above our hat brims and had gone from friend to foe. Buck had sweated through his coat, and I wanted to rest them in the shade for a bit. We walked upstream until we found a stand of suitable willow and oaks for shade. We loosened their cinches and hitched them close enough to water, as Jimmy and I went further north, scanning for tracks, and Gwen watched them. When we were almost out of sight, I turned back to look at her. She was staring back at me, and when she saw me turn, she lifted her hand and waved, smiling. Even from here, it caused my blood to rush, and I shook my head at her, smiling, and turned to keep walking, and something hit me across the face and knocked my hat into the mud.

The rough bark and leaves told me right off it was a branch, and when I recovered enough to see what had happened, Jimmy was pushing limbs out of his way and just releasing them with no regard for where I was behind him. I yelled at him to stop and picked up my hat. Looking back, I could see Gwen sitting on the bank, holding her knees and laughing. Grunting to myself, I walked past Jimmy and showed him what he was doing, and to not release a limb unless I was aware of it.

"Sorry about that, Gideon," he said sheepishly.

"Do it again, and I'll give you a cowboy shampoo," I smiled down at him.

"What's that?"

I pulled my pistol out and started to smack him with it, and he dodged out of the way and smiled, "Okay, okay."

We followed tracks along the creekbank, but this time we spotted a group of turkey hens. They sprinted off through the high grass of a pasture into some thick woods. Jimmy wanted to hunt them, but I told him that there would be no gunshots on this trip, so that we would come back in a few days. He nodded dejectedly and said he wanted to catch some to raise.

I shook my head at him and said, "Good luck."

Once back in the saddle, we skirted the town of Elliot and headed north toward Griswold. After about two hours of slow walking, we were on the outskirts of Griswold but with no horse track sightings. Dozens of rabbits and a pair of what Gwen told me were prairie chickens were the only signs of life on our trip. We rested the horses again at the same river, just about four miles north of where we crossed earlier. While we were lounging in the shade, Gwen saw something that made her get up and walk off through the river trees and into what looked like a small orchard. I thought maybe she needed to use the ladies' room, and I lay there watching Jimmy throw a stick for Chunk. When she came back, she had something in her shirt and was holding it up so it wouldn't spill out. She dropped to her knees near me and dumped out a half dozen ripe persimmons onto the bank. Taking her knife, she cut them open and sliced open the seeds. She handed me one half of the first one, and I flipped it over to see the cut side. She pointed at the white pit and then at her knife. I wasn't sure what she meant at first, but she drew in the sand a butter knife shape, a fork, and next a spoon. Pointing to the seed, then to the knife, she said it meant a harsh winter. I squinted at her suspiciously, and she cut the seeds out of the other persimmons and put them in her saddlebag for some reason.

"Cold and a lot of snow," she signed to me.

"Did they teach you that at Hogwarts?" I asked her, and she gently pushed me, smiling.

A couple of more hours, we were at the county barn, and so

were Lew and Becca with a beautiful black mare.

“Where’s Luke?” Lew thumbed back behind him to a stand of trees with a cell tower behind it.

“He ate some berries he found up at Farm Creek earlier and has had the trots all afternoon,” he grinned. Jimmy and Chunk bolted across the road to harass him. Nothing like being kicked when you’re down by your friends, I thought of Gwen laughing when the branch hit me earlier.

“What happened to your face?” He asked about the scratch on my cheek.

“Life lesson,” I told him, and he looked to Gwen as if she struck me. Just as likely as a branch hitting me, I suppose.

“I’m going to ride up, drop off the mare, and give him an invite. Wait for me here in the shade. If I’m not back in an hour or you hear gunplay, come a-runnin'. He got too close to our place, so I want to let him know we know where he is as well.”

“It thought you agreed to leave the horse here. He may not take kindly to you crowding him,’ I pointed out. Lew just shrugged and took off northeast, trailing the black.

We all took refuge across the street at a farmhouse. There was a stand of oak and maple trees to the side of the house that provided enough shade for all of us. About forty-five minutes later, I saw Lew coming through the old cornfield, and he waved to us. We tightened cinches and mounted up to meet him. Mr. Torres was happy to get the horse back and would be at the house for lunch the day after tomorrow, he told us. He had a bag on his saddle horn and patted it.

“Let’s overnight at the park and have a picnic.” I nodded, and he led off.

We came over a low hill, and below us was a small lake. "This is Farm Creek Wildlife Area," he told me as the boys raced off toward the pier. He smiled at me and shook his head. By the time we got down there, they were both soaking wet from being in the lake, and Chunk Norris was dripping on the pier. Even though it's early October, the heat of the day sent them into the water, and Becca scolded them for not taking care of their horses before going to play from the lake shore. They left the water in a rush, unsaddled them, and let the horses roll on the grass. She made them take care of ours, too, so the lesson would hit home, and Lew gently chided her for disciplining the boys. She looked at him and asked if he would like her to find something for him to do, since he wasn't starting a fire for cooking. That focused him, and Gwen and I walked around checking the place out. Out past a building, there was a herd of white-tailed deer eating. This early, it was a group of five doe and yearlings, and they didn't seem to pay much attention to us.

One thing that really seemed to help Earth thrive was the lack of humans, I thought glumly as I looked over the fallow fields and abandoned farmhouses. I wondered whether civilization would catch up again before these large silos collapsed, or whether trees and native wildflowers would reclaim these fields. As the sun dipped lower, the heat was checked, and the butterflies and bees flitting through the air helped me enjoy this beautiful new world. No traffic, no pollution in the skies, no noise had been a boon to us survivors. The night skies were amazing, with stars and meteor showers; the Milky Way no longer competed with city lights, Mr. Davenport had been right about that, and the breeze only brought natural scents to your nose now. No chemicals or runoff fertilizer had gotten into the water, making it taste sweeter. The very air seemed to invigorate you with its cleanliness. Maybe we didn't need more people again, I mused as Gwen reached out her hand and held mine.

She smiled at me and handed me her hat. Looking up, she ran her hands through her hair and shook it loose from the day's heat. I reached over and grabbed a handful of it at the nape of her neck, giving it a slight pull. She closed her eyes and moaned. I gave her another gentle pull, and her eyes flew open, looking at me, and she winked, a devilish smile playing on her lips. Her giggle caused the feeding deer in the meadow to look our way. I was lost in my wicked thoughts of her when I heard screaming from the lake. The deer bolted and snapped our attention that way. Gwen and I ran down to the water and saw Jimmy and Luke jumping around, screeching, and rubbing their skin.

"Hold still so I can get them off," Lew growled at them, and they ignored his warning as they thrashed about.

"Leeches," Becca said to us, grinning at the boys.

'They won't hurt them, will they?" I asked, never having any experience with them before.

"No, but it will teach them not to headlong into unfamiliar waters again." Lew was busy with his knife, peeling them off carefully and flinging them to the ground, where Chunk was attacking them.

79 Maryn

The day of the lunch came, and after giving us the details the day before, Granny had everything in motion. Sara and I went to the house and got the dining room ready for company. Doc got the large leaf from the attic and dropped it onto the table, extending it. Gid and Gwen wouldn't be there, and Becca decided to skip it as well. The Torreses did not know about her yet, and we could explain that Gid and Gwen were off hunting when, in reality, they would be just outside, hiding in case something went wrong. By the time they walked into the yard, Granny had everything ready. She had Doc smoke a couple of pork tenderloins, and she made mashed potatoes and field peas along with homemade biscuits.

Beto walked onto the porch, shaking hands with Lew and Doc, took off his hat, and nodded to the women. After the introductions, Granny put the four boys at a little table outside on the wraparound porch. Of course, she fed them first while chatting at the big table. Beto, as he insisted we call him, was just in front of thirty, I guessed, and had a little grey in his light-brown hair. His mustache made him seem serious, but he was quick to smile, and his soft, light gray eyes were kind.

Doc asked him about what's gone on with him since this disease hit, and it was about what you'd expect. His wife's family, along with his own from Spain, he hadn't heard from. He believed it might have started in Eastern Europe, since they warned him before he heard anything about the illness over here. His wife's brother, Pedro, had come up from New Mexico to help with the boys after his own wife had died in the sickness. The marauders from Atlantic had killed Pedro, he suspected, and left him lying in a soybean field a couple of miles from his home a few months back, and they had been isolated since then. He told us that he had seen some men looting houses near Griswold in late spring and that one of them rode the pacing horse; he saw the tracks near our house. "I knew it wasn't the same rider now because the tracks weren't as deep as when they left the town, and I saw these same men not long after that. They no longer need horses." He looked at Doc, who nodded.

"They were a problem and endangered us here," Doc said, reaching for the salt.

"I wonder if you think the same about me," Beto wondered aloud.

"Well, we don't want to judge too hastily. We aren't bloodthirsty savages, but we like to know if there are any goats mixed in with the sheep, so to speak."

Beto smiled at this. "I assure you, Doc, I mean you no harm. I would very much like us to be friends without conflict. No reason we can't behave as neighbors did before the sickness."

Doc set down his tea and replied. "That's how I hoped we could leave here today. We are willing to live and let live, and to give a willing hand when you need it. To seal the deal on this, I've put together some things you may very well need at your place." He waved to a bag leaning against the wall.

"I'm embarrassed that I only brought a bottle of wine," he said, looking at the size of the bag.

"Never mind that, think of it as a late homecoming present. I'm older and don't get out much as I used to; that's why I didn't know you moved in over there. The best gift would be for us to get along and work together. Now tell me, do you have enough hay for your horses through the winter? I think it's going to be a tough one this year."

After lunch, Granny sat at the table with Lew and listened to Beto and Doc talk. Sara and I went outside to find the boys in the yard, taking turns running from Chunk Norris while holding a stick. When he got tired of them running instead of throwing it, he would trip them up and take it, causing them to chase him for a bit. They laughed and shouted, and we sat in the swing in the shade.

"How many people do you think are like the Torreses?" she asks suddenly.

"What do you mean? European?" I joked.

"Hiding out, alone in this world, wondering if they're the last people on earth," she looked at me. "Plenty of them, I bet, have no idea how close they live to other people who will help them."

"Well, you know, not everyone is willing to help; most probably want to take advantage. I would think your distrust of strangers would be especially high considering."

"It was until today, but it's sad thinking there may be people out there without anyone and scared." She looked despondent. "I wonder what happened to those boys' mother?"

I didn't know what to say to that, so I just kept my thoughts to myself. In a few minutes, the screen door opened, and Beto and the others walked out onto the porch. He nodded to us and shook hands all around and stepped off the porch with the bag Doc had packed for him. He called the boys, they readied the horses, and they were off. He turned around one more time and waved his hat to us, and they set off for home in the warm afternoon.

Doc and Lew argued about the Torres situation well after we went to bed that night. I'm not sure what Lew wanted to do about it, but he cautioned against revealing the shelter or inviting them in so soon. Becca sided with Doc, and we left them to it. Sara and I went to talk to Granny for a bit and found her at the oven, making a cake for Nate's birthday tomorrow. I asked if she needed any help.

"You could tell your father that mercy is not a weakness and that to help out his fellow human beings is not a crime," she said, checking her timer and looking over at me.

"Have you tried telling your *son* anything lately?" I asked sarcastically. She sighed and threw her dish towel over her shoulder. "Sara, honey, how old are you?"

"Just turned twenty-four in February. You're trying to play matchmaker with Mr. Torres?" she joked.

"No, I didn't realize you were that much older than Maryn, though. I want you two to be especially careful wandering around away from the house, with no telling what's stalking around here. According to Mr. Torres, he's seen several people out looting homes. Not just men either, so don't think just because someone's a woman that you are safe with them. Are you starting to get comfortable with the rifles?" She didn't wait for an answer and went right on, "Shooting is a critical skill for everyone nowadays, make sure you are working on it too."

"I am Miss Ruth. I don't ever want to be in that situation again. We've all been working on it, including Luke."

"Luke isn't the one that I'm worried has caught Beto's eye," Granny said matter-of-factly.

“Miss Ruth, I-I-ugh, don’t know what you mean,” she said, scarlet running across her cheeks like a prairie fire.

She looked at both of us, “What I mean is if you decide to move off with a man, you'd better know how to defend yourself and your family. Whether that’s the flashy Spaniard or some other beau you girls scare up, the same principle applies. Sometimes a man isn’t what he appears, and you will have to protect yourselves even from him if you choose unwisely.” She huffed off, yelling at the boys, and Sara looked at me and grinned.

“You think he was looking at me with interest?” She asked, referring, of course, to Beto.

“Probably would have seen it yourself if you weren’t so busy thinking of him and you naked together,” I teased back, and she burst into laughter.

80 Llewelyn

The old man wouldn't budge on Beto. He wanted to welcome them into the shelter, but he didn't understand why I was reluctant. "Hell, you brought Nate here with no qualms. What's the difference?"

"I saw Nate and the others in a life-threatening situation and needing help. Those folks seem to be doing fine, and I only want to keep an eye on them for a bit before revealing the shelter. We are at risk if this place is discovered. People are actively seeking to harm us and anyone else they can take advantage of."

"The only thing I saw Beto take advantage of was Ruth's mashed potatoes at lunch. He's just a victim like all of us, Lew."

"Maybe," I conceded.

"I've sent Gideon and Gwen to keep an eye on them for a bit, and Becca and I are going to check along the river for any activity. We know there are people on the other side up to no good, and I'm concerned they may start rebuilding the outpost they had. When Gid gets back, ask him about what he's seen, and if you still feel comfortable about Mr. Torres, then invite him along; it's your shelter after all."

Mama was in the kitchen and handed me a bag of food for us while we were traveling.

"Everything okay, son?" She looked at me worriedly.

"Try to convince Doc to be cautious with Mr. Torres, will you?"

"You think he would hurt us? He seems a decent enough man. He has two little boys to take care of," she reasoned.

"If you had two little boys to take care of, what would you do to ensure their survival?" I asked.

She wiped the already clean table again. "Anything," she said, looking up at me, and I nodded.

"Thanks for the food, we'll be back the day after tomorrow, late. Maybe cook up something good around here?" I teased.

"Nate's birthday is tomorrow; can't you wait until after?" she pointed to the cake on the stove top, cooling.

"Nate's had a hundred birthdays without me being with him; he'll be fine."

She swatted at me with her towel, smiling. "Getting old is a privilege that not everyone gets to enjoy, and if it weren't for us old folks, the wheels would fall off around here. Wouldn't do you any hurt to heed our advice."

"Did Macbeth a lot of good listening to three old people, didn't it?" I grinned at her, and she reached for her switch. I swiped my finger into the chocolate icing she's making and put it in my mouth, dodging her.

"OUT!" she feigned outrage.

"I love you, Mama," I called back over my shoulder.

"I love you, baby." I heard as I closed the door and headed up.

Jimmy and Luke have our horses saddled and ready in the yard when I come out. Becca was mounted and ready, settling into the saddle. I told Chunk Norris to get away from Alice. Of course, he doesn't listen, and Jimmy has to hold him. She still tried to kick him when I turned her, and we took off to the gravel road. As soon as her hoof touched the rocks, Alice decided to have a rodeo, and we whirled around with her bucking until the other side of the road. I get her under control, and I can hear Jimmy and Luke cheering in the background. Becca looked at me and shook her head.

"I don't know why you ride her; she doesn't like you or anyone else." She looked serious.

"Gideon thinks we should get rid of her," I told her.

"Well, she's not Gideon's to get rid of, is she?" She pouted. "She does seem to especially hate you."

"I don't feel like you hate me when you're bucking under me," I winked at her, and she giggled.

"Maybe I buck under everyone," she smiled, and I shut up with a grunt. She kicked Two with her heels, and we took off. The afternoon heat was in full swing, and the horses were sweating by the time we reached where Finn was buried. I wanted to look in on him and make sure no animal had dug him up, but his grave was intact, and we continued to a small grove of chestnuts and oaks across Highway 6 to camp for the night. I got the horses unsaddled and picketed, and Becca laid out our sleeping bags and was in the little creek when I got to the edge. It's a spot just wide enough to stretch out your arms and almost touch both banks, but it's deep, and she beckoned me in. Stripping down, I eased into the cool water.

The next morning, we were sitting on a high-rise above the city, looking across the river into Nebraska. We watched for a couple of hours, then circled the central area and headed south, using the trees and small hills to observe Council Bluffs and, when possible, Omaha. The riverboat casino provided a good lookout, and we had lunch in the shade on the top deck. The casinos were broken into for some reason, and we avoided them even though they were taller than the boat. When we left the city, it was hard to see across the river because of the flat terrain and the thick trees on this side, so we rode south to check the bridges for signs of life. Deer flitted in and out of the trees, and we did spot a small pack of feral dogs under the I80 bridge, but they didn't see us. Late that afternoon, we reached Highway H10, and Becca told me there was a toll booth on the other side of the river.

"Can you see anything from the bridge?" I asked her.

"I don't remember. I've only been here once. There's an Air Force base over there somewhere. We were on a field trip to watch some jets land one year in school. Some air show or something—we watched it from a park over there, but I didn't really care about it. I was more worried about why Bobby Gault liked Samantha Reeves more than me." She smiled as I shook my head.

"Were you always so hot for the boys?" I teased.

"Well, I knew I needed something, but I didn't know it was an older man who chokes me just right and fills me to bursting." She shot back. I'm the one who choked; the water I was drinking from the canteen came pouring out of my nose and mouth while she giggled.

"That explains your Bob Seger fascination then," I said after regaining my composure. She laughed out loud about that and sidled up to kiss me. Two stepped away when Alice swung her head over, and it was a wise decision as she showed her teeth.

"No telling what we could do in the saddle if you had a horse that behaved." She slapped Alice's flank lightly.

I got down to check Two's shoes for rocks or sticks after walking across the field. Satisfied, I walked over to Alice, and Becca said, "I'm going to ride ahead; I see some trees by the bridge I can pee in."

"Just go here, I don't see a crowd." I waved my hand around at the empty highway and fields.

"A girl has to leave some mystery for her man, especially for the older gentlemen callers that I dig." She giggled and swung into the saddle. She took off up the road while I had my back to her, checking Alice. Her front right hoof has a stone wedged against her shoe, and I fished out a wooden dowel that I had Doc carve for this very task. I gently wedged it out while keeping my shoulder at a healthy distance from her teeth, then put my tool back up. I grabbed the horn and started to swing up, and I heard gunshots from the bridge.

Grabbing my rifle, I sprinted to the sound of shots fired closer to me this time, probably from Becca's AR—the sharp crack of her 5.56 repeatedly. Thank God, she's alive, I thought.

A round kicked up dirt near me, and I dropped over on the south side of the road and ran to the trees at the river's edge because I had no cover here. I couldn't see over the road, but I heard Becca still firing, calmly and methodically. That galvanized my theory that she hasn't been seriously wounded, and I slipped into the trees and looked around. I heard the loud boom from the north side again, and I slowly walked forward. When I got under the bridge, I saw two men kneeling in the trees. They stood when I saw them, still facing away from me. I stepped to my left so both men were in my line of fire, and squeezed the trigger on the first, then switched to the second before he could react. They are both on the ground before the noise of the shots fades. Why did they stand up like that, I wondered?

"Becca? Don't shoot, we're clear." I yelled out. She doesn't say anything, so I backtracked the way I came. Breaching the embankment, I saw Becca standing there with another woman's arm around her neck, pistol pointed at her head.

"Who are you, cowboy? Come closer so I can get a look at you," she asked as I cleared the road and raised my hands to show her that I posed no danger.

"Death," she said as I got close enough for her to recognize.

"I remember you now. I don't meet many men who impress me. My daddy, that cub you had with you that night, maybe, but you for sure. For as many men as I've known, that's not a lot." Denise laughed again. "Want to reconsider taking me with you?"

"I'll consider it if you let her go."

"Well, I'm not sure I believe that."

"Believe this, that lady means a great deal to me, and I couldn't let it go if someone were to harm her."

"You kill those two idiots?" She glanced toward the bridge.

"I did."

"Wish you wouldn't have done that, it's hard-to-find quality help nowadays."

" Those men weren't quality, or it would be my blood pumping into the river mud right now instead of theirs. I saved your life, and I want to redeem it with hers, right now," I told her.

"You didn't save shit; you just dragged it out longer. I've had to struggle since you put the lights out at our little party at the jail. The dregs are all that's left, as you can see, I can't depend on them too much."

"You have to know if you shoot her, I won't leave you alive."

"I know, I've seen your work, handsome. The thing I'm curious about is how I can get out of here alive," she said with a smile.

"Leave her, and we'll call it a draw. Stay on your side of the river, and we'll stay over here, and we won't run into each other again. Fair?" I slowly lowered my hands so I'm closer to my pistol in case this goes much further sideways.

"You're just going to let me walk across that bridge, huh?"

"If you leave her unharmed, I give you my word, there'll be no repercussions, and you can just go. We know the alternative." My hand was an inch from my pistol.

She dropped her arm and shouted, "Deal!" Becca took a step away from her, and I'm tempted to fill her captor with holes.

"Deal," I said, and she winked at me, turned, and walked up the road and over the bridge. Becca stepped beside me and raised her rifle.

"No." I pushed the barrel down, and the woman raised her arm in salute and disappeared over the other side.

"We're shut of her, let's head home. Are you hurt?" She shook her head, and I wrapped my arms around her.

81 Gideon

Gwen and I came into sight of the barn, and we could see Jimmy and Luke throwing a ball back and forth. They had managed to slim down Chunk Norris considerably during these weeks. They stopped and ran over when they saw us riding in.

"Want us to put up your horses, Gid?" Jimmy asked.

"Welcome home, Gwen," Luke says before adding, "Lew and Becca aren't back yet."

Instant chatterboxes. "I'll see to the horses; you two punks get that dog out of here before those donkeys see him." Right on cue, they started to bellow. The sound shattered the calm here and rolled over the fields. Chunk looked satisfied with his tongue lolling out and a grin. The boys took off, calling for him, and as quick as an arrow, he was gone. By the time we got to the gate, they had calmed down, and I got off to pet them. The dog may not have been the only thing to set them off. I had taken to scratching them every time I rode in, and they got spoiled to it and would run to me when I showed up.

I told Doc that Mr. Torres had gone straight home and that nothing out of the ordinary had occurred. He and the boys made sure the horses had feed and water. He had them throwing lassos for a couple of hours, and then they went inside. No lights were on; they used a hand pump to water the horses and bring water into the house. We didn't see anyone else. This morning was much the same, so I'm not sure what he's looking for, but we wasted a whole day watching a man piddle around his farm.

"Where's Lew?" I asked.

"He and Becca left out soon after you did to check the river for trespassers. Should be here tomorrow at supper time."

I nodded and went on inside to get cleaned up for supper.

The next day, after collecting eggs and checking the cattle, Jimmy brought a note that was pinned to the front door of Doc's house. It was from Beto, and he thanked us again for the meal and the supplies Doc had sent with him. He also wanted to invite us over to see his horses and to talk about maybe breeding them with some of our stock.

Doc asked me to head over and invite him to another meal to discuss horse breeding.

"The main thing I want you to do is check out his operation. He probably isn't fixed for supplies like us, so don't mention eating while you're there. Look around as much as you can and have him come back over for another meal to question his ideas about the stock. Ask Ruth what time works best for her and give him the day. Be careful and learn as much as you can."

I asked Granny if she would pack us some food. "For you and Gwen?"

"Luke and Jimmy, too. They would like to see those boys," I smiled at her, and she smiled back and hugged me.

"Being considerate is something I worried you may not grow into, and now look at you!" she exclaimed, trying to embarrass me.

"No, I just thought I'd bring them in case I didn't feel like tending to my horse, or I need someone to collect firewood." She frowned at that and sent me out of the kitchen with a scowl.

I asked the boys to bring in the food she had prepared, and we mounted up and rode out, with Doc and Nate sitting on the bench as usual. It was just before midday, so that we would arrive early in the afternoon. The sun beat down on us like an open furnace, and the heat waves shimmered in the distance. After the initial excitement wore off, the boys and the dog settled into a despondent pace. I ask them to ride ahead and scout for us.

Luke asked what they were looking for. "What was the greatest danger to your people before the white man moved into this country, Luke?"

He and Nate had been going through an encyclopedia, history books, and tourism info that Doc had stashed away for some reason to learn a bit about his tribe. Nate explained to us how important it is to know your ancestry, but Lew told him that everyone here was American and that nothing else really mattered. I tended to agree, but Nate thought it helped Luke, and he was interested in knowing, so all good.

"Sioux, maybe," he told me, "They and the Cheyenne were probably the most likely to go to war with my people." I nodded at that.

"The Sioux were fighters for sure, both of you lope ahead and make sure none are hiding in ambush," I told him. They looked ahead at the trees curving along the creekbank.

"Did you eat any of Mr. Nate's birthday cake?" Luke asked me, grinning at Jimmy while waiting for my answer.

"No, I didn't see any," I said, irritated that I didn't get a piece. Both boys guffawed at that.

"What?" I asked.

"We snuck back in this morning and ate all of it," Jimmy snickered, and Luke grinned at me. Little heathens, I thought.

"Go check out ahead before I decide I would rather hang two cake-stealing pecker heads," I growled, and they took off laughing. Gwen grinned at me, amused at how they had hogged all the cake.

Luke and Jimmy were both armed with .22s and were well-trained in using them, so no worries about them doing anything foolish with a firearm. They also had bows that Doc and Lew had taken from a sporting goods store in Council Bluffs and were eager to use on some live game. Small recurve bows that they had both practiced with, and to be honest, both were better than I was with Mr. Davenport's old bow. Boredom was something that you must battle even now, and maybe they could scare up a rabbit or two for us to drop off with Beto. They disappeared into the trees with Chunk in hot pursuit.

Gwen smiled at me and reached over and took my hand after the boys left a dust cloud. She liked to see them cut up and have fun, and she had spent a lot of time with Luke to get his horse used to Chunk running around his feet without throwing the boy. The pinto that had belonged to Tommy Hodges was now Luke's favorite, named 'Mix'. I think the boys were half in love with her and Becca both, and Jimmy almost treated Maryn like his mama. Sara got along with them, too, but she wasn't much for riding or tomfoolery like they were. I bet she was still pissed about me dousing them with water the other day. I smiled to myself at that expression.

"Let's rest the horses for a few minutes when we reach the boys," Gwen said, noticing me watching the boys off.

"Don't sulk over chocolate cake,' she said, digging it in deeper.

"They have crossed the line with that," I told her.

"What are you going to do? Tattle tell?" She's joined the dog pile on me, and I gave her a rueful smile.

"People who keep sweet things from me learn to pay for their mistakes," I winked, and she blushed. Turning her horse, she kicked her toward the tree line, and I followed close behind.

Jordan Creek was just ahead, and I couldn't see or hear the two knuckleheads even when we followed in behind where they entered the trees. We walked the horses for a couple of minutes, and then I heard the crack of a small caliber rifle, then another. I kicked Buck into a gallop, heading flat out toward the sound of rifle fire. I pulled my rifle from the scabbard, looking for danger, and found Chunk barking at something by the creek, while both boys stood alone on the opposite bank. Jimmy held his bow, and Luke his rifle.

"What the hell is going on?" They turned to look at me, and both started jabbering at once, pointing. Chunk was below the cut of the bank with something in his mouth, swinging it back and forth—a snake. There's an arrow stuck through it about halfway down its five-foot-long body, and it's smashing into the ground and water with every swing. Chunk thinks it's had enough and lets go of it, and its rattle was still making a low sound as it dies. Shredding from teeth, an arrow, and at least one bullet hole has ended the danger of the snake, and both boys darted after it, and I yelled for them to stop. I got down and walked across the creek to where it's quivering on the ground and cut its head off. Pulling the arrow out, I crossed back over and saw the dog whining.

"Check that dog for a snake bite," I told them, throwing the bloody arrow down in front of Jimmy. They snatched the dog up, and sure enough, on his snout, there is a bleeding hole where it looks like one fang got him.

"Go catch your horses," I told them, and squat down to look. His left side is already starting to swell under the puncture. The boys brought their horses over, and I sat Chunk on Jimmy's lap and told him to ride home as fast as he could and get Doc to look at it. "It's about two and a half miles that way," I point southwest. "Both of you, no fucking around, straight home, you understand?"

They nodded and galloped off. I went back over and skinned out the snake hide where it's not damaged, then rolled it up in my saddle bag after cleaning it as best I could. Gwen watered our horses while I finished up, and we got back on the road, headed to the Torres place.

He was in the barn when we rode up and came over to shake hands. He recognized us from the creek and said he was happy to meet us fully clothed this time. We both laughed at that, and he stabled our horses, and I told him about the dinner invite.

"I don't want to be rude, but we had a snake bite our dog on the way over, and that's why the boys aren't here. They were looking forward to seeing your sons."

"They get on well, and my boys will be disappointed to hear that. I got them out fishing right now, so I'm not sure what time to expect them." He shrugged.

"The old man wants to make sure you are fixed for provisions and that you are serious about breeding your horses," I rubbed the neck of one of his fillies, she knickered, and went back to drinking.

"I do, and I am. I may not be stocked enough to make it through a long winter, though. I'm interested in trading or working for things we may need, if he's interested in that?"

"Mention it at dinner, and I'm sure something can be arranged. He won't have you starving out here, I'm sure of that, but what he needs is something he hasn't shared with me yet." We walked out of the barn and didn't seem interested in inviting us in.

Mounting up, he looked up and spoke. "What did you do with the snake you killed?" I patted the saddlebag where the skin was. "May I see it?"

I opened the bag and fished it out for him. He unrolled it and asked me if he could tan it out. "Sure, I was going to practice with it, but if you're efficient at it, go right ahead."

He nodded and rolled it back up, and we turned and rode out back to the shelter. We didn't see another soul there, and I was anxious to get back and check on the dog. We rested the horses again at the same creek, but this time we didn't see any snakes.

82 Maryn

The boys thundered into the yard, stirring up dust and Doc's ire until he realized the emergency. He carried Chunk down to the infirmary, and I followed. Becca was still gone with Lew, and Granny was in the next room over in the laundry. She bustled in to help, and when she saw how swollen his face was, she gasped. Doc gave him a shot of antivenom and an IV, but that was all he could do for now. By the time the boys were back from putting up their horses, Doc had Chunk resting on the bed. His dirty fur left mud smears on the white sheet, mingled with his drool, which dripped from his swollen lips.

The boys told him what happened, and he looked at them sternly. "Either of you been bitten?"

They both shook their heads, and Jimmy said, "Chunk grabbed the snake after we shot it, so it was never close enough to us."

Granny hustled in and ran us out of the room. When I looked back before shutting the door, she was on the bed rubbing Chunk down with cold rags. I went upstairs with the boys and made sure they put the horses up, even though they were anxious to check on the dog. I saw Luke's saddle thrown on the ground, and Jimmy hadn't put his blanket where it would dry. I picked them up and told them to get Sara and bring her out, and we would all go to the creek for a picnic. They wouldn't leave until they knew Chunk was going to be all right, so I sat with them on Doc's bench, instead.

Lew and Becca rode up before Doc came out, and I could tell something had happened. Becca dismounted, and Lew took the horses to the barn, and I followed him.

"What is it?" I asked while loosening Becca's saddle.

"May have solved one problem from the west," he said.

"Did you have to kill anyone to solve this particular problem?" I asked half-kidding.

"Maryn, I probably didn't kill enough to be honest with you."

Well, I guess that's what I get for asking a flippant question. We walked back to the shelter in silence, and he gathered up the boys and took them below to clean their weapons. Becca was just back up from checking on the dog, and she was drinking a glass of tea on the bench usually reserved as Doc's spot. Sara was peppering her with questions, and she told us to wait, and they could tell the tale one time at supper.

Becca went to shower, and it was just Sara and me out when Gid and Gwen rode up. They stopped to ask about Chunk, fielded Sara's questions about Beto, and then went to stable their horses. They too went below, and Sara and I stayed and watched the shadows crawl across the yard.

Doc finally came up, had a pull on his bottle before supper, which was odd, and told us he couldn't tell yet whether the dog was in the clear. Nate came in from the creek, carrying his sketch pad and charcoal, where he'd spent the day drawing flowers and trees. Doc slapped his knees, stood up, and said, "Welp, let's eat."

Granny had the supper ready, and I realized how hungry I was, but our group looked despondent today. Lew outlined the shootout with the Omaha woman, Denise, and the agreed-upon rules. I could see the consternation on Doc's face after hearing how close his granddaughter came to being killed, and I knew he and Lew would argue later. It seemed they had been disagreeing a lot lately. Different philosophies, I suppose.

We looked in on Chunk Norris before heading up, and then Gid went into detail about his visit with Mr. Torres. Lew thought it was odd that the boys were gone, but Doc pointed out that our boys are mostly MIA all day. He gave what little info he gathered, and he and Gwen went off to the creek. I went back down to help Granny, and she put me to work making a pecan pie.

"Do you worry about Lew?" I asked her when I set the pie in the oven.

She looked over at me and said. "Of course, he's my son; I'll always worry about him."

"I mean changing. I see it in Gid."

"We'll all have to change to survive this baby. Truth be told, they changed Llewellyn in the desert, and he hasn't been the same since he was wounded and saw those men die. The very same incident in which he saved Doc's son. Well, after a fashion. That boy didn't really come back either. This world takes the boys and girls you raise and changes them so much that sometimes you can't recognize them. Your father is especially skilled at staying alive and killing people, but he's far from the sweet boy I gave to the army."

"It doesn't bother you that he's a killer?" I asked, astonished.

"Didn't you kill the woman who shot Finn? Baby girl, we're all killers now. Sending folks out to kill is still killing. I hate to think there are mothers out there heartbroken about my son ending theirs, but I prefer it that way, wouldn't you?"

"Yes."

"I already lost one son, and I'd sacrifice everyone else's on this earth for my other one to live. Until the world gets on its feet and even beyond that, your children will be killers, too. Remember this talk when that time comes. You must accept that there's pain in this life, and knowing your child is in danger is one of the toughest. Love them and show them the best way forward, but understand that time and circumstances chip away at and shape a person; all you can do is lay the foundation. Llewelyn is a good man at the core; the world has honed his abilities and sanded down his charm some, but he is in there."

"Charm? Next, you're going to be telling me he is polite and a good boy. Paints in the morning and writes sonnets in the afternoon after tea. Composes works of art on the piano and has a fine palette for wines, particularly from the Bordeaux region?" I smiled at my joke, but she did not; instead, her frown lines flashed a warning.

"Your father is charming and is full of generosity. He's more of a whiskey man like these other two rogues here, and I believe he is competent with a guitar. He was one hell of a finger painter, and his schoolwork was always put on the fridge to be admired, not just out of love but because it was good. The biggest part of him, though, is wild, and he got that from my daddy. The Sackett boys were a wild bunch, and he got such a dose that it caused problems between him and his father almost from the start. Gid has it too, in a way it's a defense mechanism," she poured us a glass of tea.

"What do you mean by a defense mechanism?" I asked curiously.

"How many times have you woken up from shooting that woman since it happened? How often does it affect you? How many tears have you shed over taking that life?" She looked at me sternly.

"It does bother me, we aren't supposed to kill people, even awful ones," I said defensively.

"True. There's killing that must be done, though. You think Lew worries over the men and women he leaves dead in his wake, or Gideon, either? If they do, it ain't much, and that keeps them doing the hard thing. They have a dash of cruelty and so far, with a healthy dose of good luck, have kept them — and all of us — alive. In the end, we must remember that their being alive and returning to us is the most important thing, not what they've had to do to get here. They don't take advantage of or abuse this trait, and sadly, it's needed for us to succeed. Justice is carried in a gun holster, and the law is whatever the men who wield them say. It's no different in Texas than here, so you can't run away from it. People are the same no matter where you go, and it's the times that change how they take advantage of you. They've always wanted your resources, whether it be money, land, or labor. Paper money has been replaced by other people's possessions, food, and even people themselves, all used as chattel again. It took gunpowder to blow that wretched practice from this country once, and it will probably take that again. That's another topic, though, and many years in the future on a large scale. Our part in this is to stop it where we can and to flourish as best we can. The last advice I have for you is this: cherish that boy's memory, grieve for him for as much or as little as you need, but don't give a second to that trash that took his life." She reached out and squeezed my hand, causing fresh tears to flow.

I nodded and went to hug her. She held me while I cried, just like she had a hundred times before. Her embrace was the safest place in the world, and I hoped I could pass that along at least to my children and grandchildren one day.

83 Gideon

When Beto Torres and his sons rode into the yard this time, I was there to greet them. The boys were excited to see their new friends, and even Chunk was managing to lumber around a bit, though his face was still swollen. He had kicked up such a fuss inside the infirmary that Doc sent him up top, cussing the whole time. The boys reunited with him, and he never tried to go back inside again. Even though he walked a little wobbly at first, he had managed to survive and sent Jimmy and Luke's spirits soaring. The visit that came two days later boosted their week and sent them into a frenzy. The Torres boys, affectionately nicknamed 'Bet and Neto', were just as excited to see them, and they ran their horses into the yard, stirring up dust, and received a stern reprimand from their father for their behavior.

They took the lecture like pros, then dismounted and ran off with our wild bunch to the creek, Doc yelling at them to be back in an hour to eat. Not sure they heard, Chunk tried his best to keep up as they ran across the field.

We all shook his hand after he dismounted, and Granny gave him a warm welcome and dismissed the boy's behavior. She always took the side of the little ones, and I loved her for it, even when it was cross-purposes with me. She ushered us inside, and after tea was poured, except for Lew and me, they started catching up. Gwen sat beside me and reached her hand into mine. Beto mentioned he was making the boys something with the snakeskin I left with him. He said it would take a few weeks, but he would bring it when it was finished.

"The next time I catch them monkeying with rattlesnakes, I'm going to skin them, and you can have their hide." Doc grumped, and Granny shot him daggers from her eyes.

Beto flashed his smile and said, "They are boys. Boys live dangerously even before this mess." He smiled at Doc, and he dropped his sour look.

Nate asked about his homeland in Spain, and they talked back and forth. Beto said he's from an area around Jerez de la Frontera, and I thought Doc would fall out of his chair.

"You mean Jerez?" Doc asked incredulously.

"Yes, we call it Jerez, you know it?"

"I honeymooned there with my wife, Rose, many years ago. Well, we were really in Cadiz, but we took the trip to Jerez to see the dancing horses at the School of Equestrian Art.

"My cousin raises some of their horses." Doc looked at him, shocked.

"Those aren't the horses you brought here, are they?" Doc looked ready to jump on a horse and ride over immediately.

"Sadly, no. The Spanish government is restrictive about what horses can be exported. To be honest, I carried mine to Portugal and brought them over from there. Same bloodlines, just different shipping port," he smiled brightly at his trickery.

"I'd love to see them," Doc says, almost with youthful exuberance.

"Any time, I enjoy showing them off."

Nate asked about the area and his family from there. Beto told Nate he'd brought several books on family history, and that piqued Nate's interest. Soon, he had Nate and Doc enraptured.

Lew went out to get the boys, and they chatted about the family background, horse breeding, and the area's history. They talked of battles and revolutions, and it made my mind wander because those things were gone forever. Someday, this era we live in will be written in history books, unless the world devolves further into anarchy. The full mounted assaults, fortress defenses, and great raids were a thing of the past. History may repeat itself, but it would take hundreds of years to repopulate the world enough for large-scale battles. It was more likely that a nuclear power plant would melt down and poison us all before that could happen, or some other calamity.

Lew fetched the boys in, and Granny fed them on the front porch after getting them as clean as possible from creek mud. They laughed and cut up at the table, something Granny would never have allowed inside. She grinned when she came in and proclaimed that everyone was now allowed to eat, since she had fed the boys.

The brisket Lew had resting in the oven went down like the Titanic, and everyone was all smiles after the meal. Doc had also put some burgers on for them to take home and have later for supper. We had chairs and benches set up under a giant beech tree that Doc claimed his daddy planted as a boy, and the party moved out there. The humidity wasn't bad today, and the temps had started to recede, so we took advantage of the nice day. A strong breeze helped keep it cool, and soon the boys were back at the creek.

Beto looked around and said, "I don't want to seem out of line here, but it seems you have another place you really live at and just meet me here. Careful and wise. I appreciate caution when dealing with folks."

"What makes you think that?" Doc queried.

"That brisket didn't smoke itself in the oven, and I don't see a smoker around. The grass isn't walked away from the house like it would be if you had boys constantly on it, either."

Doc nodded. "That's observant and true. We want to get your measure before revealing our actual home. Don't misunderstand, this is my home too, where I was raised and where I raised my family, but we are secreted away in a more defensible area."

Beto smiled. "Are you suggesting my place isn't secure enough?"

"I'd have to look at it, but Lew would be better at that than I. He's our tactics and strategy guy. Letting him have an unencumbered scout of your place would probably benefit you. You could always bring your family here if you wanted; we have plenty of room. Understand that this offer is no-strings-attached. Please don't feel you have any obligation to do what I or anyone else suggests, because you're concerned about hurting feelings. We grow 'em rough around here, so we don't slight easily, and we believe a man has the right to do what he thinks is best for him and his family without our judgment. We will continue to help no matter what you decide."

"I appreciate that. Llewelyn, your expertise would be welcome whenever you have the time to ride over. Also, thank you for the supplies you brought on your last visit and for the food this time. The boys enjoyed the sweets, and the medical supplies came in handy when Neto cut his hand on a hatchet. I will need hay for my horses this winter and maybe some more food stores for us if it's a long winter. I don't have any fuel for my tractors to bail with, and the season is late." He looked embarrassed.

"That's a problem we can easily solve. Diesel isn't that hard to come by around here, and Gideon is our premier hay master. Hell, he loves baling hay, don't you?" He turned his laughing eyes on me, and I felt my face start to blush as he knew I hated dealing with hay.

"Better than the Fourth of July," I shot back at him.

They laughed about that, and plans were made to get the equipment, fuel, and people over there to help. The hay from this season wouldn't dry enough to be used, but Doc assured him that there was plenty in his barn for his stock as well as ours. We chatted around the shade for a couple of hours. Sara spoke with Beto briefly and seemed moon-eyed over him; he was polite and easy to talk to, and he shook hands all around, hugging the women except Gwen, who held back. Sara seemed to linger a little too long in his embrace, and he whispered something in Granny's ear that made her throw her head back and laugh.

He thanked Doc again and spoke. "I appreciate you helping me stay on at my place. It's hard to refuse your invitation to stay, but I would like to be at home for as long as possible. I still have hope for some of my family getting here, and I wouldn't want to leave a note sending anyone looting my abandoned house directions here."

Doc nodded his head and spoke. "Some of your family like a wife?"

"No, my wife died in childbirth some years back—her and our daughter both," he said, full of sadness.

Doc wanted to kick himself for asking now, I could see. He hurriedly apologized for bringing that up. "Damn, I'm sorry to hear that. Maybe that will teach me to mind my business in the future."

"It's been years, and that's life. Nothing anyone could have done," he nodded and kicked the dirt with his boot toe.

Doc rushed on to get past the awkwardness, "Like I said, no strings attached. Stay at your place and visit as much or as little as you like. We have an open-door policy here, and I understand your hesitation about leaving your own place. Don't do without —we have plenty here and are willing to share. Mrs. Ruth will hide both of us if she finds out those two lads of yours didn't get enough cookies and fresh milk." We all had a chuckle at that, especially her, and she pressed a bag into his hands apart from the burgers Doc had cooked for him to take home.

"Take these, Sara baked them for you and the boys." She made a point of letting him know who the baker was.

He lifted his hat to her, and she blushed a deep red. The boys were already mounted and waiting to leave when Beto mounted and waved them over. He handed Bet the bag, and they turned and waved to us with the sinking sun on their backs.

84 Maryn

We worked for two solid days at Torres' place, riding back and forth in Doc's truck. Gid and Gwen just brought clothes and set up camp at Walnut Creek. When the work was done there, we came home and started harvesting and putting up from our garden. The Torres boys helped with that and we had it done in a few days. Doc sent them home with so much produce that it had to be loaded in the truck. Doc also took Beto on a tour of the shelter and its grounds. He complimented Doc on his vision to set all this aside and admitted that his son was the genius behind it. He sent Beto off with a new rifle, as well as the vegetables and smoked meats from his smokehouse.

The boys wanted to stay for a few nights with Luke and Jimmy, and he relented after Granny scolded him for not letting them enjoy her cooking after all the hard work they had done. She was the force around here, and we all bent to her wishes in the end. She wouldn't miss an opportunity to let the boys run wild when they could before the cold weather sent everyone indoors.

Lew and Doc went over several ways to improve his position at home, and Beto wanted to start as soon as possible. Doc promised to bring the backhoe at the end of the week and start putting up fencing to keep the animals out once it's done. Ditches, fences, and redoubts would encircle the place when finished, providing it with much greater security. He ate supper with us for the first time at the shelter that evening, then decided to spend the night after enjoying a few glasses with the men up top. The boys were over the moon, and Granny made sure they had something to sleep in that night in the tent.

Sara informed me she wanted to visit Beto that night and asked my advice. “I want you to do whatever will make you happy.”

“His sadness and loneliness call to me, doesn’t it you?” She asked nervously, either because of her plan or because of my disapproval.

“You think he feels the same way?” I asked, surprised at how fast she had made the decision.

“I believe he does. He's probably worried about taking me away from here and how everyone will feel about it. His gaze lingers, and I feel we have something,” she sounded as if she had considered all of it.

“No one here is going to feel differently about him or you, for that matter, you both are adults. Doc would say something along the lines of ‘A man needs a woman and vice versa. Boys need a mama, etc., etc., and Granny will be ‘baby if you’re happy with him, then be happy with him,’ and no one else will bat an eye. Do what you feel is right; if he agrees, go with it. I’ll miss you being here, but I get it.” My own loneliness swept over me at the thought of her leaving, but I wouldn’t try to sabotage her happiness if she found some.

The next day, she acted strangely and blushed when I asked her about the meeting. “I’ll tell you later, but he’s going to want me to go back with him.” She winked and almost skipped away like a little girl. Must have hit it off, I smiled to myself and headed to the kitchen to help Granny get things going.

Later, Sara hugged me, and I walked her over to Doc’s truck so she could ride over with him. I stopped at the driver’s window, and he looked in the rearview and saw her put her bag in the bed before opening the passenger door and getting in.

Doc cranked his truck and looked over at her.

“The hell is that?” Doc growled.

“My things, “she said, looking at him in the rearview mirror.

“You are going to him, honey?” Doc asked as she settled in.

“I am, and I’m staying there,” she said defiantly.

“If you’re sure, you can do anything you want. I won’t try to stop you. You need to say goodbye to the folks before we pull out of here?” He pondered.

“No, I already said my goodbyes. You are the last one I needed to see. Thank you for taking me in and saving my life. I’ll never be able to repay you, but I do appreciate it. Beto and I have something, and we intend to make a life together. I’m glad you don’t have an issue with that.” She sat there unwavering in her conviction, ready to defend her feelings.

Doc just smiled at her and said, “If it makes the two of you happy, then I’m happy as well. Wring every bit of happiness out of this life while you can; it's fleeting and hard most of the way.”

I stepped back and waved to them, and they waved back, taking off up the road. Beto and the boys said goodbye in the backyard. Lew told him they would bring the equipment over and start work soon, and they rode off, cutting across the pasture toward home.

The next couple of days, Granny and I made extra food to bring with us when they decided it was time to do the dirt work at Beto’s. After loading the backhoe and tractor, we packed the prepared food into the back of the truck, where barbed wire and metal posts were already stacked.

The work started as soon as we had everything unloaded. Doc ran the backhoe over the ground Lew had already marked out with spray paint the day before. Gid, Gwen, Becca, and the boys started on the fencing and driving posts into the ground. Lew spelled off Gid on the post driver, and by dark, the posts were all set, and most of the ditches were dug. We stayed overnight there in his cramped living room, and after getting the wire run the next morning, Doc proclaimed it was time to head home. Doc decided to leave the backhoe here in case Beto needed it to make any changes, and we headed home with everyone in tow. Nate and Granny were sitting on the benches and waved to us as we pulled into the yard, welcoming us home.

It was Halloween the next day after we got the fencing done at Beto's, and it turned out to be the last warm day of the year; the cold air coming down from Canada had finally broken summer's back and made it release its grip on us. The next morning, we woke up under gray clouds and cooler weather. The boys took the end of the warm weather the hardest, and they complained nonstop about it. Halloween turned out to be a showdown between them and Granny.

She stopped them from running away from the breakfast table and gave them another task before their usual chores. Wear boots and a shirt outside from now on.

"Granny, my feet are as hard as turtle shells. I don't need boots." Jimmy complained.

"Until they are as hard as your head, you'll be wearing them in the cold, or you can wear my switch on your backside." Her stance and deepened wrinkle convinced them to stamp into their boots and take off. Becca and I laughed at the speed the boys peeled out after her threat.

She turned her glare toward me, and it softened instantly. "You spoke privately with Sara. How is she getting on over there?"

"She said everything's fine except he beats her." The look on her face of sheer incredulity was almost enough to make me burst out laughing.

"WHAT?" she screeched, her wrinkle back and deepening.

"Beating her insides, her words, not mine." I heard Becca chortle with laughter. Granny slowly relaxed her face and almost smiled.

"The boys aren't the ones that can catch a switching around here; you almost caused me to have to take a trip over there with a rolling pin." She huffed at being tricked and looked at Becca. "Since we're being vulgar in here, how are you and my son doing? You still trying to keep it a secret from the old man?"

Becca's mouth hung open for a second until she snapped it closed hard. I thought she might knock her jaw askew. Granny laughed at her discomfort and plowed on. "I'm not asking how he is in bed, I've seen him naked all his life, I know he has a hammer that's big enough to be called a sledge, I'm speaking in general. Do you argue often, are you happy with him, that sort of thing?" Becca was silent as the grave as her face started to redden, and her throat worked, trying to swallow.

"Honey, are you alright?" Granny put her hand to Becca's forehead, and then she looked into her eyes. "I've embarrassed you now?" Granny demanded. "I thought it was all fun and games to be shocking this morning?"

"W-well, his pen-, I mean hammer, as you mentioned, is something I didn't expect you to bring up, and it caught me off guard."

"Oh, it's only funny when you two make a dirty joke to an old lady, but the medicine is bitter when given back?" She hooted with laughter. "Sit down, dear, before you faint and hit the floor. I want to make sure my boy doesn't need a whipping for not treating you right."

"I didn't even know you knew about us." Becca managed to mumble after sitting.

"Honey, even your old grandpa isn't that blind, and I'm sure everyone realizes it by now. Hell, you're twenty-five, twenty-six, aren't you? Tell the old man and be done with it. He's still going to love you, and he may even be happy about it. Either way, no more sneaking around playing hide the sledge." Becca steadied herself before speaking.

"You're right, he does need to be told. As a matter of fact, I'll tell him about Llewelyn and his magic sledge tonight after supper. Do you have a special meal that could help him take the news a little better? I don't want to explain to him how your son finished me off three times a night without something on his stomach to help him get through that."

"Well, for starters, I would leave out the part about the magic sledgehammer and just tell him how you feel about each other." Granny and I both laughed at her jest. She needed to give it back to Granny, and now there wouldn't be any more reservations between the two of them.

We heard Doc shout from the doorway, "If you three are done cackling like magpies in there, maybe I can get you to come outside and see something amazing."

Opening the door to the shop, I was assaulted by black-and-yellow swirls in the air. For as far as you could see, butterflies fluttered overhead.

"Monarchs migrating," Nate said as he admired the sight. I had seen them on TV before, but I didn't know there were this many in the world.

"Late this year," Doc said around his pipe, "but plentiful. I have never seen so many in my life."

"You mean there haven't been this many in two hundred years?" Gid asked slyly, and the grin on Doc's face widened.

After the march of the butterflies, as Doc called it, the day started in earnest. Chores, cleaning, and laundry never wait, and at the end of the day, we were all looking forward to supper. We ate and went upstairs like always, but this time Lew and Becca huddled together in deep conversation before asking Doc to join them. After hearing the news, he sat back down at his spot and lit his pipe without a word. He threw back his whiskey and stood after pouring another.

"Everyone, give me a second, I've got something important to say. My granddaughter has turned her back on Iowa and the Midwest by giving her heart to a Southerner. This would disappoint me under ordinary circumstances with an ordinary man, but that's not the case. Llewelyn became linked with me years ago in a foreign land, and having his other family here has only made it better. The day after tomorrow, he will marry my granddaughter and become part of my tribe. Hell, out of all the people left in the world, you folks are who I would choose to live the remainder of my life with, anyway, so it turned out for me. I realize everyone here has lost folks, but this family will endure and flourish. Thank you all for being here and for what you do to make all our lives better. Congratulations to the soon-to-be newlyweds." He raised his glass, and everyone shouted "CONGRATULATIONS" loud enough for the coyotes to hear from the cattle pasture and answer back with mournful notes.

The next morning was Halloween, and Granny went all out. Cookies, homemade candy, pies, and Doc planned to grill ribeyes later. He was dispatched over to collect the Torres bunch and bring them back for the festivities. Granny put the finishing touches on her "haunted house" for the boys in the wing of her sleeping quarters, and it worked, with young Neto running hysterically out into the open embrace of Sara. They told ghost stories, and we sat around a campfire outside in the chill, enjoying the starry night sky, the boys daring each other to run out into the dark, seeing who would go the farthest.

The next day, Granny was busy taking down the decorations, so I made breakfast. She came to help with the evening meal, and Lew asked me to come up to him. We walked to the barn without a word, and Gid was already there with Gwen just out of earshot.

"I wanted to talk to you two in private for a minute today and gauge your thinking about the wedding. If there are any issues you want to get out of the way, let's address them right away. Maryn, anything?"

"I hope you and Becca are happy, that's all. You're our father, why wouldn't we want you to be happy? I love you and want Becca to have love, too. Seems you both are happy, so what could be wrong with that?"

"Gideon, you got anything?" Lew stared at him.

"Nothing from me. She must love you for some reason, and that's good enough. She does love you, right?"

"She does," he said.

"I thought so because the man who showed up in Wisconsin is gone. That man would have never taken us by the hand and invited us to share our feelings and shoot rainbows out of our asses. She's made you soft, and I'm afraid you have sugar in your tank now. You're going to be braiding hair next week and giving makeup tutorials?" Gideon joked.

"Soft?" Lew lunged for him, and they grappled, Lew roaring, "I'll show you soft, boy!"

"You already have," Gideon managed while trying to stay upright and not get taken down. Gwen hadn't been paying too close attention to the conversation, and when she looked and saw them struggling together, she instinctively reached for her pistol. Both men saw her and stopped immediately.

Gid put his hands up and told her, "We're just playing around."

She removed her hand from the gun and shot us with one of her brilliant smiles and a sign to us. "Of course you are, both of you are the same age, eight." I translated out loud while she signed. We had a laugh at that and walked out of the barn with Lew's arm around my neck and headed back to the house.

85 Gideon

A week later, Beto, Lew, Gwen, and I were in a stand of trees west of Macedonia deer hunting. Beto and Gwen had both killed small bucks earlier, and we had field-dressed them and stashed both in the truck bed. We got here before daylight and wanted to see if we could thin this herd out a little and send some meat home with Beto to help with his supplies. I was waiting for a corn-fed doe to move away from a willow tree by the river to take her. She heard something from the west and turned to look that way, and when she did, I sent my arrow across from my side of the riverbank, striking her right in the heart. She bucked for a few yards and fell over into the high grass. I sat still with Gwen about ten yards to my right and gave her time to die. I wonder what made her turn and look, so she would give me the shot, as Gwen stood up beside me.

She kissed me on the cheek, smiled, and motioned toward the bridge. I put my hand up and touched her. I squatted down, and she did the same.

“Did you see what she was looking at?” Gwen shook her head, and I told her to wait a second. We sit tight for five minutes, and I ask her to bring her rifle, and I’ll carry my bow in case we see another one on the other side. Something feels weird to me, but I can’t put my finger on it.

“Does it seem as if something’s wrong to you?” I ask her. She shrugged her shoulders, and we quietly slipped out of the trees and crossed the bridge. We stopped again on the other side and waited. The feeling won’t leave me, and I glanced back at our side of the river, and Lew was standing there looking at us.

He opened his hands to ask, “What's going on?” in a gesture, and I felt silly for being overly cautious. I heard it then—a horse neighing. I looked north and, through my binoculars, saw a horse with its ears pointed toward us. It stepped out of the trees, and I saw a splash of white on its coat, red and wet on the saddle, and something hanging from the off side of it. Alarm bells went off in my brain as I turned to show Gwen. She looked past the cemetery to the little stand of trees behind it, nodding.

"I'm going to go up there, stay here, and cover me in case the owner is using the horse for bait," I told her. She settled behind her 5.56, and I took off. I pointed the direction I'm heading out to Lew, and he glassed the area; he saw it, too. He took off along the side of the river parallel to me. Before I stepped into the open of the cemetery, I glassed the appaloosa horse again through my binoculars and saw a person on the ground on the far side of the animal, his foot stuck in the stirrup. I walked over cautiously, pistol in hand, and checked the area. I placed my hand on the horse's neck and spoke to the gelding softly. He knickered again and rubbed his head against my arm when I looked around at the tangled stirrup. I waved to everyone to come up and bent to the older man, probably in his fifties, who was sprawled out with his arms flung above his head, and his face was lacerated. I slid his boot off, and his leg hit the ground, causing him to moan loudly. The horse shied away, freed from the weight, and walked off a few yards to turn and watch us. I spoke softly to her and got over to the saddle and loosened his canteen, knelt again by the old man and dripped some on his cracked and broken lips. His eyes fluttered, and he opened his mouth for more of the liquid.

He coughed and hacked some of it back up and whispered, "Shot me...ambushing bastards."

By the time Lew and Gwen made it over, I had his shirt off,

and I could see he wouldn't make it. "What's your name, mister?" I asked him after giving him another drink.

"You have any whiskey, young man?" he asked.

"No, sir, I don't," I ask his name again.

"Jim Haskins from over in Underwood, I could take dying a little easier if I had some whiskey," he sputtered.

"Mr. Haskins, my name is Llewelyn, and we'll do what we can for you, but it ain't much, I'm afraid."

The old man nodded, and I went to get the truck so we could bring him home, but Beto was already heading our way when I turned to go. We put Mr. Haskins in the bed, and I unsaddled his horse and dropped his bridle. I would come back for him after we got him home.

We had him situated in the infirmary, and Doc provided him with whiskey. Lew sent us out to the room while Beto, Doc, and Becca tended to the man. Lew relayed the story to us when he left the infirmary. Several riders had set upon Mr. Haskins while he was out tending to his sheep. Four men, he thinks, but couldn't be sure. The first warning he had was a round through his midsection that knocked him off his horse. He managed to climb back in the saddle and took two more rounds before he could get up to speed to leave them behind. One of those hit his liver and sealed his fate. After not being able to hold on anymore, he slipped from the saddle, and the horse dragged him several hundred yards until we found them.

When Gwen and I got back from collecting his horse and the deer that had been taken that morning, Lew was digging a hole in Doc's family cemetery for him. I took the animals to our processing barn, and we got to work skinning them out. Jimmy came and got us when they were ready to put Mr. Haskins in the ground, and we washed up the best we could and got there in time to see the men lowering him with ropes under a chill rain. Lew covered him with the backhoe hoe, and Nate read the Bible.

"Did you at least get him a drink of whisky before he died?" I asked Lew.

He nodded as we piled the dirt over the man. Doc stood there with his hat in his hand, about the saddest I had ever seen him.

"Did you know him, Doc?" I asked while shoveling.

"We went to school together, a touch over sixty years, now I suppose."

"Why didn't we ever see him or any sign of him? His place isn't too far from here," I asked, shocked that he could have run a small ranch this close to us, and we never found anything to indicate it.

"He just got back last week. His daughter had a place near Storm Lake, and he lived there until two weeks ago. A preacher killed her and her husband and burned the place down while he was out hunting, according to her. He gathered up what he could and came home, just to be murdered himself."

The preacher's twist surprised me. I heard they diddled kids on the regular, but flat-out murder? The Lord does indeed work in mysterious ways if He lets trash like that plague humanity.

86 Llewelyn

At first, I suspected some Omaha trash was to blame for the old man's death, but they came from the east and returned that way after ransacking his home and stealing his horses. Once they got on 80, I lost the tracks, and with the rain, it wouldn't do much good to keep looking. I was at an impasse about what to do. They could be a mile down the road or one hundred. Couldn't stake out the entire interstate waiting for them to show up again. They probably went in different directions every time to raid; that's what I would do, so predicting where they would be is almost impossible. I sent the old man and boys off to collect what's left of Mr. Haskins's livestock and bring them back here while we tracked the murders.

I took Gwen and Gideon with me, checking both shoulders of the highway while the rain pelted our slickers. The rain slowed, then stopped after a couple of miles, and we pushed on. Late that afternoon, Gideon found tracks heading southeast after we passed Indian Creek. Five riders and eight horses in total, so this was the bunch we were after. They had foolishly left the road and left the tracks we found before getting back on the feeder road and heading down 560th Street toward a town called Marne. We followed them until they took a gravel road, crossed a small branch that I suspected was Camp Creek, and then cut across a field. Near dark, the rain had stopped, so we camped beside the small creek, and I looked at the map. Not wanting to believe it, but it looked like they were heading toward Atlantic.

That town should have been a warning to anyone using it as a base, given what we left behind, and it didn't make sense why they wouldn't have just used the road until Marne. We left before full light, and I understood the direction when I saw a man standing outside a house, pissing in a yard with horses around back. I stopped the other two and signaled to them an enemy ahead. We looped wide around the house in the trees and set up south of them, and I left them in a copse of trees about one hundred yards away from the house. I waited in the roadside ditch about fifty yards farther up from them, closer to the home. An hour slowly crept by, and the cold water in the ditch was starting to work on my feet. With no thought to security, they poured out of the house, warm, bellies full of stolen food and coffee, no doubt. The thought burned through me, but I knew the next time they would breakfast would be in hell.

They rode bunched up, trailing the three stolen horses that Mr. Haskins described, and I knew this was the right outfit. I was right to send Doc after his livestock, since this bunch was too lazy to bring the sheep, and only three of the five horses he had. I waited until the first three almost passed me, and I stepped out of the ditch.

"Howdy," I said with my rifle at my shoulder.

The closest horse snorted and shied, and the middle rider tried to swing his gun around, and Gwen or Gid shot him from the saddle. The farthest rider from me lost control of his horse, and his pistol hit the ground, spinning in the morning sun. The last two sat there immobilized by fear or shock, and I shot both, watching them drop out of the saddle. The tall man closest to me got his horse under control and pulled his pistol. I swung my rifle at him, but before I could fire, his horse bucked, causing his gun to go off, the round striking the unfortunate horse right in the back of the head, instantly dumping the rider onto the gravel road. When he tried to stand up, I shot him in the head and saw the other man, who had lost his pistol, riding fast across the field. I heard the rifles crack from the trees, and he went sailing off the back of his horse into the mud. Gideon walked over to make sure he was finished, and I checked these three. The two in back I mistakenly took for women were actually a small teenage boy with just a wisp of a beard starting on his chin and an older woman with all her teeth missing. I noticed they rode smaller saddles and made a mental note to get them for the boys. All four of these were dead, so I gathered up our horses and met Gideon and Gwen at the bodies in the road. They had caught up all the horses except the one that was still running away.

The saddles were in good shape, so we took two horses and freed the others from their saddles and bits. They weren't much worth a damn, and we took five, two from the outlaws and the three that belonged to Mr. Haskins. Four saddles, two 30-06 bolt-action rifles, and eight pistols, a variety of calibers, also made the trip back home. We didn't make the same mistake and followed the road through Marne, then took roads that ran south along Indian Creek until it turned west, then back south to Beto's home.

We ate a meal with him and Sara, and I told him we intended to leave the other three horses with him for his hospitality, but he wouldn't hear of it.

"I can never repay the kindness you folks have shown us; take all the horses with you," he insists.

"Honestly, I don't want the aggravation of driving them home. I need the two black mares to haul the saddles back, or I wouldn't bring any of them," I told him in front of his fireplace, wet clothes steaming on the drying racks. "Got some pistols if you need them as well."

"Is it going to be like this forever? Every stranger you meet is probably trying to kill, rob, or both?" He looked ruefully at his sons playing checkers in the breakfast nook.

"It will be in our lifetimes, at least," I admitted. "Not saying all people are bad, but be wary of them."

"Even you?" He jokingly asks.

"Not me, I'm an old house cat." He chuckled at that.

Beto offered to drive us home in his truck, which had fresh fuel from Doc's, but I refused. I needed to take a look at the ground on the ride back, but from a truck seat, I couldn't track anything worth a damn. We spent the night there, but I didn't sleep well as I kept seeing that boy's face.

Maryn told me what my mama said about not having dreams of the people I killed, but she was mistaken. I did dream of the dead sometimes, and that young boy wasn't much older than Jimmy, and now he would never be any older. I fished an old .22 revolver out of his belt and found that it wasn't even loaded. I set it down on his chest after closing the cylinder; his green eyes flew open, and he choked on blood coming from his mouth.

"Why did you have to kill me? Why? I'm fifteen this month. Why?" The blood continued down his face from his mouth.

"Sorry, kid. You live by the sword; you die by it."

"I don't have no sword mister, just this old gun I stole from my granny's house. I didn't even load it. I never hurt nobody."

I looked away to the old woman, and it was my mama lying there with my round shot through her chest, eyes accusing me.

"You killed us. All you've ever done is bring pain to our home, ever since you killed that boy on the river in high school." She pointed back at the young boy with her blood-covered hand, and he changed to Gideon lying there.

"Why? Why kill your only son?" I woke up, reaching for my rifle on the edge of tears. I had never dreamed anything so real. I could smell the cordite in the air and horses, even the shit that had been evacuated from one or more of them. The real smell of battle. They didn't put that in poems and stories about the piss and shit everywhere, but it had clung to me in that freezing ditch and every other battle I had been in.

The next morning, we rode into the yard just about the time the rain started. The boys took our horses and were ecstatic over having smaller saddles that would be theirs. While they were busy in the barn, I recounted to everyone else what we had seen and done, including stopping at Beto's place on the way over.

"How did you come by those small saddles?" Nate asked.

"The previous owners no longer need them," I said coldly, wondering why he would mention that. A strange mood must have grabbed him, and I suppose he was allowed; he was adjusting like everyone else. Maybe the pressure of this new life had taken its toll on him, and he was despairing? I hadn't been back to sleep after the nightmare, and the cold ride this morning hasn't improved my mood, and I unfairly lashed out at him.

"I know you disapprove of the violence we partake in, Nate, but the world is left with desperate people who are suffering. Some are extremely dangerous, and if you don't understand that, go outside and let's look at that fresh mound of dirt in the yard that used to be a man who was minding his own business," I told him evenly without losing my temper over his judgment.

Turning back to my mama, I said, "Beto's family is in good health and wishes us the best."

"Did he say when he's coming back this way?" she asked.

"Friday, if that were fine with everyone," I told Mama.

"He's always welcome here. I wish he would bring his family down to be safer," Doc grumbled.

I wasn't going to argue with him in the chill and my temper being out of sorts, so I took the horses into the barn with the boys and sent Gideon and Gwen inside to clean up. I needed some more time to calm myself and to shake whatever had a hold of me after those killings yesterday. Becca came out and stood in the corner until they finished and returned to the shelter. She came over and embraced me, soaking and all.

"In a mood, huh?" She smiled at me, and I just grunted.

"Let's get you naked and see if that will improve it some," she winked, and I followed her back, scanning the horizon and seeing more darkening clouds in the western sky.

87 Gideon

Gwen and I hunted on Thursday, so when the Torres clan showed up on Friday, we had plenty of meat to send them home with. The fresh meat we killed today would replace what was in the smokehouse. We took the boys; they had both killed deer with their bows, and Gwen and I each shot a snow goose on the river north of Henderson. We worked all day and into the night to get them processed so Doc could hang them the next day.

Of course, the boys rode up first, completely ignoring the scolding they got weeks before from Beto about doing that very thing, and before their father could tell them any different, they had Jimmy and Luke down to the creek. It was too cold to swim, but boys are drawn to water and danger like moths to a flame. When he rode in with Sara, he was already shaking his head at their antics, but his smile was warm for everyone as he dismounted and greeted us.

Sara looked in fine condition and seemed happy. Doc and Granny went out of their way to make sure she didn't feel awkward about her decision to leave, and it seemed to set her mind at rest. We chatted outside for a few minutes until Granny scolded us about standing around in the cold like damn fools, and we hustled inside. I took their horses, and Gwen and I walked them to the barn. Instead of stabling them, I decided to mount them and check on these knuckleheads.

Gwen and I were shocked to find them gone. Bet and Neto's horses were ground-hitched and cropping the dried grass and knickered softly when we rode up. I dismounted, looking around at the empty trees and fields. I glanced at Gwen, and she shrugged her shoulders. Putting my hand on Neto's black,

I saw they knocked the grass over, getting down and heading to the creek. I looked over to the bank, and a rustling sound and movement from my right warned me. I reached for my pistol and stopped when I realized the boys had hidden in the tall grass to ambush me. They rushed me, giggling, trying to topple me to the ground. I pushed Luke, who reached me first, and just moved out of his way, and he almost fell into the water, flying past with his own momentum. Bet and Jimmy hit me with their shoulders at nearly the same time from my left, and I felt myself start to tilt over until Neto crashed into me on the opposite side and saved me. Soon, I had them sorted out, rolling in the brittle grass with Gwen laughing in the background. Little monsters, I thought as they started to get to their feet. Granny doesn't spend enough time beating these miscreants. They flew at me again, but they had lost the initiative with the failed execution of the ambush, and I handled them easily enough. After flinging the Lord of the Flies around for a bit, I made them tend the horses. Walking back, I explained the ambush was great, but the timing was off. Jimmy complained that I was stronger than them.

"I'll always be stronger than you and will always have a bigger dingus too. That doesn't mean the four of you couldn't have overcome me. The execution was sloppy, and that's the only reason you ended up in the grass instead of me. Work on that, the four of you. Teamwork and coordination are the only way to defeat a stronger enemy unless you're smarter than they are."

"Your mind is the greatest weapon," he repeated a lesson from Lew.

"Well, maybe not yours. Your mind is like the knife you left outside on the creek bank for a few months, dull and rust-stained, like your underwear." I grabbed Jimmy in a headlock and rubbed my knuckles gently across his scalp while he squealed, and the other boys piled on me, and we all ended up in the muddy field laughing and dodging Chunk's teeth.

When we got home, Granny was none too happy with our appearance, and she told Gwen that she was responsible because boys didn't have enough sense to "pour piss out of a boot with the instructions on the heel." Gwen laughed at that and agreed with her assessment of our intelligence —or lack of it. Cleaned up, we got right to eating and listened to their news. Not much was happening at their place, and fortunately, it's the same here.

The weather had turned cold, Doc predicted snow soon, but we had the crops in. The hay was stacked, and all the feed we could find was put up guarded by a mean tomcat that lurked in the shadows of the barn, fighting a constant war against mice. Jimmy had caught him in a wire cage at a neighbor's house a couple of miles west of us. He wasn't just ruthless with mice; he would also peel your skin back if you got too close.

This was the time for inside work, storytelling, watching the rows of DVDs Doc had stored, and repairing gear for the following year. A plow tine needed to be rewelded, Beto brought an old 1893 Spanish Mauser with a bolt that wouldn't slide smoothly, and endless minor tasks that we now had time to do.

Sara sewed the boy quilts with Granny and Maryn, while Beto helped us shoe the horses. They stayed about eight days, Beto taking the boys back to his place every few days to check the stock and make sure the auto feeders stayed full. Our chickens had to be moved inside, and their egg production slowed in the cold weather. We had to change our breakfast diet to include powdered eggs, but overall, it was a happy time. After the outdoors chores were done, we exercised, shot, cleaned, lounged around, played board games, wrestled, and hustled wood for Doc's smokehouse. We had plenty of food and sent a truckload over to the Torres' place. Doc was afraid of heavy snow this year, and about three days after they went home, he was right.

The Wisconsin snow was plentiful, like I said earlier, yet it was just more civilized. There were no shoveled sidewalks here. This snow was a different beast. The wind that accompanied piled it up against the shop wall and barns, and over a foot of snow fell in two days, and the only people who were happy about it were Maryn and Granny. The women loved the way it looked, blanketing the ground, and honestly, I did too, but the shine wore off with the boys as soon as they realized we still had to tend our animals in it. The snow went from ready ammunition to launch at each other to a hazard and a hindrance when doing chores in it. We couldn't give ourselves away with the snowplow, so the roads stayed covered and had to melt on their own.

We didn't see Beto again until Thanksgiving. The storms had broken, and the snow had mostly melted, allowing them to head over in his truck. We feasted and laughed during the holiday. Sara looked well and broke the happy news that she was expecting. We all cheered that, and the celebration was taken up to the shop where the men smoked and drank now, since the snow and cold had driven them inside. Granny had to threaten the two boys moving out of their tent and into a bunk inside, and Doc finally relented and let Chunk Norris sleep with them in their room. They made a pallet on the floor, and all three of them piled into it every night.

Lew sat next to me that night, and I had my first whiskey. He looked at me strangely, raised his glass, and said, "To my son." If I didn't know any better, I would say he's proud of me and getting misty-eyed. He quaffed his glass, and I did the same. The liquid hit me like lava, and I almost sputtered. He smiled and gave me a wink before getting up to hug Gwen and shake Beto's hand. What the hell had gotten into him, I wondered. He sat beside Maryn, whispering to her, and she wiped her face to hide tears. I'll ask him later what he was going through. Instead, Granny came over, and I questioned her about it.

"Your pa is just maudlin, is all."

"What does that mean?" I asked.

"He's seen you two grow up over the last several months, but missed you all your lives. He loves you, and he knows the bitterness of not being able to change the past. Regret is brutal to face. You're young, but if you live long enough, you will make decisions that burn you like a brand. Even when you make the best decision in a situation, or you aren't completely responsible for it, consequences must be lived with. Your sister lost her young beau, and the chances of her finding anyone suitable are slim around here. Think of this: while he celebrates your um, companionship, with Gwen, he mourns her sadness and loss." She finished her tea and stood.

"Thanks, Granny, I never thought of it like that before," I told her.

"Don't feel guilty about your happiness, but don't forget about her suffering either. Life is different for her than it is for you, and that's not your fault. Life is just like that. Someone is always up while someone else is down. Just be aware of her pain and loneliness. Have a kind word ready every chance you get —not just for her, but for everyone that needs it.” Enough seriousness from her, I supposed, because she switched gears. Maybe she was facing her own consequences? “I saw the look on your face when you drank that whiskey. Are you going to be able to walk to your bed, or do I need to carry you like when you were a baby and would fall asleep on the couch?” She chortled at that and took off.

The drinking went late into the night; Doc got the drunkest I ever saw, except for the day he declared that Becca and Lew were a couple, and the next day was an easy day for everyone except those with sore heads. A slight rain kept us all in, except for chores, the lion’s share of the day we spent lounging around, nursing headaches, playing games, or chatting. Gwen and I went to bed early so we could be alone, as she was feeling down herself. I asked about why she had the blues, but she shook it off and slid up against me in the bed, refusing to say. The next day, the Torreses left and returned home, promising to return at or before Christmas.

88 Maryn

Once Sara was gone, I felt lonely again, but we were so busy that I didn't have time to focus on it. We worked like crazy to get the Christmas presents ready for everyone since Doc had declared the hides from the deer and cattle were ready to be sewn. Granny decided everyone needed new chaps since Luke had cut his leg on a branch earlier while riding his horse, so we got to it. We weren't used to working with leather, and it took a bit to master, but the chaps turned out great. After much measuring, cutting, and sewing, we managed to give everyone a customized pair unlike the ones from the western store. She got the Torreses' measurements while they were here for Thanksgiving, so we were set for Christmas when they came.

Beto managed to find an actual sleigh with bells and all, and came into the yard on Christmas Eve, causing a commotion. The boys unloaded the packages from the sleigh without much thought, focusing on going for a ride, which Beto did so often that he had to switch the horses out. The boys had gotten a break from being cloistered indoors and seemed to be enthusiastic for the first time since Thanksgiving. We all got a ride, and I can still remember the snowflakes brushing my cheeks and landing on my eyelashes that night. We had to stop and let Chunk in the sleigh so he would stop chasing the horses, and Granny held him close to her chest and laughed while he snapped at snowflakes. The most magical Christmas I ever had before or since, truth to be told. Everyone was in great spirits, and for that night, there was nothing wrong in the world.

Walking into the kitchen that Christmas Eve was burned into my mind, and I carried it with me all the days of my life.

Granny was using her apron to pour hot chocolate from a pot into mugs, the smell of cinnamon coming from the ovens, the laughter, and the rosy look on everyone's face from the frosty rides in the darkness was etched in my memories, sending my despair and pain to the back of my mind for a time.

The snow was still falling when we awoke on Christmas morning, and we all gathered up top to witness the world blanketed. It still fell and piled up in the grey dawn, looking like a full day of weather. It seemed like a postcard outside, and for the first time in a while, I was happy, and the anguish over Finn lessened.

Sara was glowing in her pregnancy and showed off her small bump to our delight, but underneath it all, Granny was worried about her safety. Becca was the best chance of helping her with the delivery, and she made Beto promise to bring her here for the birth. Bet and Neto loved her, and they seemed like a happy family trying to put their lives back together, and Granny made them all promise to get her here in time for delivery.

Nate flourished during this time with his books and teachings. The weather seemed to be his ally, and he shone during this spell of indoor days and storms raging. Jimmy and Luke were the opposite. The holiday gave them some respite, but the days of summer, running wild and barefoot, left them with little enthusiasm for being stuck indoors, away from sunshine and warmth. They struggled to focus on Nate's studies and Doc's long-winded stories, and the only reprieve was physical exercise with Lew and Gid.

That Christmas morning, they were excited about not just their new chaps, which they all donned immediately and swaggered around like old west cowboys, but Beto had fashioned the rattlesnake hide that Gid left him into hat bands for Jimmy and Luke. He sewed the rattle into a leather strap and added a buckle for the other hero, Chunk Norris, to wear. They slipped them onto their hats, and each one shook Beto's hand for the personalized gift. They all ran off to play in the barn with Chunk jumping in the snow like a deer, and left us in peace for a few minutes while Gid and I cleaned up from breakfast. Chunk had been lying in his customary spot in front of the wood-burning stove up in the shop while everyone sat around it jawing, but wouldn't miss a chance to get outside with the boys.

The next day, they returned home with a fresh supply of food, and Doc pleaded with them to move in and bring the horses down. Beto even had Granny applying guilt about the upcoming baby, and he was on the cusp of breaking, it felt like. He promised they would return the following week for the holiday, but that wasn't to be. It wasn't until the end of January that we saw them again. The weather turned terrible, and the snow piled up. Weeks of fighting to get to the barn and back again kept us close to home, and the same for them. Lew took Becca off in mid-January to check on them. Gid wanted to go instead, and they even got heated over it. In the end, Lew and Becca went and were gone for four days.

When they came into the yard on the fifth day, they looked haggard and half frozen. Gid slipped and sprained his ankle in the barn putting up their horses, and Gwen had to help him back home. Lew informed us the Torreses were fine—just as stuck inside as we were—and in good health. We stayed put for another ten days, and just like it came in, it was gone. A couple of days in the high fifties, and the world turned to mud instead of snow and ice.

Three days later, Jimmy ran in shouting at riders on the horizon. Beto brought his bunch in, looking bedraggled. It was early afternoon, and they were mud-spattered, and the horses were blown.

"Come on down, have any trouble on the road?" Doc asks to help Sara down.

"Yes, the creek is flooded, and we had to backtrack and take the long way. The mud has dragged the horses down, and they're exhausted," Beto said, swinging down. "My truck is stuck in the ditch along the road by the county barn." The horses weren't the only things worn out. They came in from the drizzle, and all had hot showers. Even Neto and Bet were soon asleep, and they didn't rouse until suppertime.

89 Llewelyn

Early March arrived with howling winds and freezing rains. Doc nodded and assured me it's about right for that month, and he goes so far as to wonder why a woman would have babies this time of year —a jab at me because the twins' birthdays were at the back end of the month.

My opinion on them staying at his place has shifted after living through the past winter. Experiencing the hardships of surviving with animals and the dangers the weather presented, I pitched in with Doc and everyone else to get him to move over with us. I joined the others in urging him to bring his family in, but for some reason, he remained resistant. It had gotten to the point where if he were there alone, I would have just avoided the place altogether, angry over his stubbornness. Of course, with Sara and the boys there, that was not possible, so I tried to hide my irritation with him and carry on as we had been.

I rode over around a week later to check in on them, and the creek was still swollen with floodwater. It had become a contention between Gideon and me over these trips, but I finally had to tell him how I felt.

"I wouldn't risk you or your sister for a hundred Betos and Saras. There's danger not only from people but from the terrain itself right now. Hell, you almost broke your leg in the barn, so sit tight, and I'll go check on them," I explained to him.

He didn't like it any, but he could be angry in the shelter, and I could accept that. The nine miles to their place had turned into an Odyssey of ice, mud, storms, and flooded crossings, and it had become tiresome to trek.

Sara smiled as I got down from Alice and welcomed me inside for coffee. She was showing now and had never been prettier. She was there alone; the boys were out with Beto, looking for a horse that had gotten out and escaped. I hurriedly drank down my cup, dumped the dregs on the ground outside, and asked which way they went. She pointed north, and I saddled back up and went to look for them. I met them a mile away, heading back with the errant horse trailing by a rope. They were all mud-spattered and disheveled. Beto is soaking wet, jeans and coat.

"Howdy, what happened?" I asked as they rode up.

"She broke through the fence and then got stuck in a creek bottom northeast of here. I had to get down and push her while the boys pulled with their mounts to get her out." He flashed his smile and seemed embarrassed.

"It happens, hell, let me get out of your way, looks like you're ready to get home."

He nodded, and I fell in behind them. I rode over next to Neto, who I noticed was falling asleep on his mount, so I could catch him if he did. Good thing, too, a quarter of a mile, and he was swaying and almost lost his seat. I put my hand out to stop him from toppling, and he grimaced, embarrassed to have nearly fallen asleep on his horse.

After he warmed up and changed into dry clothing, I helped him mend his fence and sort out his horses while the boys washed up and went to bed. He said he had them out well before daylight, and they were exhausted. After finishing up, I told him I was heading back to the house and asked him to consider moving his family back with me. He ducked his head, and I thought he was going to balk at the idea, but he surprised me by nodding and looking me in the eyes.

"You are right, we need you, and I won't let my pride endanger my family anymore. Once the ground hardens up enough where we can load things in the truck, we'll be over. Ask Doc to drive over when he's able, pull me out of the ditch, and we'll get loaded."

He reached up his hand to me, and I shook it from the saddle. "I'll tell him, and he will be pleased, hell, everyone will. If you want to ride your stock over right now, you can, and we can always come back for your gear," I told him.

"No, I'll get it together and have it ready to be loaded so we aren't doing any waiting around when he brings the truck," he told me.

"Suit yourself," I said and tugged my hat to Sara as she waved from the doorway.

I made it home that night, exhausted, and skipped supper to get some sleep. I told everyone about Beto's plan to move, and we got to work making the space ready for them to move in. Mama made sure they had plenty of supplies. Doc laid out plans to expand the barns for his horses and to build a new grazing pasture for his livestock. Becca and Maryn brought out the surplus clothing we brought from Council Bluffs for them to look through and choose what they want, and the boys are talking about building an outdoor shelter to accommodate the four of them, plus Chunk.

It drizzled for ten days and grew cold. When the sun finally came out and warmed up for a change, you could almost walk around outside for a bit shirtless, which the boys tried right off until the old lady caught them.

“I swear I have never seen two boys rushing to the grave like you two. Get inside and put on some clothes!” She chided them, and hearing those exact words she used on my brother and me took me back years. She chased them inside and left Doc and me alone on the benches.

“How long until we go and fetch them?” Doc pulled on his pipe, and I considered my answer.

“Well, he wants it to be dry, so we don’t have any problems in his yard with the truck, you know, we did a considerable amount of dirt work there, and he’s worried it won't be dry enough to pull out his truck, but we can always come back for it. He doesn’t want Sara riding either, so...” I let that hang in the air.

He nodded and clenched his teeth on his old pipe. When the boys came back out, I rounded them up, protesting, to help me in the barn. They complained they didn’t have enough time to play because Mama made them come back inside.

“Should have come out here ready to play, then. The old lady isn’t going to let you get sick. Think how long you’ll be stuck inside with pneumonia,” I explained to them.

“I’m too tough for illness, Lew. I can sleep out here in this mud with no problem,” Luke bragged.

“Wouldn’t bother you a bit?’ I asked, and he shook his head; Jimmy agreed, explaining in detail exactly how tough they were. I grabbed them both, tossed them into a mudhole, and watched with amusement as they crawled out of the shallow pool, surprised.

"If you can sleep all night in the mud with no worries, then you can shovel horseshit with a little on your clothes, right?" I knew Mama would make my ears ring when she found out about this, but these punks needed to be taken down a peg or two.

I waved them on, and when we got inside, I saw Gid and Gwen had already gotten it cleaned up, and the boys rushed off in loud exultation before I could find them something else to do.

"I was going to get the boys to clean this out. How come you did it?" I asked him.

"Because I wanted to, and it needed to be done. They aren't the only ones tired of being inside." He's not wrong. I've noticed tension mounting between him and me for some reason. Maybe it was cabin fever, or perhaps we are too much alike to get along. I turned and left, time to find something else to occupy me for a couple of hours; he wasn't the only one tired of being indoors.

When I went back inside, I found the boys sitting with Nate in the living room, going over some Native American lore. I heard him mention Custer on my way through to find Maryn. It was a year ago today that her mama had died, and I wanted to check and make sure she was okay. I found her sewing with the old lady, and both had been crying. I could tell from the moment I put my head in the room that they might not be done, so I left them to it, not saying a word, and went to clean my rifle again.

The next few days, the rain set in again, and the wind howled outside. Doc became more irritable, and even Nate had had enough of the inside weather. They both got an ass chewing from Mama for going out in the rain because of their ages, and it hurt their feelings. They decided to sulk in Doc's new lean-to instead of his customary bench and curse the weather and their predicament of being bossed around by a mother hen. Doc groused about getting Beto here, but I reminded him that not only did the rain need to stop, but it also had to dry out. His grouchy mood worsened at that, and he vowed to drive the excavator over there if he had to and pull the truck out with the bucket. I grinned at his bitching and went to check on the boys.

A couple of days later, I woke from the nightmare of the boy on the gravel road again, asking me why he had to die. This time, Maryn was there too, and she joined in with the others, asking me why I killed so many. My brother Charles stood on the road, but he was still a kid and had a bullet hole in his chest that smoked.

"Why does everyone have to die around you? You couldn't save Jess or me, and you really didn't save Doc's son, did you? You only got enough of him out to suffer and die here. Is Maryn going to be next? Why did you let us die?" He pointed his finger out, and I followed it and saw Becca sitting on the gravel, bleeding, holding her stomach. She looked up at me with tears in her eyes and asked, "I loved you, but it didn't matter, did it?"

Gid and Gwen were leaning against some structure, both shot and bleeding, and looking at me accusingly, and he said, "A father is supposed to defend his family."

Becca looked up at me, standing over them with a rifle, and cheered me on, "You got rid of everything that is in our way, you killed them. They just held us back, you know? Baggage." Her smile was haunting, and her grin turned maniacal as she reached for me and clasped my arm. I snapped awake in the dark, and she was gently pushing me.

"Lew?" she murmured to me.

"I'm okay," I said, swinging my feet off the bed onto the cold floor. No more sleep for me tonight, I thought, as I reached for my watch and it read three fifteen. I got up, washed my face in the bathroom, and headed to the kitchen for some coffee. Mama was sitting in her chair already with a cup.

"What causes you to be up this early?" She asked me.

"I suppose I could ask you the same," I replied, grabbing a cup and sitting down across from her.

"Something in my bones, I suppose. A terrible feeling. Ride out and check on Sara and the boys for me today, will you?" She closed her eyes and leaned her head back before saying, "Something's wrong."

I saw the cakes sitting on the stove top from the twins' birthday yesterday. I nodded at her and sat with her in silence for a few minutes. When I got up to leave, she hugged me and told me to be careful, and that no matter what, we were moving them here today.

"I'll bring them back no matter what. Even if we must come back later for their things, okay?"

"I suppose since the twins' birthday passed yesterday, we will be back on trash rations again. The food has really started to suffer around here since you just don't put in the effort," I told her once I was out of reach of her dish towel. She smiled at me and shook her head before standing.

"I'll send the old man with the truck when he gets his lazy bones up and around. You can eat in the barn tonight, I'll make you up a nice batch of poke and grits," she smiled at me, and I left out chuckling at her old joke, 'poke your feet under the table and grit your teeth' was something she used on us as boys when we complained about what was for dinner.

I woke the twins up and roused the boys, too. Becca was getting out of the shower when I came from the kitchen, and she volunteered to go as well. The seven of us mounted up and started well before daylight. I didn't like bringing the boys, but hell, everyone was tired of being indoors and stuck at home, so I just left the old folks there. The past few days of no rain and warm sunshine should have lowered the creek, and the ground had firmed up considerably. Doc said over a cup of coffee in the kitchen, he would head over around noon, meet us there, and haul their stuff back here in his truck and trailer.

The boys were excited to be set free for the first time in a long while and to see their friends. The weather was cool but not cold, and they rode off with their jackets unbuttoned, rattlesnake hatbands flashing in the predawn. Becca admonished them about their coats, and they had to stop and button them up.

As we neared the county barn where I'd left his black that time, I saw his truck still in the ditch and smelled smoke. The horizon was marked by a dark plume, and fire made the low, grey clouds overhead glow. We crested the first small hill, and I wondered why in hell he would have a fire lit that big. The old lady was right, something was wrong, and I feared his barn had caught fire from a kicked-over lantern, so I had everyone wait here.

"Sit tight, I'm going to go take a look," I told them.

Mounting the low hill on my stomach so as not to skyline myself, I saw the home burning. There's a dead horse in the back yard I don't recognize, and some of the grays are still in the corral. Why wouldn't they have taken the horses, I wondered? I stood up and ran my binoculars over the place, noting the bodies stretched out in the yard, smoke bellowing from the home, and a wide swath of mud coming from the yard and back toward us. They must have come from the north or east, so why come this way, I wondered. The likely scenario flashed in my mind; they must have tortured it out of one of them back here, and the marauders set off. I ran back to my horse, mounting her while she was moving with me and kicking her to the end of the road. The muddy tracks veered southwest before they reached the gravel road, and alarm bells rang in my head as I feared they were heading for our place, while my horse's hooves thundered on the muddy ground.

ABOUT THE AUTHOR

Kellan enjoys fishing on the Neches River and hunting the woods between Jasper and Zavalla, Texas. He has traveled extensively and met all kinds of dangerous and interesting characters, some of whom you will find in these pages. Kellan enjoys hearing from his fans, and if you see him out on the water or at your local grocery store, make sure to say hello and share your story. Feel free to reach out on social media and give your thoughts on his work.

www.ingramcontent.com/pod-product-compliance
Lightning Source LLC
LaVergne TN
LVHW100501110826
845146LV00002B/477

* 9 7 9 8 9 9 4 9 4 9 8 0 1 *